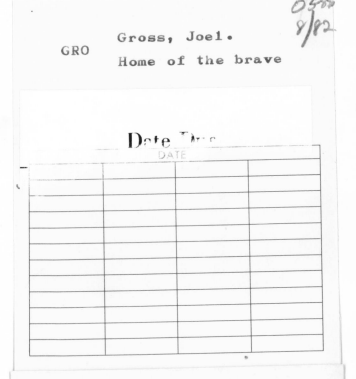

GRO

Gross, Joel.

Home of the brave

0588
8/82

Date Due

DATE

MAYWOOD PUBLIC LIBRARY
121 SOUTH 5th AVE.
MAYWOOD, ILL. 60153

© THE BAKER & TAYLOR CO.

HOME OF
THE BRAVE

HOME OF THE BRAVE

JOEL GROSS

Seaview Books

NEW YORK

The people and events described or depicted in this novel are fictitious and any resemblance to actual incidents or individuals is unintended and coincidental.

Library of Congress Cataloging in Publication Data

Gross, Joel.
    Home of the brave.
      I. Title.
PS3557.R58H6   813'.54   81–84529
ISBN 0–87223–771–0   AACR2

Designed by Tere LoPrete

This book is for my mother and father

We may affirm absolutely that nothing great in the world has been accomplished without passion.

—HEGEL, *Philosophy of History*

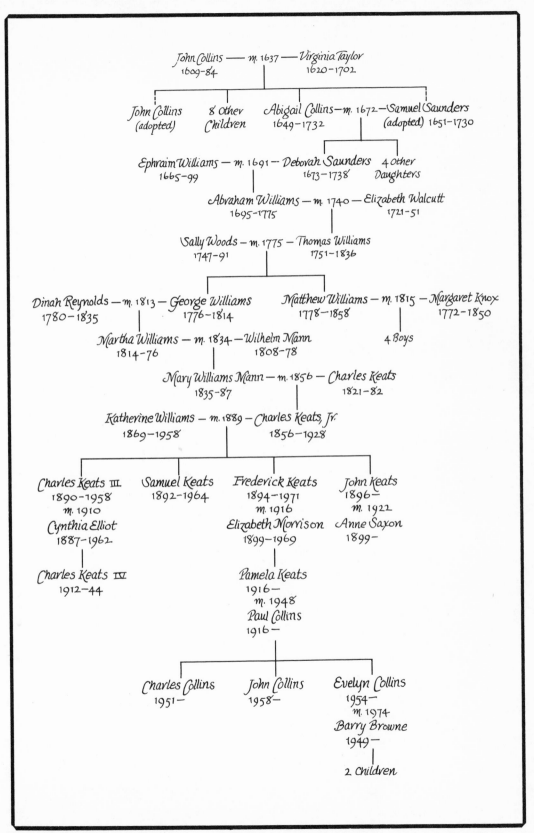

PART ONE: 1637

A House at the Edge
of the River

ONE

On the second Wednesday in January of the year 1637, Virginia Taylor lowered a large wooden bucket into the icy water of the brook behind the house in which she'd lived for the past three years. Though she wore no gloves, and the full pail was heavy, and the northeast wind tore at her from the bleak forest's border, the girl made no sign of complaint. Goodman Silvester's enormous mastiff ran to her, barking and stretching its neck, yearning for a pat or a bone. As dully as she had pulled the bucket out of the brook, she now patted the powerful dog. Like herself, the poor beast was an exile from England, living among a heartless people. And in this valley of the great river called by the Indians "Connecticut," the harsh syllables in the Algonquian tongue meaning "Long Tidal River," they were as far removed from her native land as any resident of hell.

Taking little steps over the frozen mud, careful not to spill water or trip out of the wooden clogs she wore over her ancient shoes, Virginia was suddenly struck by a sound, unexpected in the cold, gray air. It was midmorning. Men were out in their allotted fields, picking stones off the hard January ground. Some took this time of sleeping earth to thresh grain, or help their women with dressing the flax or chopping firewood. A very few brave ones went clamming, risking the cold for the sake of the hot, healing broth. Almost no one went hunting, though the forest teemed with big game, moose and bear and deer made clumsy by the snow. It was easier to barter English cloth and kettles and axes with the Indians, who hunted these woods on snowshoes and were eager to trade their wealth of fresh-killed meat and bloody pelts. Few Puritans hunted for the sport of it. In a land where men farmed and fished with their muskets at hand, it was no pleasure to shoot at animals that might be on any of a dozen different tribes' hunting grounds. While the men went about their mundane, methodical tasks, their women labored inside. Up a half hour before dawn, starting up a great fire with the embers of the night before, women and children were at their morning tasks around the enormous fireplaces of their wind-swept homes. By the light of tiny leaded glass windows, they spun and sewed and wove and dyed their cloth. Before the hearth they cut great chunks of meat for the stew that would simmer over the fire the rest of the day. Butter was churned, hams were pickled, bayberry tallow was melted and poured into candle molds. Shoes were mended, boards were sanded, newly discovered chinks in the walls were stopped with twigs or mud or clay. All the while babies screamed, or nursed, or slept; corn was pounded, bread was baked, pewter was polished. In the Silvester house, as many as ten people clustered about the hearth at one time, all save the two- and four-year-olds busy at their assigned tasks. But there was little protest at the close quarters in the dim light. No one was anxious to leave the relative warmth of the crude clapboard house for the bleak outside.

So the sharp, brief crack heard by Virginia made no sense at first. The men were too far off for her to have heard their axes; and this was no sound of splitting wood. She turned around to the vista of empty fields to the south, to the village green to the north, to their close-by neighbors, the little weather-washed houses sharing the southernmost edge of the square around which their village was built.

And then a crimson flash from the far end of the village caught her eye. Mesmerized by the bright, growing dance of color against the gray sky, Virginia put down her bucket and took a few steps toward the distant vision. In that moment, the dog brushed against her leg and ran off, racing for what she watched in wonder.

Fire.

Virginia ran, heedless of the frozen ruts, unaware that she was screaming out an alarm as she pushed herself through the cold air. She passed the deserted meeting house, the blessedly empty pillory and stocks, the whipping post, which Goodwife Silvester seemed to mention to her at least once a day. Long ago, when she was thirteen years old, in England, she'd been removed from a world of minstrels and actors, jugglers and clowns and dancing monkeys—her brother's beautiful world—and transported with him like a slave to the terrible New World. She'd been in Boston only a year when the Silvesters moved from that paradise of one-room huts and fanatical preachers to this village, which its founders had dared name Contentment, but in that year she'd witnessed a dozen fires. The thatched-roof, wattle-wall structures burned up in a minute; and one of those Puritan hovels had housed her brother, sitting in chains for his sins. Contentment, with its population of forty families, numbering less than three hundred souls, had already built a better prison than the one in which her brother had perished. Every house in this village was built of heavy oak timbers, with roofs of boards and shingles, like the best houses in Boston. There had not been a fire in the town since the day it was laid out, three years before.

The fire came from the trading house, the only house built by the work of one man, and separated from the rest of the town by a thicket of young buttonwood trees. It was a log house, not much higher than six feet, and as Virginia burst through the leafless branches of the trees, she saw that the fire had already destroyed it. Now it was nothing but a magnificent bonfire, radiating waves of heat and light against the implacable cold.

The mastiff was there, and half a dozen other dogs, chasing each other around the fire. It was the sound of the fire-wracked oak wood that had first drawn her eyes to the terrible blaze, but now that she understood this, she was faced with another mystery. Handsome Sam Blake, the half-English rogue who ran the trading house—kept outside the confines of Contentment, so that its inhabitants would have little contact with the heathen Indians—stood quietly in front of the flaming ruin. He was naked to the waist, and his back had been severely whipped. The exposed skin was striped with fresh welts, and faintly blue from the cold, but the man didn't appear to be shivering, or cringing. Virginia had been whipped once, in full view of the village, shortly after her fourteenth birthday. She had thought that the humiliation of being tied to the whipping post, being stripped of bodice and chemise, condemned from the meeting-house's balcony by the town's magistrate and the Reverend Master Brown, was far worse than any pain she would have to endure from the whip. But she had been wrong. With the first of seven strokes on her bare back, she had forgotten everything but the physical agony. The lashes were spaced by moments, but these bits of time were interminable in her anticipation of pain. Virginia wondered how the man could bear to stand so still and straight, when she herself had to be carried away from the whipping post, fear having driven her into blissful sense-lessness.

But that Sam Blake stood secured between two stout free-men, facing the burning ruin of his home, was only part of the mystery confronting the seventeen-year-old girl. Two guards-men, dressed in full armor—clumsy cuirass, neck-constricting gorget, greaves that would stop any arrow but made it nearly impossible to walk through a marsh or a wood—held great swords ready in their gauntleted hands. But ready for what? The burning house seemed a display for the group assembled before it: Contentment's parson, magistrate, a half dozen members of the magistrate's guard, not counting the two men in armor, and the two freemen holding on to the beaten man. And more wonderful than this, more amazing by far, was the smaller group, composed of three Indians—one old male, carry-ing a long smoking pipe like a badge of office, and two braves—all standing to the side of the Englishmen, watching the burn-ing house without expression. None of the Indians wore paint or wampum, but the braves were bare-chested, wearing open deerskin capes over their breechclouts and leggings, and their powerful bodies and glistening black hair excited Virginia. But this was no exotic play staged by her brother and his friends in

London. These men were real Indians. And the old male, in his robe of fur, seemed like nothing so much as a phantom, a demonic spirit of the imagination, long held in check by the dour, civilizing Puritans. Virginia could not imagine what the savages could have to do with a punished Sam Blake, what they could have in common with the terrible men of Contentment.

Suddenly, Sam Blake turned.

Virginia had seen him from behind, catching enough of his right profile to recognize the strong features of the only non-Puritan in the village. But now he had turned to his left, away from his burning home, his wild eyes looking straight to the forest.

She stepped back, not to hide herself from the men, but to distance herself from the horror of the man they had punished. Sam Blake had been branded, and though this was not the most terrible punishment in the arsenal of men, it had long had a special significance for her. Virginia's brother had been branded, the first time he had been caught stealing. She had been eight years old then, living in glorious squalor on the top floor of a narrow house filled with actors and sinners of every denomination. He had not taken much, and he was young and humble, and the sentence placed the burning letter T for thief on his left hand, instead of cropping his ears, or hanging him. But Virginia remembered her brother's shame at the disfigurement. He never let her touch the brand mark, no matter how she begged him. And when they were outside, he either wore gloves or kept his left hand beneath his cloak.

Sam Blake's branding was far worse than her brother's. The Puritans of Contentment had branded his left cheek, ruining his looks and making it impossible for him to make his way anywhere else in the world. Two young men had been branded in previous years by the magistrate's orders, both of them indentured servants. Their branding had been done in the square, under the assembled eyes of the village, so that their pain and humiliation would teach some godly lesson to the people of Contentment. They had both been runaways, and had been branded on the hand with the letter T, marked as thieves for attempting to steal the years of their lives that had been sold to their masters.

Sam Blake's cheek was branded with an *F*, but what this had to do with the burning of his house, with the magistrate and his guard, with the parson and the three Indians, Virginia couldn't imagine. She watched as the man twisted out of his guard's grip, and as the magistrate ordered his men to let the prisoner alone. Only the parson followed the stumbling man to the edge of the wood. He said nothing to the man, but gave him a bundle of clothes to cover his nakedness. Then Sam Blake was gone, lost in the impenetrable forest before his home was fully reduced to ashes.

Like so much in her four years of bondage, she could understand only a tiny part of what she had witnessed: that Sam Blake had been inhumanly punished, that he, like herself, lived among ferocious madmen, in the worst place in the world.

Sunday came at last.

Virginia hardly noticed the morning chores. She wore the heavy black gown that her employer lent her for Sabbath meetings, and her ugly little white linen cap, freshly washed the night before. No one would look at her cracked black shoes. She sat in the very last row of the meetinghouse, farthest from the twin stoves that warmed the front-row benches. But the cold didn't bother her. She was glad to be as far from the Reverend Master Brown and his interminable sermons as possible. Even though she sat erect and still on the backless bench, her eyes facing front, she heard almost nothing of the service, of the hymns, of the sermon. This was Sunday, and on Sundays she allowed herself to dream.

Her father had been a seaman, sailing under Sir Walter Raleigh, and her mother had been the most beautiful woman in London, living under the care of blue-liveried servants, always waiting by a great window for the return of her husband from the sea. Their house had sat on the edge of the Thames, and all the windows faced the river and its endless procession of sailing ships. She had been born in a room papered with a rainbow of colors, while tropical birds in gilt cages sang a welcome to the world. Noble lords and ladies had visited, of course, each in robes and boots and blouses made the night before. They brought presents for the newborn: sweetmeats and black-eyed dolls and angora shawls. If only her father had come home, if only her mother hadn't died, if only her brother hadn't been so desperate to feed the two of them.

Virginia shut her eyes tighter against the flood of unpleasant memories threatening her dream. She was named Virginia, in honor of the Virgin Queen, Elizabeth; surely that suggested a girl of gentle birth. Naturally her brother's name was Walter, in honor of the man under whom her father had served. What did it matter if she'd never seen her father, if the mother she could barely remember had fallen upon hard times? Surely this didn't belie the facts of her origin.

And if all her facts were simply bits and pieces of her brother's imagination, what did that matter now that he was gone? As far as she was concerned, the entire city of London might just as well be a fancy for all the importance it had in this world to which she'd been condemned.

Virginia's mother had died of consumption. Though Virginia had an endless parade of images which she assigned to this person, she had no true memory of a woman who'd died before she was three. Walter, twelve years her senior, raised her with the help of a succession of spurious aunts and cousins, all of them female, and most of them, like Walter, members of the acting profession. Walter had been on the stage since he was a little boy, his slender frame and high-pitched voice keeping him in ladies' parts till Virginia was five. By the time she was seven, she had seen Walter in a dozen parts. In his own long blond hair or wearing a black wig, he played heroes and villains, a duelist with an Italian foil or a knight with a broadsword. She had seen him stabbed and bleed the fresh animal blood, worn in a bladder under his cloak, that brought the audience to its feet in horror. She had seen him create miracles, fall victim to a terrible fate, take away a princess in his arms. Walter had died and come back to life; he had won and lost fortunes; he had drifted back and forth from the Spanish Main —all in the space of a two-hour performance. It was no wonder that the Puritans allowed no plays to be performed in their colonies. In the New World, dreams were a waste of time; worse, they interfered with the relationship between God and man. How could one follow God's path, search for a role in God's plan, when one's head was filled with fancies?

As Virginia had learned in four years of Sunday sermons, try as she might to shut them out—in the daily Silvester family prayer and study sessions, in endless lectures from her mistress, in a dozen trips to the stocks in Boston and Contentment— God's pledge of salvation for the children of Adam had been withdrawn. Man was doomed to suffering, corruption, and death. Only the Puritan elect were exempt from this fate, and they only because their lives were spent in spiritual searching. Life was a trial, during which one's worth was tested. Everyone must prove, by virtue of thought and deed, that he searched for and accepted God's calling, or else face eternal doom.

Her brother had raised her with none of these values.

When she was eight, she appeared onstage, dressed up like a queen, her face painted, her hair sparkling with fake gems. She loved the laughter of the crowd, the love of her brother's friends and fellow performers. Backstage, she watched a magician make dice disappear, a juggler suspend half a dozen balls in the air. Virginia rarely sensed her brother's anxiety: the dread lest they be turned out of yet another house, the worry of finding a decent bit of food for them. She had little experience of real luxury. Bright colors and witty words were far richer to her than mansions; liquor and laughter and sexual love weren't mysteries or abominations, but the lifeblood of an existence that made her present condition seem worse than death itself.

Her brother's troupe fell on hard times around about her twelfth birthday. Though the Puritans, themselves the victims of persecution, couldn't close down the theaters, there was enough uneasiness in the land to bring about a lack of business. Actors were out of work. Minstrels left London for far-flung courts. Actresses left the stage for the arms of "protectors." And Walter Taylor stole.

For many months they survived. Petty thieves, regardless of the dreadful penalties over their heads, were numerous. Walter was not a highwayman, except of course in his former life on the stage. In London he stole bread, a cloak, a pocket watch from an old gentleman who'd strayed from his coach. The fact that he had once been convicted, and had the letter *T* branded on his hand to show it, deterred him from too daring a crime. He might be hanged for assaulting a shopkeeper with a knife, so he never bared a weapon. All his crimes were quick, paltry, yielding nothing more than a means to survive for a few days more.

He was finally caught by a baker's assistant, who knocked him to the ground in full view of a London street crowd. Walter was beaten by the crowd and arrested. Two days later he was sentenced to hang. Only when the facts of his having supported his twelve-year-old sister reached his judge was this sentence changed: Together with Virginia, he would be transported to the New World colonies for life.

Like the majority of convicts sent to people England's new domains, Walter had no way of paying the four pounds passage fare to New England. He and Virginia were given free passage in exchange for a seven-year bond of service from each of them; when their ship arrived in Boston, the captain would sell their contracts to the highest bidder. They were not quite slaves, for their servitude would not last for life. But as indentured servants, they could be bought and sold and bartered and handed down in a legacy for the duration of their seven years service. Though the custom of indentured servitude was common throughout the English world, and the great majority of these bondservants were not even convicts but poor people looking for a passage to a better life, there was never a doubt in Walter's mind that he would not endure such a thing for seven days, much less seven years.

In Boston, the siblings were separated at once, their contracts bought by different families. Walter left his new house the night he arrived, but in Boston in 1633 there was nowhere to run, save the ocean or the wilderness. And so her brother was brought back, and flogged; and he walked out again, was put in the pillory, and lectured on his duty, and the family who'd bought his contract sold it at a loss to a farmer without sons. It was this farmer who'd eventually sent him to the prison shack, in chains, to starve him into useful humility and obedience. The third night in this one-room hovel, Walter died, unable to crawl out of the burning building in his chains.

Virginia always found her mind wandering back to that night

of fire and death, when she'd discovered that she was alone in all the world. Sitting in the meetinghouse, bringing back the beauty of her early childhood, she was eventually bested by the ugly memories of adolescence. Against her will, she remembered the six-week crossing to Boston from Bristol, with her brother kept in leg irons, cursing his fate. Trying to ignore the image, she saw quite clearly, behind her shut eyes, the entire population of Boston, hundreds of terrified people, rushing out into the night, watching the prison shack burn, caring only that its flames not spread to their own homes. And other memories were always there, waiting their turn to plague her: Goodwife Silvester, swinging her cane, howling at her for laziness; Master Silvester, refusing to let her sit at the makeshift table where even the youngest children sat on benches; being pelted with frozen mudballs by the village children, who laughed at her for being a servant and a nonbeliever.

Only then, where there was nothing beautiful to contemplate, when the world of fancy was overtaken by fire and death and humiliation, did she open her eyes and succumb to the sermon. Even two hours of instruction in the ethics of purifying the debased Church of England was preferable to remembering what she had endured, and what she had yet to face in the three remaining years of indentured service.

Opening her eyes to the preacher at the end of the meetinghouse, Virginia caught an unusual sense of tension from the cold, huddled Puritans all about her. Everyone was still, but it was not the usual respectful, accepting silence. The rapt attention shocked her into a swift scramble for comprehension. Out of the jumble of words she heard "fornication," and she remembered Sam Blake's branded face, and his horror.

"Why was he not simply whipped, and fined ten pounds?" the preacher was whispering into the silence. "Was not that the punishment of Goody Barret, herself a member of our community? Was not her crime in some way more terrible than Blake's, in that she had fallen from so great a height, having lived among us and worked among us and chosen the path to salvation? And have not adulteresses walked off from the judgment halls of other communities with hardly more than a stern lecture and the obligation to exhibit their crimes with a badge of

cloth? Were we not too harsh with this man? Why did we whip
him, brand him, burn down his house, ruin him utterly? What
was his crime that his punishment was so severe?"

The Reverend Master Brown turned his back to the congregation, as if drawing up strength from the heat of the fireplaces,
and turned around with sudden fury. He was through whispering.

"What was his crime?" he shouted, and everyone in the meetinghouse felt as if the question had been hurled his way. Virginia knew the answer, of course. Sam Blake's crime was that
he was not a Puritan. That he wore his hair long, that he liked
drink, and women, and that he cared nothing for the world to
come. "What was his crime?" shouted the Reverend Brown,
moving along the narrow aisle between the benches. "His
crime," he said, suddenly speaking more quietly, more slowly,
as if patiently explaining the riddle of the universe to a class-
room of idiots, "his crime was the first step to destroying God's
plan. Destroying our Zion, our New Land of Israel in the Wilderness. Not fornication. He was not punished simply for that.
Sam Blake was the agent of Satan. Yes. Do not doubt it. The
agent of Satan, sent for one reason, and that reason was to
destroy us, our community, our example for the world. You who
do not know the Indians do not understand their role on this
earth, do not understand why they are here and for whom they
work. But I know the heathens. And it is I, following my calling, who have for today—and only for today—prevented them
from fulfilling Satan's goal."

Virginia listened, perhaps with a better ear than anyone else
there. The preacher spoke out the details of Sam Blake's crime:
He had fornicated with an Indian, a heathen, with a daughter
of the devil. Not out of lust, but out of design. The girl was the
daughter of one of their chiefs. She had been promised to the
son of a neighboring band, of the same Algonquian tribe; a
young man who was both orator and warrior, and who had long
been looking for a cause with which to unify the half dozen
bands of his people. And not only had Sam Blake fornicated
with the heathen, he had impregnated her, and had stolen two
canoes, made of the best northwoods birch, and two dozen
beaver pelts, all belonging to the girl's father. The girl had not

survived the trip from her village to Sam Blake's house of logs;
perhaps Blake had drowned her, or slit her throat. No matter
that he had sworn that her death had been the result of expo-
sure to the cold. His purpose was at all times clear to the Reverend Master Brown: Satan had entered his weak soul and
directed it to rape, steal, murder—in order to incite the
heathen. The devil would never be satisfied until the example
of Contentment, a community of God following the dictates of
the Old Testament rather than the pope-loving, bishop-ridden
Church of England, would be exterminated. This was Sam
Blake's role in Satan's plan. This was his crime.

"Only by rooting him out of our community," said the
preacher, "only by burning down what was his, by branding
him for what he was, by whipping and humiliating him in front
of the heathen girl's own family, could we remain in this place
to do God's will. Had his crime been fornication, he would have
been punished for that crime alone. But his crime was the attempted destruction of God's chosen people, the deliberate in-
citement of the murderous hordes of Indians to kill God's elect
on earth. And we must never be afraid to do God's will."

"I would agree with that, Preacher," said a sharp, unfamiliar
voice from the back of the meetinghouse. Virginia turned violently to her left. She had not heard the door open, not felt the
white man in deerskin clothing brush up against where she sat
at the end of the last bench in the congregation. "If you want to
live in this part of the world, it's a good idea not to be afraid."

With those words of contempt he walked up to the Oxford-
educated man of God and handed him a blood-soaked bundle
of hides. "You showed the Indian you were scared," said the
man. "And now this is what he shows you."

The stranger ripped away the wrapper, leaving in the
preacher's hands Sam Blake's severed head.

TWO

The meeting had never been broken up so decisively. Everyone spoke, many got to their feet, all interest in the service was gone. But only the magistrate remembered that order must be restored. He took hold of the head, rewrapped it, and shouted at the arrogant young trapper: "Leave this meeting! Get out of this place, and hold your tongue as you leave! At once, I say! Go!"

Two members of the congregation, Ashton and Halloway, took hold of the trapper and escorted him down the narrow aisle, while the magistrate followed, bearing the bloody package. As the procession passed Virginia's seat in the last row, she heard the trapper hiss at the big men who held him: "Take your paws off me," and then they were gone.

The Reverend Master Brown began a hymn in his tuneless voice, and the congregation followed automatically, waiting for instruction or revelation. But the meeting was soon over, and the minister had said nothing about the terrible interruption of the Sabbath service. He walked to the doorway of the church, followed by the silent congregation, one row at a time, beginning at the front and ending at the back, everyone pausing to greet the preacher with words that said nothing.

Virginia walked quickly across the common, her eyes to the ground as her mistress had instructed her, and caught up with the Silvester family. "Take Mehitabel," said Goodwife Silvester by way of greeting, thrusting the two-year-old into Virginia's arms. The baby didn't protest or squirm. Her four-year-old brother, Joshua, took hold of Virginia's tattered shawl and whispered up at her: "Did you see the head?"

"Quiet, Joshua," whispered Virginia. But the oldest girl, Martha, had already caught him.

"Joshua's talking, Mother," she said. "About the head!"

"Thank you, Martha," said Goodwife Silvester.

"I'm sorry, Mother," said the four-year-old.

"Be still," said Goodman Silvester. Turning to Virginia, he added: "He has the courage to speak because he knows you will listen to any nonsense. If you don't slap the boy's face when he's insolent, he will grow up like a heathen. How many times must you be told, girl?"

"I'm sorry, sir."

"Hurry home," said her mistress. "The child doesn't weigh so much that you can't be home before us. I want to see the fire blazing when I enter. I'm too sick to run, but you're not. Go ahead, go!"

"Go, go!" said Mehitabel, laughing into Virginia's face. Joshua was ordered into line behind the eight-year-old twins, William and Thomas, and next to the oldest son, Jonathan, who was a month shy of his eleventh birthday. Martha, who had just turned thirteen, tried to rule the household as her mother's viceroy, for Goodwife Silvester was often too unwell to leave her bed. Ann, the Silvesters' six-year-old, held on to her big sister as they followed the stately walk of their parents. There had been six children when Virginia's contract had been bought by the master in Boston. The birth of Joshua had nearly killed his mother, and a hard-working servant girl was urged upon the family by their parson. After the birth of Mehitabel in Contentment, Goodwife Silvester was confined to her bed for four months, during which time she accumulated enough bad temper to fuel a lifetime of violent rages. Virginia had heard the Reverend Master Brown caution Goodman Silvester that another child would kill his wife, and that God wanted no more children, neither male nor female, from their union.

"Go, go!" said Mehitabel again as Virginia slowed down to catch her breath in the cold air. All the children save Mehitabel were dressed like miniature versions of their parents. The boys' cloaks weren't lined with scarlet like their father's, and the girls wore no black felt hats like their mother's over their ugly little white caps, but otherwise their study, many-layered costumes were identical. Mehitabel would surely soon be dressed in her sister Ann's old clothes; everything from tiny boots to tiny gown had been saved, with other family treasures, in one of the many chests the family had carried from England to Boston to Contentment. As far as Virginia was concerned, Mehitabel's only saving grace was that she had not yet been transformed into a tiny facsimile of mother and sisters. Dressed in clumsy smock and blankets, the large baby was endearing in spite of herself. Dressed like her elders, she would be a small tyrant, petty and overbearing and cruel.

"I'm going, Mehitabel," said Virginia. "Like a horsey."

"Go like a wolf, go like a bear!" cried Mehitabel. The farther the two moved from the family, the more childlike and exuberant the two of them became.

At the far end of the common, near the wide front porch of the magistrate's enormous eight-room house, the child's wildly swinging fists managed to tear off Virginia's cap. The wind picked up the light linen covering and sent it flying, even as it tore at Virginia's loosely tied long hair. Mehitabel laughed as the pretty servant's face reddened in fear and her blonde hair danced in the wind.

"Quiet, child. I have to get it. It's not funny!"

It would be her fault if it blew away, irretrievable. She would be punished for carelessness. Holding the child, she ran in her clumsy clogs, keeping her eyes on the white linen jerking and hopping through space. Catching on a fallen branch, it stopped long enough for her to bend low and almost touch it; but at the last moment the breeze picked it off the deadwood and sent it tumbling away.

Virginia lifted up her head, searching for the cap, and as she turned left she saw it held up before her eyes.

"It's a real pleasure to meet a white woman with a head of blonde hair," said the trapper.

Mehitabel laughed, and hit at Virginia's cheeks, and turned

her face back and forth between the servant and the trapper.

"Please, sir," said Virginia, reaching for the cap. "Thank you, sir."

But the trapper pulled his hand back, teasing her with the cap. He had a reddish-brown beard and green eyes, dark blond hair that was longer even than poor Sam Blake's, and about his throat was a deerskin thong of black wampum beads.

The magistrate and the two freemen who'd escorted the trapper out of the meetinghouse looked down at them from the wide porch of the magistrate's house; Virginia's flying coif had interrupted an important conference.

"Why in the name of all that's holy you Puritans want to hide your pretty hair behind these ugly things is beyond me. But then, I'm not one of your elect," said the young man. Each word threatened to put him in the stocks, or tie him to the whipping post, but all Viriginia could say was: "Please, sir. I am not a Puritan."

"Tell me your name, and where you live, and I'll give this rag back to you. With my blessing," he added, bowing with comic extravagance, a courtier in deerskin. Save for her brother, he was the handsomest man she'd ever seen.

"Virginia. I am a servant. To the Silvesters, sir."

"I am John Collins, and here is your cap, and from this day forth I am the Silvesters' servant's servant." In an undertone he added, "God save the King," and then he turned about and ran back up the steps to the magistrate's porch.

Silently, Virginia mouthed the forbidden words—"God save the King"—too stunned to understand why. King Charles was universally loathed by the Puritans; he and his archbishop, William Laud, were the most hated men in New England. Though the colonists were still Englishmen, of course, they longed for a God-sent plague to rid the earth of their persecutor and purify England of all license, frolic, and lechery.

"Shameless girl!" said Goodwife Silvester, catching up to her.

"How long do you intend to stand there like a harlot?" said Goodman Silvester. His wife took Mehitabel out of Virginia's arms.

"Hit her, hit her!" cried Mehitabel.

"Put your cap on!" cried Goodwife Silvester.

"I'm sorry, Mistress," said Virginia.

"She's not sorry, Mother!" said Martha. "Look at her hair! It's not even tied!"

"I am sorry, please believe me, it just blew away, Mistress!"

Martha, all of thirteen, slapped the family bondservant across the face.

"Martha!" said her father, very angry.

"I am sorry, Father. I didn't mean to. It just happened. It was her insolence, and something in me just made me do it. She just stands there, she doesn't tie her hair, she doesn't put on her cap—even now. I'm sorry," she said again.

"Take your children," said Silvester to his wife. "And instruct our Martha in the way to treat a servant."

Virginia hurriedly shoved her hair back inside the cap, keeping her eyes to the ground. Worse than being slapped by the young girl was the fact that the young man, John Collins, must have seen her at that moment.

"Look at me, girl," said her master.

"Yes, sir."

"You spoke to the stranger. What did he say?"

"Oh. Nothing, sir. His name."

"He came over to tell you his name?"

"He picked up my coif."

"Yes, girl. And he told you his name. And then what did he say?"

"Nothing else, sir."

"What did you say?"

"I thanked him, sir."

"And nothing else?"

"Nothing, sir."

Silvester turned his dull gray eyes to the magistrate's porch, and found the young stranger's eyes on his. Slowly, he turned back to his servant. "You are lying, Virginia. I watched you from ten yards. You spoke. He spoke. There was talk, girl, and you deny it. You stood there, your hair uncovered, your eyes not on the ground but looking directly at him, like any London harlot. Again and again you have been taught, but you are still vain, lazy, shameless. You will be punished. Go to the house, and attend to your mistress."

* * *

Goodman Silvester was a rich man in the community of Contentment, but not because of the work of his hands. Unlike most Puritans, he retained close financial ties with England. His family, brothers and cousins and one ancient great-uncle, were all staunch believers in Mammon. They were tolerant of their wayward relation, though they certainly thought him crazy to travel to the other side of the world to set up the New Zion. Though they had nothing but fashionable distaste for the short-haired, somber Puritans in their midst, forever agitating for stricter religious controls, they made an allowance for the one Silvester who had discovered himself one of the elect, and sent him to the New World with silver plate, linen tablecloths, napkins and bedsheets and bibles and cookware of the finest quality. In the absence of banks in the New World, the Silvesters, with their hidden cache of silver buckles and brooches, English and Dutch gold coins, and the contents of their household chests, were among the half dozen richest families in the community. The magistrate had four indentured servants, and the Sanders family had three; but in the entire community of nearly three hundred souls, only sixteen people were bondservants. The Reverend Brown had more windows, and the magistrate's house was far larger, but the Silvesters had a massive frame-built chimney, with a fireplace seven feet long.

"Hurry, lazy girl," said Goodwife Silvester, as Virginia labored to raise an enormous fire-blackened iron pot onto a tripod in the corner of the hearth. Empty, the pot was difficult to raise; with it filled nearly to the brim with the Sunday stew, and her body tense from the threat of punishment, Virginia felt as if one wrong move would crack her neck. With the pot secure on the tripod, she carefully moved the heavy weight along the hot hearth, pushing it gingerly over the great fire.

"And what are you looking at, Martha?" shrilled her mother. "The servant's not the only one who works in this house. Pull out the table. Take down the dishes. You know what to do. Help her, Ann! Jonathan, bring in some more logs! Virginia! What are you doing? Stir it, don't tap it! And get my warming pan! I'm cold!"

Virginia hung a kettle of water from the thick black lug pole over the fire. Bars and hooks extended from this pole, supporting pots and kettles. A baking pan, black with soot, sat at the back of the hearth warming yesterday's bread.

Try as she might to busy herself with thinking over the tasks at hand—stirring the stew, warming the bread, preparing the precious tea, shoveling hot coals into the mistress's warming pan—Virginia couldn't rid her mind of the day's horror. Sam Blake had returned to haunt her. The entire community had been presented with his terrible head, a reminder of their guilt in sending him into the wilderness. John Collins had made his contempt for all of them clear; even his flirting with her had been contemptuous. She was a servant, and he had called himself a servant's servant! But that was meant in jest. His handsome face made it plain that he was no one's property, and that he regarded all of them as weak, fanatic remnants of the old country, not worth their place in the New World.

"Bring me the tea!" said Mistress Silvester, even as Virginia approached with a hot pewter mug. The children were now busy pulling out the table from its position on the far wall and setting it up before the hearth. A bench was placed on each side, and the room's two chairs were placed at opposite ends. A silver knife was put before each of these places, set also with white linen napkins and two different sized spoons. Master and mistress had pewter plates, silver beakers, and large pewter goblets for ale. Though there was ample silver for the eight other residents of the house, the other places were set with earthenware bowls and wooden trenchers. Children and servant were allowed no knives, nor any other utensils but wooden spoons. The small parlor room, situated on the other side of the chimney with its own much smaller fireplace, was used to exhibit the unused silver, pewter, and glass of the household, and for those rare occasions when husband and wife wished to entertain the magistrate or the parson or some traveling dignitary from one of the other three new towns on the Connecticut River. Here too was the parents' feather bed, covered with rich Flemish rugs and curtained off from the cold with heavy English wool. Martha and Ann shared a rag-stuffed mattress set up on a home-built frame of cords and wood in the main room; they pulled this up before the hearth, and enjoyed the warmest sleep in the house. Virginia slept on a pallet kept in a box during the day, and unfolded on the hardwood floor near Mehitabel's crib in the corner of the main room. Now that the baby was no longer nursing, she had no more business in the room that was parlor, parents' bedroom, and "borning room" all in one. The four boys slept on one huge bedstead in the loft, reached by a staircase set against the chimney. The house had a lean-to addition against its south wall, used as a scullery, buttery, and storehouse. There was a small cellar, where wine and ale were kept, and also barrels of brine in which Virginia pickled fresh cuts of meat. It was a terribly crude house compared to what the Silvesters had had in England; but in New England, it was a palace, and in a town not four years old, it was a wonder.

"Light the candles!" said Mistress Silvester. "William, go out and see if your father's coming! Not you, Thomas! You needn't be your twin's shadow! Bring me the bible! Lazy girl—why aren't you stirring the stew!"

There was hardly time for her to complain about the scarcity of light in the hall, the insufficiently hot fire tended by Virginia, the lack of speed with which Thomas brought over the Good Book. Goodman Silvester returned, letting in a blast of frigid air. He looked about the room, and his eyes rested on the Sabbath table.

"There will be no place for the servant," he said.

"Yes, sir," said Martha, rushing to take away a spoon, a wooden plate, and an earthenware bowl.

"Listen," said Goodman Silvester. This was an unnecessary admonition. They suspected that he had come from the magistrate's house, and that he had spoken to the man who had brought the severed head to Contentment. "No one shall leave this house after daylight. No one shall mention the name of Sam Blake, nor his murder. No one shall question me or anyone else about the wisdom of Sam Blake's punishment. The name of the man who has come to Contentment is John Collins. He is not to be spoken to by any member of this household. If you, Virginia, speak to him again, you will be whipped. Now bring out the bread and we shall say grace."

Her head throbbing, Virginia got on her hands and knees and used a long-handled shovel to pull the baking pan out of the fireplace.

Master Silvester had only a superficial resemblance to most of the Puritans of Contentment. Silence and meditation were virtues that he believed in only in theory; he enforced this theory on his children, and occasionally on his formerly pretty wife. But he found it difficult to remain silent once there was something to say, be it the arrival of a baby in Boston or the results of a sensational trial in London. Perhaps it was his money that made him different. He had three hired men who worked his fields, and he spent more time with affairs of the community than with the state of his crops. But certainly he, like all Puritans in Contentment, never looked down in any way on those who performed manual labor. Blacksmiths, tanners, weavers, carpenters, and joiners were, in theory, as worthy as any man of property of being members of the church, full voting freemen in the community; unlike the developing social systems in the large Virginia plantations, in New England the colonists did not like to play the landed gentleman, the lazy country squire.

But there was no escaping the fact that certain Puritans were wealthier than others. Master Silvester spent his days differently from the town's wheelwright or spinner. He might well be appointed the next magistrate of the town, and as it was, he carried on much of the correspondence between their community and others in the New World. Against his better judgment, he had told all of them, wife and children and servant, tales of the Dutch in their tiny island settlement of Manhattan —three hundred people huddled behind a crude wooden wall, praying in a church made of brick that the Indians wouldn't slaughter them in their sleep. Though it would have been more instructive to present the dinner table with an Old Testament story or a New Testament parable, the master gossiped about highwaymen outside of London, about the young French noblemen learning to trap beaver in the northwest with savage Indian tutors. Even the hated Spanish, the most serenely Catholic people in the world, presented him with stories that he couldn't keep to himself. Virginia, though she was stung at not being allowed to eat at their table, served the master his bread, waited for an end to grace, and hoped that no one would ask a question. The story would come of its own, out of the master's unstoppable lips.

"You will stand at your empty place, girl," said Master Silvester.

"Don't slouch," said Mistress Silvester.

"She's making an insolent face, sir!" said Martha.

"An insolent girl makes an insolent face," said her father. "But you will mind your own affairs, Martha. There is hot food on your plate. Eat it."

"Yes, sir."

"Would you like to tell us why are you standing and not sitting?" said Master Silvester. "Why you are fasting? Why you are being punished?"

"No, thank you, sir."

"Tell us, Virginia," said the master.

"Because you are angry with me, sir," she said, keeping her eyes on the fire.

"I am not angry with you!" shouted Master Silvester. "How dare you twist around the truth even now! You lied! I caught you in a lie, and it is for that that you are being punished! Lying! Do you understand?"

"Yes, sir," said Virginia.

"What was the lie?"

"I'm sorry, sir," said Virginia. "I'm sorry if I lied. I don't remember how I lied, or what I said anymore. I'm very sorry." She would have gladly told him what the lie was at that point, if only he'd get on with the story: what had happened to Sam Blake, where John Collins found the man's head, why they were all to remain inside after daylight. He had always been strict with her, but not nearly as mean as his wife; this inquisition was more in the style of Mistress Silvester, and she found it especially frightening, as if even the soft corners of her world were turning hard.

"You denied speaking, when you had spoken. You said there was nothing exchanged between the two of you, but there was. Even now the mention of the stranger unsettles you, because you carry secrets that you refuse to reveal. You are arrogant, you are insolent, you are obstinate, and you will be punished until you learn to conduct yourself like the bondservant of decent, God-fearing people."

"Martha," said Mistress Silvester, "you will watch the baby

tonight. Virginia will sleep in the scullery. Perhaps the January air and the lack of a pallet or a blanket will remind her of who and what she is supposed to be."

"My *dear* wife," said Goodman Silvester, suddenly angrier than any of them had ever seen him. "How *dare* you presume to tell the girl what to do? *I* am talking to her. *I* am punishing her. *I* will not *tolerate* interference in my own affairs, do you understand?"

"Yes," said Mistress Silvester, hating him for his anger, for she knew it came from unfulfilled lust. She had given him seven children without a single miscarriage, accepting his desire without complaint since she was a girl of nineteen. Not yet thirty-five, she felt like an old woman, always out of breath, her bones aching from the cold; she was sure she would die before she was forty, and this only because of his desire. He had not touched her since the birth of Mehitabel, but she knew that he would not be able to restrain himself forever. Every time he asked how she was feeling, she understood him to be asking how much longer he would have to wait—either for her to become his woman again, or for her to die and leave him to take another.

"You don't know the reasons for my wish to punish her, you see," he continued, his tone milder, but the anger quite apparent. "This stranger, this John Collins, this Christian heathen, as godless as any Indian, has not only chosen to insult every man, woman, and child in Contentment with the disruption of our meeting, but has decided to make a special example of me. He wanted to buy the girl's contract."

Virginia turned to face the master, unable to conceal her astonishment and her anxiousness to understand what had just been said. But the master was now more than eager to talk. He wanted to let the words out, so that they would not twist apart his insides.

"Just like that, can you imagine? The girl's contract. He said he had need of a woman. A woman! I had a good mind to strike him, the nerve of him, with decent people in the room, even the parson. But the magistrate wouldn't have a quarrel. It seems this stranger is important just now. He's lived and hunted in this area and all about here for years. He knows the Indians, he speaks to them in signs, he has some of them for friends—and he's come here to tell us that we have to go to war with them."

Joshua, the four-year-old, interrupted boldly: "I don't want any more stew, please. May I give mine to Virginia?"

"No, Joshua," said Martha. "And quiet, your father is speaking."

"But I'm not hungry," he whispered.

"Joshua," said his mother, "leave the table and go stand in the corner. One more sound out of you and there'll be a caning."

His father watched him slide off his seat on the bench and walk slowly to the corner, his eyes downcast. Virginia wished she could crush the little boy in her arms, to return his love with her own; she had experience of the twins' early kindnesses to her, and remembered how this had been beaten out of them, slowly, inexorably. Now, at eight years old, they would never offer her food when it was being denied her by their father. Not out of fear exactly, but out of a harshly learned system of what was right and what was wrong in the Puritan household. There were rules, and they had learned them; and they had learned not to question the authority that was the foundation of their lives.

"He's a crazy man, this John Collins. Without religion, without respect, a typical youngest son of a Catholic family. Probably his oldest brother is a baronet and they're waiting for Charles to turn the country over to the pope."

"Is he really a Catholic?" said his wife.

"He looks it. He's fanatic. He's no respect for our church, or our parson. And he's crazy for war. He wants to kill the Pequots. He says it's they who killed Blake, not the Mohegans —as if he could tell the difference by looking at the way they'd cut off the head. And when I asked him how he knew it was the Pequots, he looked at me—cold, like a killer—and he asked me if I was the Silvester who had a pretty blonde bondservant. I couldn't even answer before he offered to buy her up. He showed me gold coins, he held them up to my eyes as if I had never seen a sovereign before. He offered eight pounds. I really think he was serious. He thought he could buy the girl just by offering a couple of pounds more than she cost."

"Why did the Indians kill Sam Blake?" said Mistress Silvester, interrupting his angry rambling about Collins. For a moment it seemed as if Silvester would have to reprimand his wife once again; that her question might have stopped up all talk for the duration of the afternoon. But he let it pass.

"I don't know. Maybe Collins killed him and said it was the Pequots. How can anyone know the truth when you speak with liars, men who have nothing of God in them that they don't pervert? He claims it was the Pequots' way of showing contempt for our laws. They cut off his head to mock the Mohegans and to mock us. There have been other killings, a month ago and more, and Collins blames them all on the Pequots. He blames them for taking his canoe, stealing his pelts, he blames them for killing a Dutchman east of Saybrook, on the Sound, he blames them for burning out a trading post a hundred miles northwest, with two Frenchmen missing, both of them his friends—probably Catholics. There was a killing in Wethersfield, a farmer—Collins blames the Pequots for it. A family in Hartford fought off a war party, scared them with their muskets, and they were Pequots. Everything that's ever happened along this river or along the Sound, on either side, where the Dutchmen are, or the Frenchmen are coming with beaver from New Canada—everything is the Pequots' fault, and he wants a war. The man is crazy. Anyone who would walk two days through frozen forests with a man's head in his hands must be crazy."

He had not yet explained everything when the drumbeat from the meetinghouse began—the three short beats and the two long ones signifying danger. Virginia wanted to know how Collins had come across the severed head, not realizing that it had been delivered to his camp as a deliberate provocation. She wanted to know how one could navigate a canoe through frozen rivers, not realizing that the Pequots had picked up his canoe under its winter nest of hides and dead branches near his permanent house on the Saugatuck River, nearly sixty miles away, and carried it off on their powerful shoulders. She was confused, too desirous of knowledge to be frightened. Everyone jumped up from the table and ran to look out the tiny windows as men began to run out of their homes and make for the common.

(27)

Silvester was a brave man, and perfectly willing to meet his fate at any time. He wrapped himself in his scarlet-lined black coat, loaded and primed his prize flintlock musket, strapped on his sword, and walked out the tiny front door without a word. This was the Lord's work, and not a question of man's paltry hopes and wishes.

"What did that man tell you, girl?" said Mistress Silvester. "Did he say the Pequots were near?"

"No, Mistress."

"You'd better tell the truth, Virginia," said Martha. "You're already to be punished. You'll sit in the stocks if you keep on lying."

"I'm cold," said Mistress Silvester, pointing at the warming pan at her feet. Virginia hurried to take it to the hearth and replace its contents with hotter coals. The twins and Joshua jostled one another at the windows, looking for Indians, laughing at the huge, ancient matchlock muskets of the poorest townsmen.

Suddenly, the door burst open, and Martha screamed.

But it was not an Indian.

"Virginia," said John Collins, a musket in his right hand, his eyes wide with humor. "Don't worry. It's only a drill. My idea. To see how ready the men are." He smiled winningly at Mistress Silvester, at her children, but only Joshua and Mehitabel returned the smile.

"Are you an Indian, sir?" said Joshua.

"Hush!" said Mistress Silvester. "If you please, sir," she said to John Collins, "we are not receiving visitors in the absence of my husband."

"That's too bad," he said, still not having any idea of the trouble he was creating for the pretty bondservant. "But really, I wasn't calling on you. I was calling on my pretty friend Virginia."

"Please, sir!" said Virginia. "If the mistress wants you to leave, then you must leave. Don't stay on my account, please!"

"I used to like a coy woman, back in civilization," he said. A round of muskets was fired, bright little sounds carrying through the still air. Two moments later, a second round was fired, while the first rank of musketeers reloaded, fingers made clumsy by the cold. "Don't be afraid," said John Collins, ignoring the mistress and her children, taking deliberate steps to where Virginia knelt at the hearth. "It's only a drill, like I said."

"I'm not afraid," she protested, but fear made her drop the warming pan and get suddenly to her feet.

"I only came to say good-bye. I'll be back. Not for two or three months, but I'll be back."

"All right."

"It's a long way where I'm going. Not many white men. It might be that I'll never see you again, and that wouldn't be at all to my liking."

"No," she said, not to corroborate his words, but to prevent him from getting closer. For a few moments more, he remained in place, and his words reached her as if through a distance of yards, not inches. She shut out the awful possibility of what might take place, choosing to dwell on his soft muffled words: He lived in a little house on a river called Saugatuck, which ran into the mighty Sound where great ships sailed. When it was warm enough, he would bring a great fur-laden canoe across the Sound, and trade with the Dutch on their rich little island called Manhattan, and return to New England with guilders and Dutch cookware and gunpowder, and these he'd trade in the trading posts and five tiny new towns along the Connecticut. "Why did you come here?" she said, not realizing that she had interrupted him in mid-sentence, or that the mistress was shouting at him to leave, or that her own words seemed shaped by hysteria.

"I was hunting not two days away, and the Pequots left me with the man's head. I knew Blake, you see. I knew where he was from, and who had killed him. No matter what they say, I'm a decent man. You remember that. I didn't come here for any other reason but to warn Englishmen like myself, even if they're Puritans."

He put his musket down so quickly and so silently that Virginia's terror fastened itself on this action, as if by holding on to the moment she would stop his next movements.

But the girl could no more stop the handsome young man than she could stop the passage of time. His hands reached up and plucked off her coif, and then slowly, patiently, his fingers ran through her hair, pulling it out of its knot so that it fell wildly to her shoulders.

The mistress was out of her chair, but there was no sound now, not from Martha, not from anyone in the room; and the drilling men on the common, desecrating the Sabbath day for the first time, no longer entered Virginia's consciousness, no matter how they fired their guns or shouted their puny cries of mock warfare.

"You'll forgive me," he whispered. "But when a man goes into the woods, there's no one can say he'll come back. And you're very beautiful."

He kissed her.

John Collins moved his hands from her hair and placed them on her cheeks, and he kissed her mouth, without roughness, and then he let her go, his reddish-brown beard retreating from her field of vision, the black wampum beads about his throat diminishing in size as he moved back through space.

"Good-bye," she said.

It would have been easier for her had she screamed, had she thrown something at him, had she collapsed in a corner senseless with rage. But as the man picked up his musket and left, closing out the winter winds and the threat of violence behind him, Virginia remained in place, her hair loose, her back warmed by the great fire.

Not for four years had anyone remarked on her beauty, had anyone but the smallest of children shown her something of kindness. It mattered not at all how they would punish her, how they would chastise her. In that kiss she remembered that joy existed in the world. Those hands that had touched her, those lips that had stopped her breath belonged to the race of men. She was right, she was human, and it was those about her—the men, women, and children of Contentment—who were wrong, inhuman. Virginia was not in love, but she was enlightened. In this cold place on the far side of the world, there was a remnant of the life that had been snatched from her. Until John Collins returned, all she had to do was survive.

THREE

———◈———

Everything of importance was written in the bible.

The laws of ancient Israel were perfect and wise. Proverbs, hymns, and parables were always available for the people of Contentment. In a world savage with lust, hunger, and passion, the bible was a bedrock of sanity, an inviolable structure to frame the meaning of their lives. As the children of Israel were the Chosen People, so were these children of Contentment chosen, and as with the Hebrews, the bible was their Book, their Law, their Way.

When Goodman Silvester returned from the drill on the common, he was quickly apprised of what had taken place in his absence. It was not told to him in a way that suggested a stolen kiss, a fleeting moment of youthful daring. Neither his mind nor that of his wife allowed the possibility of innocent impulse. Demons preyed upon weak souls, bringing sin into the world. John Collins had entered Contentment, bringing with him disrespect, irreverence, arrogance. Virginia Taylor had welcomed him, had allowed him to touch her, to kiss her; she had wished him farewell. This was the work of a devil, and Silvester turned to his store of biblical knowledge for guidance.

"Resist the devil and he will flee from you," he said to her, but the words from James were not uttered in solace.

"She must be whipped," said Martha. "Just like the last time, Father. She must be whipped in the square."

Silvester didn't hear his daughter, so busy was his mind with searching for biblical direction. "Ye cannot drink the cup of the Lord, and the cup of devils," he intoned, quoting I Corinthians, and the very passage used by the Reverend Brown earlier that day.

"She is a wanton, sir," said Mistress Silvester to her husband. "It would not surprise me if she knows the man better than she admits. If she had met with him in the woods, like an Indian harlot. She has never followed our way, no matter how we have instructed her. It is not just the devil in her, it is London, it is the Old World and its ways."

"Babylon. She is of Babylon, the habitation of devils," said Master Silvester, inaccurately quoting from Revelation.

"If you have gotten yourself with child, girl," said Mistress Silvester to Virginia, "you will have made a bad bargain for yourself. You will not only be whipped, but you will have earned yourself another two years of bondservice to pay off your fine."

"I have done nothing," said Virginia.

Mistress Silvester slapped the servant across her face. "Do not contradict me! You have gone too far already!"

"But I have done nothing!" said Virginia, refusing to let go of her insolence. It was as if the young man's kiss had reawakened a rebellious spirit long since beaten down. Not for any sensual reason, of course, not for any romantic, overwhelming notion. She had simply caught the sense of the young man's freedom, a freedom that had once been hers. "I have done nothing and I won't be whipped!"

When she had been whipped before, it was at the magistrate's orders. She had been put to work for many hours with the coarse, wide-toothed hackle comb, cleaning and straightening the fibers drawn from flax. The work was very tiring, and the dust had collected in her throat and eyes, and she had put aside the hackle comb for a moment of fresh air. Martha, then all of eleven—to Virginia's fourteen years—found her at the side of the brook, and ran to tell her mother that their bondservant was shirking. Mistress Silvester, pregnant with Mehitabel and dangerously irritable, went out to castigate her. "I am only taking a breath of air, Mistress," Virginia had said. "Surely even among the elect that is no crime."

The words had been brazen enough to shock the goodwife into striking out at her with her cane. Virginia danced away from the blow, and pulled the cane out of Mistress Silvester's hands. Then, not knowing quite what to do, she tossed it into the brook and ran off to the woods. When she was finally brought before the magistrate, the fear had all blown away. But the sentence, so implacably cruel for the crime, brought back the fear, and taught her a lesson: not to respect her masters, but to loathe them; not to honor their example, but to shut it out from her mind. The seven lashes on Virginia's back brought about an obedience founded not even on fear, only on a desire to avoid the pain of a beating. This was not the same as fright, she assured herself. The Silvesters were too much a known quantity to be a source of fear. A beating would be painful, and a missed dinner, a cold night in the unheated scullery, a sharp word were never pleasant, but they came about for reasons she understood. If mistress wanted the floors washed again, there was no point in explaining that they had been washed an hour previously; if master found the stew not cooked long enough, it was folly to explain how many hours it had hung from the lug pole over a roaring fire.

And so Virginia was not so much sullen as she was cautious. It was not a great surprise to her that life was unjust, that Martha could sit when she could stand, that master could accuse her of smiling at Goodman Sanders's second son, that mistress could scold her for bringing a cold foot stove, when it had been hot enough to burn the servant's rough hands.

And so now, in the wake of John Collins's kiss, their anger made perfect sense. There was no doubt that she would be punished, and that the more she protested, the worse the punishment would be.

But a demon had, in fact, taken possession of her. Not Satan, not Beelzebub, but a nameless devil of defiance had her in his grip. She was a good English girl, not a slave, she said. She loved God, she loved her King, she loved her country, and she would be damned before they accused her of anything wrong.

The twins retreated from her anger in amazement. Joshua began to cry, and Mehitabel to laugh. Martha watched in fascination, clutching her sister Ann's hand. Only Jonathan, the eleven-year-old, had anything sympathetic to say.

"He forced her, he did," he said. "She never wanted it, but he just did it. He had a gun, and he's a big man, Father. It wasn't Virginia who did it."

"I didn't do anything!" she said for the tenth time, and when little Joshua approached her, bearing her dirty coif, she took it from his hands and threw it into the fire.

Master Silvester took her by the arm, not even pausing for her cloak, and pulled her outside into the frigid air. "Silence," he said as he hurried her to the magistrate's house, but it was not she who wanted to talk. "You will be surely whipped, girl," he said, out of breath with rage. "With your pretty hair, your wanton looks, your wicked eyes." The pressure on her arm grew violent, and the girl twisted in his grip. "You can't get away, girl," he said. "I will teach you discipline. I will teach you to properly honor your master, as it says in Malachi. I will show you, as it says in Ephesians, to be obedient to him who is your master according to the flesh. You will learn, Virginia, and you will cease your tempting, you will quit flaunting yourself before the good men of this town."

A trio of townsmen passed them, their black capes flying, astonished at the sight of the furious Silvester, walking with his hand on the servant, and she with her hair loose and wild.

The magistrate's three bondservants wore the blue livery that distinguished them not only from the freemen of the town, but from the other, lesser servants. One of them was sent for the parson, while another prepared hot cider in the separate, chimney-equipped kitchen—the only one in Contentment. But even before the Reverend Master Brown could join them, Silvester blurted out his charges.

"I didn't do anything!" said Virginia, staring into the magistrate's cold blue eyes. "I never do anything but my chores, sir! I am a good girl, no matter how they provoke me with harsh words and blows! I won't be whipped now! I will die before I am whipped, because I have done nothing!"

Biblical phrases flew fast and furious in the wake of this

defiance. The magistrate, harsh on the battlefield, and fanatically devoted to setting up the New Zion in the midst of the many enemy nations of Indians, was yet kind in the face of domestic crises. His wife was young and beautiful, even after six children, and he saw nothing terrible about a kiss. Worse than this, in Silvester's eyes, was the man's refusal to see the devil in Virginia's wild hair, defiant looks, and beautiful tears. The magistrate quoted Proverbs: "Pleasant words are as a honeycomb, sweet to the soul and health to the bones." Master Silvester quoted Romans: "Who art thou that judgest another man's servant?" He claimed that the magistrate was being bewitched by the servant's youth and shape—by her false innocence. The magistrate quoted Exodus, recalling the severity with which the Egyptians treated the children of Israel. Silvester countered with Genesis, reminding the magistrate of the subtlety of the serpent, and the manner in which Eve led Adam to his fall.

"You don't propose to compare your servant to Eve, Master Silvester?" said the magistrate. "Or is it that you wish a theological conversation? There are certainly enough opinions, even among the good neighbors of Contentment, on how we Puritans should regard those first chapters of Scripture. But first I think you should send this girl home, and let her alone. Just allow her to spend the rest of the Sabbath in a restful, contemplative manner."

At this point, the Reverend Master Brown joined them. He astonished Virginia, after a history of three years of dread-producing sermons and black looks, by being totally in agreement with the magistrate. "Hatred stirreth up strifes: but love covereth all sins," he said, choosing to quote from Proverbs, and then adding his own, extrabiblical injunction: "If it's the girl's pretty looks that stir your heart and your wife's against her, you are guilty, sir, of a terrible sin. There are other bondservants in this town, nearly a score of them, and nearly threescore others in apprenticeships or some other sort of service. None has the sad face of yours. She is your chattel for three more years, and you have rights over her body, but not her soul. And you will ultimately answer for any sin you commit in the name of discipline."

Virginia understood. There was to be no public whipping. When Master Silvester demanded that the girl be disciplined in some fashion—even if only forced to stand on the meetinghouse porch with a placard about her neck bearing the word INSOLENT, a punishment meted out to servants, apprentices, and children with great regularity—the magistrate reminded Silvester that judgment had been passed.

"Virginia," said the magistrate, "you have been insolent to your master, and for that you have rightly been deprived of your dinner. Bear in mind who you are, and the distance between you and those for whom you work. Humility, gentleness, respect—these are the marks of a good servant. Never again let me hear that you've spoken back to your master in such fashion. Do you understand, girl?"

"Yes, sir."

"All right, then, Master Silvester. As you are not yet magistrate of the town of Contentment, you will have to be satisfied with my verdict. The girl will miss the dinner she has already served you. That is the end of the matter, sir."

The magistrate had, indeed, ended the threat of a public whipping. Unlike the last time Virginia had been sentenced, she had not "assaulted" a pregnant woman, her mistress, and had not made cynical remarks about the Puritan elect. But if the threat of public shame was over, the reality of private punishment could not be stopped.

"The magistrate thinks you should have the day for contemplation," Silvester said. "You shall contemplate in the cellar, with the cider and beer and pickling meat."

Once home, the master stilled all questions by ordering Jonathan to raise the trapdoor to the cellar. "Would you like me to bring up some beer, Father?" said the boy, who loved the adventure of climbing down the rickety ladder and roaming about the cool dark space with only the light of the open trapdoor and a single candle for guidance.

"Raise the trapdoor," said Master Silvester. Before the boy did this, he turned eagerly to his father to ask once again if it could be he who went down. Silvester fixed him in place with a terrible glare. "Jonathan, you will go into the scullery and lower your breeches and wait for me to come to you with a cane."

"Yes, sir," said Jonathan. He understood that it was not cruel; he had erred. His father had had to repeat his order, and he had stupidly ignored the order while asking a favor. Now he would have to quietly assert his strength, his dignity, his worth. He would be caned, but he would not cry. As he left the hall through the front door—the scullery could be entered only from the outside—he heard his father order the bondservant down the ladder.

"Yes, sir," she said. A candle hadn't been offered her, and she knew better than to ask for it—she knew better than to ask for anything. Stepping off the ladder, she examined the cellar quickly, taking in the barrels and chests in the large subterranean space. She had to stoop, because the ceiling was five feet high and she was a quite tall girl—nearly five feet and five inches. The cellar trapdoor was slammed shut, and she was in total darkness, alone with the enormous quantities of food and drink stored up for the long New England winter.

She was hungry, but couldn't have touched the meat in its barrels of brine. To pass the time, and try to shut out the dark and the damp cold, she conjured up the preparations for a meal she would have loved to cook for her brother. Back in England, where men were free and women beautiful and any dream was possible, she and her brother and his friends had been hungry much of the time. Meat was a great luxury. Here, in this cellar, was more meat than a hundred Londoners would eat in a year's time—and this meat was but a reserve against the unavailability of fresh game.

But there was always fresh game, in every season.

Meat was the main ingredient at every meal. There was a plenitude of turkey, pigeon, deer; for ninepence, one could buy a half of venison. For a penny, one could procure a score of pigeons. The occasional white man who hunted outside Contentment would often leave three quarters of a moose where he had shot it with his musket and butchered it with knife and axe; there was no point in taking more meat than his family could eat, and it would be nearly impossible to sell what was so

readily available. Though the Puritans grew grain, and culti-
vated gardens with native vegetables and English imports,
there was nothing as easy to procure as meat, and nothing as
satisfying to a group of people who had once considered it a
luxury to have it once a week. Even Virginia, downcast and
resigned to the years of indenture, often found herself dwelling
on the daily plenty available even to the lowest of servants.
When fish was served, on huge platters, simply as a change for
the breakfast table, there were inevitable groans. Lobster was a
poor man's food; clams and mussels, unless used in a broth,
were most often thrown to the hogs. Virginia had never seen
the master eat vegetables; he made it a point of pride that he
didn't have to, now that he had come to a land of plenty.

For her poor brother, she would have taken fresh-killed venison and mixed it in a mortar with eggs and spices. He loved
sugar, and so she would have added raisins, currants, dates, for
the Silvester larder was rich with preserves, both native and
imported. He loved a fiery taste, and she would not have
skimped on the salt, or the pepper, or the garlic. She would have
boiled this over the fire, and then cut the meat into tiny chunks
and cooked it in a stew of wine and raisins.

Virginia tried to conjure his face, tasting the hot, fragrant
stew. She remembered his clothes, his gorgeous doublet, his
tight breeches striped with gold threads. But the face wouldn't
come. She couldn't remember. Then, in the cold, in the terrible
dark silence, she felt panic for the first time. What had happened to her brother, after all? What if she could not imagine
his face because it no longer existed, because his very soul did
not exist, and he had simply been burned alive and thrown into
the ground, and now was ashes—his body ashes, and his soul
air.

"Please, sir!" she called out, not very loud, but her voice
echoed about the gloomy space, frightening her further.

Of course his soul existed, she told herself. Not in the way
the Puritans imagined it—where everyone save themselves
went to hell. Her brother could not have gone to hell, because
he was gentle. Moreover, he believed. He had told her this
many times: Christ was good, compassionate, understanding.
And her brother had been good, truly good. He had helped
herself and others—with words, with food, with understanding.

So what if he had been an actor, a rake, a man who had known many women? That didn't mean that he was in hell, no matter what the master or the parson might say.

But now a shivering took hold of her. She was breathing quickly, and without a steady rhythm. Her hands were cold and her forehead was damp. Still, she couldn't conjure her brother's face—a face that she had been able to dream about every night since his death nearly four years before, simply by wishing it. Closing her eyes more tightly, sitting on the ground, her back against a cider barrel, she felt her heart race. Her heavy linen undershift seemed to scrape against her skin; her gown felt unbearably weighty, as if it would crush her to the earth. Through the darkness, waves of black and gray assaulted her shut eyes. "Please, sir, let me come up," she wanted to say; she wanted to scream, but now there was no way to make her throat and lips and tongue work. All she could do was huddle in terror, retreating into a nightmare where her faceless brother floated, a bag of bright clothes, his features blasted along with his soul.

"Girl!" said a sharp voice, the master's voice, and Virginia opened her eyes and found herself staring at a line of beer barrels. It was light in the cellar, she realized slowly. "Where are you, girl!" she heard again, not a question but a command, and very slowly she eased herself up, and hit her head against the ceiling.

"Please, sir," she said, and she turned around and found the master standing, his head stooped, one foot on the last rung of the cellar ladder. "I don't feel well, sir. I would like your permission to come up, sir."

The master held a bayberry candle on a pewter dish, and he walked to where she stood, holding her head, her eyes twisting at him in pain. "Why are you looking at me that way, girl?" he said. But his words weren't angry now; they were anguished.

"I am afraid, sir."

"Such a brave girl—I don't believe you're afraid," he said. "Perhaps you're hungry."

"I don't know, sir." There was no daylight coming through the open trapdoor, and no sound of the children or the mistress in the busy hearth room. "Is it night, sir?"

"Yes, girl. Night." And then the master, his hand on the pewter candle dish shaking the light, reached under his doublet for a large hunk of brown bread. "Here, Virginia."

"Thank you, sir," she said, taking the bread, and pausing before putting it into her mouth. Perhaps this was a trap, she thought. Mustn't she say grace?

"Go ahead, girl. Eat it," he said, his voice strangely gentle. Virginia shoved the bread into her mouth with her rough, dirty hands. Her throat was so dry that she nearly gagged. The master watched her closely, not offering his help, but exhibiting an anxiousness that she couldn't quite fathom. "It's late. It's the middle of the night. I thought I heard you."

"I'm sorry, sir," she said, chewing the bread, her throat clear.

"I must have been wrong. You were asleep, I think. Besides, the cellar doesn't go under the parlor. I couldn't have heard you, could I?"

"I don't know, sir."

"Perhaps it was Jonathan, crying in his sleep. He didn't cry when I caned him, and I know I hurt him. I know he'll remember his place the next time. Maybe he was crying in his sleep, and it was he who woke me." Suddenly, the master turned from her, moving so quickly that the candle nearly blew out. No longer was his voice calmly explaining the reasons for his having woken. He let out a harsh explosion of breath. "May God help me!" he said. "Help me!"

Virginia watched in astonishment, her body still racked from her hours of troubled sleep in the unheated underground room. The master had gotten to his knees, his back to her, and was knocking his head against an oak-wood barrel.

She had never seen anything like this. Even on the endless crossing to the New World, where men began to chew the filthy leather of their shoes for sustenance, where wives turned in horror from their husbands' corpses, she had never seen anyone try to break open his own skull. And she was sure that this was what her master was attempting to do.

"Master Silvester!" she said, and she took hold of his shoulders from behind and pulled him with great force from the hard barrel.

He fell over onto his back, dazed at the cessation of pain, at the sight of her wild concern. His forehead was bruised, but

Virginia could see at once, even in the bad light, that the inexplicable fury within him was far greater than any physical wound.

"Get away from me," he said softly.

"Are you all right, sir?" she said. But she stepped away from him.

"Don't you touch me," he said, even more softly, and slowly he got up on one knee, the fingers of his right hand to his bruises. "You're not ever to touch me, do you understand?"

"Yes, sir."

For a moment it seemed as if he would rise up and knock her down, that the fury within him could be satisfied only with violence. But he finally turned his eyes from hers, and picked up the candle dish where he had set it down, and slowly, without looking back, went back up the ladder and out of the cellar. A moment later the trapdoor slammed shut, leaving her in darkness.

She spent the next hours trying to understand. How could he be such a mixture of bizarre tenderness and violence; how could he come to her in the middle of the night with a hunk of bread, and then succumb to a fit of self-destruction?

But Virginia had no answers, and the questions only added to her fears. She tried to sleep, and managed what seemed like a few minutes before the trapdoor was opened and little Ann called down to her in a trembling voice: "They're wanting you, Virginia!"

And it was that day, Monday, that her punishment began in earnest.

The work load that had always been expected of her was intensified specifically for chastening. There had always been sweeping, scrubbing, washing, polishing. She had always to feed and look after the children, bring water into the house, empty chamber pots, split firewood logs, make soap and candles. There was always mending to be done, whether it was repairing a chink in the chimney wall or sewing a patch on Mehitabel's smock. To fill eighteen hours of the day with work was not difficult, even without being punished. Simply preparing the meat, the sauces, the hearth fire, the dough for the makeshift oven; simply cleaning out the monstrously heavy iron cookware with icy brook water, or preparing lye from wood ashes or urine, or cleaning the chicken coop; simply dressing the flax, or sweeping out the chimney, or working a quilt—any and all of these could fill every moment of the day. The cows had to be milked, dyes had to be set, fowl cleaned, baskets woven, wool spun. Few tasks were unimportant, for the Silvesters, with all their wealth, still could not simply purchase whatever they wanted. Durable goods could be bought, either from Boston or from abroad, but it would take many months or even a year for an order to be delivered. Nothing could replace manual labor; and when Mistress Silvester became too unwell to continue her very hard work, there was nothing to be done but get a girl such as Virginia—at least until the Silvester children would be old enough to work the household themselves.

It was this fact of her being essential to the household that once gave Virginia solace. No matter how often she'd been scolded for "dreaming" or "lazying" or "shirking," she knew quite well how important she was to the lives of the family. At the end of the long day, she had been able to breathe deeply, with a sense of satisfaction; she had made the day possible for nine people—had fed them, cleaned for them, clothed them, warmed them.

But with the first day of punishment, even this satisfaction was taken from her, because there was to be no breathing space, no chance to imagine anyone was thankful for her efforts, for the entire family was united into one chastising arm.

"Martha will help serve the breakfast," mistress ordered that first Monday. "Jonathan will help. Virginia will stay at the hearth and ladle it out, but she is a godless girl, and must not approach the table while we eat the Lord's bounty."

She took her breakfast in the scullery, where she was to take all her meals from that day on. Here there was no chair, no heat, and the food was leftovers, and cold. But she had little time to dwell on her lonely meal.

"Hurry, lazy girl!" was mistress's constant complaint. Virginia scrubbed the black pots with a caustic soap and icy water, she brought in freshly split hickory logs for the hearth fire, she prepared a foot stove for mistress, burning her hand when one of the hot coals fell from the shovel. "Clumsy girl, stupid girl!" said mistress. "Hurry, now! Jonathan is gathering stones in the fields while you relax before the fire! Go ahead, go! I want to see you run to him!"

She threw on her cloak and ran to join the oldest son, six years her junior. Quickly, she began to pick up the stones scattered all about, which the hired men would use to build fences. "Are you all right, Jonathan?" she asked him at one point, remembering that he had been caned the day before.

But he didn't answer her, much as his eyes showed that he'd have liked to. She understood that he had been forbidden to speak to her, just as Joshua and Mehitabel and the twins had been forbidden. But the oldest girls, Ann and the horrible Martha, were allowed to speak to her—with the voice of their mother.

"Get inside, girl!" said Martha, coming out to the fields. "Your mistress wants you, and you'd better run! She'll take the stick to you if you don't! Go ahead, run!"

Virginia ran, listening to Martha's laugh fade into the wind. She was tired, and felt as if a chill had taken hold of her lungs from the night in the cellar. Very much out of breath, she ran into the house, shutting the door quickly behind her.

"Look how long the girl leaves the door open! You'd think she was trying to kill me!" said Mistress Silvester. "Come closer, lazy girl. Let me see your hands!"

"Yes, Mistress," said Virginia, exhibiting them palms up. They were cold and filthy and scraped from the field stones.

"How dare you come to serve me with such hands!" said Mistress Silvester. "Do you think I want to eat your filth! Get outside and wash, and come back in here—quickly!"

Virginia ran out, closing the door behind her, and then walked slowly to the brook, trying to catch her breath. She plunged her hand into the icy water, breaking the film of ice with the tips of her fingers. Standing up swiftly, she rubbed her hands on her stiff cloak and ran back inside.

"The fire is dying down, lazy girl!" said Mistress Silvester. At once, Virginia went to the hearth and used the bellows to pick up the flames. She put on another hickory log, and then Mistress Silvester barked at her again: "Now go out and wash your hands again! I won't be eating ashes, thank you!"

Virginia did as she was told. She washed again, she served her mistress some broth, she spent an hour spinning together equal parts of indigo-dyed wool, white lamb's wool, and black sheep's wool to create the all-purpose "Puritan gray" wool that clothed every member of the house. Then it was time to scrub the spotless floor, while the mistress shouted at her to work faster. The chill in her lungs bothered her, but there was no sense in mentioning it; there was no pity in this house.

Master Silvester was harsh with her too, but his harshness had an altogether different ring from his wife's. Often, he would send her out of the room while they ate, even if she had duties to perform with fire or ladle or long-handled spatula.

"Tell the girl to face the wall," he'd say to his wife, not deigning to speak directly to his servant. "Her face displeases me."

"Turn round and face the wall!" mistress would say, as if Virginia had not heard the master speak. The momentary gentleness in the cellar, when he had offered his bread to her, seemed like a useless dream now. He didn't speak to her, he tried not to come near her, he seemed to have a true aversion for her presence; an aversion that the children had to pretend.

It grew dark early, and the whole family gathered about the hearth from five till nine o'clock. Supper was served at five-thirty, except on Sundays, when it was an hour later, to accommodate the late afternoon church service. After she had cleared away the dishes and added a log to the fire, Virginia was banished to another part of the house for more work. The family didn't want her in their presence. While Mistress Silvester performed some fancy needlework, Master Silvester listened to the twins read from the bible. Joshua played with Mehitabel until one or both of them grew bored. Jonathan and Martha copied out lengthy exercises, trying to improve their penmanship. Ann read from a battered chapbook, one whose ballads and tales had been approved by the Puritans. There was no school in Contentment other than the home, and it was here, at Mistress Silvester's knee, that the servant had learned a smattering of what was taught to the children. Virginia could read and write, if slowly; she could fly through the hymnal, and rejoiced in the fact that she could write out her thoughts or send a letter—if only there were time, and pen and paper.

"Go on, lazy girl! Into the scullery with you! Take one candle! We don't want you here. You're not to go to sleep until you've finished!" And the mistress would sentence her to an endless evening of spinning or sewing by the pale light.

"Watch out for the Indians!" said Joshua as Virginia left them, wrapped in her cloak, going outside. He was not supposed to speak to her, but they let it pass as insults flew.

"Don't waste the whole candle!" said Martha.

"Don't dream the night away, girl. I want the work finished!" said Mistress Silvester.

"She will dream, Mother!" shouted Martha. "I always see her, even in broad daylight, she dreams with her eyes open! She dreams of that stranger! I see it in her eyes!"

"Tell the girl to go!" said the master, and finally Virginia would be allowed to leave, cradling her candle in both hands, walking slowly through the utter blackness of the New England night to the freezing shelter of the scullery.

Once inside, she worked quickly, racing the candle to its end. She never finished the work she was supposed to do—that was hopeless—but the cold impelled her to work with speed, if only for its warming effect. When the candle died, she would settle on the floor in her dark cloak, trying to rush the morning light. She didn't dream of John Collins, though she often thought of him before sleeping. He was mentioned daily in the house, as another way of taunting her, and the question of when he would return, or whether he would return at all, was as good as any other in forestalling thoughts of the cold.

Under the rough cloak she wore a gown. This was good wool, though ripped in many places and faded and filthy. She had no time to look after her own person, so busy was she with her mistress's orders. The gown was composed of a skirt, which opened down the front, and a bodice with a pair of separate sleeves, tied at the armholes with English cord. Under the bodice was a chemise, filthier and more ragged than anything she would have ever worn in England—even as a tiny child, living in poverty. Her mistress and Martha and Ann all wore petticoats under their underskirts; Virginia had only the underskirt, so that there was no shape to her ragged gown, and one less layer of warmth. Mistress also had a smock of heavy linen, which she wore next to her skin; and when mistress worked, or affected to work, she put on a lovely, embroidered apron, covering her entire outfit.

So the layers were not enough to keep Virginia warm. The coif she had made to replace the one she'd tossed in the fire was useful now, locking in the warmth trying to escape from the top of her head. New wool that she'd been working on would sometimes find its way to her chest in the middle of the night—she had been expressly forbidden to do this, and had to wake before light to make sure that she put it back in its place. But more than anything else, Virginia relied on the passage of time to warm her. No matter how bad the day, or how cold the night, she always knew that there was one day less of her period of indenture. No matter how bizarre the master's conduct, how hateful Martha's words, or how eager the mistress was to use her cane, time was passing. A steer was slaughtered in January, the first lamb of the year was born early in February, and late in the month trees were pruned—a necessary seasonal step before the sap would begin to run.

And then it was the first day of March.

Soon they would begin to plant peas and radishes. Hay seed would be sown. The icebound streams would melt. Neighboring Indian bands would appear on the outskirts of town, wondering what had become of the white man's trading post. And John Collins would return.

But the slowly lengthening days, the occasional breaks in the cold, also brought about a change in the Silvester household.

The children, save for Martha, had grown weary of hurling insults at Virginia—or not being allowed to talk to her at all. Mistress Silvester, feeling a bit healthier as the earth warmed up, let up on her persecution of the servant girl. Indeed, on more than one occasion she attempted to soften a punishment or a harsh word thrown at the girl by her husband. Toward the middle of March, the mistress took a brave step.

"I don't believe that she thinks of that stranger at all, sir," she said to Goodman Silvester. "And truly, I think she has tried to repent her insolence. Perhaps we can allow her to sleep next to Mehitabel once again."

"How dare you, woman?" said the master. "This is my house, and I alone know what to allow and what not to allow, and that girl must never be allowed to sleep with any of us. Do you understand me?"

"Yes, sir," said his wife. She clamped her mouth shut and hoped that he would not quote Genesis—"Thy desire shall be to thy husband, And he shall rule over thee"—as he did on any occasion that remotely suggested rebellion.

But there was no time for the master to speak.

The forty-pound kettle hanging from the green-wood lug pole over the hearth fire suddenly moved; they all heard the crack. And a half moment later the lug pole itself cracked in two, letting the kettle fall into the flames, spilling the midday stew into its center.

"You stupid girl!" screamed Martha. "I told you the lug pole was weak! Mother, she doesn't listen to me! She only listens to what she wants to do, and she never listens to me!"

"Well, girl! What are you standing there for?" said the good wife. "What are you looking at?" Even after all her training, the servant girl was like a block of wood, incapable of getting to work without being told what to do. Mistress Silvester was so angry, particularly after having just stood up for her in front of her husband, that she nearly got out of her seat to take the cane to the girl.

But then two of the dozen candles burning against the bleak day blew out, and she saw that Master Silvester had gotten to his feet, his face white with fury.

The door had opened quietly, and standing on the threshold was John Collins, a smile on his face, and his flintlock, loaded and primed, in his hands. "Sit down, Silvester," said the young man. "I wouldn't want to be responsible for so many orphans all at one time."

"Please tell them, sir," said Virginia. "Please tell them the truth. Tell them that you don't know me, that this is not my fault."

"Sure, Virginia," said John Collins. Silvester had not yet taken his seat, and the young man could see that he would have to get out of there quickly. The fanatics weren't necessarily great fighters, but they were unpredictable, substituting fervor for courage, impelled by a mad urge to fulfill God's plan. "This isn't the girl's fault. I hardly even know her. Is that right, Virginia?"

"Yes, sir, but please. Why must you point the gun?"

"Take your cloak, girl," said John Collins. "You're coming with me, and no one will get hurt."

"Yes, sir," said Virginia. She would never forget the look on Silvester's face at that moment. A passion of hatred had exploded in his austere frame; he was not listening to the words being spoken, but rather struggling, like a fly stuck to honey, amazed at his inability to break away. But something more than the young man's gun kept Silvester from springing at them, something more potent than fear.

Only when she was outside with John Collins, her arm caught in his powerful grip, did she realize that she was never coming back—that she was free.

FOUR

———◆———

She had not taken her clogs, and already the cold wet ground was seeping through her ancient shoes. "Are you abducting me?" she said, when they were ten yards from the house and he had let go of her arm.

"Sure I am—I'm a buccaneer, and this is the Spanish Main, and you're my prisoner," he said. "Now you better run."

"Where?"

"Just keep up, Virginia," he said, and then, as he had done once before, he pulled off her white linen coif and threw it to the wind. "Come on, don't you want to go?"

"Yes," she said. "Yes, I do." And then she ran so fast, following him across the common, that she couldn't take the time to turn and look toward where Goodman Silvester screamed across the deserted ground. He *was* abducting her, after a fashion, but she realized that her crime was being irrevocably forged nonetheless: She was running away.

But just as the breaking of the lug pole over the hearth fire, the sudden silent appearance of the young man in the Silvester home, the absolute willingness to follow the impulse to flee with him all carried the insubstantial weight of a dream, so did the scene before her. No one was coming out of the houses to stop them.

"You look better already," said the young man, not at all out of breath. She couldn't think of answering him; it was enough to keep her heart from dancing up into her mouth as she followed his long easy stride with short, quick steps. They were running toward the great river Connecticut, along whose banks Contentment was built, as were Hartford, Wethersfield, and Windsor a few years later. They passed the meetinghouse, the large green where the townsmen had been drilling in preparation for the Indian raids, the jailhouse. No one came at them with drawn swords, with harsh words, with muskets at the ready. It was not possible that three hundred men, women, and children were so engrossed in their midday dinner that they could not have heard Silvester's shouts for help.

Contentment had built a wharf of great oak timbers, and every year this was extended. The river here was deep enough for great ships, and the town's leaders, including Silvester, were sure that Contentment would grow in time to be a great city. Though Boston had the advantage of several years' head start, Contentment had access to the great Sound by way of the river, and was therefore at the same time on the inland waterway that would someday connect the New Zion. Because of the importance of the river in their lives, a guard was always posted along the wharf—not just to look for Indian canoes, but to be alert to any Dutchmen or Frenchmen in what were often contested waters.

And sure enough, as they crested the little rise of earth just before the waterfront, Virginia saw the guard, and stopped. It was the second son of Goodman Sanders, doing his civic duty, a musket in his hand and a pipe in his mouth. "He sees us," said Virginia, getting out the words between gulps of air.

"Follow me," said John Collins, taking hold of her arm again.

And the dream continued: The Sanders boy smiled at her, a bit gravely perhaps, but it was a smile nonetheless. And then slowly, deliberately, he turned his back to them and continued to watch the river.

"But he saw us!" said Virginia, still not understanding.

"It seems I've made a very bad bargain," said Collins. "For four pounds you should be able to do more than just look pretty."

"What bargain?" she said, but he was pulling at her now, and she had to look down at the steep, irregular ground as they hurried down to the riverbank. Perhaps a dozen yards from the guard, a large Indian canoe, loaded with a deerskin-covered cargo, was tied to the wharf. Collins let go of her hand and, getting to his knees, pulled the canoe effortlessly alongside the wharf and held it still.

"Get in," he said.

She thought of protesting. Though she had seen white men in these long swift boats, she still thought of them as primitive vessels. The idea of a boat made from burning out the inside of a tree was of a piece with half-naked brown bodies, incomprehensible guttural cries, swift, silent movements through endless forests. Stepping into the dugout was like putting her first foot forward into a barbarous realm.

But nothing could be worse than what she was leaving. "All right," she said, as if it had been up to her to express her will, and she put her right foot into the gently swaying boat.

It was like trying to stand on water. Virginia let out a worried cry, reached out for Collins to support her, and promptly fell flat on her back into the bottom of the boat. Terrified of the wildly shaking canoe, she tried to raise herself up, holding on to the sides of the boat, but this only increased the shaking. Suddenly Collins joined her, stepping into the canoe while holding its sides, and getting to his knees at its slightly thicker end, opposite from where she was trying vainly to rise.

"Go on, sit up," he said, shaking his head from side to side. "Just sit, nothing's going to happen, for the love of God." She watched as he untied the boat and picked up a long paddle. "Sit up, girl," he said, and Virginia sat, holding tightly to the sides of the boat, looking carefully at Collins and nothing else as he pushed off from the wharf and began to paddle downriver with the gentle current.

"This is fast," she said. The only boat she'd ever been on was the stinking slave ship that had been given over to the transportation of indentured servants. That was huge, tall-masted, like all the great English ships that had visited Boston during her year there; those incredibly rugged sailing ships had dwarfed the tiny two-story city. And if those boats had represented the Old World with their majesty, their cargoes of precious tools, and their sick masses of refugees, convicts, and servants, this savage dugout represented the New World: It was fleet, silent, its power stemming from its closeness to—and not its distance from—nature.

They went over a tiny wave, and the canoe lifted and fell, as simply as a log, not struggling any more than a drifting leaf, eager to go with the flow, to simply join with the forces around it. John Collins scarcely paddled now; he seemed to be using the paddle like a kind of tiller, and only occasionally would he lean forward and make a wide powerful arc through the water, adding to the force of the current.

A minute later, Contentment and its wharf had disappeared.

Since she sat facing him, Virginia had the wind at her back, and watched the scenery retreat rather than advance. But she was not about to try to turn around in this makeshift shell of birch wood. His handsome presence was not merely reassuring; it was charismatic, the materialization of a dream.

"There's not a thing to be afraid about. This canoe's good enough to cross the Sound. In a storm, in winter, in the middle of the night."

"What's the Sound?"

"Just a great big body of water where Englishmen and Dutchmen and Frenchmen trade with each other in the daylight, and slaughter each other at night. It's where the ocean slips into the New World, girl. A great enormous saltwater inlet. The Connecticut runs into it. So does the Saugatuck, where my house is. I can see Long Island on the other side of it, where the Pequots like to cut off white men's heads. There's hardly a wave to be afraid of, and more fish than the whole world could sit down to eat. Do you like fish?"

"No, sir."

"That's too bad. You'll have to learn to like it. And prepare it. The Indians eat fish, you know. They eat it, they stick it in the ground so the earth goddess has something to eat too. And one thing you'll learn very fast where you're going is that if the Indian does it, it can't be too bad for you."

"But where am I going, sir?"

"John Collins is my name, Virginia. You call me by my Christian name, and that'll be the extent of our religious practices, all right?"

"I don't understand," said Virginia, moving slightly off the boat's hardwood bottom. Collins sensed her discomfort, and threw her a blanket.

"Bunch it up and sit on it, so you don't feel the damp."

"I'm a little afraid. To move, I mean."

"Listen, if I tell you to do something, you just do it. I'm no Indian, but I know canoes just as well as any of them. Look," he said, and he got to his feet. The front of the boat lifted precariously off the water's edge.

"Please! Stop! Sit down, sir! Please!" Virginia thought that she was about to be pitched into the water, dragged by the current to a cold and violent death.

But John Collins wouldn't sit. "Look," he said. "Feel the boat? Feel how it moves with me? We're not going to tip because I'm keeping my balance. That's the whole trick to these dugouts. Just pay attention to where you want your weight. Now if you want me to sit, quit crying. Did you hear me, Virginia? Quit crying!"

Virginia did as she was told. She shut her mouth, and closed her eyes to the terror about her, refusing to give him any more excuse to rock the boat. Immediately, he sat down.

"Now do as I tell you. Move yourself off your bottom, slowly, hold on to the sides of the boat, and just get that blanket under you, girl."

"I'm comfortable the way I am, sir," she said, but he warned her that he'd be back on his feet in another instant if she didn't do what he'd demanded.

"Yes, sir," she said, and quickly she moved herself from her steady position and shoved the blanket under where she sat.

"All right," he said. She looked so suddenly relieved that he began to laugh. Virginia looked at him sharply, unused to the sound of laughter. John Collins put in his paddle, and threw back his head and laughed and laughed. For no reason that she could ascertain, she felt herself blushing, as if a joke had been performed at her expense. It seemed an eternity since she'd last heard laughter. It seemed impossible that she herself had ever laughed at all.

But in a space of moments she felt herself transformed. Incredibly, her lips twisted upward, and she let out a single astonished snort of air. Not a laugh, exactly, but it was as if something had pushed her to the top of a hill, and now all of a sudden she was falling down, effortlessly, madly, deliciously.

Virginia laughed, and she understood that her fear of capsizing the boat was comical, and she let her titters and giggles grow to a convulsive roar, laughing and laughing without restraint, laughing so that there was no sense to it, shrieking away four years of sobriety and servitude. She laughed until there was no longer a Boston, until Contentment was ripped from her mind, until all the world was simple, painless, until the tears that filled her eyes were not for her brother or for lost London or for the long years of hardship to come, but simply for joy, and its concomitant possibility—love.

They traveled south for four hours of bleak daylight. Virginia lost her fear of the boat. Soon she was getting on her knees, turning around to face the wind, edging forward and backward in the crouched stance he showed her. Sometimes the current was swift, and they rushed forward with great speed; sometimes the water was slowed by a fat finger of land, or by some mysterious crosscurrent. They went through whitewater, and though Virginia shut her eyes and held on to the sides of the boat with all her strength, she was less afraid than she had been stepping into the boat in calm water just hours before. She had grown used to John Collins's insouciance. He was not arrogant, but nonchalant; not foolhardy, but sure of his prowess. There was abundant evidence that he could handle the canoe in all the dark and stormy waters of which he'd spoken. And when she took hold of the spare paddle in her own strong hands, and began to stroke at the water from the front of the boat, she realized there was no mystery to the primitive craft. More important, she realized that its rudimentary nature was its source of strength; that she was no longer afraid because she could understand the simple forces at her disposal. Paddling furiously, she propelled the boat faster. Though John controlled the boat's direction from his more important seat at the rear, her paddling on the left did make the boat turn slowly to the

right; paddling on the right turned them to the left. Rounding a
bend in the river, he droned directions at her: "Left, left, left,
right, left, right, left, right," and every stroke brought her closer
to an awareness of the canoe, and a sense of its dignity and
security.

Virginia had questions for John, questions that went back to
the first time he'd blown in from the wilderness and retrieved
her coif. She wanted to know who and what he was, of course,
but first she had to know how he had come to take her away,
why no one had stopped them from leaving Contentment, why
he had dared take her into his arms and kiss her that terrible
January day. But for the moment there was time for nothing
but the trip. He showed her how to hold the paddle, how to slip
it into the rushing water, how to get the most power out of its
pull. Three times she dropped her paddle into the river, trying
to follow his instructions for changing hands, and each time he
laughed, as if there were not a worry in the world that need
concern the two of them. And indeed, as he slowly maneuvered
the boat up to where the paddle floated and retrieved it for her
with comically exaggerated gallantry, she felt as if they were
the only two people in the world. What cares could there be in
a place inhabited by fish, flocks of birds, deer so silent and
beautiful it was heartbreaking to imagine their slaughter?

"We won't reach the village tonight," he said, guiding the
canoe to the shore. "By myself, I'd go in, you see, but not with
you. It would be better for you to see it the first time by daylight."

The bottom of the canoe ran aground, and John pulled the
boat closer to the bank with his paddle and then jumped out
onto the land.

"What village?" she said.

"You think it has a name?" he said, pulling the loaded boat
fully onto the shore. "Come on, get out. See what the earth feels
like under your feet."

"All right," she said, and she got out of the canoe, lightheaded from fatigue and hunger.

"You look a little tired out," he said. "They swore up and
down what a worker you were. Said you were worth your
weight in gold. I paid gold, too."

"What do you mean?"

"Why don't you sit down," said John. "Lean against that tree. I'll make us a fire and get some food going. Excuse me if I talk so much. It's just that most of the time I'm alone, you see. I told them just to have someone to talk to would be worth it, if you see what I'm saying. Sometimes I get into a talk with an Indian, and I feel like screaming. Not a talk. I mean with two or three words, and drawing pictures in the air and on the ground. Sign language is not the same as moving your lips. It's just not satisfying. You're cold. It's amazing. You forget how delicate your own kind are."

He was gathering deadwood and flinging it in a great pile near where she sat. Behind her was forest, tall, bleak, and impenetrable. Before her was the river, very wide at this point, its flow made gentle by the easy pathway. Here one could paddle upstream, he told her, but in many other places it was either portage or find a quieter tributary.

"Why don't you answer my questions, sir?"

"I asked you not to call me that, didn't I?" he said. "John, all right? It's a good solid name, and it's what I want to be called. Why don't you give a hand with the fire?" he added, and took out his flint and steel from a pouch at his belt and tossed them to her.

"All right then, John," she said. She would ask him again, calmly, so that he would tell her what she needed to know. Virginia wasn't frightened. He had shown her no cruelty. In most ways, this day had been as wonderful as any in old England, when her brother had lived and she'd been the happiest and freest of children. But as she struck the flint against the steel, showering sparks into a bit of rag and tiny dry twigs, she felt the nervousness rise up in her. For all his cheerfulness, she knew nothing about him, about why she was with him, about where they were going. For all the strength of her attraction to him, she felt her resentment growing, an anger that would instantly evaporate if only he would tell her what would take place on the morrow. It was true that he had taken her out of Contentment, away from the Silvesters for all time. But she was not being returned to her former life. This was not London, and the nameless village which he'd mentioned would not be in any books, or on the tongue of any civilized man. She was completely alone in this world, more alone than she'd been as a servant. Whatever tiny pockets of civilization existed in this wilderness were to be denied to her as well, for she had become a runaway, and could not go back, except to be flogged and branded. She could find no friends, no family, no English people at all save John Collins. It was becoming infuriating to have him refuse to answer her, even as she grew more and more intoxicated with his presence.

Finally, the sparks caught fire, and the twigs burned in the slowly darkening March air. Virginia selected some dry branches from the pile and added them to the fire.

"Isn't it funny to think that there are mud floors in England, because wood's so scarce? And look at us—we could burn up everything in sight and the country would never notice it."

"I never had a mud floor, sir," she said.

"Calling me sir again, are you? I have a mind to take you across my knee, Virginia, if you keep up with that, do you hear?" He added an old cracked oak log to the fire, and warmed his hands over the flames. "The Indians just burn away the brush, you know? Not at all afraid of the consequences. You can see this isn't Indian country, because the brush is so thick. They like to keep it open, not just for planting, but for the game. Indians eat real well, better than the richest Englishman. And they live longer, too. Don't get gout, like my father."

"I want you to tell me something," said Virginia, suddenly turning on him, her face white against the flames. "No more of this just talking. I want to know."

"Know what, girl?" he said, as if he were willing and able to tell her whatever she wanted to know, if only she knew how to ask. But her questions were hopelessly confused by an infatuation she didn't comprehend.

"What you said. I mean about the gold. You paid gold. For what? Why didn't the Sanders boy stop us? Why did nobody come to stop us from running away? Who are you anyway? I know it's John Collins, but what does that mean? Why did you kiss me? What did you come for?"

Even if her words had been straightforward and calm, he would not have had a chance to listen to her. There was a great commotion beating out of the sky. The bleak sun was suddenly blocked by a flock of birds so densely packed, so perfectly mar-shaled, that the man to whom she'd been addressing her wild questions seemed to vanish into blackness.

"You hungry, girl?" said John Collins, walking through the dark toward the canoe. Virginia didn't answer. She'd seen vast flocks of passenger pigeons before. The Puritans didn't like them. They weren't like birds at all, but like some unnatural pestilence, peculiar to the New World. Not only was everything a bit larger here than in England—giant strawberries, lobsters, and codfish were the norm in New England—but everything came in greater profusion. Birds could be netted, clubbed, or shot, but one had no need of a million birds blocking out the sun for hours, alighting only to eat the hardship-raised crops.

"I wanted to talk," said Virginia with annoyance, more to the birds than to John Collins. It was not his fault that they'd arrived.

Slowly, he unwrapped his flintlock and loaded it with bird-shot. Unlike the far more common matchlock musket, the flint-lock could be loaded and primed days ahead of its firing; the matchlock employed a glowing match—niter-soaked cord—and this had to be lit, and kept out of the rain, before shooting. His large, man-killing shot replaced with birdshot, John pointed the flintlock upward and pulled the trigger. This pulled a piece of flint against a bit of steel, sending sparks into the enclosed powder pan, igniting the charge; the resulting controlled ex-plosion sent shot through the musket's barrel and into the birds.

It was hardly like shooting for sport.

Birds rained down from the single firing. Perhaps a dozen of the small passenger pigeons crashed to the ground, some dead, some wounded, some dying. One, its wings beating wildly, fell into the fire and burned up there, even as its fellows flew by, oblivious to the deaths in their midst. John finished off one or two more with an Indian club, and threw them into a pile at the edge of the fire. As the birds continued their journey overhead, he gutted the fallen birds and mounted them on a green-wood spit over the fire. When the birds had finally gone by, the sun had set, and the two of them were alone at the fire's edge, each with roasted pigeon on a trencher, slicing off wings and breasts with a shared knife. He had a pewter flask of Holland gin, and drank from this steadily but in small quantities. Virginia drank river water, and stared steadfastly into the fire. Eating was not to be mixed with talking, she had been taught. Besides, the man certainly knew by now what she wanted to know. He would tell her when he was ready, when his beautiful hands were through tearing apart the delicate parts of the birds he'd killed and was now eating with pleasure. Unless he wouldn't tell her anything at all.

"You're looking ready for sleeping," he said.

"I am tired, sir," she said, correcting herself almost at once: "John."

"Very good! Virginia Taylor. Of London. On her way down the mighty Connecticut River with John Collins, also of London. And other parts of our mother country. Not to speak of New France, New England, and, of course, my favorite place in the world—my house on the Saugatuck."

"Why did you come for me?" she said, breaking her vow to herself not to question anymore.

"I needed you," he said. The fact that he had answered at all was as shocking to her as his words. "You're very beautiful, you truly are. Even with those foul clothes, as ugly as they are dirty, you're beautiful. Soon you'll have clothes, Virginia, beautiful clothes."

"Where will you get clothes from?" she said, realizing at once it was the very least of her concerns. But she was so anxious to keep up the catechism that she preferred to ask questions related only to his own words.

"From the Indians, of course," he said. "There are thousands of Indians whom the English haven't killed. And they have beautiful clothes." John threw the remains of his meal into the fire. Standing up, he added a few more branches to the flames, and looked at her. "If you think you're tired now, imagine the trip upstream. Are you cold? I used to wonder how the Indians did it, always walking around half naked. Of course, the Pequots feel the cold less than the Mohegans. I've seen braves wearing nothing but beads in the snow." He brought her a blanket from the canoe and wrapped it about her shoulders.

"Thank you, John," she said.

"I didn't think of shelter. We could sleep in the canoe. Sometimes I travel with more equipment. A wigwam just isn't worth putting up for myself. I don't mind the cold. We could sleep in the canoe, there's plenty of blankets, and we'll be off the ground, and I'll keep the fire going. It's not that cold, is it?"

"I'm all right."

"You should know. Of course. It's just that I'm not used to this. This is what I came here for. Did I tell you I was in France? Not just New France, but France."

"Are you a Roman Catholic?" she said gravely.

John laughed at the question, and at the expression on her face. "I was born a good English Christian. My father was rich, and whatever the King was, he was. My mother wasn't rich, but her family was far more important than my father's, and for some strange reason, the poorer that branch of the family got, the more Catholics they developed. It was like a disease. It hurt my father more than his gout. More than me, even. I mean, *I* was disgrace enough, but for his wife to go Catholic! And very Catholic. But to answer your question: I am not a Catholic. Do you feel better now?"

"I feel the same," she said.

"I see. You're tolerant. Very commendable." Once again he was laughing, and he took another sip of his Holland gin, and he shook his head at her in wonderment. "Listen, I wasn't going to inherit anyway. Not a second son—I was a fourth son. And not cut out for business, or for the clergy. But I haven't told you my sin. I killed a man. In a duel. It was quite fair. He wounded me. But I killed him, and I had to leave the country. It was my mother who helped, actually. That was part of the irony. With her Catholic relations living in France—English people, not French—they helped me there. And my good old gouty father had the sentence reduced—I was sentenced without ever being in court. But I was pardoned in exchange for spending the rest of my life out of England. So here I am—give or take half a dozen years. I wasn't about to spend my life in France. My father wouldn't send me any more money. So off to New France, to the Indians, to the woods, to the beaver, to vast riches which I haven't quite gotten hold of yet—and freedom. Of a sort."

"Who did you kill?"

"What's the difference? I was eighteen, he was thirty, and it was he who had challenged me. He was from a good family. That was the problem, that was the only problem. Do you have any idea of how many people I've killed since then?"

"No."

"Well. Do you want me to try to add it up?"

"No, you needn't—"

Suddenly he pulled her to his chest, just as he had done in January, when the Silvester mother and children had stood by in astonishment. But now they were alone, lit by a lone fire in the midst of black woods, farther from civilization than a ship on the ocean, like two tiny stars separated from the constellations by an eternity of sky.

"It's all right," he said. "I only want to hold you."

She could feel his passion through her shut eyes, her terrified breathing. But she didn't protest. A beast howled in the distance, while nearby frogs croaked out a chorus of mocking laughter. Slowly, she lost her fear of the embrace. She opened her eyes and let her senses take in the night. His beard was soft, and she could smell the gin on his breath. The water slapped at the shore. Beyond his embrace the world was wild, and dark, and cold. Against her will, she let out a shiver of pleasure. Without thinking, she raised her hands to his shoulders; she held him.

"Do you like me?" he said.

"Yes." Now she had to fight herself to keep from letting go. What she was doing was bad, sinful. What she was feeling was a reflection of his own lust, and the feeling itself was a sin and must be fought. She remembered the women who had come and gone in her brother's life in London, and how he had enjoyed them; and how beautiful they'd been, and good. But she remembered the often quoted passage from Galatians, "The flesh lusteth against the Spirit, and the Spirit against the flesh." But even the pastor had spoken well of love between man and wife. But she didn't know if she was feeling love, or lust, or simply wanting a warm space against the cold. She didn't know if she was embracing the handsome young man because he had taken her out of Contentment, or because she was remembering her brother in his arms.

"Are you cold?"

"Not now."

"I came back only because of you. Not to trade, though I traded. Not to bring news of the Pequots, though I brought news too. Only because of you, Virginia. Do you understand?"

"No, sir," she said.

"I'm twenty-eight years old. I have some gold, I have a house, I have furs and wampum and a bigger fireplace than the Silvesters'. You should know that I'm never going back to England. Not only because of my sentence. But because to me, this life can be good. Life here. I know you don't believe me, but I think you can find it good too." He let go of her then, and got to his feet. Once again, he added some dry wood to the fire. "I need you," he said. "I came back for you. I want you to be my woman. My wife."

"Please," she said, looking up at him as if he were mad. "You're kind. I do like you. You're doing me a great honor by speaking to me like this. You don't know my family, and you're the son of a rich man and I'm a servant."

"Is it that you don't want me?" he said suddenly, not at all angry, just wanting to end the prolonged proposal of marriage.

"I don't know you. I hardly know what I'm saying. This morning I was a servant, now I am a runaway. I'm in the wilderness. I have no one. How can I think? How can you think of me as a wife, when you don't know me at all?"

"I know you," he said. John dropped to his knees and took her head in his hands and brought their lips together. He kissed her, thrusting his tongue between her shut lips, pulling back her hair from where it fell over her ears and eyes. She was shamed by the sharp sensation of desire taking hold of her. Though she was seventeen, her body was largely a mystery to her. Hidden behind layers of stiff clothing, it wasn't to be touched, to be thought of, to be treated as anything other than a vessel for her soul. When she'd begun to menstruate more than three years ago, she'd been slapped for daring to bring up her problem in direct terms to Mistress Silvester. These delicate things were to be spoken of obliquely, and then shut out, ignored, until such time as the mysteries of conception and childbirth were to be revealed.

"You're beautiful," he said, and she couldn't think of his endearing words, or the way her own mouth was opening wide to
receive his teeth and tongue, as ravenous as any of the invisible
animals of the forest about them. Virginia felt as if she were
struggling at the edge of a precipice. All her thoughts were on
her struggle to understand the desire growing within her; at
any moment she would shut her eyes and fall.

John kissed her neck, her hands, her eyes. Slowly, he brought
their bodies to the blanket-covered ground before the fire.
While he spoke to her of love, she remembered the tiny sensation of pleasure she'd gotten from exchanging glances with
Goodman Sanders's son in Contentment, and how she'd hidden
this sensation deep within her as useless, shameful, and vain.
While he talked of her pale skin in the firelight and struggled to
open her skirt, she remembered Goodman Silvester's sighs of
pleasure from the bedroom, before the birth of Mehitabel. Even
at fourteen she'd heard the sounds of his pleasure drifting
through the thin wall and found them not only terrible, but
wonderful too; though she'd never heard the mistress's cries of
delight, she couldn't help but believe that delight was there,
ineluctable in the consummation of everything that was hidden, adult.

But she was not married. And if she was not a Puritan, she
was still a decent Christian girl. The myriad memories of
drunken laughter, cries of delight, beautiful painted faces of
girls who had probably been no older than she was now, ran
through her; there, at the edge of the forest, she remembered
London, the legacy of all that was sensual, romantic, daring.
Virginia quit struggling, quit thinking. This was not a question
of right and wrong, but of feeling, and what she felt now
couldn't be contained by her thimbleful of theological learning.

"I know you," she said, affirming his desire, telling him of
hers even as she admitted it to herself. The ground was uneven,
and it was cold even by the fire, but there was no thought of
discomfort. She didn't think of trying to please him, or pleasing
herself; she didn't have an exact notion of what was happening
within her, what was making her heart race more than any run,
than any terror. Virginia didn't feel her heavy underskirt
bunched up under her waist, didn't feel the rough blanket

against her naked backside. All her concentration was on this young man, his green eyes searching for her love, his hands touching her in a way that she had never dared to touch herself, until the whole world seemed to tremble, until the entire universe threatened to end in a single moment of unbearable pleasure. And then, for a moment, there was no world: no fire, no woods, no night, no shame, nothing but the consummation of desire. She cried out, but didn't hear herself, and she shook with a joy so intense that it astonished her lover. The Indian women he'd slept with never pretended to do anything other than submit to his pleasure; and the prostitutes he'd had in Europe either felt nothing and showed it, or felt nothing and pretended that they'd enjoyed it as much as he. But they weren't good actors. Now, when he finally entered her, her body was so alive to sensation that he couldn't tell if he was hurting her or pleasuring her to madness. But though Virginia had already climaxed without understanding how such a beautiful thing had come to pass, the shock of his penis entering her twisted the fact of her personal passion into a shared, blissful sense of loving. She understood something: This wildness was bound to love; this unbearable ecstasy had a meaning as strong as any church.

"I love you," she said, the first time she'd ever said that to anyone but her brother, and the words, like her actions, were beyond thought, beyond logic. He was inside her. Her passion surrounded his passion; their desires were mated; their flesh was momentarily one flesh, and this union could not be evil, this pleasure could be nothing other than good. She had never seen his nakedness; had never seen any man's nakedness. But when the man ejaculated deep within her the sensation was not a surprise. This was the stuff of life within her, this was the mystery, and it was familiar to her. She was passionate, she was longing for release, she was in love with the idea of freedom; but what had brought her to joy was the sense of recognition. This was love, and she was part of it, she was part of the generations of man. And no one could tell her that she had sinned. No one could tell her that the universe was eclipsed by anything other than the holiest, most human of actions.

FIVE

Had she been a member of the Puritan congregation rather than an outsider, had she had experience of fumbling lust or shared in the moral outrage of a community directed at an adulterer, she might have woken to a sense of loss, or guilt, or shame. But her life's experience was built upon a stronger foundation than a studied morality: There was the memory of a life before transportation, and a life after it; the fact of a life of feeling, and a life of repressed feeling; life with her brother, and life without him; a free life, and a life of bondage.

So when Virginia woke, her feelings were directed only at preserving the beauty of the night before, retaining the sensation, holding on to the ecstasy that seemed her human birthright. And because this was the first time she had experienced such love, she woke to an awful sense of mortality. This surprised her, that she should think of the possibility of death at the moment of first love. When she saw John, moving easily in the early dawn, readying the first meal, loading the canoe, she saw him in a mortal light. What had been so beautiful must needs be fragile; and she felt, with an intensity that shook her, that her life was bound up in his, that there could be no meaning without his existence. She must protect him. He was not immortal; at twenty-eight he seemed far older than her seventeen years. His beauty and his arrogance and his strength were ephemeral, like everything else that lived in the world. The fact that life and love could not last, that they were but moments in the eternity about them, added a poignancy to her feelings, a bittersweet sensation that made her want to hold him at once, for neither of them would last forever.

When they had eaten, and pushed off from the shore, he asked her how she felt, whether she was comfortable—not too cold, not too tired?

"I'm fine, but I'd rather not paddle," she said. Virginia sat in the front of the canoe, the rising sun reflecting off the clear water and warming her. She wanted to watch him, and would not be able to do this if she paddled, facing front.

"There would be those who think I took advantage last night," he said. "But I don't think of it that way. This isn't England. There is no special ceremony for marriage that I would want to take part in, not with the Puritans. The magistrate would have had to marry us, because that's the way they perform such things. Without a minister. Very dry and serious. Not even a wedding ring. They only have a feast at a funeral. Did you ever go to a Puritan funeral feast?"

"No. I am a bondservant, you remember."

"A runaway bondservant," he said. "And you still didn't answer me. What I said last night. If you'd be my wife."

"I am your wife now," said Virginia. "I thought you knew that."

John Collins put in his paddle and let the canoe drift downstream. He looked at her as if he were drinking her in, finding greater and greater pleasure with every moment. "You're more than I thought," he said finally. "You're going to make me very happy."

"I don't know how, but if you tell me, I will do it," she said.

"I am amazingly lucky to have found you, and found you out," he said. "Do you know, I was going to go to the big frontier trading post in New France—Montreal—and try to get myself a wife from one of the wife boats. It's not easy. You don't have long to make your choice, and my French is not the best. And the girls are peasants. You only have to pay their transportation costs and propose marriage, all at once. In the same breath. With about five hundred French trappers all trying to do the same thing—look for a beauty who won't mind living in the woods." He had a sudden thought, and laughed. "Do you know, that's what I was going to do with you. If you didn't want me. Or if I had made a mistake about you. I would have taken you to Montreal when it was warm enough to travel that far north. I would have taken you there and sold you to a trapper, or a marriage broker."

"Thank you very much," she said. "Sell me? If I'm a runaway, what does that make you? You're in every bit as much trouble as I am with the law, if there is any law here, and if you wanted to get rid of me, I certainly wouldn't have allowed you to sell what you never owned."

"Oh no?" he said. "I wish you'd stop calling yourself a runaway, Virginia." From under his deerskin blouse he pulled out a pouch, and from this he removed a paper. "Do you know how to read?"

"Yes."

"Well then, take a look—and don't you get it wet," he said. John edged forward in the boat and got close enough to the front to hand her the paper.

"Please sit down," she said. The boat was rocking again, and she was no longer simply afraid for herself, but for him too.

"You can read it, go ahead. There's the magistrate's seal. You're not a runaway. I bought your contract. Four pounds, in gold. For the next three years, you're my bondservant."

Virginia found her name, and the name of her former master, and the magistrate's seal; but the flowery script was difficult to read in the too-bright light, and she wanted to know at once what it all meant.

"You see, they're not all bad, the Puritans," he was saying. "They knew why you were treated so badly. Silvester needed a woman more than I did. He was in agony, or so they said. Not just because his wife was no longer his woman, but because of you. Everyone knew it. If he hadn't been such an important man, he would have been called to task long since. But he hadn't actually harmed you, not physically. He had lusted for you, and the magistrate and the parson were more than happy to get rid of you. They sold your contract on his behalf. That's why no one stopped us. As far as they were concerned, you belonged to me."

Virginia was too astonished to speak. That she could have been an object of sexual desire to the austere Silvester seemed fantastic to her; but if she could believe John's words, everything about her last years made more sense. No wonder her mistress loathed her; no wonder Silvester went out of his way to exhibit his antipathy. And the night when he'd come down to the cellar to offer her a bit of bread made sense too: He had wanted her, the way John had wanted her last night; and the master had hated himself for such desire.

"But what did the magistrate think you wanted me for?" she said finally. "Who were you that you had need of a bond-servant?"

"A stranger with money who could take you out of the community. That's all that he cared about. He didn't know what I had in mind, and maybe I didn't know either. Not exactly. But whatever I would do would have to be better than what that family was doing to you. Even if I sold you to a marriage broker, or just let you look after my boy."

"What boy?" she said, conjuring at once a wife who must have died, a woman whom he would always remember. In that same moment she realized how much she needed desperately to know all about him: what his life had been like in England, in France, in the New World; whether he had liked his brothers; whether his father and mother were good and kind; how he had fared in the crossing to America. Already she had pledged herself to him, after a fashion; but he had no idea of this. She must tell him what he already meant to her, how her growing love for him had already replaced any desire to return to England— to go anywhere at all where he could not go. And she had so many other things to share with him: her brother's stories, memories of her experience before an audience, tales and poems and jokes and songs. She wanted him to know everything about her, to understand why she loved him, feared for him, desired him.

"An Indian boy," he said. "Johnny, I call him. He's seven. I've taken care of him since his parents abandoned him—Pequots.

He was three then. I've got a Micmac woman who looks after him. She doesn't know any English, and her language is different from the Pequonocks and Sasquas who live nearby. The boy tries to be an Englishman, you see. Because then he can be my son, and he'd rather be my son than some Micmac squaw's little bastard. He doesn't know that his parents just left him. He thinks they're dead. And he doesn't even know that he's a Pequot. He's got no clan, no Indian name, no parentage—he loves the King of England. I know he'll love you right away. The Indians don't think too much of white women, but Johnny doesn't like to think of himself as an Indian, so he won't be prejudiced in that way." John began to paddle swiftly, a great smile breaking across his face as he looked over Virginia's head to a point on the opposite shore. Virginia turned around, but could see nothing at first.

"What is it?" she said.

"Broken Nose," he said. "My best friend in this part of the world."

Then all at once she saw the Indians: three powerful, bare-chested braves, paddling swiftly toward them in a great canoe. Their paddles hit the water in unison, soundlessly pulling their way across the river. Even with her limited experience of Indians, she could see that these were very different from any of the savages who'd come to Contentment. These were darker-skinned, with wide foreheads and painted faces; most strikingly different was the way they'd shaved their heads, save for a long central strip of bristling black hair.

"Don't speak," John said to her. "Don't say a word unless I ask you to."

"Are they friendly?" she said.

"Of course they are," he said. "Now, not a word more!"

She watched as John backwatered his paddle, turning the boat about to line it up with the approaching Indians' much larger canoe. John smiled, a huge, manufactured twisting of lips that seemed less related to happiness than to an exhibition of it. The Indian in the bow returned the smile, an even more grotesque parody of this usually spontaneous expression of pleasure. His nose was, indeed, broken, flattened into the ugly broad planes of his savage face. Both John and Broken Nose now touched their fingers to their smiling lips, and then brought their fingers up to their eyes, spreading their hands open and then turning them about, palms outward.

"Hey, Broken Nose, you old ugly bastard, good to see you," said John.

The Indian answered him in his own language, as harsh and incomprehensible a barking of syllables as Virginia had ever heard.

"I'm glad to see you agree with me, Broken Nose, you old devil you. What's for dinner, you blaspheming son of a savage? Are we going to sit around here and freeze, or are you going to invite us back to your twenty-wigwam village and get the squaws to cook up some food?"

Once again Broken Nose spoke, his eyes fastened with total concentration on John, his hands moving swiftly to his lips, to his eyes, to the sky, to the water, in signs that Virginia comprehended no better than his words. She marveled at his composure, and at that of his fellows. Not only did they show no fear, but they showed neither curiosity nor impatience, nor emotion of any kind. She shivered in the cool March air, even with the bright sun, and with the heavy gown and cloak and blankets about her. The Indians were on their knees in their huge dugout, and she could see the elaborately beaded moccasins and breechclouts they wore on otherwise naked bodies. She wondered if they were truly not cold, warmed perhaps by the exercise of paddling, or protected by a natural thickness and coloration of skin that she didn't possess. Virginia thought it just as likely that they *were* cold, that only training as elaborate and severe as any in Europe prevented them from wrapping themselves in the furs piled in their boat. If this were the case, she thought, they were formidable. Not like animals, warming themselves in the sun, true creatures of nature; but human beings, with frailties. Then their composure was learned, intelligent. Their savage clothing was chosen out of a tradition, a culture, and not because they hadn't the civilization to make doublets and jerkins. It was possible that they weren't simply pale shadows of men, incomplete, closer to the kingdom of animals than to that of the white man. When smallpox, a white man's disease unknown to the Indians, had broken out in

Contentment, it had been contracted by a local Indian band—a tiny group of no more than fifty men, women, and children, related to more powerful bands of the same northern tribe—and had killed every single one of them. The Puritans had rejoiced at the destruction, taking it as a sign from God. This was to be the New Zion, and just as the God of the Hebrews scoured the land of Zion of enemies, so would God rid New England of the heathen. For the first time, Virginia saw clearly the horror of this thinking. As Broken Nose spoke, and moved his eloquent hands, and leveled his intelligent eyes on her lover, she understood what the colonization of the New World meant for the Puritans, and for the Indians. The New Zion would be complete only when every naked, muscular body was clothed in Puritan gray; when every harsh syllable of the myriad Algonquian dialects had been converted to English; when every brown face had vanished; when every wigwam was replaced with an English village; when every Indian path was a New English highway; when God, through his chosen people, had removed this primitive sprinkling of heathen people and put in their place a mighty Christian nation.

"Come closer to me," said John suddenly. "Come on, to the middle of the boat." Even as he spoke, Broken Nose stood up, his powerful muscles alive to the shifting waters beneath his boat, and stepped from the bow of his boat to the bow of theirs. Virginia had never seen anyone move with such speed and agility. One of his fellows handed him his ash-wood paddle, and then he motioned for Virginia to get away from him; he did this with a bizarre courtliness that could not, however, disguise his distaste for the white woman.

Quickly, Virginia clambered over the center thwarts, keeping her back to the savage, and getting close to where John knelt, his hands on his paddle, eyes front and serious. Her clumsy shifting of weight nearly capsized the canoe, while Broken Nose's difficult jumping from one boat to the other had hardly added a ripple to the waters about them.

Then, without another word, John began to paddle, and with fury. She turned around to see Broken Nose at the bow, his large left hand at the top of the paddle's handle, his right hand very low, skirting the water as he pulled it back with rapid, even strokes. In a moment, they had built up a terrific speed, rushing with the current through twisting miles of rapid water. At their side, the two braves in the larger canoe paddled even more swiftly, keeping up with them at great expense to their bodies; but their faces showed nothing of wear, or excitement.

"Where are we going?" she said softly to John.

"I shall speak," said John loudly, as if addressing Broken Nose. "But you will only answer, my beautiful wife, or they will be angry. Bad manners for a squaw to intrude, and especially among their tribe."

Broken Nose turned his head, exhibiting the same polite, forced smile that was now on John's lips. Because his friend had spoken, he spoke in response, his sharp, arrhythmic words having as much meaning for John as John's had for him. Perhaps, thought Virginia, the savage is mocking my hair, or clothes, or smell; but no, she thought not. She couldn't believe that the words were anything but serious, steady, sure.

"That's right, Broken Nose, just keep on paddling," said John, letting out a little laugh. The Indian responded at once with a similar sound; not a laugh exactly, but a facsimile of one. Softly, John spoke now to Virginia: "Don't worry, darling. They're wonderful, this band. Come down for the pigeon roosting. They eat about a thousand birds in a month, and that's it for the year. Next month it's greens. Wild plants. They cook the leaves and eat them. Then it's shellfish. Oh, they'll be tapping the maple trees soon. All the squaws get fat that month, and very glossy and handsome. Broken Nose saved my life. Killed a Pequot before he killed me. With his little axe. Tomahawk. But don't be afraid. We'll stay with them this afternoon and night, do a little trading, and tomorrow we go home. And you'll have new clothes, like I promised."

Near the entrance to the Sound, they landed both canoes and portaged them, Virginia explicitly asked by John to help with the carrying, so as not to offend the Indians. It was all right for John to talk to her, and even with her, he explained, but only as long as he initiated the conversation. It was a black mark on a man's reputation if his woman spoke out of turn, especially in the presence of other men. Virginia bridled at this idiocy; it seemed more like a rule from the town of Contentment than from this strange, eerily serene civilization that she had never known to have existed at all. But she was resolved to learn what she could, do as she was told, at least until such time as she had the tools and the power to contest such customs.

The canoes were monstrously heavy. Even though Broken Nose and John held opposite ends of hers, the middle still pressed down on her raised hands with deadening force. She felt the blood drain from her wrists, from her arms, but saw no way to make a complaint, and nothing for her to do but endure it as the others did. Even John's breath became louder and shorter behind her as they climbed a hilly ground, then walked through a salt marsh spotted with bayberry bushes. Then another hill, steeper than the first, with the Indians breathing evenly at her side, carrying the canoe as if it weighed nothing; or perhaps as if it weighed ten tons, but showing that it made no difference to them at all. Broken Nose's perfectly proportioned back showed no signs of strain, and his moccasined feet seemed to have eyes of their own as they marched steadily, finding the surest ground. Virginia began to wish that she had less clothing on herself; the exertion was making her overheated. She began to think that she would have to quit before getting to the top of the hill, disgracing her husband as well as herself.

"There," said John. "Strong stuff you are. Go on, we're putting it down. Look, there's Long Island."

Virginia looked where he pointed and saw a vast body of water, the great Sound, and in the distance a fringe of land. But the land was blurry, and the ground beneath her swayed. She held on to John, and said without thinking: "We're not going there. Not to Long Island."

"You're not," he said. "Pequots are too strong there."

"Don't you go either," she said.

"Virginia, are you all right?" he said, for her tired face had grown suddenly pale, and her eyes were wide with horror. He could not know that the sudden fear in her was for him, and for their life together. What she had woken to that morning was a sense of love, and of life's claim on it; what she had seen across the Sound was an end to both.

"Please promise that you'll never go to Long Island," she said.

"What do you mean, Virginia? I go there all the time."

"Promise it to me, swear it to me," she said. "Please, John."

"Virginia, you're not to act this way in front of the Indians," he said sharply, insistently. "We will talk about this later."

Broken Nose was lifting one end of the canoe, and John rushed to pick up his end. "Go on," he said to Virginia. "Help us. It's only a few minutes more."

The village sat in a clearing, without a stockade or a sentry. To make up for the way he'd spoken to her, John filled the minutes with good-natured chatter. He told her that it would have taken an additional two hours to wind their way by canoe to the village, and the rapids they would have had to run might have capsized the boats and ruined his cargo. Broken Nose's people were of the Niantic tribe, John explained, but he didn't know what that meant, or how many of them there were out-side of this village. "Tribes don't really have names, except the names that other tribes call them. The way the Pequots are called that by everyone around here. It means something like wolves, or killers, or murderers of men—I can't be exact, be-cause I don't really understand most of what they tell me through signs. I speak a few Algonquian words, but nobody this far east understands me. In Unquowa, on the Saugatuck, I can make myself understood a little better, but not much. It's like I speak English, and say a few words in French—sometimes they can understand me a little. But even in fifty miles, or twenty miles, the languages are that different, like English and French. And if you go farther, where it's nothing like Algonquian, in New France, near Montreal—even you could tell that it's different. That's like a Greek going to China. And that's how different they look, too. Broken Nose is an Indian, but in New France he looks as different as I do from the people there. And he believes in different gods, different customs, different traditions."

A squaw at the edge of the village spotted them and let out a shrill cry. All at once, a half dozen Indian women came out of their wigwams and ran toward them. Two of the squaws, short powerful women in deerskin skirts and capes, took charge of Virginia's canoe, and two others relieved Broken Nose's friends of their portage.

"I'm going to have to go with the men," said John. "They'll take care of you."

"Yes," she said. She wasn't afraid for the moment. Nothing would happen to her lover as long as he stayed on this side of the Sound.

The squaws were very ugly to Virginia, having the same savage planes to their faces that their men had, but with little of their grace. Where the men's strength seemed free, warlike, invincible, the women's thick-limbed power had all the glamor of beasts of burden. Broken Nose spoke to them briefly, sharply, indicating Virginia with a nod; there were no smiles now. He left to go off with John to their sachem, with two other women carrying the contents of John's canoe behind them on a flat frame of hides and poles.

One of the squaws spoke to her, making a flurry of signs at the same time: a finger to her nose, another to the side of her cheek, a hand moved about her clothing with speed.

"Whatever you say," said Virginia. She followed them into the heart of the village. Wigwams were erected on either side of two distinct rows, the rows forming an elongated cross. Children, boys and girls in clean, brightly painted clothing, ran about; seeing Virginia, they ran up to her with great excitement. Like the youngest Puritan children, these Niantics hadn't yet learned to hide their feelings, to exhibit an absolute neutrality to the chaotic world.

There were no more than twenty-five of the wigwams, all of them nearly identical, large dome-shaped structures made up of woven mats covering long pointed poles held together with bark. Virginia thought she'd be taken into one of these, perhaps given a little food and a chance to rest, but quickly saw that she was being marched out of the village, past the last wigwam, to a very small, low structure of logs covered with sheets of bark.

"I don't understand," she said, forgetting for a moment her weariness and her terrible premonitions about the island on the other side of the Sound. The squaws signified their desire to have her remove her clothing, but as this made little sense to her, she hesitated, looking wonderingly at the tiny hut, no more than three feet high and six feet square. A young bare-breasted woman, wearing only a ragged skirt, tended a fire near this hut, on which rested a bed of stones and several small pottery vessels filled with steaming water. Virginia was too distraught to notice that this woman was of a different nation, much taller and longer-limbed than the other squaws, and that she was a slave, the keeper of the steam hut. The women began to take off her clothing. Once the gown was removed, they grew angry over Virginia's lack of cooperation, and the mysteries of buttons and pins. One took out a flint-bladed knife and cut away at the dirty layers of clothes. Virginia was too shocked to feel the cold, and too frightened. Never before had she been naked in front of strangers, and as these women jabbered about her in their ugly language, never letting go of her arms and hair, she felt as vulnerable as a newborn.

The slave woman got on her knees to open the steam hut, and the squaws forced Virginia to the ground and then pushed and prodded her inside. While the hut was open to the daylight, she could see herbs hanging from the low roof, but almost at once the slave woman shoved in a steaming pot of water, obscuring her vision with clouds of vapor. A moment later the woman returned with another pot, and then a third, each adding to the heat and steam in the room. Finally, the woman added hot stones from the fire, holding them on thick slabs of green wood, dropping them into the steaming water; and then she shut up the opening.

Naked, Virginia began to sweat.

Steam filled her lungs, her eyes.

For a young woman who hadn't been allowed a bath in many months, it was absolutely terrifying. Dirt ran out of her pores, and her heavy odor—so distasteful to this tribe, whose customs demanded great personal cleanliness—mingled with the aromatic herbs and vanquished their smell. But Virginia didn't relax, didn't imagine the purpose of the hut. She felt imprisoned. She tried to get out, to find her husband. Somehow her delight in their union must be responsible for this. In some way this steam was related to the hell promised her by the Puritans, a foretaste of eternity. She was shouting and hitting at the shaky walls when the slave woman returned and pulled her out. The daylight dazzled her, as did the rush of cold fresh air; but only for a second, for the squaws lifted her bodily and plunged her into an ice-cold stream on the other side of the steam hut, forcing her head underwater.

Virginia was certain now that this was a punishment, that they had dragged her out of the hut for trying to break it down, and that this was the way they planned to tame her, by freezing her to death in water, or drowning her altogether. But in another moment she was being pulled out, and the slave woman was beating at her body with twigs and rubbing her skin with the harsh inside of an animal hide. This through, the squaws motioned her back into the steam hut. Virginia dropped to her knees and did as she was told. Freshly heated stones were added to the steamy water, and once again she was in darkness, drinking in the vaporous, aromatic air.

And so it went, time after time, steamed until she thought she'd go mad, then released only to be shocked by the ice-cold water, then beaten and rubbed and returned to the steam. Virginia wondered if it all meant nothing, if these savages were every bit as childish and unintelligent as she'd been taught; if this whole ceremony of steam was but a game, a romp for the Indian women. It seemed that the cold immersions grew less frequent, that they were keeping her for longer and longer periods of time in the steam hut, and as the heat and water and rubbing cleansed her, she found herself relaxing, against her will, lulled into a stupor of acceptance. All her life she had been retreating farther and farther from civilization, she realized: from the structured life of a home she couldn't remember, to her brother's wild existence, to the primitive village of Boston, to the desolate frontier of Contentment, to this ultimate wildness.

When the slave woman came for her, she was very docile, removed from her own body, content to observe what they would do to her next. Nothing made sense to her, so she would not think. She had had parents, and they were gone; she had had a brother, and he was dead; she had a husband, but she knew that he too would die, and soon. Life was ugly and nasty in England, violent and mean in New England, and here in the wild it was incomprehensible.

She was taken into a wigwam, surrounded by squaws, chattering in their strange language about her blonde hair and pale skin and long, delicate limbs. They rubbed her body with sweet-smelling oils while she lay on thick furs, staring up at the circle

of sky in the center of the domed roof. Grease was applied to
her wet hair, adding luster to its thick texture. A skirt was
found for her, of deerskin, and so painted over and beaded that
it reminded her of her childhood, when she'd gone on the stage
as a princess or a fairy queen. Though none of the squaws had
paint on their faces, one of them began to paint Virginia's
cheeks and around her eyes. The women wrapped a loose
blouse about her, also of deerskin, and patterned with many
colors of beads in the shapes of fish and stars and slivers of the
moon. She was brought hot corn soup with bits of unfamiliar
fish floating in it, and she ate greedily, feeling more and more
like an inhabitant of a dream; but also stronger, more beautiful,
more a part of this new world.

Her hair was combed, and combed again. She was given
moccasins, softer than any shoe or boot she'd ever put on. Paint
was applied to her arms, to her fingers, to her fingernails. Virginia sat up on a bolster of hides, while a woman lit a fire in the
center of the wigwam against the encroaching cold blowing in
with the darkness. Once again, food was brought her. In a rude
wooden bowl were hot beans smeared with fat; she ate them
with a wooden spoon, amazed at their sweet taste. They'd been
pit-cooked in maple syrup and were the most delicious things
she'd ever eaten. She drank a warm herbal liquid, unfamiliar to
her, but sweetened too, and the sugar and the warmth of the
fire, and the unparalleled state of her skin and hair—clean and
fragrant and rejuvenated by the steam and the cold and the
rubbing—added to her euphoric passivity. If these people were
savages and she was civilized, she was happy now to have let
them remake her in their image. No matter that the paint on
her face and body was primitive, the deerskin clothing ruder
than the work of a tailor, their language awful to her ears—she
felt overwhelmed by a superior force, by a people kinder and
more direct than the English among whom she'd lived for the
last four years.

Broken Nose barked out commands from outside the wigwam, and immediately her wooden bowl was taken from her
hands, her hair was combed one last time, and all the squaws
pulled at her and then pushed her before them out into the
clear, cold night.

She saw John at once, standing alone in a circle of braves, his bearded face and full head of hair and fully clothed figure enough to distinguish him, the foreigner, even from a hundred yards away, in the light of a dozen bonfires and a nearly full moon.

The squaws accompanied her, ringing her, saying nothing to her or to each other now that they were under the scrutiny of their men. Perhaps a hundred Indians stood in a larger circle around the selected handful of braves who surrounded John; as Virginia drew closer, she saw that their bodies were painted, and that John's deerskin was new, and heavily beaded. An old Niantic man, his face painted more thoroughly than any of the braves, and the only Indian male there with a robe over his bare chest, stood facing John, just outside the ring of braves. He spoke three sharp syllables, and the ring opened as Virginia approached, and the squaws who'd accompanied her pushed her forcefully into the ring, next to John.

Virginia braved a quick look at him, marveling at John's gleaming hair, freshly combed beard, fragrant smell. John glanced at her, and she could see that his will to remain as impassive as the braves failed, if only for a moment. More than ever before in her life, she felt beautiful. There, utterly in the wilderness, under the clear night sky, surrounded by a congregation of savages, her lover's composure was broken at the sight of her: clean, anointed with paint and fragrances, wearing clothes that were sensual, exotic, cleaving her from her four years in Contentment with one sure stroke. She felt his desire for her, even as he turned his eyes back to the sachem, attempting to restore his dignity before the village.

"I love you," he said clearly, as if speaking to the sachem, but Virginia understood that the words were for her.

"And I love you," she said.

The sachem responded at once, rolling out deep, rhythmic phrases that were punctuated by monosyllabic cries from the congregation, exactly as if they were in church and the congregants were chanting "Amen." Because the words made little sense to her, she concentrated on the feeling in the old man's face as he made his pronouncements. His eyes were wide with wonder, as if he was as enthralled as she by the ceremonies now taking place; as if, indeed, it was an exploration, an entrance into a new world.

Virginia felt it was right to turn to John now, not surreptitiously or fleetingly, but to look at him, to absorb his image at this wondrous moment and remember it forever. He turned to her and took her hands in his. The sachem lifted a cup to John's lips, and he drank; then the old man brought the same cup to Virginia's lips, and she drank. The liquid was sweet, very cold, and the taste lingered long after she swallowed. All fears and premonitions fell from her. She was not tired, not filthy, not enduring a hard fate; she was joyous, she was exhibiting her love to the world. The sachem put his hands on their heads, and the entire village erupted in a frenzied chanting.

John pulled her suddenly into his arms, and kissed her before the crowd. She shut her eyes against the night, and felt herself joined to this man at this moment, becoming even more a part of his flesh and spirit than she had the night before. All at once, she was pulled away from him and hoisted in the air by a half dozen squaws. For the first time, she heard Indians laugh; the squaws, the braves, the sachem, the whole village was laughing as she and John were carried by their attendants to what that night would be their bridal chamber. The contract they had entered into wordlessly the night before was now sanctioned by native law, by a ceremony of union as clear and comprehensible as the force of nature. They had entered into matrimony in the New World, and its inhabitants had celebrated and sanctified their passion.

SIX

John and Virginia took five days to travel sixty miles east along the northern coast of the Sound to the Saugatuck River, to the small house with the great fireplace that John had built with his own hands.

They traveled twenty miles one day and four the next, not keeping to a schedule or going deliberately quickly or slowly. The weather was fine, and the March sun reflecting off the water browned their faces and hands and warmed away the winter chill lingering in their bones. Every afternoon they dug holes in the beach and piled in hot stones, covered with seaweed; in the seaweed they steamed clams, which Virginia had never tasted before. The Puritans fed clams and mussels to their hogs, disdaining shellfish as a lowly food, fit for beggars, and Virginia was astonished at how delicious and unique a treat the clambake was.

But everything about the journey was unique. They were man and wife, allowed the pleasures of each other's bodies. Choosing to beach their canoe for a brief meal in the middle of the day, they would put aside their pemmican meat—a gift of the Niantics—and fall into each other's arms on the sand. Duty gave way to pleasure. Nothing need be done but what each desired. The sun didn't have to be chased with chores that had to be done before darkness. It was entirely possible not only to forgo rising before dawn, but to sleep blissfully under the pale morning light, listening to the crackling logs of the campfire.

It was not only the nature of time and duty that was turned about; it was the very nature of space. They saw no other human beings after leaving the Niantic village. They had the vastness of the Sound, the vistas of the New England beaches, the distant Long Island shores; they had vast flocks of sea birds, shellfish sitting idly in pools, an occasional sprinkling of crimson flowers viewed on a far hilltop, away from the beaches, where spring flowers foolishly pushed themselves into the world before their time. In place of the cramped quarters of the house in Contentment, with ten people clustered about the hearth, Virginia could contemplate the miles, the silence, the freedom. Still, neither of them was silent long. For if Virginia had been surrounded by noise, it had been the noise of other people's conversation, or the noise of her mistress's anger, or the heavy banging of iron pots; and John wanted talk desperately.

"Often I see ships here, in the distance," he said. "The tops of masts, looming over the horizon. There's less traffic since the Pequots slaughtered an English crew at the beginning of winter. On the east end of Long Island, where pirates sometimes come."

She reminded him that he was not to talk about Long Island, or the Pequots, but only about their lives together in Unquowa, on the Saugatuck. He told her about the Dutch admiral who'd captured an entire Spanish treasure fleet—eight treasure ships and nine galleons filled with spices and hides—bringing home more than three hundred thousand pounds' worth of booty. She told him about life in London, about how the audience would howl with pleasure when she appeared onstage, a little girl in the clothing of a queen. He spoke to her of French châteaux, and the cold weather in New France, much worse than in New England. She spoke to him of arriving in Boston in the "strawberry time," when the weather was so hot and the air so moist that she thought she'd been taken to a tropical land; until autumn came, swift and violent with cold sleet and then snow, falling in quantities that she'd never dreamed possible.

"That's it about this place," he said. "Anything is possible. Everything is bigger, quicker, more abundant. More wonderful, really. I would never have met you, never have had the chance to love you in England. Everything is old there, and constrained, and crowded together. I swear to you, you'll never miss the old country. Not when you understand what we have here."

But she couldn't accept his feelings about the New World, not completely. Virginia was perfectly resigned to remaining where she was, because she was with him, his wife. The fact of their love was more important than geography, than wide spaces and plentiful game. He spoke to her so possessively of the bright sky, the wooded hillsides, the romantic coves and great harbors of the New England shore, that she knew that he would fight for these things; and Virginia wanted nothing so badly that she would fight for it, except for their love. Though they saw no hostile Indians, he told her more about the seven-year-old boy waiting for him at home; even if the Pequots had never killed a white man, he would have hated their tribe for abandoning the boy, leaving him for dead. He had been three years old, traveling on his mother's shoulders, part of a band of Pequots, perhaps a hundred of them; they had come south along the Saugatuck in the spring, probably to do mischief to the local Sasquas. Some of them contracted smallpox, or what was thought to be smallpox, including the three-year-old, and the large war party abandoned all the sick and fled the area, terrified of the disease. Everyone died except the boy, who had had nothing worse than a childish fever. The Sasquas took him in and cared for him, but would not adopt him; they would adopt any other tribe's child, but not a Pequot's. They were not afraid that his parentage would be discovered; they believed his character to be foreordained and, like all Pequots, he would grow to become a murderer, and they did not want him to live with their tribe. John Collins adopted him, at the same time buying a Micmac squaw to care for him. He tried to explain to Virginia his reasons for such an act of altruism, claiming that he needed company, that the squaw took care of all the work, that many tribes in the area respected him for his decency, if not for his courage.

"What kind of foolish things are you telling me?" she said. "You took the boy because he was going to be abandoned. And you're a wonderful man."

"I'm not so wonderful," he said. "I'm hardly ever with the boy."

"Don't call him that. Call him what you call him to his face: Johnny. I won't confuse you. You wanted a son, and you took him in, and you have a son, and I'll love him just the way you do."

"Yes," he said passionately. "I know you will."

But she knew she'd never love the boy the way she loved his adoptive father. And John's passion worried her, unless it was directed her way. She knew he would always hate the Pequots, and that expense of feeling worried her. More than once he'd predicted war, a war of white men and Mohegans united against the Pequot tribe, and she knew that he would want to be in the first rank of men fighting the hated tribe. Even Master Silvester had thought John Collins a fanatic on the subject of the Pequots, and Virginia understood that fanaticism revealed itself in different ways among different men. The Puritans had a vision, a fanatical vision, one that they would die for; but so did her husband. And if John Collins's life was not built around religious idealism, it still was structured by certain inescapable beliefs: that this new land must be free to all who wanted to live on it; that every man in New England must be judged according to his deeds; that the white man must show himself as brave, as fierce, as intractable in dealing with hostile tribes as any of the Indian nations.

Listening to the man she loved, Virginia understood that he was capable of terrible violence. Though he spoke of growing rich and fat surrounded by their children, Virginia could see the unsettled future in his eyes. While for Virginia their love was a beginning and an end in itself, it was mostly a beginning for him. His love for her had brought his hatred into clearer relief; he must make their home secure. John wanted a family, he wanted generations of strong, straight-backed children, eager to make lives in the endless wilderness. But first he had to secure this foothold, this tiny house at the edge of the river.

"The Puritans don't understand the difference between Indians," he told her. "They're nations, separate and distinct, and they're prepared to be as civilized as we are. Except for the Pequots. They insist on war, and the white man has to make his force felt with them. That's the only way we can have this land, the only way. The destroyers have to be destroyed."

"But you sound as superstitious now as the Indians," she said. "Your own boy is a Pequot. Could you see him killed for the sake of New England?"

"*Virginia*," he said, as if to block a torrent of anger. But quickly he turned his eyes from her to the slowly moving countryside. She did not understand, he told himself, and he would save his anger for when it would be needed.

"I'm sorry if I upset you," she said. "Perhaps I shouldn't mention Johnny at all."

"You may mention Johnny, and you can yell at old John," he said. He looked at her again, her eyes turned bravely toward him. She was after all still so young, for all her experience of the Old and New Worlds, of suffering and joy. He wanted to reassure her then, to tell her that all would be well, that he had not meant to show anger, that in the sphere of their lives that dealt with death and destruction she must never have a part.

"I don't want to yell at you," she said. "But perhaps you can beach the canoe for a minute. Over there, if you want."

"I want," he said, and quickly he did as she suggested, paddling into a shallow, rock-bottomed pool adjacent to a sandy beach, shaded by a huge hill covered with bayberry bushes.

And this was how they spent most of their honeymoon, wordlessly exploring each other's love, not searching for the facts of pain and hatred that nestled within their memories. Virginia had heard long ago, without quite understanding what it meant, that the honeymoon of newlyweds did indeed follow the orderly changes of the heavenly moon: With each day, love would grow stronger, reaching for a fullness; but this fullness, like its lunar model, must needs diminish. Inevitably, the honeymoon was a time of greater and greater happiness, and then greater and greater sorrow, as the lovers returned to the diminished realm of reality.

So with the start of any argument, any flashing of her husband's pain, any premonition of an awful future, any remembrance of her brother's death in this New World, indifferent to any human suffering, Virginia wondered if the moon's fullness had come and she was now witnessing its waning.

But always, this fear would vanish, this conceit would evaporate when they made love. Her feelings weren't waning; neither were her hopes, her moments of happiness, her love. This was not the beginning of a half month of happiness and a lifetime of drudgery and toil. This was the beginning of a love that would fire her life, that would sustain her always. They made love, and the world truly was new, and free, and beyond all concern with the old. And in five days of travel to the house John Collins had built, Virginia learned to ignore the fear, the irrational reaction to distant half-human sounds, the sense of journeying into a wilderness so removed from civilization that it seemed impossible for them not to be swallowed up, transformed into trees and rivers and birds, into the very fabric of the world around them. In its place she found the courage to embrace the moment, to celebrate the freedom that she found so hard to accept as hers. Just as her love for John had brought about a terrible fear of his mortality, of the fragility of human life in an eternity of death and birth, so did her joy call forth an awareness of the chaos about her; a chaos which had always managed to destroy. But she took instruction from her feelings now, deliberately. Loving, making love, holding on to John, listening to his words, watching the sun in his beard, watching the sweat on his chest as he stroked the ash-wood paddle in the coastal waters, all these were the moments to dwell on, to live in, to be joyous for.

And so, when they had finally reached the end of their journey, had swept upriver against the current of the Saugatuck, paddling furiously and laughing all the while, and Virginia finally saw their house, she ignored the dread that stole over her. Shutting her eyes for a moment against a stabbing of pain, she refused to believe that Johnny was gone, that the Micmac squaw was butchered, that inside the tiny house was nothing but destruction.

"It's a little small," he said, and she opened her eyes, and he jumped out of the canoe and pulled it after him onto the marshy land. "Hey, boy! Hey, Johnny!" he yelled.

She got out of the boat onto the land, looking slowly at the rude logs that had been planted in the earth in a wide perimeter about the house; perhaps a quarter acre had been fenced in on three sides, the open side being the sharply curving river. From the high ground on which the house rested, one could look downriver to the Sound, and upriver for a mile. The soft ground felt shaky after so many hours in the canoe, and she looked searchingly through the tiny windows of the house, hoping to see movement.

"This is crazy," he said, not at all worried. "Usually Johnny's all over me by now. He doesn't go too far from the stockade. Unless Biki's taken him to the Sasqua village."

Virginia saw it all quite clearly: the boy dead, the woman hanging from a crude gibbet, John grabbing his musket and running off to war. But she forced this vision down. "Who's Biki?" she said.

"The squaw. It's what we call her. I don't even know if it's her name, or her clan, or if it just means 'woman' in her language. But she comes when you call her that."

There was a huge woodpile against the stockade wall, and next to it an even larger hill of kindling wood. Virginia tried to believe that it was true: They were at the Sasqua village, they were fishing, they were planting peas and radishes, they were alive.

"Come on up to the house," he said. "Aren't you curious to see what it looks like? After all, you're now mistress of everything in it." She forced herself to watch his broad back bend over a burden from the canoe, remembering that he was alive, that they had not made love for the last time, that perhaps even now his baby was growing within her. There was joy in the world, and she shut back her dark vision and joined him in picking up some of the cargo, and then the two of them began to ascend the hill to the house.

Suddenly, there was guttural noise behind them, the sound of the savage, and instinctively Virginia dropped her bundle and threw herself before John. Let them kill her first, she thought. She could not live by herself, not only without the man she loved, but simply alone—alone in this distant universe.

"What's the matter?" said John, laughing with pleasure. He took her hands and turned her about. "Come, meet Biki," he said.

(87)

They were not Pequots, not savages with drawn bows. A short, wiry, long-haired woman, dressed in a deerskin skirt and a Puritan's gray bodice, but without sleeves: Biki, the squaw who watched Johnny. She was calling out in her awful tongue, not to attack, but to attract Johnny's attention.

"Hey, Biki, you lovely old Micmac. Take care of my son, did you? Johnny? How's Johnny? Good, huh? Glad to see your English is improving. This is Virginia." He pulled his wife close to his side, and smiled. "Virginia Collins. My wife. Woman. Yes, you understand?" For emphasis, he brought Virginia yet closer, and kissed her cheek. The squaw jumped back and laughed. Then she turned around and ran straight for the river, and then she ran all the way back.

"I think she likes you," said John.

The little boy crept up so silently, it seemed to Virginia like a dreamlike refutation of her vision. He was quiet, and moved with infinite care, a pretty boy with tiny dark features, dressed, unlike his adoptive father, in Puritan gray, a suit of good cloth that must have cost a pound and was now ragged and dirty and too small.

"Hello, Father," he said with great dignity. He did not look at Virginia at all.

"Johnny! Where did you come from?"

"From the woods."

"Wait till you see what I brought you."

"Hello, Johnny," said Virginia.

Johnny turned to her, his face wild with wonder. "You speak English," he said, as if this were the greatest surprise of his life.

"Yes, of course. I am an English woman."

"God save the King," said Johnny, meaning every word. "God save the King!" There was no question about his joy. Here was someone like himself, he seemed to be thinking. Someone who can speak and act like an English person.

"Oh, yes," said Virginia, picking him up with a spontaneous show of feeling. He was after all a very small boy, and very much alive. "Yes, Johnny. God save the King!"

* * *

The fireplace was indeed as huge as John Collins had promised. Its length and depth would have served a hall five times the size. As it was, it seemed more like the relic of a mansion, its carefully matched field stones worthy of the magistrate's home in Contentment. The tiny shelter built about it, though it was sturdy, might have been put up in a few days, a quick defense against hostile surroundings.

"One day I'll build a fine house here," John said soon after they'd all entered. "Myself or my children, right, Johnny?"

"I can build a house," said Johnny.

Biki said something to Johnny: short syllables of varying pitch, almost like a song, whose melody was as ugly and indecipherable as its words. Johnny sang back to her, shaking his head sharply.

"Biki wants us to eat, but we're not hungry yet," said Johnny.

"Maybe Virginia is hungry?" said John.

"Are you hungry, Virginia?" said the little boy. She marveled at the fact that he had no accent, or at least no other accent than that of his father.

"No, I'm not," said Virginia, wishing that she could be called something else. If John was his father, she must become his mother. Pulling the boy closer to her, she asked him if he'd like to see the clothes they had for him.

"Oh, yes, I would like that," he said, but she could see that he wanted to waste no time with bundles, with material things. He had a need of one thing, and that was to talk. Perhaps he had little use for Biki's language, had learned little more from her than simple commands about eating and drinking and sleeping. He was not only English-speaking, he was English-loving; his eagerness to embrace the world of his adoptive father was touching. Here in Unquowa there was no one who spoke his language. She was the first person to speak out words to him in the language that he thought of as his own, other than the father who had taught it to him. "Do you know how to count to a hundred? I can count to a hundred, and I can count it backwards, too."

"Really?" said Virginia. "That's remarkable."

He counted quickly, too quickly, stumbling over the syllables, and getting to a hundred in the space of a minute. John wanted to stop him when he began to recite the numbers backward, but Virginia smiled at her husband and shook her head. They were making friends.

Meanwhile, Biki was busy at the hearth, building a fire from hot embers, though it was a warm day and in the small space the four of them warmed one another. As John showed her about the house—the trunks and boxes that doubled as tables and chairs, the rolled-up pallets on which they slept, the great quantity of French and Dutch cookware, the very valuable books from printing presses in London and Amsterdam—he spoke to her about his dream of generations. The fireplace would be the center, the unchangeable core of whatever would come later. At once, he would set to work, building out a second room on the other side of the hearth, doubling their little space. But that was simply the beginning. There would be a porch one day, a second story, a kitchen with its own stove, its own oven. There would be rooms for sleeping, rooms for sitting, rooms for sewing and spinning, each with its own lights and hearth and furniture.

"This is wonderful, John," she said. "Already it's wonderful, as long as you're here."

Though there was an abundance of fresh food, they dined on pemmican meat, the gift of the Niantics, because Johnny thought of it as the food of the adventurer. Made from the leanest—and therefore most tasteless—meat, it was dried and then subjected to a long beating; cranberries were pounded into it, together with bone marrow and hot fat. The result was wrapped in animal skin, and would keep for many weeks.

"I'm going to be a trapper too, and a trader, I'm going to go out with my father and live in the woods," Johnny said, still marveling at being able to speak English to another human being. "I can spell. I have a book. Do you want to see? We have a bible here with mistakes. It's very funny, that's what my father says, but we can't show it to any Puritans. You're not a Puritan, are you? I never saw a Puritan. I never saw a white woman either. You have yellow hair. I like it."

John interrupted his talkative son, and Biki ordered the boy to eat. He explained to Virginia that he owned one of the famous "Wicked Bibles" published in 1631, with the terrible error in the fourteenth verse of Exodus 20: Instead of "Thou shalt not commit adultery," it read "Thou shalt commit adultery."

"What does that mean? That word? You said you'd tell me when I was older."

"Are you older now?"

"Of course I'm older, I'm older every day," he said. But still the little boy wasn't allowed to know the meaning of the word *adultery*. Curious, he was looking over the color and texture of Virginia's hand and arm. "Why are your hands browner than your arms?"

"From the sun, boy," said his father. "Leave Virginia in peace.'"

"It's all right," said Virginia.

"She's so much whiter than you, Father. I'm English too, just like my father, but I come from the Indians, because I look like them. But not like Biki. I don't look like Biki, do I?"

"No," said Virginia. "You look just like a little English boy."

"But don't little English boys have yellow hair? Or brown like Father? I have black hair, see, like Biki, and my skin is dark, much darker than Father's."

"Well, there are so many people in England, all different kinds of people with all different colors of hair and shades of skin."

"Are there wigwams?"

"No, of course not," said John. "I told you that."

"And the houses are really big? Did you ever see a castle? Are the castles really like this, made out of stone, all over of stone?" He was up on his feet, putting his hands on the fireplace wall.

"It's just that he's not used to talking for a long time," explained John. "Not in English, and English is what he likes. He's a good little English boy, isn't that right, Johnny?"

Virginia got to her feet and took hold of the little boy in front of the blazing hearth. "Johnny," she said, "I want to tell you something. An English custom, all right?"

"Yes."

"This is what's done in England, and so I think we should do it here too, since we are all English people. You see, when a man with a son marries a woman, the woman becomes just the same as a mother to the child. Do you understand what I'm saying, Johnny?"

"I understand."

"Johnny, your father and I have gotten married. We are husband and wife, and that makes me your mother."

"You are my mother?" said Johnny, looking at her with trembling amazement. He looked over to Biki, stirring a huge pot of Old World manufacture over the fire; and he looked to his father, alive with anticipation and pride.

"Yes, Johnny. I'm your mother now," said Virginia, and the seventeen-year-old girl took the little boy in her arms and held him to her, just the way she'd held each of the Silvester children, until they had grown old enough to find her their inferior. But this was different, far different. The little boy was hers, and for precisely the reasons she had told him. If no English court had married John and Virginia, no English court had overseen John's adoption of the Pequot child either. Virginia had become a wife, and now she was a mother to her husband's child, and there in the tiny space of civilization within an endless sea of wilderness, she felt a power, a unity, a strength. From a rootlessness of despair, she had joined with this young man, and now, sharing their lives, they shared a family.

In some ways the tiny log house's interior reminded Virginia of the cramped backstage quarters of the London theaters she'd performed in as a child. Every inch was crammed with treasures, props for living, exotic and practical. Especially in the dark, when Biki snored, and Johnny slept in silence, John's whispering reminded her of the swift words spoken backstage, offering encouragement or information or solace.

They shared a pallet, not five feet from where their son slept. Ten feet away was the squaw, her back to them, and rising in rhythm with her snores. The only source of light was the dying fire in the hearth, illuminating little more than the field stones of the fireplace. There were four windows, and their glass revealed only blackness; pitch-blackness, as if no stars shined, no moon wandered across the skies.

"I won't be just a trapper anymore," he whispered. "To the Puritans I'm more a trader now anyway. Let the French boys run into the woods for the beaver. I can go to the beaver post at Montreal, and over to Long Island and to New Amsterdam, and trade back and forth. That's the future for us. Fourth son's got to be smart. They say ten thousand English are coming over this year and next—mostly Puritans, but they still speak English. Think of what that'll mean for us. Books and clothes and English flowers and vegetables and people to talk to. What I want is for us to be smart, you see. Make the most of getting here first. I figure on buying a ship maybe, a sailing ship, and going to the Caribee Islands. That's where the richest colonies are, you know. That's where the English live like kings."

"Where are the Caribee Islands?"

"In the Caribee Sea," he said, laughing softly. "It's far away, where it's warm, and black slaves do all the work, and white men live in great mansions by the sea."

"Why do you want to go there?"

"Well, it's not like I have a definite plan. Someday, I think. It would be good to be able to have a ship, and take over things we have here in abundance to trade for their rumbullion."

"Do you mean hard liquor? You want to trade hard liquor?"

"I want to *drink* hard liquor, but also trade whatever I have left." After a moment he added, "I love you. More than I could have ever imagined possible. I won't want to leave this place. Not for trading, not for anything."

"So don't."

"Once in a while. Only to keep us healthy and wealthy, all right?"

"But not for war."

"What?"

"John. Not for war, please. Don't leave us to go to war."

"There is no war, thank God," said John. "Don't talk about war when it hasn't happened."

She said nothing further, feeling his anger grow. They were still for a long time, and she waited for him to come to her, certain that he would want to make love with her, no matter how close the others were, no matter what his mood. For how could anything be more important than lovemaking? With the blackness outside, and their world a tiny speck floating in a universe prepared to erupt and engulf them at any moment, how could anything be more important than sharing what they had, what they both acknowledged?

But he made no move to take her into his arms. "What will

(*93*)

you trade for the hard liquor?" she said softly, to see if he was awake.

"Barrel staves."

"Who will cut the barrel staves?"

"Our servants, our slaves."

"We will have no slaves, John," she said. "Don't talk about slaves when you've freed me from slavery."

"You weren't a slave," he said, turning to her; if it hadn't been so dark, he could have seen the tears of vexation in her eyes. "You were an indentured servant."

"No slaves."

"The Puritans own slaves."

"I hate the Puritans."

"The Indians have slaves. Biki is a slave. I bought her from the Sasquas."

"She will not be a slave, not in this house. She can come and go if she wants. She is not to be our property, do you understand?"

"There are to be no slaves in this house, is that right?"

"Yes."

"And I am not to go to war?"

"Yes, John."

"Anything else? Any other orders, my dear wife?"

"Yes," she said. "You are to love me more every day. More and more, and always there'll be room for more."

"Yes," he said. "All right." If she had waited another moment, he would have taken her into his arms, but she had no desire to wait. This was her man, and she wanted him at that moment, and so she brought his face to hers and kissed his astonished lips, and he felt her tears against his cheek, and he blamed himself for crimes he didn't understand. Of course he would go to war, if the English banded together to fight the Pequots. He was a man, after all, living in a land that must be made safe for his wife and children, and the generations thereafter. But if she cried, it was his fault. He had taken her away and exposed her to love, and for all his show of mastery and confidence, her tears cut through him like daggers.

Softly, she ran her hands over his clothing, she loosened his deerskin shirt, she placed her hand on his growing penis, feeling his breath come faster, his desire quicken in the still, dark space.

"Our children," he said. "They will cut the barrel staves."

"And bring back rumbullion," she said. "To make the Puritans drunk? What sort of man of business are you anyway?"

"I'm not," he said. "Not a man of business." And then there was no more talk, just the mutual astonishment of their young bodies, once again growing to pleasure, up a path so steep with sensation and desire that it brought them very near to pain. But it was not pain, not at all. She placed her fingers over his lips, to show him how loud he was, but he was past caring. The squaw wouldn't wake, and if she did, she'd hardly be surprised. As for Johnny, his dreams were simple, and kept him deep in sleep, where everyone lived in the tales of his father's home country, all with red beards and yellow hair and pale skin and speaking English, only English, just like the King and Queen.

Please, he thought, begging her to be happy, to cease crying, to never cry again. For as he merged his body with hers, as they moved their torsos with a rhythm that was never learned, but sure, and perfect, he wanted only for her to be happy. She must not cry. He would do anything and everything in the world for her, for she had become the center of his life. It was not possible, he knew, that a girl of seventeen, poorly educated and of unknown parents, could have so bewitched him. But then, neither was this possible: this warmth around his penis, this gentle pressure running through every part of his body, this inescapable desire for release running against as strong a desire to stay forever, just where they were, at that point of hysterical pleasure before the explosion of joy that was no less miraculous than the possibility of conception itself.

Later, when he had fallen asleep in her arms, Virginia examined her feelings, trying to assuage her hurts, the way an animal licks its wounds. She fought back her fears now with the realization that she had been proven wrong; that the little house had not contained death and destruction, but a little boy, loving and in need of love. Still, she knew that there would be nothing that she could do to stop John from going to war, if war came. But even this fear must be shunted aside, so that she could live. Perhaps war would not come. If it did, there was no way to be sure that it would kill her husband. Holding him tighter, she knew that only her life of misery made her so full of dire premonitions. Only her life as a victim sat on her back now, telling her that such joy as she now experienced with this man in her arms could not endure forever. Such joy must be as short-lived as the moments in which their bodies merged together, moving in tandem to a world beyond time, before returning inevitably to earth. This was her greatest fear: that to be as happy as she was was impossible, inhuman, and could not last, not in this world. But there was no other world that she wanted. Not in heaven, not in any world to come, or world that was past. She would have John, only John, always John, or she would have nothing.

SEVEN

John Collins was not a farmer. In Connecticut March was the time to sow hay seed, plant radishes and peas, set goose eggs, and perform a hundred other tasks of the season. But this house, and the land around it, was made rich by his trapping and trading. The Sasquas provided them with food, though they had little need of it: John fished and hunted, and the squaw Biki had a vegetable garden in its own stockade.

Because he was a man of property—owning gold coins, iron pots and kettles, two dozen newly manufactured flintlock muskets, as well as dozens of ancient muskets in good repair—he had leisure as well. This was something greatly prized among the many Indian nations, but rarely observed in the Puritan towns. The warm weather turned suddenly cold, and a snowstorm blew in from the northeast, locking the four of them up in the tiny house for a day. Whereas the Silvesters would have used the time to shell corn, to dress flax, to make soap, John passed the time telling stories and whittling a dog out of a stick of wood.

John could be industrious too. When the warm weather returned, he bought the help of a couple of Sasqua braves with a good iron spatula, and together they chopped down the trees that would serve to extend the log house. All three worked from dawn to dusk, ignoring a light drizzle, stopping only for a meal at midday. Virginia spent the time acquainting herself with both Johnny and Biki, the child helping her to communicate with the squaw. "We will teach Biki English," Virginia announced to the little boy. "Wouldn't it be nice if she could understand what we are all saying?"

"Biki can't speak English," said Johnny. "She's a Micmac. She's an Indian."

"But that doesn't matter. She can learn."

"No," said Johnny, as if the point was very important to him. "She can't learn English. It's not possible."

But slowly, to Johnny's amazement, she proved that it was possible. By the first week in April, Biki had learned to say "Good morning," learned to call the sun, moon, trees, river, house, and hearth by their English names. Meanwhile, Virginia worked on Johnny's reading and writing, using the "Wicked" bible and an English translation of Sir Thomas More's *Utopia*. In the middle of the rainy month, she helped Biki dig an asparagus bed, and went with her to the Sasqua village to buy painted straw baskets, paying with white wampum beads produced by a tribe on Long Island. At the Sasqua village, Biki pointed to a pregnant squaw and then to Virginia. "Yes," said Biki. "You. Boy."

"I hope so," said Virginia. Her menstrual period was a week late, but she had none of the signs she'd witnessed with Mistress Silvester. She felt fine in the morning, had a healthy appetite, was in good humor—was in love, and thought of nothing so mundane as nausea.

"Boy," said Biki again, and she put her hands together as if holding an infant and rocking it gently to sleep. Virginia wondered how old Biki was, if she'd ever had children of her own, if she'd ever known love.

"Or girl," said Virginia, trying to get Biki to repeat the word and, more important, understand what it meant. Drawing the attention of a group of Sasqua children, she was able to illustrate the new word. But now that the yellow-haired woman had granted their importance—by noticing them at all—the curious children wouldn't let off following her about. They had seen other white men besides John Collins, but rarely; and none had ever seen a white woman, or such blonde hair.

Virginia allowed them to follow her and Biki home, a distance of two miles along a narrow path through the woods. Since the children, like their elders, preferred running to walking, it was a small distance even for the youngest of them, and Virginia was comforted by the fact that a friendly community was close by.

Through an annual, largely symbolic gift to their chief, the Sasqua village accepted a responsibility for the safety of the Collins house and its inhabitants. But even without the Holland gin and glass beads, the leaders of the village would have protected their neighbors from a war party; for without John Collins they had no regular supply of cookware, and no ready outlet for their furs, for which he paid them well, in fathoms of black and white wampum.

And so there was cause for accepting the fact of peace and serenity. The new room was finished, and bright Sasqua blankets covered the floor and walls, and husband and wife were alone with their pleasure throughout the long, quiet nights. Only the intensity of her happiness got in the way of her hopes; only the same gloomy refusal to believe that life could be sustained at such a level of joy haunted her.

"You're leaving soon, aren't you?"

"Just for a short time," said John. "I want you to miss me."

"Why can't they all come here to trade?"

"Who? The Dutch in New Amsterdam? The villages on Long Island? The fur traders of Montreal? There is nothing here for them, except me. I don't have anything to trade unless I travel."

"But this could be a trading post, couldn't it? Right here. We can build another house, and fill it with things the Indians want. They come here, they bring us furs, then white men come and buy the furs with whatever the Indians want."

"No, it won't work," said John. He didn't choose to explain the reasons. His wife was pregnant, her breasts and belly slightly swollen, her eyes bright with the promise of a new life. It was May. Biki had planted melons, pumpkins, and potatoes, and the young English apple trees outside the house were just beginning to bloom. They had lived together for less than two months, but already a clear pattern had developed in the way he chose to treat her: Virginia was not to be exposed to the things she feared. "They wouldn't want to come here, darling."

There was a rumor he'd heard the day before from a Sasqua brave. A Pequot band had been cheated out of their share of the proceeds from a sale of beaver pelts by a half-English trader who'd simply vanished with the gold. What happened next was unclear: Either the Pequots had ambushed the Dutch traders who'd bought the pelts, and killed them, or had failed in their ambush and had themselves been slaughtered. In either case, the Sound was not going to be the happiest of places for a man with a canoeload of pelts. And Virginia's idea of creating a trading post at the edge of an unimportant Sasqua village made no sense for precisely that reason. Profits were made by traders willing to risk their lives carrying their cargoes through dangerous routes, with ready muskets, and friends in many strong tribes. His latest trip was to take him first to the Dutch island of Manhattan, where he'd trade beaver and otter pelts for gold, cookware, and gunpowder, then to the dozen bands with whom he'd long traded on the north shore of Long Island, trading cookware for more pelts, and giving the most hostile band, a subgroup of the Naragansets, liquor and gunpowder and some very old matchlock muskets. These fiercest of his clients protected him, not only against the Pequots who were in the area, but against the occasional Dutch cutthroats, half traders, half pirates, long since banished from New Amsterdam.

"But promise that you won't go to Long Island," said Virginia.

"Yes," he lied. "The important thing for you is to leave Biki to her work. You rest, do you hear me?"

"We don't even know that I'm pregnant."

"I know," said John. "All my wives looked like that after the first month and a half."

"What wives?"

"Do you expect me to remember all those names? There must have been a hundred of them."

"That's not funny," she said, suddenly bursting into tears. John apologized, and held her. "That's not funny at all," she continued. "There's never supposed to be anyone else, not before or after, do you understand? You're my whole life, and I want to be your whole life, and I don't think it's very funny, not when you're getting ready to go away soon, leaving me for someplace dangerous."

"You see," he said evenly, "you're even acting pregnant. Listen to yourself. Crying over a little canoe trip."

He was right, after a fashion. Her words had been too wild for his little joke, too wild to protest his journey. After all, he was a trader. It was his trade that would bring them soap and clothing and perhaps even a looking glass. But then, she was not protesting his trip so much as trying to hold on to what she had; she was not angry at his joke, but at the awful possibility of an end to her joy. She supposed this was a sort of selfishness, but she didn't care. There had been no chance for selfishness during her terrible years with the Silvesters. She wanted her man, her love, her baby, her home; whatever threatened this she would fight with all her heart.

John left a week later, on a cool bright day, his canoe loaded with beaver and otter pelts, wampum, muskets, and a few gold coins. Virginia walked barefoot into the water, up to her knees, holding on to the boat, feeling his impatience to be off, and resenting it. It was the first time she felt that she loved him more than he loved her. But when he turned to look back at her, his eyes squinting in the bright light, she knew that she was wrong; it was stupid to compare their different ways of loving.

She had thought she'd be afraid to sleep alone in the new room of the small house, surrounded by blackness and the sounds of the forest. But she had no trouble drifting to sleep, and slept deeply.

During the warm days of May, she would often walk along the river to the Sound, watching Johnny pick up clams and collect them in a huge basket. Biki fished with a net in the river, and the Sasquas provided them with a constant supply of wild turkey, either as presents or as a way of securing future credit from John. So they were all well fed, and Virginia's mind was busy with teaching Johnny to read and Biki to speak. The great fears that had so preoccupied her had strangely vanished, as if the life growing within her refused to be disturbed by womanish premonitions; her baby demanded quiet, and good food, and a dreamless sleep.

John had promised to be back within four weeks, but even

when five weeks had passed, Virginia remained calm. She felt that if anything had happened to John, something unmistakable would have happened to her; something within her would have died at once.

"Boy," said Biki late one morning, rushing up from the river's edge to where Virginia sat in the sun. "English," she added, but Virginia was already up and running, not even thinking of the child in her womb, but only of Johnny, and the look of terror on Biki's face.

Johnny was down at the river, shouting to a group of men in a longboat coming upstream from the Sound. "Hello, hello!" he shouted, for these were white men, like his father.

"Johnny, get away from the water," she said. But like her adopted son, she couldn't take her eyes off the men in the boat. Beyond them, looming like a great prehistoric beast, was a three-masted bark flying English colors. The larger ship carried cannons, and was anchored in the Sound, afraid to enter the river. There were four men in the longboat, two of them struggling with the oars, their little sail made useless by the windless day.

"Englishmen," said Johnny.

"Please, Johnny, come here," she said, and the little boy stepped back and took Virginia's hand. He was not afraid, but he held her hand tightly, possessively.

As they grew closer, she could see their quilted vests, worn as a light armor against arrows. The men were bearded, sunburned, in filthy doublets over white linen shirts. Three of the men were young, her husband's age, and wore long hair; the fourth was an older man with stiff-backed bearing and dead eyes. It was this man who spoke as they drew closer.

"Hello, Goodwife. God be with you."

"Hello!" said Johnny. "Throw me your rope!"

"Isn't that an Indian boy?" said one of the young men.

"More likely a half-breed," another laughed. Neither made any show of courtesy, or any attempt to keep their words from Virginia.

"We're looking for the home of John Collins," said their leader.

"And who are you sir? And what are you wanting with John?"

"I am Captain Wendell. From the Massachusetts Bay colony."
Johnny was pulling in the big boat with the rope they'd thrown
him, and wrapping it around one of the posts driven into the
ground for that purpose. "Is this the home of John Collins?"

"Yes, sir."

Biki had joined them silently, her eyes on the strangers,
watching their every move with suspicion and loathing.

"I think Collins likes the ladies, that's what I'm thinking,"
said one of the young men. "But tell me something, pretty lady,
where in the world did he find an *English* woman?"

"I am his wife," said Virginia, with as much gravity as she
could maintain.

"John Collins has no wife," said one of the younger men. "But
if that's what you want to call yourself, you go right ahead.
You're pretty enough to say whatever you want."

"You, sir," said Captain Wendell to the young man who'd just
spoken, "will remain with the boat. And you keep silent. Mistress Collins, I apologize for my men. They are idiots, and you
should take their words for the words of idiots and nothing
more."

"Please, Captain," said the reprimanded man. "I'm sorry,
Mistress Collins, I'm very sorry. Please let me come in. I want
to see a house. See something human."

"You will stay with the boat, sir. The discipline will be good
for you," he said.

"My husband is not at home," said Virginia.

"You're very young to be a married woman," said one of the
young men.

"All right," said the captain. "You are specifically ordered to
say nothing further to this young woman. Do you understand?
All of you? You will be silent, or you will sit in the boat with
your friend."

"Is there some special reason?" said Virginia. "Is there some
danger? Isn't that a warship?"

"It's a boat with three cannons, Mistress Collins. It leaks, and
it lumbers, and it's the only one we've got. I'm sure your husband is in no danger. He has more friends than any white man
in New England. That's why we have need of him. At once."

"Everyone is an Englishman," said Johnny to Virginia.

"Yes, Johnny."

"Hey, boy, that's some suit you're wearing," said one of the young men as they walked up the hill to the house. Johnny wore a doublet and breeches, but was barefoot, and his long, straight, black hair reached his shoulders. "All you need now is a feather."

"What for?" said Johnny.

"A feather? To put in your hair, of course."

"I don't wear feathers, sir," said Johnny. "I am an English boy. In England there are boys just like me. Just as dark-skinned."

"Only after they've been roasted."

"Mother," said Johnny, catching up to where Virginia walked with Captain Wendell. Once again, he took her hand.

"I told you he was a half-breed," said the taller of the two young men. He himself was fair, as blond as Virginia, but his face was pockmarked, and his long hair was thin and stuck to his greasy scalp. "She must have got herself a big brave until Collins came along."

"He said I should wear feathers, Mother," said Johnny, his voice quivering with indignation. To his mind there were two types of people in the world, English and non-English, white men and Indians, men as perfect as his adoptive father and men who lived in wigwams and belonged to no mysterious civilization across the distant sea. "He said you have to be roasted to be dark like me."

But that was not all he'd said, and she'd heard every word. How could the captain say nothing further, how could such ruffian garbage be allowed into her house? She would not be treated as if she were still a servant, still under the rule of the Silvesters and people like them.

"You really think she'd do it with an Indian?"

"I knew whores who'd do it with a monkey," said the fair-haired one. "Indians and monkeys are pretty much the same."

All Virginia had at hand was the wood bowl from which she'd been drinking a warm herbal tea. Without thinking, she turned about and pushed this empty bowl into the young man's face.

"Get off my land," she said.

"Mistress Collins!" said the captain. "That wasn't called for." She had bloodied the recruit's nose, and his hand was reaching for his sword.

But then little Biki flew at him, her hands at his neck and eyes, her knee in his groin as they tumbled to the ground. The captain and the other recruit drew their swords at once, but Biki had already accomplished what she'd set out to do: The young man was nearly senseless, and his sword was in her hands as she slowly and carefully got to her feet.

"My father will kill you," said Johnny evenly, staring directly into the captain's eyes. "Even if you are English, he will kill you."

"Tell the Indian to drop the sword," said the captain.

"I will do no such thing," said Virginia. "Who do you think you are to come to my house and talk to me and my boy like that?"

"If you do not tell the Indian to drop the sword, I will kill her," said the captain. "I will disarm her and kill her as surely as I speak."

Biki's serious face suddenly broke into a smile. The heavy sword in her hand wavered a bit, and then finally she let it fall to the ground with a laugh. Before the fallen recruit could retrieve his weapon and get back to his feet, an arrow seemed to materialize out of the air, landing with enormous force an inch from the sword hilt.

They all turned, and saw that they were surrounded by five Sasqua braves with drawn bows, eager to kill any enemies of John Collins. One brave spoke, and gestured fiercely. The captain dropped his sword, and ordered the recruit who was still standing to do the same. But the young man panicked. "They're going to kill us," he said. "They're going to burn us alive." Wildly, without a plan, he raised his sword and threw himself at the nearest brave.

It would have been easier to kill him, but the attacked brave simply stepped out of the way of the sword, dropped his bow, and grabbed the recruit as if he were a child. The brave wrenched his sword arm behind his back, and stepped on the back of the man's knees, forcing his face to the ground.

"Thank you," said Virginia to the braves.

One of them spoke to Biki. She answered him, her words coming slowly, with careful enunciation, so that her different dialect might be understood.

"We have forty men in our bark, and heavy arms," said the captain. "We have come in friendship, seeking the help of your husband. I am sorry for the stupidity of my men, but they are new recruits, inexperienced in every way. And they have no religion, no fear of God, but only of men. Two weeks ago they saw what it meant to deal with savages, Mistress. They have not gotten over that yet."

"Men go," said Biki, pointing to the white men and to the river. The braves had come up along the riverfront, and had subdued the lone man there easily; a brave now brought him up the hill to join the others, holding his pinioned arms as if he were weightless.

"Yes, Biki," said Virginia. "Men go."

The captain wanted to talk further, to explain why they needed John Collins, to relate the latest news of the Pequots on Long Island and along the New England coast. But Virginia wouldn't listen. If John wanted to talk with them, he could visit them in their three-masted bark. They would have to leave her land, and at once.

Not till the Englishmen had gotten into their longboat and begun to vanish down the river in a blaze of reflected light did Virginia begin to cry. Johnny held her, and Biki took the two of them into the house, away from the imperious Sasqua braves.

John returned two days later, just before dark. They had been terrible days for Virginia, not least because of Johnny, driven to the riverfront to sight the three-masted ship in the Sound, his eyes hard and sad and unforgiving. He had wanted all Englishmen to be creatures of wonder and goodness, able to command armies and weave stories and dredge up magical weapons from their store of civilization. All his life he'd known the Sasquas and the Pequonocks, and loved them, but always at a remove; he was the son of an Englishman, special, better. He had seen the honor commanded by John Collins, the unique place given him in the Indian villages, a lone white man. And while he had followed the lead of his father in admiring the physical prowess of the braves in running, in wrestling, in ignoring extremes of hot and cold, he had always assumed that this admiration was that of the king for his subjects, of a father for his not quite developed sons.

All this was shattered now.

The Englishmen he'd seen were brutes. They were ugly, stupid, clumsy with their words, and even clumsier with their weapons. A squaw disarmed one; braves surprised the rest with ease. A killing had been prevented only because the white men were not worth the glory of a killing; they were like dumb beasts compared to the Sasqua braves. For the first time in his life, Johnny felt more of a kinship to the Sasquas than to the nebulous idea of England. Of course, John wasn't ugly, and Virginia was nothing if not kind and gentle and patient. And he was not of the Sasqua nation. Even in their clothes he wouldn't be taken for one of their tribe.

But he was dark, and his cheekbones and his coarse straight hair were closer to the Sasquas, the Pequonocks, the Micmacs, then they were to the English. And he would refuse to be sorry about this anymore. Sasquas were brave, potent, full of knowledge of the woods and of man. He would be proud to be possessed of their experience as well as that of his father.

Virginia understood something of this change in Johnny, and tried to help him understand that the world had good and bad people in every country, in every race. But she had other concerns as well. She hated the men who had come in their warship even more than Johnny did. Not simply because they had insulted her. Not only because they had come to get John's help. Mostly she hated them because they had shown her how simple it was for white men to die. This was not an empty land, with a few simple folk eager to be the slaves of civilized colonists. This was a populated country; or rather, it was a continent populated by many nations, each of them strong, each of them different, each of them prepared to slaughter invaders.

John lived in Unquowa by the grace of the local Indians. She had seen that clearly for the first time. He was an outlander living in a foreign country because he had made friends, and because he supplied these friends with useful things. But pots weren't vital; the Sasquas had lived without iron cookware, and could live without them again. Virginia knew from John that they were a proud people, and willing to defend themselves; but they weren't especially warlike. They weren't a tribe that lived by subjugating others, by stealing the bounty of weaker tribes, by making slaves out of a free people and selling them to white men; they weren't like the Pequots. Or at least, they weren't like the vision of the Pequots given her by her husband.

Still, they had handled the English soldiers as if they were toys. And her husband was determined to go to war with far worse than these Sasquas, with Indians whom all other tribes feared. She hated these Englishmen because they had shown her how arrogant was their claim to this land, how blind were their eyes to the power of the Indian nations. One old man with his raw recruits, even with one hundred more like them, even with two or three barks and twenty cannons—what chance had they on the land, in the silent forests, where a hundred tribes ran swiftly, with bravery and dignity and power? This Old World rubbish wanted to exterminate the Pequots, and this was revealed not only as an impossibility to Virginia, but also as an outrage. The inner lives of these people were so hidden from her eyes that she couldn't imagine that John understood them in any real way either. The Sasquas and Pequonocks who lived nearby, who spoke to them in signs, and sold them turkey and hides—what did they really understand about them? Perhaps John knew a bit about their festivals, about the way in which they chose a leader, about how they sanctified a marriage or a birth or a death. But even about these neighbors, he knew little that mattered. What did they feel was their reason for being on earth? What did they love? For what reasons did they go to war? What was justice, freedom, friendship to a Sasqua? If John didn't know this much, how could he know enough about the Pequots to determine to destroy them?

Johnny saw him first, tying up his canoe at the end of the day. He ran to him, out of breath, filled with a hundred questions and demands. "Father," he said. "Father, you're back!" Quickly, clumsily, he told him about how the Sasquas had helped them, about how the Englishmen in the big ship in the Sound had behaved, about how they had insulted them, about how they must be punished.

"They were men under strain, son," said John, picking up the boy and putting him on his shoulders. But almost at once he had to put the boy down, because Virginia saw them and ran down the hill, ignoring her pregnancy, wanting only to embrace her lover.

"I will tell you about everything," he said.

"Later," she said.

"Much later," he said.

They all ate a meal of chunks of fish and beans, cooked in a sweet sauce. Biki was silent, her face without expression, as if she could feel the discord in the air. Johnny wanted to be reassured, to be told that the men in the ship were bad and that his father would hurt them the way they had hurt him. But all John would say was that he had been on their ship, had spent a few hours with Captain Wendell, and would hold further discussions with him on the morrow.

"Is there going to be a war?" Johnny persisted.

"There already is, son," said his father. "But let me see what you've been doing. Let me see you read something."

"It's too dark to read."

"Light another candle."

"I don't want to read now, Father," said Johnny. "I'm tired, and I want to go to sleep."

"Then go to sleep," said John coldly. "If that's how you greet your father, go to sleep, and go right now!" He pushed aside his bowl, stood up in the small room, and walked out the door, followed by Virginia.

"Where are you going?" she said.

"Nowhere," said John. "Where can I go?"

The moon had risen, a half-moon, but its light didn't reveal the glories of June, the violets and wood anemones, the bright columbine illuminating the rocky hillside beyond the stockade. Johnny had told her about an Indian custom he'd learned from Biki, perhaps Biki's way to get him to understand her pregnancy. Virginia wanted to tell it to her husband, to see if he knew about it, to see if such a custom could possibly be practiced by the Pequots. In late summer, Johnny had told her, Indians went barefoot, removing their moccasins so as not to hurt the earth's pregnant belly just before it was to give birth to the harvest.

But she didn't tell him about the custom, thinking him unreceptive at that moment. He reached for her hand, and they walked to a boulder overlooking the black river, audible below them.

"I must tell you now," he said.

"All right."

"There have been separate skirmishes, three or four of them, between Pequots and Englishmen. Two times on Long Island, once on the Sound, once past the English fort at Saybrook."

"You said you wouldn't go to Long Island," she said.

He didn't bother to answer her. There were things he wanted to tell his wife, his partner, so she would understand why he must leave her once again. But all Virginia could think about was that he had lied to her, and that he had more passion in his heart for anger and violence than he had love for her.

He told her about the Pequots' ambush of some men from the bark in the Sound, and how they had slaughtered three Englishmen without warning. He told her about the poor Englishman caught past Saybrook, and horribly tortured: how he had been fixed to a stake, how they had chopped off his feet and his hands, how they had separated his skin from his body, placing hot embers under the skin.

"Please don't tell me any more," she said.

"You must know why I have to help Captain Wendell."

"The English torture too," she said. "They chop off ears, they brand, they tear people limb from limb. What is it that the Pequots want? Let them have it. Let them have it, and stay with me. Let them kill Captain Wendell and all his kind. We can stay here, we can have a big family, we can stay friendly with the Sasquas. We will be safe."

She had let go of his hand and stood up from her seat on the great stone.

"Come here," he said.

"No."

John came after her, moving quickly in the dark, and turned her about with great force. He brought his lips to hers and tried to bend her will to his, tried with a kiss to make her see that his way was correct, that his actions were imperative, that she must bow to her husband's authority—just like in the Silvester family.

But she hardly returned his kiss. She was angry—angry that he had blown up at Johnny, angry that he could want to leave her again, angry that he wanted to risk his life, angry that he had murder in his heart.

"I'm not finished explaining, Virginia," he said. "You're much too hard on me, when all I want to do is for you and our family. In Wethersfield they just killed ten people, women and children too. I don't know what they did to the women before they killed them. I'm not like the others, the Puritans, who think it's their right to kill the heathen, to make it their country, with their God. I want the other Indians to live. It's only the Pequots, the murderers. How can I not leave you and fight with the other white men? Even the Mohegans are joining us, because they know the Pequots have to be destroyed."

"And what if you're destroyed? What if they destroy you?"

"They won't," he said. "Our cause is just, and we have better weapons. If we're lucky, we can surround them in their sleep, and have done with them all at once."

He chose that moment to try to draw her back into his embrace. She allowed him to hold her, closing her eyes and listening to the rushing of the river below. Perhaps it was her love that made her so angry, perhaps it was her pregnancy that wouldn't let her see him in any other light than selfish and cruel. Certainly she understood the words that he was saying: that the Pequots were a menace to all white men in New England and it was his duty to be part of the war against them. She wondered if her anger was simple selfishness. If he died, she would be alone in the world, a woman without a town, without a guardian, with a newborn baby and a seven-year-old Indian boy to raise. But she didn't think she was selfish. It wasn't selfish to demand love as pure and overwhelming as your own.

"I will come back, you know," he said.

"I don't know. And neither do you."

"I will come back," he said again, and he took her hand and walked with her back to the house, to their private room on the opposite side of the warm hearth. She lit a single candle and slowly undressed, watching his smile return as he examined her swollen breasts and belly. Virginia remembered how he had first kissed her, how she had known what he was about to do, and had been unable to stop him, though it meant great trouble for her. She had wanted the kiss, as much as she had wanted him to return to her and take her away, exactly like a knight in a fairy tale. And she had loved him, she decided, right from the start, though she hadn't known it at the time, so afraid was she of the consequences. She couldn't allow herself to let go, to allow her feelings to embrace him, until she was gone from the Puritan town.

Now, alone with her husband, she found herself twisting away from him, not in body, but in spirit. Her feelings were withdrawing deep into a shell, and as he spoke words of love to her, fondling her body, she was suddenly sure that he was wrong: He would not come back. That was the reason for her anger. That was the reason for her body's refusal to join his in passion. John Collins would not return, and she would be alone with her memory of love, alone forever.

EIGHT

———◆———

John Collins showed his wife where he had buried a clay pot stuffed with gold coins of four nations. He visited the Sasqua village with Johnny, and gave them presents of wampum, gunpowder, and muskets, thanking them for helping his family. Biki was presented with an angora shawl, imported from the mother country. Two mornings after he'd returned, he was picked up by the longboat and taken off to the warship, leaving the canoe perched upside down on posts near the front of the small house.

"Good-bye, John," she said to him, and tried to remember the passion of their first days together as he held her in his arms. But she could feel his attention was elsewhere: He would have no peace until the killing was finished, until he had destroyed the Pequots or they had destroyed him. This saddened her more than anything else. She felt as if this might be their last moment, their last embrace as a loving couple, as man and wife, as the parents of an unborn child. And he ruined the moment. He didn't have the sensitivity to feel her need for loving, her desire to be acknowledged as the focal point of joy in his life. All he could think of was murder. Even as he kissed her, even as he held her, his only lust was for blood.

That night, she castigated herself. She had been unfair to him. It was not murder she had felt in his heart, but fear. He was brave, he was courageous, he had rescued her, he had rescued Johnny, he was a good man, the best of men, and she had slandered him. Of course he loved her, as she loved him. John was better than she, unselfish, a part of the greater community of man. It was only such a man who could bring order out of chaos, who could make life safe, meaningful for the thousands of colonists who would come to this new land. He, not she, was good, she insisted, shutting her eyes against the flow of tears, against the terrors of the night shared by her husband on the Puritans' warship, and by herself in their home.

But the days grew warmer, the sticky nights longer. She moved her pallet into the main room, to share the floor with Biki and Johnny, to calm her taut body with the sound of their easy sleeping. Still, she could do no better than sleep in snatches throughout the night. And as she lay flat on her back, eyes open to the black, still air, trying to imagine a tiny, perfect baby sleeping inside her, she trembled for John. Beyond all deciding whether she was angry, whether he or she was wrong about his going off to war against the Pequots, she simply worried: Virginia wanted him back, whole and healthy. It was at night that she conjured the terrible images of the dread Indian warriors: their fiery arrows, their tomahawks, their tortures. She prayed for him, after a fashion, appealing to a nameless force to bring home her husband, to allow him to witness the birth of their child.

Three weeks went by without word.

The walk to the Sasqua village grew more difficult as the humid weather tired her pregnant body. Biki tried to get news from the sachem, but he had no news to give her. All the signs of the powwow, or medicine man, were positive; there would be a great victory over the Pequots, he assured them. But Virginia wasn't reassured. She couldn't sleep; she imagined disasters but couldn't identify them. All her images were blurred, and based on memories—the fire in Boston that had consumed her brother mingling unaccountably with the deliberate burning down of Sam Blake's trading house in Contentment.

Later she was to learn that the memories of fire had rele-

vance to her present. The English force had surprised the main
body of Pequots at their fort on the far eastern north shore of
the great Sound. Surprise won the day. Since the English intent
was not to reform, or even to punish, but rather to exterminate,
their night attack worked superbly: Eight hundred men,
women, and children were roasted, burned, or asphyxiated by
their flaming fort. A few lucky ones were shot by the inexperienced musketeers. Perhaps one hundred others, mostly
elderly men, and women and children—for most of the braves
insisted on fighting till the end—escaped the circle of fire and
Englishmen, and their Mohegan and Narraganset allies. Over
seventy-five miles of marshy coastal land the refugees were
tracked by the zealous Englishmen, fueled by the Puritan vision of creating a safe homeland for the New Zion. Many died
along the way, but a few survived, urged on by fate to the
swamp five miles west of the Sasqua village, where the riotous
English soldiers surrounded them and burned them out, shooting all but a dozen, who were taken prisoner and eventually
sold to West Indies slavers. Somehow, the Pequot leader, fierce
Sassacus, eluded capture, though months later he was killed by
a Mohawk band currying favor with the Englishmen. The day
the Pequot leader's head was exhibited on a stake to the Puritans of Connecticut was a day of celebration, and the anniver-
sary of the burning of the Pequot fort was declared a feast day
for all.

But though Virginia's home was close to the final massacre,
though many Sasquas caught glimpses of the pathetic Pequot
remnant—their dark skin blackened and blistered, their legs
hardly able to support their own weight—she herself remained
in a limbo of ignorance. While Biki and the Sasquas and the
Pequonocks and Johnny would have definite feelings about the
way in which the swamp massacre took place, Virginia held
back judgment. She waited for John, for a sign that he would
come back. For not all the English who had burned the Pequot
fort had survived the attack; and not all those who'd survived
had participated in the swamp massacre. Many English, Mohegans, and Narragansets were adrift in the area, combing the
forests, river paths, valleys, and marshes for Pequots. And no
soldiers visited the Collins home, eager for the company of a

white woman after killing so many half-dead Indians. The Sasquas and the stockade and John Collins's orders saw to that.

A Pequonock brave reported the news of John's homecoming on the third day of August. He was a runner, very long-legged and long-muscled, his body glistening with perspiration, his eyes preternaturally calm, as if the solitary distance run through summer forests had transported him beyond the ordinary cares of man. Biki spoke to him in signs.

"Man home," she said finally. "Man lives. Man home. Two days. Three days. Man lives."

Biki insisted on sharing their meal of corn, beans, and squash with the runner. They ate outside, all of them cross-legged on the cleared ground, watching the river below them. "He's strong," said Johnny to Virginia about the Pequonock, who never raised his eyes from his bowl while he ate; but when he finished he looked at Biki and Virginia and smiled broadly, formally, and remained seated, waiting for the others to finish.

It struck Virginia then that it was not just the white man who was oblivious to murder and hate and destruction; it was all men. Surely this serenely handsome brave knew of the swamp massacre, of the mutilated bodies, of the fierce warrior people sold into slavery. And even if he had not personally killed a single Pequot, or urged his people to join in the killing, he knew of the atrocities, he breathed the murderous air, he heard the cries of their dead in the long nights—and it affected him not at all. The way he ate, the way he composed his formal smile, the way his beautiful body moved with grace—all this was obscene to Virginia. People had been murdered, lives and souls had been brutalized all about her ever since she was a child; and now the complacence of this brave, this young man who had done her the service of telling her that John Collins lived and was coming home, drove a cold wedge of fury deep within her heart.

Just as the Pequonock had said, John returned. Two mornings later Johnny saw the three-masted bark, and ran down to the river to wait for the longboat. Virginia joined her son at the shore. John was not much changed: He was simply a bit thinner and very tan, his hair bleached by the summer sun.

"I told you I'd be home," he said.

She held him in her arms, but it was not the same as before.

He never told her of the night of burning flesh, of the great victory that made the region safe for white men, coming in greater and greater numbers over the next forty years. She never asked him. The force that had allowed her to hold judgment in abeyance till his return now relaxed. Virginia judged him and found him wanting. He had not loved her enough. He had not heard her. Murder in the name of a false ideal had a greater attraction for him than their love; he never said he was proud of having participated in the massacre, but she knew that he was. Virginia understood that her fears about his never coming home were partially realized: His body had returned, alive and eager for joy. But the joy was never to be shared by her. What had not come back was the love that had united them, the mad passion that had broken her away from a life of restraint to a life of bliss. Now the bliss was dead, the passion gone.

"Are you all right?" he asked her, and he kissed her, and she kissed him, and they made love that night, and he told her that he wanted to stay home, to be with her, to establish a trading post just as she had suggested. "Safe Haven," he said. "I would like to call our home, this house, this land, Safe Haven."

And life was safe, and children came, and there were good years, and there was prosperity and health and many comforts. But all her life Virginia remembered her seventeenth year, and the husband who had come for her like a god, the man who had lifted her to an ecstatic realm. That man was dead, but she remembered his pure spirit and their love all the days of her life.

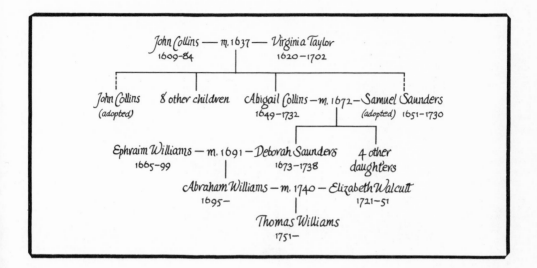

John Collins — m. 1637 — Virginia Taylor
1609–84   1620–1702

John Collins   8 other children   Abigail Collins — m. 1672 — Samuel Saunders
(adopted)   1649–1732   (adopted) 1651–1730

Ephraim Williams — m. 1691 — Deborah Saunders   4 other
1665–99   1673–1738   daughters

Abraham Williams — m. 1740 — Elizabeth Walcutt
1695–   1721–51

Thomas Williams
1751–

The Family of
John and Virginia Collins
1637-1775

Within a year of the marriage of John Collins and Virginia
Taylor, Puritans settled the fair region ten miles west of Safe
Haven. These immigrants, fueled by religious ardor, built a
sturdy meetinghouse and laid out a township of six square
miles, and farmed the land and fished in the Sound. Safe
Haven, with its godless young couple, its adopted Indian boy,
its Micmac maid, was a house and a trading post forbidden to
all except those members of the congregation selected to buy
goods for the entire community. But this restriction collapsed
of its own weight over the years. Virginia bore nine children in
a dozen years, all of them healthy, spirited, and wild. One by
one these children entered the little school in the Puritans'
town, learning to read and write and cipher. They made friends
with the other boys and girls, incomplete Puritans, not yet
beaten into compliant replicas of their parents. Two of the Collins girls married young men of the prospering new town, and
were eventually accepted into the Congregational Church of
their husbands. John, the adopted Pequot boy, went north to
New France, to try the life of a trapper with an old friend of his
father's. By 1665, the year the town's Puritans hanged an old
widow for witchcraft, John and Virginia lived in a greatly en-
larged two-story house, still wrapped about its original field
stone hearth. Their youngest child, Abigail, was nearly sixteen;
she and her brother Roger were the only children remaining at

Safe Haven. Two of the boys were already dead, drowned at sea on an expedition to the West Indies. The firstborn son had long since taken up residence in India, a buying agent for a Massachusetts Bay trading company, whose activities ran afoul of England's colonial trading policies. Arrested and sent back to England for trial, he died of typhus during the long sea voyage. One daughter, the next to oldest girl, had converted to a fanatically religious Puritanism and gone off to join a community of like-minded worshippers clustering about a famous minister twenty miles north of Boston. Their wildest son had a taste for warfare; he'd served with the colony's militia in numerous Indian skirmishes, and had gone off to enlist in a British regiment in the dangerous far south colony of Georgia.

And so with only Roger—lame since an accident in infancy—and Abigail living at home, John and Virginia took in an orphaned young Puritan boy from the neighboring town. Two years younger than Abigail, Samuel Saunders grew from a trading-house servant to a fiercely competitive man of business. Though the neighboring town had as fine a harbor as Safe Haven, ships with contraband preferred to anchor at Safe Haven: Samuel Saunders saw nothing wrong in buying and selling West Indian rum, in purchasing from English smugglers cloth made in Spain or France; though it was not true, as some claimed, that he didn't refuse to sell Sasquas muskets and gunpowder.

Samuel married Abigail in 1672, three years after the neighboring town had become the seat of a just-created colonial county. Safe Haven too was a part of this county—at least one could place it within the county's borders on an official map, even if the trading post had no legal status in the colony. The neighboring town received a new name—Fairlawn—to replace its earlier Algonquian designation, and quickly became a gathering point for travelers and traders. And so, if Safe Haven was not written on the map of Connecticut, it was still a far different place than it had been when Virginia was first brought there by her new husband. Still surrounded by forest, still without close neighbors save for two tiny Indian bands, the house at the edge of the Saugatuck River was alive with children, with traders, with the daily arrival of boats of every size and description. At night the sounds of the forest still drifted through the tiny windows of the house, but it was comforting to know that a civilized town stood ten miles away, where fellow Englishmen followed established law, and where violence —even against nonbelievers—was repaid with violence.

But though Fairlawn had meetinghouse, schoolhouse, courthouse, and regular market days, it would be incorrect to suppose that its inhabitants followed the news of the ever-jousting world powers with rapacious interest. The accession of William of Orange to the throne of England in 1687, ridding the Empire of a Catholic despot, was greeted with more interest in London and in Boston than in little Fairlawn, where the news was eclipsed by an outbreak of smallpox. The death of Virginia Collins in 1702, at the age of eighty-two, was more talked about than the accession of Queen Anne to the throne. Erecting the first great bell in the turret of the Congregational Church in 1707 had more moment for Fairlawn than the union of England and Scotland in the same year.

Still, even remote little Safe Haven, with its hard-working master—Samuel Saunders had been in control long before John Collins's death in 1684—felt the distant thunder from Europe. Settlers fleeing religious intolerance or economic devastation took the brave step of crossing the ocean, adding to the little clusters of Europeans living along the Atlantic seaboard. Some of the settlers in Fairlawn weren't Puritans, or had became Puritans simply for the sake of being allowed to live in the community. Together with the large families of the time, they swelled the resources of the single meetinghouse, the long since apportioned lots of land. Settlers began to band together, leaving Fairlawn for rich land beyond its jurisdiction. When a dozen families had become neighbors, they began to think of importing a minister. By 1715 one of these little groups had taken the incredible step of bringing over an Anglican minister; for these farmers, removed from Fairlawn's regulations, began to long for the old English church service. Fairlawn itself allowed an Anglican minister to enter its domain ten years after that; and in the year of Samuel Saunders's death, 1730, a large turreted Church of England was erected on the outskirts of the town.

Samuel Saunders died an old man, with a good deal of money, and only one heir. All his life he had wanted sons, but Abigail had blessed him with daughters—five of them. Only the eldest, a widow, lived at home, with her child, Abraham Williams, old Samuel Saunders's grandson; the child was quiet but ambitious. Abe was thirty-five when the old man died, leaving him the Safe Haven estate, and the responsibility of caring for his mother and grandmother, Abigail Collins Saunders, now eighty years old. His mother's four sisters were scattered about, three of them having married and borne children, but they hadn't figured in Samuel Saunders's life once they'd left home for Virginia and England and New York. Safe Haven had been his passion, the home and business around which he'd built his life. Only those who wished to remain in or near the house mattered to the old man. One daughter had moved only as far as Fairlawn, marrying a wealthy landowner and associating with cousins in the prosperous town—children of Virginia and John Collins's two daughters who'd married into the town and been accepted by its Congregational Church. But for Samuel Saunders, this daughter, with her silly chatter of England as if it were "home," with her affected manners and accent, might have moved as far away as China. He cared only for Abe, even if he would not carry the Saunders surname into history.

Abe Williams tried hard to please his grandfather. Because his own father had died when Abe was a young child, his grandfather was his greatest influence. He filled him with economic theories, with visions of a great mercantile empire, a fleet of ships that would sail from Safe Haven to the Orient and return with rare silks and spices. But Abe was a prosaic boy: He understood that their money came from buying smuggled goods, and that bigger ships sailed to the greater harbor at Fairlawn. They owned not a single ship, but possessed a great quantity of gold coins, currency of five countries. And the area about Safe Haven itself was becoming a kind of disorganized, second-rate Fairlawn. Farmers who had settled to the north and west of them had taken the name of the trading post and house as the name of their region; long before Samuel Saunders's death, the once-a-month postman who connected Boston, Stamford, and Fairlawn began to make a stop in Safe Haven. A

Congregational meetinghouse was built a mile up the Saugatuck from the Safe Haven home in 1724; a much less austere
Church of England was built half a mile to the east of the
Saunders home a year later. Abe Williams understood that a
town was being formed all around him, and instead of dreaming of fleets to China, he bought land, and sold it to the new-
comers. He was a quiet man, who buried his grandfather,
grandmother, and mother without having yet brought home a
wife for their approval. Without expanding the base of his
grandfather's trade, without currying favor with his rich Fairlawn relations, without attempting to join in the rough politics
of the Safe Haven meetinghouse, Abe Williams grew rich, rich
in gold and richer still in land.

Everyone imagined that the sober Abe would marry a rich
widow. There was nothing about him to suggest a passionate
nature. If he were to marry at all, it seemed likely that he'd take
a woman whose estate included lands, or ships, or capital waiting to be employed by his expert hands. But he surprised the
town by marrying a nineteen-year-old girl when he was in his
forty-fifth year. Her name was Elizabeth Walcutt, and she had
a way of walking about the town of Safe Haven with her eyes
on the ground and her steps short and silent. She wanted no
attention. Her father was an English yeoman, her mother was
Irish. They'd immigrated to the Connecticut shore when Elizabeth was three years old. Abe gained no material benefit by
marrying her. Everyone spoke of her remarkable beauty, but
mostly in unflattering tones; she was blamed for having bewitched an older man into committing a folly.

Married in 1740, the couple remained childless for ten years.
The gossipers worked hard, but there was little with which to
attack the beautiful Elizabeth Williams. They lived simply,
without friends, keeping only one servant for the large house at
the edge of the river. Abe kept a single apprentice in his office,
helping him look after his quiet little empire of rented farms
and waterfront lots and deep forests. Elizabeth still kept her
eyes on the ground when she walked in town, and carried her
beauty more as if it were a curiosity than her great asset. She
wanted no talk about her, and no malicious slander of her
middle-aged, dour-faced husband. Like Abe, she was a

thoughtful, methodical person, eager to create a world buffered from change, violence, and poverty. She wanted no part of fleets to China, or of any venture that contained much risk. Because her memories of England were of hunger and want, she dreamed of no greater civilization than she found in Safe Haven. When her husband was fifty-five and she twenty-nine, she had effectively shed her youth; her beauty had become bloodless and cold. She seldom visited her parents.

And then, in the year 1750, she became pregnant.

She had already experienced four miscarriages in the past ten years, and had little expectation of a successful pregnancy. Still, as in all the other times, she did the correct, methodical things. Though she wasn't tired, she took a two-hour afternoon nap. Though she wasn't hungry, she ate meat pies and soups twice a day, and three eggs for breakfast. After her second month, she extended the afternoon nap to three hours. When she had been pregnant four months, longer than she had ever carried a baby in her womb, she began to think of a name—a boy's name. She thought of Samuel, after Abe's grandfather, but didn't like it; it was too common, too ordinary. She liked Abiah, and she thought Jedediah was a strong name too. Jedediah Williams sounded like a man with a future, a man with substance, who would grow on the experience and wisdom of his parents, who would become a magistrate, a governor.

But Elizabeth was never to name the boy Jedediah. She died in childbirth, in February 1751, and Abe, fifty-six years old, named his baby boy Tom. There were those who claimed the boy resembled his great-grandfather, Samuel Saunders, and others who saw in him the reincarnation of his father's father, Ephraim, dead at the age of thirty-four. But as he grew into young manhood, under the harsh but steadfast supervision of his old father, his handsome features and arrogant disposition reminded no one of any of the Saunders or Williams family, living or dead. And though there were no portraits left of the man, Tom's great-great-grandfather had left a legend behind him: John Collins, the fierce Indian-fighter, the brazen loner who had followed no one's lead but his own. This was the name that Abe Williams began to intone to account for the behavior of his son. No one else in Fairlawn or Safe Haven had a son so rich, so bright, and so eager to lose everything in 1775.

PART TWO: 1775

A House on Fire

NINE

The sloop from New York had taken a week to sail to Safe Haven, dragging its forty tons through windless March weather. First onto the Long Wharf, latest and most popular of the town's cargo landings, was Tom Williams, windburned and filthy in his gentleman's clothing. The Hog Tavern was a mere fifty yards from the shore, and served liquors of all kinds—even those boycotted by the Sons of Liberty and their sympathizers. Tom wanted a bowl of old Madeira. The mood in New York City had made it impossible to drink anything but rum distilled in New England or beer brewed in New York.

"Why the hell don't you watch yourself, Mr. Silk Stockings?"

Tom had been so anxious to get off the wharf and into the tavern that he had broken into a jog, his handsome face alive with sensual anticipation. But now he stopped short. He had lightly brushed against one of the many cartmen unloading cargo from the ships crowding each other along the wharf. And the cartman, a Southerner, had actually put out his huge hand and touched it to Tom's shoulder, as if to stop him. But Tom had stopped himself. He had been insulted. A familiar madness took hold of him, and when he spoke the sense of his anger was overshadowed by joy.

"I don't need to watch myself, pig face," said Tom. "It's scum like you who've got to watch out when I'm coming."

For a moment the cartman could think of nothing to say. He looked about to see if Tom was perhaps accompanied by a platoon of red-coated soldiers. But Tom was alone. Among the dozens of cartmen and crewmen running about the bales and barrels and crates, no one took notice of them. He could stick his knife into this gentleman's side and no one would lift a hand to stop him.

"What are you," said the cartman, "a ship's master? An officer?" He didn't like the look on the gentleman's face. If he wasn't afraid, there must be a reason. Breaking the pretty boy's face wasn't worth a flogging or a keelhauling, or getting pounced on by a dozen crewmen.

"I'm a gentleman," said Tom. "Wearing silk stockings. And you are a pig face, an ass licker, a thick-nosed oaf. Shall I go on?"

"Are you British?" he said, at a loss for words. He was still trying to understand how their roles had reversed, how this thin-framed boy could be urging him to fight.

"Whatever you hate, that's what I am," said Tom.

"I'm a Whig," said the cartman.

"You don't know what a Whig is, pig face."

"I'm a Whig, and a patriot, and if you say another word, you Tory bastard, I'll kick you into the water."

Tom slapped the man across the face. "You called me a Tory," said Tom, smiling. The cartman took a step back, squaring his shoulders and touching his cheek.

"Now what did you go and do that for, you bastard?"

"I'm not a Tory," said Tom, and he stepped closer to the big cartman and brought his closed fist up under the man's chin, sending him into a three-wheeled wagon. But the man was not hurt. He still looked disbelievingly at the gentleman.

"You must be crazy," said the cartman. "I'll kill you, boy. I don't care how rich you are, I'll kill you."

And as he moved away from the wagon, raising his right fist, puffing his fat face up with fury, he seemed perfectly capable of murder. The cartman swung mightily, not at Tom's face but at his belly. Tom stepped aside, as if changing partners at a dance, and grabbed the man's swinging arm as it jerked harmlessly into the air. With enormous force, Tom twisted the arm behind the man's broad back, simultaneously kicking into the back of the man's knees.

Suddenly it seemed as if every man on the wharf had stopped working. They were surrounded. The cartman had fallen to the rough planks, bloodying his hands as he scrambled to his feet, clawing against an ancient cask. He was no longer wondering at Tom's nerve. This was absurd, to be slapped and punched and twisted to the ground by a fop. As sailors, porters, merchants, and fishermen shouted encouragement, the cartman wheeled about and tried to grab hold of Tom.

"Pig face," said Tom, dancing out of the man's reach. As the man lunged at him, Tom kicked into his shin, and drove a fist into the man's nose. The madness was in control now, the terrible anger, the urge to break apart the world about him. He hit the big man again, slamming into the solid jawbone, jabbing at his chin, at his bloody nose. Blinded by blood and anger, the cartman swung his huge fists wildly, hurt and humiliated, but not nearly beaten. Tom would have to continue, as he had done so many times before on the waterfront: He would break a jaw, a nose, an arm; he would dance about his unskilled opponents, hitting them without a trace of reluctance or feeling. This had always been his source of strength in a fight. Even as a small boy, he had been a fighter. While the other boys threw their punches into an arm, or pulled their opponents' hair, Tom would strike anywhere vulnerable, without fear of the consequences. Most children, and many adults, showed the same reluctance to hit where they themselves were afraid to be struck. Even this thickheaded cartman had tried to hit him in the belly, afraid of striking at eyes, groin, neck. Tom knew how to box, of course, for he had trained with a boxing master in New York, and another in London. But he knew how to fight more than he knew how to box. He had the anger, the madness, the terrible urge to avenge miserable years of impotence, always waiting to explode.

And so he would have to beat the cartman till he no longer fought back, till he no longer moved, or moaned, or appeared to breathe. He had never killed anyone with his fists, but that was not because he hadn't tried. His fury lasted as long as there was resistance to be met, as long as his opponent moved; more than half a dozen men had been saved from death by being beaten first into unconsciousness.

"Thomas," said a sharp voice at the edge of the crowd, a voice that hardly anyone minded, until the tall young gentleman turned around, leaving the cartman to stumble about the wharf, holding his face as if it were about to crumble into a hundred pieces.

"You stupid fool," said the sharp voice. "You wharf rat."

An old man, stocky and vigorous, but at least seventy years old by his appearance, pushed his way through the rowdy crowd, waving his silver-headed walking stick before him.

"Hello, Father," said Tom.

The old man whipped the cane through the air; its silver head would have cracked Tom's skull if he hadn't ducked. "Please, Father," said the young gentleman, advancing warily, waiting for the next swing of the cane.

Abraham Williams brought the cane over his head, and then, instead of swinging it down, he lunged with it, driving its tip into Tom's belly.

"You should have stayed in China," said the old man as his son doubled over in pain. He moved in close now, and hit Tom with the flat of his hand, slapping the young man's face and ears and neck. "You're a disgrace. You've always been a disgrace, and always will be a disgrace." He grabbed at his son's hair and pulled him erect, so that Tom once again towered over his old father.

"Stop it, Father," said Tom, but he made no move to defend himself. Abraham Williams pushed him along the wharf, toward land, as the crowd made way for them.

"Move, go on," said the father, and as his son preceded him, he prodded him along with his elegant cane, sticking it hard into his back, looking as if he wished it were a sword, and as if only the greatest of indulgence prevented him from killing him at once.

"I want to go into the Hog," said Tom, turning about for a moment. "I need a drink."

The father raised his cane and brought it down on Tom's shoulder with enough force to make the young man cry out in astonished pain.

"It was not my fault," said Tom. "The man started with me."

"It's never your fault, is it?" said his father. "Not since you killed your mother in being born was it your fault. Not since then have you ever done a wrong thing!"

"I'm going to the Hog, Father," said Tom.

"Get into the carriage, boy," said Abe Williams. The old man ignored the servant's offered hand to help him into the waiting carriage. With effort, he lifted himself up and into the closed passenger compartment. "I said get in," he repeated dully.

"I'll see you at home, Father," said Tom.

"I'll see you in hell," said Abe Williams. He ordered the driver forward, beating his cane against the floor.

Tom watched the carriage race uphill, toward the river. His shoulder throbbed where he had been hit, and his fists were sore from the fight with the cartman. Once again his father would threaten to disinherit him. Even now his father might be running to every merchant in Safe Haven, demanding to cut off his son's credit. But it made no difference. He had stood up to the old man. Without uttering a disrespectful word, without returning a blow, Thomas had still managed to refuse him. He went into the Hog, far more pleased with his victory over his father than with his beating of the cartman.

He walked quietly into the tavern, sitting at a bench at a low table. There had been enough excitement for one day, he thought. It was too easy to meet the eyes of an English soldier without a penny for another cup of ale, or a hotheaded patriot looking for a chance to ask a young man in gentleman's clothing whether he was a Tory. Ordinarily, he would have enjoyed either such encounter. Only in a waterfront tavern like the Hog was he likely to be challenged in Safe Haven. The town was not yet so big that it offered him obscurity, even after having spent most of the last four years abroad.

"Yes, sir, Mr. Williams," said the tavern keeper, a white-faced, skinny young man devoted to the Anglican Church but known for his vociferous support of the patriotic cause. It was symptomatic of the times that the tavern keeper could serve British soldiers and Sons of Liberty at the same bench, even as he prayed in a church whose minister, quoting Saint Peter, urged them to "Fear God: Honor the King."

"A bowl of Madeira, Johnny," said Tom. "The older the better, if it's not spoiled."

"You wouldn't prefer some nice raspberry tea, would you, Mr. Williams?" said the tavern keeper softly, smiling archly. It would have been a dangerous joke to make to a Tory, or a British soldier. Patriots boycotted all goods taxed by the mother country, and some that weren't; tea, formerly the universal drink of the colonies, had become a symbol of oppression. Americans looking to unite the colonies forced themselves to drink coffee, or homemade herbal teas, or the terrible and expensive Dutch tea, even after the British had lowered the tax and the price on their fine India tea. Men who cared about such things were fighting a principle, not a price. Patriots ordered coffee because drinking English tea was a signal that the mother country had the right to rule the colonies unconditionally. Tories drank India tea because they believed themselves absolutely a part of England; the mother country had every right to tax the colonies, as the colonies existed only because of and for the benefit of England. Though many items were taxed, and became symbolic of the tension between England and America, tea remained the sorest point between them, especially since the Boston tea party, more than a year before, and the punishing of the Boston port that followed. Still, heavily taxed Madeira, British paper, silk, and wool were nearly as vigorously boycotted by patriots as they were consumed by Tories.

"I'm not wanting the wine to toast the King, Johnny. Only to drink it."

"It'll cost you."

"Come on, Johnny. What do I have to do to get my throat wet—denounce the King?"

Johnny leaned close. "There's three redcoats drinking Yankee beer in the back, and Pierpont Woods and his sister looking right at you."

"Not worried, are you, Johnny?" said Tom. But he was whispering now. "I'll be quiet. Only get me the wine."

The tavern keeper didn't see Tom's face grow red as the fact of the nearness of Pierpont Woods's sister grew more and more pressing. Tom hadn't seen Sally Woods in more than three years, soon after he'd returned from his first trip to England, and just before she broke her engagement to the scion of the richest family in Hartford. She was old even then—twenty-five to Tom's twenty-one—and the news of her broken engagement confirmed what half the upper classes of western Connecticut had always suspected: that the girl was mad. Pierpont was her younger brother, thick where she was thin, blond where she was black-haired, dull where she was bright. Tom had known Pierpont briefly at Yale, which he had entered at fifteen, and from which he'd been expelled a year later. They had never been friends, but coming from the neighboring towns of Fairlawn and Safe Haven, it was impossible that they should not become acquainted. It was the Yale connection to her brother that had emboldened Tom to speak to Sally Woods three years ago when he'd chanced upon her on a gray day at Fairlawn's lovely harbor.

"Looking at the boats, are you, Miss Woods?" he'd said.

"Go away," she'd said.

"I'm Pierpont's friend," he'd said, desperately trying to save face. "Tom Williams. From Safe Haven. I was at Yale."

"What of it?" she had said, speaking softly, looking past the traffic at the wharf to the mist-edged horizon.

"I was wondering if you might like to take a ride," Tom had said. "Sometime, Miss Woods. I've admired you for a long time."

Sally Woods had finally turned her black eyes toward him; the hollows under her eyes might have been from exhaustion, or from tears. "Tom Williams," she'd said. "You're the one who was expelled. Fighting, wasn't it?"

"It's not the way I like to be remembered," he'd said, trying to relax in her presence, letting his boyish charm float up through his nervousness. Tom had wanted to tell her about London, about the squalor and the glory, the pitiful masses of farmers streaming into the city looking for work, the sense of unlimited power and riches lurking behind every corner in that tiny nucleus of the Empire. But she didn't allow him to go on.

"I'd very much appreciate it if you'd leave me alone, Mr. Williams," she'd said. "You seem a nice enough young man, but I want nothing to do with you, not now nor at any future time.

All right, then? Please. I don't want to ride with you, or with anyone."

She hadn't even bothered to walk away. It was enough for her to turn her head back to the contemplation of the great Sound. He had never felt so rebuked. Everyone in their little part of the world knew him, knew that for all his wildness, he was still handsome, articulate, and the son of a very rich and very old man. Of course, she was much older than he, but that was her liability, not his. Perhaps the Woods family was of greater social prominence, with one uncle a baronet in England, and many cousins married into the Southern aristocracy of planters. But they weren't richer, and Sally Woods was very nearly an old maid, even if it was by her own design.

Now, three years later, she would be twenty-eight, a confirmed old maid, and it infuriated him that he was afraid to turn around to look at her, afraid of the blush that would shout at her across the little room.

"Your Madeira, sir," said Johnny with exaggerated politeness. Tom began to pull up his purse. "No, no, it's been paid for, Mr. Williams." He placed the bowl of white wine in front of him.

"What do you mean?"

"Your wine has been paid for," said Johnny. "Compliments of Mr. Pierpont Woods." Again he leaned closer. "Your Tory classmate, sir."

"Very funny," said Tom, feeling as awkward as he had that day three years past. He would have to turn around now and look at them, at her; he would have to get up, offer to join them, to buy them a drink. He was so overwhelmed by embarrassment that he had no chance to dwell on the strangeness of Pierpont Woods's extending such graciousness to him. Tom picked up the bowl and drank. "What are they drinking, Johnny?"

"Tea. India tea, in point of fact. They're lucky the soldiers are here," he said, still whispering. The tavern keeper stood up tall, and said in a clear voice: "Personally, I think Dutch tea is just as good as any from England."

One of the English soldiers looked over to Johnny and shook his head slowly from side to side. He was too drunk from Yankee beer to want a fight.

"Please send them some tea at my expense," said Tom.

"They've already had two pots," said Johnny, but Tom didn't

even hear him. Without thinking, he'd gotten off the bench and turned around in one easy motion. He saw them at once. She wore silk brocade, obviously new and imported from the mother country; in Safe Haven the farmers' wives might have pelted her with mud for being so brazenly a Tory. More than one rich lady of Connecticut wore only homespun at this difficult time, even if her chests were full of good English broadcloth, imported long before the boycotts began. Fairlawn was more typical of the old, established western Connecticut towns, in that its population had many Tories unafraid of speaking out in defense of their King. Though Safe Haven was Fairlawn's neighbor, its unusually diverse population, made up of dissenters and misfits from highly organized New England communities, made it an outspoken outpost for uniting the colonies. Here on the waterfront, where every manner of political persuasion could be met, one might be attacked by wharf-rat patriots on Monday and beaten by drunken English soldiers on Tuesday. Even so, it was generally considered dangerous to flaunt your affections for the mother country in Safe Haven in March of 1775, even at the waterfront, with English soldiers nearby.

"Mr. Woods," said Tom, forcing himself to look at Pierpont and not at Sally. He walked their way, cradling his bowl of Madeira as if it were an infant.

"Mr. Williams," said Pierpont Woods, his sober face working hard to make a smile. He stood up gravely, made a little bow, and gestured toward his older sister. "I believe you are acquainted with my sister."

"Yes, of course," said Tom. "Miss Woods. It's very good to see you again." She had aged much in three years. The hollows under her eyes were more pronounced and weary. Her black hair was less artfully arranged under her little cap, as if the fact of her spinsterhood had come home to her. She seemed to have little regard for her clothes, despite their quality. What she wore seemed irrelevant to the intense look in her enormous eyes, and when she spoke her voice was urgent, without a trace of wit or coquetry.

"Thank you," she said, examining his face for character. "Pierpont tells me that you live in a very interesting house."

Tom tried not to look quizzical. But suddenly the fact that

Pierpont had bought his bowl of Madeira and had made it obligatory for him to join them seemed bizarre. This young woman who had no interest in him whatsoever was inviting him to sit down, was asking him about his house with the intensity usually reserved for matters of life and death. Tom sat, and sipped his wine, and listened to them.

"I had always meant to come and see it during the time we were classmates," said Pierpont. "I never had the invitation, but still, the desire was there."

"It's not much to look at."

"Oh, I wouldn't say that, Mr. Williams," said Sally Woods. "It's not grand, of course, not stately, like a merchant's mansion in New Haven. But it's old. Pierpont says it's the oldest house in Safe Haven. Older than anything in Fairlawn."

"Only the hearth is original. One whole wall is probably from the same time. But it's really very plain, not at all like your house."

"I don't believe you," said Sally Woods. "You're just being selfish. Why don't you invite your old classmate home for a cup of tea?"

"My father doesn't serve tea, and the house is his."

"If it was up to you," said Sally, "you'd serve tea, then, wouldn't you?"

"I'd serve you whatever I could get my hands on, Miss Woods," said Tom.

"Really?" said Pierpont. "That's very curious. We were just wondering what side of the fence you'd be on, if there was an actual uprising."

"Not in public, Pierpont," said Sally. "We can continue this interesting discussion if and when Mr. Williams sees fit to invite us into his home."

"You really want to see the house?"

"Yes," said Sally.

"I've had a bit of an argument with my father, I'm afraid," said Tom. "But I'm certain that he'll calm down once he sees the two of you." He finished his wine, and they watched him carefully over their raised teacups. Regardless of how she had aged, her beauty retained its power over him. Tom felt clumsy in her presence. All his words sounded foolish, irresponsible.

He was conscious of the filthiness of his expensive clothing, and when he apologized for how he looked, explaining that he had just gotten off the ship from New York City, the look she gave him emphasized how little she cared about him: about his clothes, his words, his exploits. Conversely, everything she said and did carried the weight of mystery, intrigue. She was far too wonderful to care about anything ordinary. What difference would it make to her that their hearth had been shaped by John Collins in 1637? There was a reason why she was talking to him, why brother and sister had pulled him into their web and were even now deciding what to do with him. But that was all right with Thomas. For now he was content. It was fine just to walk alongside her, and understand that he had somehow become a part of her world.

"It's not much of a walk, I don't think," said Pierpont. "Half a mile, if I remember right."

"You're sure you feel like walking, Miss Woods?"

"Yes, sir."

"It's a bit wet today, marshy . . ."

"It's the waterfront," she said, her face preternaturally calm. "And you're at the edge of the river. I expect it would be wet."

Outside, she took her brother's arm as they followed the foot-path along the river. An occasional horse cart clattered by on the parallel main road, bringing produce to the waterfront markets. "May I call you Thomas?" she said. "Mr. Williams seems silly. You're so young."

"I'm not so young," he said, without thinking.

"I'm sorry. I can see that at your age you feel it better to be older," she said. "That won't last. I know."

"We're the same age, you and I—almost. It's too close to make a difference."

"Don't be silly, Thomas. You're younger than Pierpont. And to me Pierpont is my baby brother."

"You would do well to ignore her teasing, Thomas," said Pierpont, relaxing into the first-name usage in the wake of his sister. All this familiarity annoyed Thomas. He couldn't see his way clear to calling either of them by their Christian names. They were deliberately making him feel like a child.

"Did you read the governor's broadside?" he said sharply,

blurting it out like a suddenly remembered weapon at his command.

"Yes, Thomas," she said. "I read all the governor's comments, whether or not I agree with them. In times like this, it's important to know exactly where everyone stands."

" 'Trust thyself, and another shall not betray thee,' " said Tom happily. He had a facility for calling lines forth from his memory, as did his father. It pleased him when the lines were appropriate to the occasion; or when, as in this instance, they pointed directly to a subject about which all talk had only skirted.

"It's not the bible," said Pierpont, "so it must be the *Almanack*."

"Yes," said Tom. He knew that their father, Richard Woods, was famous for his arguments with Governor Trumbull. When a group of Fairfield County and Litchfield County loyalists had gathered to assert their allegiance to King George, Richard Woods had been among their most vociferous advocates. Everyone in Fairlawn and Safe Haven assumed that the children of Richard Woods, dressed in their imported clothing, drinking India tea, and socializing with British soldiers, were as loyal to England as their father. "What I'm saying is that you can trust me. All right? I don't know what you want from me, but whatever it is, it will go no further than the walls of my house."

"The governor called my father's group 'depraved, malignant, avaricious, and haughty,' " said Sally, watching Tom closely. "Those were his exact words. He said that the Tories of Fairfield County and Litchfield County were doing no less than seeking the 'ruin and destruction' of Connecticut. Then he said that violent action should be brought against them. Our own governor said that. What do you think of that, Tom? What do you think of what Governor Trumbull had to say?"

"I wouldn't worry about it, Miss Woods," said Tom. "It's just words. No one's going to attack the Tories in Fairlawn. They'd have to burn away half the town if they wanted to do that." He tried to put as much affability as he could into the words, but his charm didn't seem to have the desired effect. She measured him, and her eyes found him wanting.

As they continued along the river path, Pierpont spoke to his sister: "You heard what he said. You can trust him. I trust him."

Ignoring Pierpont, she said to Tom: "Your father—he's not a Tory, I hear."

"My father has no politics at all, just like most folks. He just wants to make money, but why he wants that at eighty is beyond me."

"What do you want?" she said.

"Me? Do you mean about money, politics—what?"

"No—what do you want out of life?" she said, taking his arm and turning him about toward the house, growing out of the oak trees behind the next turn in the river.

He understood that she was manipulating him again, moving about his desire as if it were weightless, insubstantial. What did he want at twenty-four? To shake her hand from his elbow, crush her body to his, take her pale face in his hands, and slowly, slowly bring her lips to his lips, her eyes to his eyes, her cheek to his cheek. To kiss her, caress her. The *Almanack* praised chastity, moderation, industry. Life must have no unnecessary actions. But in China, in London, in New York he'd made love with prostitutes whose every moment was immoderate, unnecessary—and wonderful. He knew what he wanted. Tom wanted to win this woman, to make love with her, to understand that she acknowledged him, needed him, desired him in the way that his body understood desire.

"I would like to be happy," said Tom.

"But how? You don't say how, Tom," she said. "You must have something you want very badly, and go after it. That's what I'm asking. What is it that you want that will make you happy?"

They had come up to the edge of the half-acre clearing surrounding the house at the edge of the river. John Collins, Tom's great-great-grandfather, would have had a hard time recognizing the site on which he had built his little log house one hundred and thirty-eight years before. The rise of land from which he had been able to look down at the changeless river, and at the impenetrable forest around them, now commanded a view of neighboring farms and homes on both sides of the Saugatuck. There were still woods, of course, but the single-file Indian footpaths had been replaced by dirt roads, often impassably muddy, but still recognizable marks of civilization. The Indian village that had stood nearby was long since overrun by settlers; the Sasquas who lived in town wore English clothing and hated their heritage, having lost touch with its meaning.

He had still not answered her question, when the words came to his lips of their own volition. In place of telling her anything as absurd as that he was infatuated with her beauty, her presence, and had been ever since first glimpsing her as a child, visiting Fairlawn with his old father, he let the words rush out: "I would like to be free," he said.

"Free," she said, and her expression became a trifle more grave. "Free in what sense?"

"I'm not sure," said Thomas, leading them up the path to the house. "As free as the man who built this place. You know, open seas, endless forests, no laws or restrictions—free."

"Yes," she said, "I understand."

Pierpont interrupted her: "Wait a moment, Sally. Let's get acquainted with the house first, shall we? No need to rush."

"Don't be ridiculous, Pierpont. Look at his face. Don't you trust that face?"

Before Pierpont could say another word, Sally had turned Tom about, so that his back was to the old house, and his eyes measured hers. "We're not Tories," she said. "Pierpont has been with the Sons of Liberty for more than two years. I've been involved since the Stamp Act—ten years. You might say I've wanted to be free since I was eighteen."

"I can't believe it," said Tom.

"I hope you'll believe it," said Sally. "We came to the waterfront looking for someone who might help us. And you walked in, and of course I remembered you, and I had the feeling we should try. And now, you see, I'm beginning to feel I was right. You said you want to be free, didn't you?"

Tom was about to explain that he had no politics, that he felt himself an Englishman from his head to his toe, even as Shakespeare was English, and Sir Walter Raleigh. But he said nothing. After all, the Sons of Liberty didn't all preach revolution. The Sons simply demanded the same rights given to Englishmen in England. It made sense to Tom that citizens shouldn't be taxed by a parliament that didn't represent them. But the fact of the matter was that the cry of "No taxation without representation" didn't excite him very much. There were fortunes to be made in and around boycotts. Smuggling carried no stigma for a gentleman of his class in New England. The idea that the thirteen colonies might unite and engage in some sort of conflict with the imperial might of the mother country was too absurd to be taken seriously, except by those who had nothing better to do than read John Locke and quote him portentously in coffeehouses and taverns free of British soldiers.

New York City was filled with such intellectual hotheads; the rabble whom they'd excited had managed to close the single decent theater in the city, on the grounds that the times were too serious to allow for such frivolity. Tom knew that, tax or no tax, boycott or no boycott, people would still be constrained by rules. No matter who passed the rules, or how just or unjust they were, people would not be free, not in the sense that he longed for. But he could not bring himself to explain any or all of this. He understood what their patriotism meant to the two of them: They were deliberately turning their backs on their father, on their loyalist town, on their aristocratic upbringing. They were the sort of people who wanted to rip down one government and replace it with another, because it would be a government in their image, not in that of their parents. And neither of them, it was suddenly clear, had any other goals or desires in the world than this notion of colonial freedom.

"Think of what it might mean, even for Safe Haven," Sally said. "You could trade directly with any country, you could buy Madeira from a Spanish boat, right in your own harbor."

"You're going too fast, Sally," said Pierpont. "That will only happen if we're pushed to it. No one wants independence if Parliament comes to their senses about our grievances."

"I want independence," said Sally. "I don't care about Parliament. I am an American, and we've already had our first congress, and all we need now is to unite." She turned her intelligent black eyes to Tom, and pulled him close. "To unite, do you understand? To come together, all of us, and make this a country, our country, and we'll be free, we'll all be free."

Tom relished the contact of her hand on his arm, he loved the power in her eyes, because it was concentrated somehow on him; she needed him. He didn't understand how or why he could be of help, and all her words had made no difference to his lack of political feelings. All that mattered was that she wanted him in some fashion, and he wanted her, more urgently every moment.

"Of course I understand," he said. "We'll all be free, Sally."

She didn't flinch when he used her first name, and she didn't take her hand from his arm as they continued up the path to the house of his father, and that of his forebears.

TEN

———◆◇◆———

The house that John Collins had named Safe Haven in 1637 had been torn down, save for the original fieldstone hearth and chimney. Logs had been replaced by a single-story frame house, sawed at a local mill in 1658 and crafted by English joiners and carpenters working off their passage money to the new land. The steep gable roof began to fall in 1677, and the rickety lean-to addition constructed without skill collapsed during the winter of 1678. A costly renovation took place during the spring and summer of 1678: Two large ground-floor rooms were added onto on all four sides, and a second story was added. A new brick chimney was built to service a separate kitchen room, and the field stone chimney was built up with care to rise over the great height of the new structure. A projecting porch was added on before the end of the century. Samuel Saunders, John Collins's son-in-law and Tom Williams's great-grandfather, enjoyed sitting there in his old age, watching the river traffic.

During the eleven years that Tom's mother, Elizabeth Williams, reigned over the household, many more sophisticated additions were made, inside and out. All the windows were replaced with diamond-shaped, high-quality leaded glass panes in hinged casements. Born in terrible poverty, Elizabeth had an urgent desire to create a sense of luxury about herself and her husband, always trying to bring this about with economy, not extravagance. Abe had never denied her anything, even though he had little interest in the plate, paintings, Turkey carpets, and faddish furniture she bought in abundance; his suspicion that much, if not most, of what she acquired for the house was in bad taste was confirmed over the years by the comments and suggestions of well-meaning friends. After all, Abe had been a widower for twenty-four years, and was not expected to know how to match furniture and tapestries and paint colors and goblets. But Abe had changed nothing since the death of his beloved wife. The only addition he had allowed was a massive front door, desired by his wife before her death. This particular door came from a demolished house, built in Fairlawn almost a century before, and was considered absurdly inappropriate by Safe Haven's modern-thinking builders. But the immensely heavy door, three thicknesses of wide boards studded with wrought-iron nails in a whimsical pentagon on either side, was Tom's joy. It was so heavy that a servant had to open it for him when he was a little boy, and he or a servant had to open it now for his eighty-year-old father. Its strength, its obduracy, linked him more with his mother and with the tales of John Collins than did the drafty old hearth with its blackened field stones.

"I would suggest that you don't tell my father," said Tom.

"I never intended to," said Sally Woods. "What a remarkable door." Impulsively, she touched the front door, and immediately the door gave way—not from her touch, but by the inward pulling of the massive weight by Isaac, Abe Williams's oldest servant, a man of sixty years.

"Your father said you are not to enter, Mr. Thomas," said Isaac.

"That's all over now, Isaac," said Tom, stepping ahead of Sally and Pierpont, and thrusting Isaac away from the threshold.

"Well, I don't know, Mr. Thomas. Your father, he gets very angry, and it's not up to me to say who's right and who's wrong," said Isaac. His look made it very clear whom he thought wrong: The son was the newcomer in his domain, the failed usurper of his master's affection. Abe Williams never had a kind word for Isaac, but the old servant knew that his master loved him, if only out of gratitude for his competence. And along with Abe, he never forgave Tom for killing his mother on his way into the world. The son's arrogance and belligerence only exaggerated what the old servant already knew: that the Lord had taken Elizabeth and given Tom as a punishment, not as a blessing.

"That's right, Isaac, it's not up to you," said Tom, and the young man pushed the old servant a foot away from the doorway, so that his company could enter the house unimpeded.

"There's laws against that kind of thing, Mr. Thomas," said Isaac. "I'm no slave, if you hear me right, sir. I'm no slave, and even if I was, you don't have to hit me when I'm only doing my job."

"Another word out of you, you black bastard," said Tom, "and I'm going to break your skull open. With my bare hands, I'm going to smack your head into a tree trunk." Pierpont and Sally had still not entered the open doorway, and Tom turned on them impatiently. "Come on, right this way."

"We could talk somewhere else, Thomas," said Pierpont. "I don't want to cause any ill feeling here."

"I said come in," said Tom. Sally entered first, and her brother followed, just as Abraham Williams, swinging his cane, clattered up to the doorway on the highly polished wood floor. His ancient, angry face was trying all of a sudden to twist itself into a welcome. He had recognized the children of the distinguished Woods family at once.

"I'm sorry, Mr. Williams, sir," said Isaac, "but the boy, he just pushed me, he pushed me hard—"

"Silence," said Abe. "Close the door."

"Yes, sir," said Isaac.

"I'm terribly sorry to intrude like this, Mr. Williams," said Pierpont. "It was just a sudden thought. Not Thomas's fault. I asked him if we could see the house."

"It's not for sale," said Abe, leaning forward and squinting at Pierpont as if to understand better what his purpose was in coming to his home.

"Oh, no, Mr. Williams," said Sally. "We don't want to buy it, just to look at it."

"What for?"

"Father," said Tom, "Miss Woods and Mr. Woods have always been curious to see our house, because it's old."

"This house will stand another hundred years. It's not old. It's made of good timber, the best. And my dear Elizabeth, may her immortal soul rest in peace, she worked so hard to make everything new and clean and comfortable. It's the best house in town, even now, even after all these years, with only Isaac to clean up."

Tom once again explained: The Woods siblings were eager to see the house because of its historical importance, its reputation for containing beautiful objects, and also because they were his friends.

"You are friendly with my son?"

"Yes, sir," said Pierpont. "We were at Yale together."

"I didn't think he ever stopped to make friends. He never made it through there, you know. Started when he was fifteen, passed all the Latin and Greek with no problem. I taught him Greek. I still read it, even with these old eyes and old head, I still read Greek, sir. He was expelled. I never went to Yale, of course. But he was expelled, and went to China. He did me a great favor and went to China." Abe paused, wondering if he might perhaps be talking too much, and looked directly at Pierpont's old maid sister. "I know your father, Miss Woods. I am honored by this visit."

"Thank you, sir," said Sally. "Actually, my father has no idea we're here today. My brother is looking for some land to invest in, using his own funds, and when we saw Tom, and remembered of course how famous his father is for his investments in land . . ."

"I am not a speculator, you know. Anyone who says that Abe Williams speculates is a liar, my dear young woman. I have always bought land for one purpose, and that was to rent it out. That was my sole reason. I am not one of these new people with a little smuggling money who want to buy and sell the same farm five times in one year."

"Not a speculator, Mr. Williams. Of course not. If it weren't for people such as yourself, the poor farmers would never have a chance to eat. The land's too expensive for them to buy. Someone has to buy it for them. You do a service to the countryside."

"Thank you, Miss Woods."

"But frankly, the talk of such things doesn't interest me, sir. I have come only to see the beautiful house, if you will permit me. Perhaps your son will be good enough to show me about?"

"Thomas, you heard Miss Woods."

"Yes, Father."

"I would very much enjoy seeing the house too," said Pierpont, looking fiercely at his sister.

"Don't be silly, Pierpont. I know you hate looking at pictures and furniture. You needn't be so formal with Mr. Williams. I'm sure he's very much like yourself—more interested in business than art."

"Yes, miss, that is precisely the way I am, always have been. Now you take my boy—you wouldn't think such a ruffian likes things like pictures, when all you ever see him doing is getting into and out of fights—but he does. Like a girl. You go ahead, Thomas. And show Miss Woods everything that your mother found for this house. Everything."

They passed quietly through a hallway lined with dull portraits. A Dutchman had painted most of the children of John and Virginia Collins, catching each of them with unnatural stiffness and sepulchral skin tones. Abigail's husband, Samuel Saunders, was there in four different portraits, at age twenty-one —when he'd first married her—and again at thirty-seven, fifty-eight, and seventy-six.

"How do you know how old he was?" she asked, and he pointed to the tiny numbers under the artist's signature. "Is there a picture of your mother?"

"Yes," he said, with an earnestness she understood at once. He would be unreliable to work with unless he believed in what they were doing, she realized. A young man who could be such a boor with an old servant, be rude and clumsy and brutal to half the people he met—and at the same time go weak at the mention of a mother he had never even known—would have to become emotionally attached to their cause.

They entered a wood-paneled room without windows, and Tom explained that it was part of the single-story house built up around the original hearth in 1658. But Sally didn't cross the large room, lit by natural light coming from opposing doorways on the room's longer sides, and approach the great field stone fireplace. She could see where Tom's reverence was directed: An enormous oil portrait of a young woman, her golden hair arranged into a fullness and symmetry that could never have existed in real life, hung between two French sconces. Without a word, she walked over to the portrait and stared at it, as if this was her only reason for coming to Safe Haven.

"Shall I light the candles, Sally?" said Tom.

There was plenty of light from the open doorways, but she wanted to please him. "If you don't mind, I'd really appreciate that. It's dark in here, and the portrait is wonderful."

"I'm told that she was far more beautiful," he said. "It's my mother, you know. She died when I was born." He lit a taper, and then lit the three bayberry candles in each of the two sconces. The candlelight did little to enhance the visibility of the dark painting. But as he lit the candles, she was struck again by his vulnerability, and its underside of anger and violence.

"Our mother died when we were small children," she said. "I know it's not the same. You never saw your mother, and that must be hard. I can still remember mine quite well, and I like to think of her when I'm worried or upset."

He took the bait. "And are you worried now?"

"Yes, of course. Anybody would be who understands what's happening." She said it all in front of the portrait, as if his mother would be bearing witness for the cause of American independence.

"Shall I put out the candles?" he said.

"All right. Your mother was beautiful, Tom." She was wary of removing her eyes from the painting for a few more moments. Only after he'd blown out the candles and begun to pace the long room did she feel comfortable about turning away from Elizabeth Williams. She turned to admire a grotesque tapestry of fat squires chasing game on poorly proportioned horses.

"Why don't you tell me what you're needing, then?" he said, trying to make it easier for her.

"Perhaps we should go into a quieter room."

"What do you mean? There's no noise here."

"There are two doors, Tom. Both open. I'm thinking of the servants."

"There's only Isaac and the cook. Both of them are too old to eavesdrop, and besides, neither one of them would care."

"Please," she said, turning her head toward the far door. He shook his head, and then gallantly offered his arm and took her off to the left, along a narrow foyer leading to a small sitting room. The chairs were upholstered in leather and finished with brass nails, in the ponderous style of the turn of the century. Here there were a few shelves for books, and no wall tapestries; someone had decided to paint the wood paneling Indian red. There was, however, a lovely tea table, with a silver tea service of very good quality. A single enormous easy chair was covered in red silk, in precisely the same shade as the overbearing walls. She closed the door to the little room.

"I need you to smuggle guns and ammunition into Fairlawn," she said.

"Is that all?" he said, trying not to laugh, or to seem at all taken aback.

"Two thousand rifles," she said.

"How many? Are you serious? What are you planning to do, start an army? There aren't two thousand people in Fairlawn and Safe Haven combined."

"It'll be dangerous," she said. "And I can't pay you much."

"Why will it be dangerous?"

"Because this is not yet a free country," she said, ignoring his question. Tom insisted: Who was she dealing with? What was special about this smuggling? Why couldn't he just remove the guns from a boat in the Sound and take them by a series of canoe trips to any of a thousand points on the shore, just the way every New England smuggler operated?

"Don't expect me to get all white-faced, Sally," he said. "This won't be the first time I've smuggled, and like you, I have my reasons to justify not paying the customs man. The whole point is to do it at night. Out in the Sound, if you know your way, there's no chance of having serious trouble. And don't worry about the money. I usually take payment in merchandise. Rifles are the easiest thing to sell. I'd rather have them than good British coin."

"We can't spare any rifles."

"Who is we?"

"And I'm afraid it's more dangerous than I've told you, or you imagine," she said. "Look, we have silver, Pierpont and I. Not with us, in Fairlawn. Family silver that Father won't miss, at least not right away. And later it won't make a difference."

"I don't want to steal your family heirlooms," he said. "Perhaps you can pay me later. Or your group. The Sons of Liberty have plenty of money. Even with the Boston port all locked up, the Sons there have plenty."

"Please don't talk about the Sons of Liberty," she said.

"All right."

"And the only ones who'll be paying you for your trouble will be Pierpont and myself. You won't be dealing with the Sons. You'll only be dealing with the two of us."

"Fine." He smiled. "But you still haven't told me what the problem is."

"I trust you," she said. "And I know that you're brave. But you have to understand that until I know that you're going to work with us, I can't really tell you everything."

"Look here," he said. "Perhaps I can make it easier for you. I don't want your silver. Maybe I'm not a great Connecticut patriot, but I don't mind helping a woman I admire do something that she believes in. We won't worry about the payment, not now, maybe never. Is that all right? I've agreed to do it. You can tell me what the difficulty is. I won't run away."

"Tom, I'm not asking you to unload a boat in the Sound. There is no boat. The guns are in New York City. I'm asking you to get them out of New York City and into Connecticut. And you have to do it within the next two weeks."

There was no helping it now: Tom laughed out loud. He didn't like the anger that twisted her lovely face, an anger of disappointment, of betrayal. "Look, just a moment, let me explain," he said.

"You won't do it?" she said, without a trace of friendship in her flat tone.

"Let me explain. You can't get anything into or out of New York City. Manhattan Island is not the Connecticut shore. There are a couple of places on the west side, the Hudson River side, where smugglers try to land, but half the time they crack up there on the rocks. Coming in from the ocean is impossible too. It's seventeen miles to the Battery from Sandy Hook. Once you're at that lighthouse, forget it. There's more customs boats than porpoises. You go north through the lower bay into the Narrows. Nobody gets through the Narrows without being seen. By the time you're in the upper bay, into the harbor, you're either legal or your ship is impounded."

"But you're not coming in from Europe. The guns are in New York. You can take them out by the East River, just as the farm produce boats do."

"The East River is the most crowded, congested, watched bit of water in America. You don't leave the wharf there and just set off whenever you please. It's guarded, regulated, and full of soldiers and sailors. And you don't even have a ship! How can you even talk to me when you don't have a ship? What am I supposed to do, float the guns in barrels down the river, into the Sound?" She could feel his anger rising, and she shut away her fears and disappointments. Tom was a boy, and she would ride his anger, flatter his manhood; she would make him do her will, because the fate of many depended on it.

"And you're angry at me?" he continued, his voice more and more indignant.

"I'm not angry at you," she said mildly.

"I saw it. I felt it. You were furious, and you had no right to be. Didn't I offer to help you? I said I would forget about money for the moment. But you have no boat! And the guns are in New York City! There are limits to what a man can do."

"I said I'm not angry at you," she said, turning her sad eyes on him. "There may not be anything you can do. It was just a thought. We didn't come to Safe Haven looking for you, remember. We came to find a smuggler we could trust. Someone who wouldn't need money right away. Naturally, we understood that there was a chance that we wouldn't find someone like that."

"All right. Then you must not be so terribly disappointed."

"I will try," she said. Sally was about to place her hand on his, but hesitated. "But don't you be upset with me, please. It was a whim, remember that. We saw you, and we thought we'd take a chance."

Tom suddenly said: "The last time we met, you told me quite

plainly that you wanted nothing to do with me. Do you remember? You told me to go away. Just go away. I'll never
forget that."

She was not angry, but she feigned anger, slapping her hands
together and looking at him with astonishment. "It was only
days after I called off my wedding, Thomas. Surely even you
knew about the wedding I refused to go through at the last
moment. You showed terrible taste in bothering me at that
time. I only wanted to be alone. You could have been King
George and I would have showed you as much interest. Think
what I must have been going through."

"Why didn't you go through with it?" he said.

"With my wedding?" Sally let out an indignant puff of air.
"What right do you have to ask me a question like that?"

"No right," said Tom. "None at all."

She had been sitting on one of the leather chairs, but now
stood up suddenly and walked to the huge easy chair and stead-
ied her hands on its elegant carved-wood back. "You want to
know?" she said. "You aren't the only one. Even today my father still asks me. In disgust. As if I've thrown my life away. An
old maid. Useless, contemptible. I don't have a function, you
see. I'm an empty vessel. I'm a ship that can't sail, a horse that
can't pull a cart. But you want to know how I could do such a
thing. My fiancé was attractive, rich, intelligent. I suppose I
loved him. It wasn't just an arranged match, two families with
common goals. I knew him. I'd known him a long time, and we
got on. We were a fine pair."

"Look, I'm sorry," said Tom. "I was stupid to ask you something like that. It's just that I do admire you. You know that. I
wondered. I should have kept it to myself, but there I am.
That's me. I don't know when to keep quiet."

Sally moved around the chair and sat down in it, sinking
into the flamboyant red silk with relief. She said: "He had no
convictions."

Tom took this in at once. It meant that the beautiful young
woman could love no one who didn't believe as she did; and
too, it meant that she could love someone like himself, if only
he believed.

But she was not through characterizing her almost husband.

"He was a coward as well, though that meant less to me. Many men are brave, for stupid reasons. And many men of good hearts, freedom-loving, with the best of intentions, simply are too afraid to hold a rifle in their hands and shoot down an oppressor." She looked up at him shyly, with a weak little smile. Sally was no longer trying to seduce him to her side, though her confession was having a greater effect on him than anything that had preceded it. "I remember hearing how you'd gone off to China. It seemed incredible that you could do that. I know you're not a boy—you weren't a boy when I heard of it, either —but still, you were younger than Pierpont. It seemed so brave. I wondered if I would have had the nerve to sail that far away on the other side of the world."

"There was nothing brave about it," he said. He had been away from Safe Haven for nearly three years, and most of them had been spent on the open sea, waiting for wind. His greatest disappointment had been that his ship hadn't traveled around the world, but had satisfied commercial obligations by retracing its own route: New York to England to West Africa, around the Cape of Good Hope, to Madagascar, to Ceylon, and finally to Canton in China. They had never even touched the coast of Japan. And of the sights he had seen, most of what remained in his memory was the picture of slaves and half-slaves of every color and creed, loading and unloading cargo to the shouts and blows of overseers; that, and the whores he'd visited in every port. He remembered the miserable shanties, the filthy mats, the swatting at insects, the overpowering odor of semen and sweat, the terrible protestations of love in languages harsh, arrythmic, alien. Usually they were very young girls, younger than himself, frail, hungry, eager to please. Always, he fell in love with them, every time he joined his body with one of theirs. It was not the same as when he'd gone to the brothels in New York and London, where the girls were English or French or German. Tom had felt their disgrace, their horror at their own lives, and felt himself shamed, a partner in their shame. On clean sheets, in comfortable houses, he had still been able to see the lives of poverty and gin, the ruined marriages and loves that had brought these girls to desolation. But in the Orient, in Africa, in exotic island ports, he had felt a bizarre kinship. Their hunger was like his; their desire to please matched his desire to be loved. And the sheer miracle of the sexual act blotted out what was alien, leaving only the bliss of physical love. When he looked at Sally Woods, he wondered what it would be like to bring his infatuation with her to love; what it would be like to make love with a woman whom he desired emotionally as well as physically.

"It was brave to get on the boat," she said. "Did you ever stop to think that you might not get back?"

"Yes," he said.

"Do you know what I think? I think if I could teach you what England is doing to America, I think you would be dumping tea off the docks in every seaport in America."

"Is that what you want from me?" he said.

"No," said Sally Woods, and because the conversation had shifted back to a seductive tone, she became hopeful. This was a time to beguile, this was a boy who could be led, and to his own advantage, and to the advantage of his country. "Tea was dumped in Boston to good cause. But that was more than a year ago. I want you for something far braver, far more important."

Tom smiled. "You think I'll change my mind?"

"I think I could teach you," she said. "You're brave and intelligent. I wouldn't have to tell you what to do. You'd know." Sally stood up abruptly, taking a step closer to where Tom stood, his hands clasped behind his back.

"I don't own a ship."

"Your father owns several."

"To ship fruits and vegetables, not guns." But he felt his attraction to her growing unbearably. And it was not charm that would win her, but reckless courage.

"But that's what the sloop brings from Safe Haven. What does it bring back?"

"Anything that New York sells to Safe Haven, and that means everything under the sun." Tom unclasped his hands and brought them slowly to his sides. Sally moved a wayward strand of black hair off her forehead. "Where are the guns?" he said finally.

"In New York."

"You said that. You didn't say where."

"Under lock and key, and under guard."

"The Sons of Liberty have an arsenal?"

"No," said Sally. "The Sons of Liberty are going to liberate an arsenal." She reached out a hand: He could shake it, he could caress it, he could try to bring it to his lips. But to do any of those things, he had to keep talking, keep allowing the possibility of this mad scheme to be part of his life. "You needn't be alarmed about that. It's all set, that part, and you're not to have anything to do with that. All I'm asking you for is to get the rifles to Fairlawn. We'll see to it that they're at your disposal in New York."

He took her hand, and she didn't resist. "So you and Pierpont are going to New York?" he said.

"Yes."

"By coach—the Post Road?"

"We have made no arrangements," she said. Her hand rested in his, waiting for him to decide. Somewhere in the old house, Abe Williams belabored her brother with proposals for land investments. Outside, wagons rolled back and forth from the marketplace, boats sailed down to the Sound, everyone driven by the winds of ambition. In Fairlawn, her father and others like him demanded protection from the ruffians who had splattered paint on their front doors, or hurled rocks through their imported glass windows. The Tories were nervous in Connecticut, and hid their gold underground, and sank their silver in buckets at the bottom of wells. But few made plans to leave their towns. British soldiers were already there, keeping a semblance of order, and many more were on the way from England. Everyone knew that the troublemakers, the zealots who spoke of independence, were a tiny minority; that the vast majority of Americans wanted only one thing, and that was order. For every Tory there was a patriot, but for every patriot there were five who cared as little as Tom Williams. Men wanted to tend their crops, women wanted to feed their babies, families wanted to grow into self-contained units of safety and prosperity. Indifference was Sally Woods's greatest enemy, and she feared that it would defeat the colonies before a country could be born out of its troubles. It was all too easy for her to imagine the red-coated soldiers marching into all the little towns, confiscating the few ancient weapons on hand, disbanding the local militias, creating imperial order out of democratic rule.

"Perhaps we can go together," said Tom, looking into her eyes, trying to wrest romance from her determined stance.

"Do you mean that you'll do it?" she said, pulling back her hand from his, but only to clap her hands together in joy and astonishment.

"I'll try," he said, without a plan, without any idea of what he would be committing himself to. "I'll do whatever I can."

"Thank you," she said, "thank you so much." She reached out and grabbed both his hands and squeezed them, and Tom responded by pulling her hands apart and moving his body to hers and embracing her. "No," she said. "Please let me go."

But suddenly it made no difference what she said. He had committed himself, and the rush of desire was running through him, powerful and sure. He let go of her, only to take hold of her beautiful face, and slowly he brought his lips to hers and kissed her. Sally remained motionless. She didn't struggle, didn't try to wrench her head from his grip, didn't clench her teeth against the gentle touch of his lips. But neither did she accept the kiss, or the embrace, or the offer of love. She looked at him, her large black eyes shocked into a passivity more frightening to Tom than any forceful reaction would have been. He understood that she had no interest in him, no desire; but her desire to fulfill her patriotic task was so great that she would remain rooted to this spot, accepting his embrace, as long as she must. Tom let her go. He was as angry as she was; but only he was allowed to show it.

"It's all right, Miss Woods. You don't have to pretend to like me. I've said I'm going to help you, and that's what I'm going to do."

Tom stalked out of the room, and Sally followed, afraid of his temper. She caught up with him as he interrupted Pierpont and Abe Williams. "I'm through with the house tour, Father. If you need me, I'll be at the Hog."

"I need you right now, boy," said his father. "Sit down."

Tom hesitated, and Sally came up behind him and put her hand lightly on his shoulder. "You have a lovely home, Mr. Williams. Your son was a wonderful guide. Very patient and knowledgeable."

"I said sit," said Abe to his son. Tom sat down in the indicated hard-back chair. "All right. Mr. Woods here wants to take a look at the Wheatley lot. Right off the water, next to Margam's—"

"I know the lot, Father. I didn't know it was for sale."

"Everything's for sale if the price is right, boy. It's about time you learned that little lesson. Go on, get up now. Show your friend the lot, and be polite. He's a business associate as of this moment, do you hear?"

"I hear, Father," said Tom. Glumly, he marched outside with Pierpont and Sally, leading the way back to the river path at a very fast pace.

Once out of earshot of the house, Pierpont stopped him. "All right, you two. Would somebody please tell me what's going on?"

"He's agreed," said Sally. "Tom has very nicely agreed to help us all he can."

"That's great!" said Pierpont. "Tom, that's wonderful!" He shook Tom's hand and pounded his back.

"He knows everything," Sally said.

"Do you think you can find a way to get them in? Can you get us a boat? What do you need? Did Sally tell you that we can get hold of some family silver?"

"I won't need the silver," said Tom, looking only at Pierpont. "As soon as you're ready, we'll go to New York and I'll find us a way to get the rifles past the British. I don't expect it to be easy, but I don't expect to get caught, either." Finally, he turned his cold eyes to Sally. "My only requirement is that your sister stay out of my way."

"I'm going to New York," she said.

"I don't really care where you go, Miss Woods," said Tom. "As long as I don't have to hear you or see you, I'll be perfectly all right."

It was a mark of their intense dedication to their cause that neither Pierpont nor Sally answered this terrible rudeness. They simply walked on, following Tom to the waterfront, where Pierpont would pretend to be interested in a choice bit of Williams-owned property, and Tom would wander into the Hog, looking for a drink, and a chance for oblivion.

ELEVEN

———◦◆◦———

There were many ways to get to New York from Safe Haven in 1775, but the only reliable one was to follow the Post Road. In good weather, without mishap to horse or coach axle, one could make the journey in two days. Every little town had a few rooms over a tavern, and some had a full-fledged inn. When it was dry, and the roadbed solid, the sixty-five miles fairly flew by, the milestones drifting one into the next with cheerful regularity. Stops were frequent, and pleasant. While the horses were attended to, the travelers traded gossip at the local tavern. Little signs and signals were given by travelers and locals, so that one could easily tell on which side of the fence the other sat—were they supporters of Parliament or of the American Continental Congress? Whether they were Tories or patriots, conjecture about British troop movements, about the possibility of imperial wrath against the American boycotts and training of militias, flowed freely.

Pierpont and Sally Woods, traveling with an Anglican priest and the old widow of a British colonel, were more often than not perceived as Tories. Local Tories angrily exhibited copies of the New York *Journal*, famous for its "Unite or Die" slogan and its "treasonous" support of the Sons of Liberty. "They dare talk about not having liberty," said one loyalist innkeeper to Pierpont, slapping at the tattered newspaper. "This preaches nothing less than rebellion, and no one puts a stop to it. These fools forget that they're Englishmen, and that only as Englishmen will they ever have liberty."

The priest lifted his cup of ale from an adjacent table and saluted the innkeeper's sentiments. He reminded all of them, and the room at large, of what Dr. Johnson had said in response to the Boston tea party: Americans were nothing but "a race of convicts and ought to be thankful we allow them short of hanging!"

Through all of this, and a score of similar comments, Sally and Pierpont kept their silence. They had enough gratification from sensing the innkeeper's wife's indignation at the priest's remark. Many of the ordinary people encountered along their route were silent and hostile to their party, and this was a good sign to the Woodses, because they knew they were taken for Tories. As they grew closer to New York, Sally especially felt the anger building in people, rising through layers of indifference. Everyone called for arming the populace; not for revolution, but for protection against any form of tyranny. This anger gave her courage, and encouragement. By the time, late in the afternoon of their second day of travel, that they arrived at the Spuyten-Duyvil Bridge in Knightsbridge, she felt no fear at what had to be done in New York. Clattering over the wood planks of the bridge, which spanned the clear waters of the Harlem River, she asked Pierpont if they could stop the night in Harlem Village. "I'm too worn out for New York just yet. Too happy. I want to be rested when I'm going to be surrounded by all those people."

Pierpont agreed, of course, and without comment. He suspected that she wanted another day of peace before seeing Tom Williams at the boardinghouse on Broadway where they'd arranged to meet. Brother suspected even more than that of his beautiful sister, but refused to ponder the consequences of his suspicion. Pierpont felt that he had plumbed the depths of Tom Williams, and found only anger, daring, and charm. There were no beliefs, no loyalty, no convictions of any kind. If his twenty-eight-year-old sister was attracted to the twenty-four-year-old boy, he was sure that the attraction wouldn't last longer than the importation of the yet-to-be-stolen rifles to Fairlawn.

They slept over at Day's, a comfortable tavern precisely nine miles from the Battery, at the tip of Manhattan Island. Up at six the following morning, they took seats in the scheduled coach from Harlem Village to Hull's Tavern on Broadway. It began to rain, a drenching March downpour, and the Post Road quickly turned to mud.

"We could be waking up in the city right now," said Pierpont. They were alone in the coach, and the driver seemed to be in no hurry to cut short his uncomfortable perch on the open driving bench.

"I wonder if he's there," said Sally.

"He's there. If he had to swim to get there on time he'd have done it."

"What makes you so sure about him?"

"He's in love with you, Sal," said her brother. When she didn't answer this, not even with a hand to her face, or the beginnings of a blush, he turned to look out at the rain. At the rate they were going they wouldn't cover much more than three miles in an hour. Once they'd left Harlem behind, they were in country as sparsely populated as much of Connecticut.

"That's the beginning of the Stuyvesant lands," he pointed out to Sally an hour later. They had finally picked up the pace a bit, and the coach had entered the Bowery Lane.

"I don't see a farm."

"You can't see a thing just yet. This is the end of it. They live much further south, closer to the city."

But the muddy road suddenly began to climb, and the rain let up just as they reached the top of a little hill. All thought of looking for the Stuyvesant houses in the gray mist vanished, for now they had a vista of the city of New York.

Nothing was distinct, save for the towering height of King's College and the lovely spire of Trinity Church rising behind it, imperious, perfect in form and expression. Though they could not clearly see houses or people, they could sense the closeness of the sea, they could feel it in their bones. And though they had been to New York a dozen times before, they couldn't help but be excited by entering it. Here, in an underpopulated land, puny settlements set up along the Atlantic seacoast from New Hampshire to Georgia, mere pockets of civilization in an endless forest, here was a metropolis. Almost as populous as Philadelphia, it was far more exciting, its twenty-five thousand people drawn from every race and creed, its streets alive with soldiers, whores, merchants, slaves, aristocrats. It was said that three thousand separate structures stood on this little bit of earth; and there were nearly that many political parties.

"What's that?" she said. "I don't remember a lake."

They could see the Collect Pond off to the west, and around it shanties, makeshift dwellings with mud floors. Pierpont explained that it was New York's water supply, an enormous freshwater pond catching rainfall in its seventy acres. "I skated there once," he said. "With a Dutch girl."

"Rich Dutch or poor Dutch?"

"They're mostly rich. And mostly Tory. More loyal than the Anglo-Dutch, and much more loyal than the simply English."

The Bowery Lane twisted a bit to the west, and they could see a collection of the shanties, almost a village of its own, with fires burning in the open, some of them smoldering from the recent downpour. Pigs walked about the rude huts and cabins, picking through the garbage in the muddy lanes. Little children ran about half naked, though the March weather was raw, and heavily muscled men pulled carts through the mud, most of them loaded with water barrels.

"They're all Negroes," she said. "I don't remember that."

"Just in this part of the city. They live near the Collect Pond, and most of them make their money from carting water down to the ships and the houses. Most of them are free."

"I've never seen so many black faces in my life."

"They should be in our army," said Pierpont seriously.

"Who?"

"Negroes, of course. There are three thousand in New York. They're not Tories, you can be sure. Not a single one of them has any reason to support the King of England."

"I never thought of that," she said. As always, thoughts and impressions were crowding in too quickly now that they were entering the city. Blacks in the American army? She had no idea if they'd be able to fight, if they could learn to shoot at the oppressors of the country that had enslaved them. And what of the white Americans? She doubted that many would want to serve alongside savage Negroes.

She had missed the sight of the Stuyvesant houses, and the coach had picked up speed, oblivious of the pigs walking sedately across their path. But soon the famous city traffic, carts and cattle and wagons of every type, began to clog the road to Broadway. They slowed to a crawl, then to a standstill.

"Listen," said Pierpont suddenly.

"To what?" They had started up again, joining the slow line of traffic past gardens and fields into the city.

"We're on Broadway."

"How do you know? I don't see a sign."

"We missed the sign, but listen—we're on a paved road. Cobblestones. They've paved another half mile since I was here last year."

"Then we're almost there, aren't we? A few minutes?" she said, fixing her hair and fussing with her collar. They were suddenly in a city, not in its outskirts of shanties, but a city of great, lasting structures. At St. Paul's Chapel, real sidewalks began, paved with flat rock for the benefit of pedestrians. The road itself was wider here, and save for the garbage thrown in the middle of it, was alive with a sense of power. This would be the American capital, she thought. This city of wealth and motion and diversity, surrounded on three sides by water, possessor of the finest harbor in the civilized world.

Peddlers with their wares and beggars with their self-pity approached the open windows of the coach, as the day continued to clear. The rain had stopped, and the feeble March sun lit the old, pretty mansions on Broadway, where some of the richest men in New York lived. Newer money, from men who'd made fortunes from smuggling and land speculation, had built homes along both rivers, those north of Wall Street able to indulge in large ornamental gardens, landscaped in the French style. Smaller homes were being built about Hanover Square and along Queen Street, where very rich families clustered in four-story mansions, many with rooftop balconies from which they could look out to sea. But the old Broadway mansions maintained their special charm; some had survived fire and storm for a hundred years, and had been lived in by generations of the same family.

Hull's Tavern was on lower Broadway, a crowded meeting place for Tory and patriot alike. Here the talk was of business first, and politics second. Unlike the venerable Coffee House nearby, which catered strictly to Tory businessmen, or Jasper Drake's Tavern, which served most of New York's monied Sons of Liberty, Hull's Tavern could be entered and left anonymously. Strangers weren't conspicuous here, and weren't bothered with emotional questions about their fidelity to or hatred of "Farmer" George, the King of England, and ruler of its American empire.

Brother and sister entered the crowded tavern through a low doorway and looked for Tom. Men turned to look at Sally, but lowered their eyes quickly; this was a gentleman's place, and though there were no other ladies in the room, it was improper to stare at an accompanied woman.

"He's not here," she said.

"How do you know?" he said. "Wait a minute." He wanted to stroll about the benches and tables, rub shoulders with the innkeeper and barmaid, look through the thicket of hats and wigs and pots of ale and trenchers of meat to see if Tom had shown up, only to sit sullenly in a corner of the room, waiting for Sally.

"He's not here," she said, so insistently that he believed her. She was actually attuned to the boy; or he was to her. If he was here, he would have made his presence known by now. She knew this. And she worried.

"We were supposed to meet last night," he reminded her.

"But we said to come here the following day," she said, "if one of us couldn't make it on time. He's not here, and there's a good chance that he wasn't here last night, either."

Tom had wanted to make his own way to New York, to give himself a chance to work on his plan. For one dollar, a boatman had ferried him across the Sound to Long Island, together with his horse, and he had ridden west across the sandy north shore, looking for a protected cove not yet inhabited by smugglers, privateers, or fugitives. While Sally and Pierpont had ridden in comfort along the western Connecticut shore, Tom had searched on foot and on horseback, skirting new farms and old estates, avoiding the camps of vagabonds who would have killed him for his clothes, his purse, or his horse. He slept at an inn on the outskirts of Brooklyn, and then returned to a protected nook of land he'd seen at twilight. A large boat, an eighty-ton schooner, would never make it through; not even a forty-ton sloop, he realized. But the cove was uninhabited, hidden, and close. Three or four small boats, the size of the smaller ferries, would easily carry the weight of two thousand rifles. Ten such boats could hide in this cove. He noted carefully the landmarks he'd need to recognize the place from the water and, satisfied, set off for Brooklyn and New York.

Brooklyn had its share of fledgling villages, some of them started by religious communities; its position on the opposite side of the East River from Manhattan, backed with endless reaches of good land, had sent more than a few respectable burghers to stake out estates. Still, for all its growing gentility, Brooklyn was most famous for its Ferry Road, and the taverns and boardinghouses and brothels all about it. Miles away from the river, pushing east into the open spaces of Long Island, it was easy to forget that Brooklyn was a city. But on Ferry Road, inhaling the odors of slaughterhouses and breweries, listening to the din of the shipyards and their ceaseless construction, picking one's way between drunken soldiers and rowdy dock workers, it was difficult to remember that over the nearest hills was farmland and pasture and peace.

Tom had found a stable for his horse, and an inn to serve him a meal, as he had more than five hours to spare before his scheduled meeting with Sally and Pierpont on the other side of the river. He wanted to fill his belly with beef and beer, rest his backside and feet, and think of nothing until it was time to take the ferry to Peck's Slip in Manhattan.

"I don't go with no English," said a girl with an accent more French than American, and a painted face more pretty than it was whorish.

"What are you, some kind of rebel?" said a huge English soldier, wearing a much disheveled sergeant's uniform. "I always said the Sons of Liberties were nothing but whores, but I never really meant it, right?" He took hold of the pretty prostitute by the elbow and dragged her to her feet.

"I already told you, I don't go with no English," said the girl. She tried to release herself from the man's grip, but could not. Tom Williams tried to control himself. This was not the time for him to make a spectacle, particularly with an English soldier.

"What are you looking at, you drunken bums?" said the big sergeant to the tavern at large. He felt vaguely threatened, not by the force of men in the room, but by his public rejection by a whore. It was only partially an affront to the British Empire; it was also an affront to his manhood. "No halfpenny colonial whore is going to tell me what I can or can't do," he said, continuing to hold on to her, but not making much headway toward the doorway.

A gentleman, very much smaller than the sergeant, and apparently about fifty years old, stood up from where he'd been eating, knocking over his bench in the process. "Let the girl alone, Sergeant," said the gentleman.

"This ain't your business," said the sergeant, but he let the girl go at once. Another man, younger and square-shouldered, had gotten up on the other side of the room.

"The preacher said there's a time to pray and a time to fight," said the whore. "Now it's the fighting time."

"Your preacher is a blaspheming traitor, and I damn him," said the soldier. "Do you hear me? I damn him!"

"Get out of here, Sergeant," said the younger man. "We don't want your kind in here."

"What's my kind, you fool? I'm an Englishman, and I can beat any one of you." To prove his point, he took a quick step over to the younger man and pushed him into and over a table laden with meat pies and pots of ale.

"I'm an Englishman, and I can beat you," said Tom Williams. He hadn't planned on saying those words, and he hadn't planned on getting up. But the madness, the anger had taken hold of him. "I'm an Englishman born in America, but if England keeps sending over pigs like yourself, we're going to have to put a stop to it." It was probably the closest he'd ever come to expressing a political idea that was truly felt, and his intensity embarrassed him.

"Call yourself an American," said the prostitute. "You'll save yourself a lot of trouble."

"Call yourself dead," said the big sergeant, and he lurched forward, leading with his left fist. Tom moved to the left, and then to the right, raising his own fists, but not deigning to strike. The sergeant swung at him three times, and each time he swung at air. Meanwhile, the man who'd been pushed over the table was back on his feet, and others in the tavern were standing now, and moving in.

"Leave him alone," said Tom. "I don't need help." And he finally hit the sergeant, lightly, a left jab, and then again, two more lefts, his fist swinging from a fluid wrist, snapping into the big man's nose, not breaking it, but bloodying it.

"I'll kill you," said the sergeant. Anger made him clumsier, the taste of his own blood leading him to swing indiscriminately, wasting his energy, accentuating his humiliation at the hands of the lighter man.

"All right," said Tom, stepping back from the sergeant, feeling the madness in his frame quieting. He remembered that he must not let anything get in the way of his making the ferry to Manhattan. There might be soldiers, watch officers, Tories, men with clubs or guns, and they must not interfere with Sally Woods's plans. "Just get out of here," he said, putting up his hands. "I don't want to kill you."

"No," said the sergeant, coming after him. "You can't walk away now, you American pig." He walked into Tom's right fist, a short, sharp uppercut; and then Tom threw three jabs with his left, and drove his foot into the man's shin, and grabbed his hair, and threw him howling onto the floor.

As in a dream—a bad dream he had already imagined, had already hoped would never take place—red-coated soldiers stood in the doorway. There was a rush for the back door, for the windows fronting on Ferry Street, as every bench scraped on the wood floors, as each table was turned over, as the single lantern burning in midday was sent crashing to the ground. Tom knew that he had to run, he more than the rest, but he was so taken aback at the sight of authority—strangers who would have power over him in his own land—that he couldn't move.

Two soldiers dropped to their knees to attend to the sergeant, but two more already were upon him, shouting at him, swinging at him with cudgels. A sharp pain exploded in his left shoulder, and then another in his belly. Someone tugged at him from behind—the girl, the prostitute with the slight French accent—but he was turning away from her, fighting. He landed a punch at the point of a soldier's jaw, he landed a kick in another soldier's groin; but then he was on the floor, being kicked, stepped on, and he felt as if the myriad pains starting up in his arms and legs and at the base of his skull were erupting into fire.

But it was the tavern that was erupting into fire.

The old-fashioned whale-oil lantern had ignited a cloth draping one of the overturned tables, and fire was spreading through the shabby wood building with speed. Once again there was a sharp pain in his shoulder, but he was not being kicked, but urged to his feet. He looked up slowly, and smiled against the smoke and the screams and the rising heat. But it was not the prostitute who was pulling him to his feet; it was the older gentleman who'd first challenged the British sergeant. Tom tried to do what the man urged, but he couldn't seem to get his legs to respond. The fire felt warm now; the sense of urgency was relaxing. What did it matter if he slept for a while, only for a moment?

And Tom did sleep, even if the sleep was troubled, disturbed by pain and a hundred worries: His father hadn't wanted him to go back to New York so quickly, not believing his story of having an important business meeting with an owner of land in the Hudson Valley; if Tom were wounded, or dead, Abe Williams wouldn't be able to grieve. And how would Sally know that he'd died, his body burned to a crisp in Brooklyn, unrecognizable, the story of his patriotic defense of a whore obscured for all time? Where was he then, if he was not dead, floating on hot sheets, a shiver of fear running through him where no fear had ever run before? How pretty that whore had been, how sweet her accent, how noble she'd been to spurn the Englishman. An American, she'd called Tom—no, not that. She'd advised him to call himself that: "Call yourself an American," she'd said.

A single candle sputtered on a blackened dish.

"What?" he said involuntarily, questioning where he was, whether he was alive or dead, what had happened to him in the past moments, what was happening to him now.

There was no answer. He tried to move, and felt an awful weariness, a heavy weight of weakness sitting on his chest. He was in a bed. The candle burned on a dish sitting on a chest of drawers. There was a window, covered by dark curtains, but it was dark outside. It was night. He had missed the ferry.

"What time is it?" he said, and this time his words were audible, and were answered by a scraping from outside the room. Then footsteps, a door opening, light.

Tom Williams sat up, trying to still the room turning about inside his head, trying to steady the vision of strange men coming up to where he lay.

"Are you all right, sir?"

"What time is it, please?"

"Late. Past midnight, sir."

"I must get to New York."

"How do you feel, sir?" The man who spoke looked familiar, a kindly gentleman in his early fifties, his eyes bloodshot in the poor light.

"I must get to New York," said Tom again. "Please. Can you help me get to the ferry?"

"There is no ferry at this hour, sir. And I am quite sure that you're not up to the trip, though it's a short one. Why don't you try to rest for a while, and we'll see how you're feeling at daybreak?"

"You don't understand," said Tom, wanting to explain the urgency of his mission. But all he could think of was Sally. Seeing her was his motivation; his urgency was to be met by her dark eyes, to be embraced by a welcome no longer indifferent. But his thoughts of Sally were soft, quiet, dreamlike. Covers were pulled up to his neck, cold cloths put to his forehead, and in a moment the candle was snuffed out, only to be replaced by a golden light, easy and comforting. The chest of drawers was bow-fronted, made of mahogany. A hardwood banister-back chair, crafted in the style of sixty years ago, sat next to the bed. The ceiling was high, and a chandelier hung from it.

He remembered missing the ferry.

Tom sat up in bed, slightly dizzy, but alive with purpose. He was weak, but he wanted food; he knew that he would be all right after something hot and wholesome was digested. Carefully, he swung his long legs out of the high bed and onto the polished wood floor. Three small Turkey carpets, poorly matched, hung on the wall. Whoever owned this house was newly rich, he thought. These carpets weren't meant for exhibition, but for walking on. He made his way to the mirror on the wall opposite the carpets. There was a bandage over his right eye, and when he touched it, he felt a dull pain start up.

"Good morning, sir!" It was the gentleman from the night before, grinning as if at some shared joke. Tom recognized him now.

"You were in the tavern," he said. "You spoke back to the sergeant."

"The both of us did. And other patriots, sir. But you stood us proud. The *Journal* will write it up: British soldiers assault citizens in drunken brawl. Lovely! My name is Laker, sir. Walter Laker of the city of Brooklyn, and a loyal American patriot. I am at your service completely."

Laker explained how he had helped Tom out of the burning tavern and walked him through the back alleys to his house, less than half a mile inland from the waterfront tavern.

The nightshirt Tom was wearing was Laker's, as were the bed, the house, and the lovely young daughter who brought him breakfast on a silver tray. Together with Laker, Tom ascertained that none of his bones had been broken during the previous afternoon's brawl. All along his right thigh, however, and about both shoulders were black-and-blue bruises, and when he moved too suddenly he experienced spasmodic pain along his shoulders and down his spine. He would have to move slowly and carefully, but he would have to move. Since he had not made it to Hull's the night before, they'd expect him there at midday.

"How far is the ferry from here?" he asked Laker.

"I'm afraid you can't take the ferry, sir," said Laker. "For today at least, you're a bit notorious. That sergeant is very much alive and looking for you. All the ferry docks are being watched. They have your description. I'm sure in a day or two it'll all blow over, but until then you'll just have to put up with my hospitality."

"And mine," said the pretty Miss Laker. "Are you with the Sons?"

"I really shouldn't be talking about who I'm with," said Tom mysteriously. He was certainly not a Son of Liberty, but he saw nothing wrong with hinting that he was involved with their plans. After all, he was on the verge of a crackbrained scheme to run British guns out of New York, if not for the Sons, then for Sally Woods—which was more or less the same thing.

"You needn't say, sir. So much is obvious to me," said Laker. "I won't ask you if you're for or against independence, but I needn't ask you if you're for or against the Congress."

"Of course I'm for the Congress," said Tom.

"And independence," said Miss Laker. "I don't see why we're all so secret. He's not a spy. Tell us your name."

"Thomas Williams."

"And where are you from?"

"Safe Haven."

"And the men of Safe Haven—how will they stand?" said Laker.

"I can't speak for anyone but myself, I'm afraid," said Tom.

"All Congress decided is so simple," said Laker. "Any man who won't agree with those two decisions should be hanged. We had out-and-out Tories in the Congress, and *they* went along with the decisions. And still there are men in New York who become furious if any dares suggest the Parliament of all-mighty England could possibly be in error. It's like Catholics and the pope. We got rid of the pope a long time ago—now we'll just have to rise up and get rid of the King!"

Tom was a bit embarrassed by Laker's vehemence. For one thing, he wasn't quite sure he knew which two decisions of Congress he was referring to, and he hoped he wouldn't be asked. "Absolutely," said Tom. "I couldn't agree with you more."

"When you hit that bastard, there wasn't a man in the tavern who wasn't a patriot," said Laker. "Do you understand me, my friend? This country is ripe and ready, and all it needs is something to set it off. That stupid oaf of an Englishman—we'll show them that they can't abuse us, even if it's abusing a prostitute."

"The whores in New York City won't go with them," said Miss Laker.

"My dear," said her father, "I think that's quite enough on the subject. I went too far myself."

"I know what a whore is," said Miss Laker. "I'm fighting for just as much as any of you are, and I can use the same words. When there's independence it's going to mean independence for women too, just you wait and see."

"My daughter is an extremist, Mr. Williams."

"As is my father," she said with a smile. "As is our Mr. Williams, I would imagine. He is here from Connecticut for the Sons of Liberty on some dangerous mission, and we shall help him, Father. We shall help him with anything he needs." She paused, and then she added, "I am with the Daughters of Liberty. We are very strong in New York, and we are growing in Brooklyn. A merchant tried to sell English wool from his boat at Peck's Slip a week ago. We stood in a line and chanted 'Traitor' at him for an hour before the soldiers came. He didn't sell a thing. And he wasn't too popular after that, either."

"I have to get to New York by noon," he said. "Can you help me?"

"You can't take the ferry," began Mr. Laker. But his pretty daughter interrupted him:

"Yes," she said. "I can row you across."

"Fine," said Tom. "I'm ready then, whenever you are."

His host insisted on Tom's finishing breakfast and resting quietly before rushing off. Since there was the possibility of danger, he wanted to round up a few friends, and take him across—without his daughter—fully armed, in a good boat, away from the ferry lines. When he had gone off, Tom asked the girl bluntly what Congress had called for in the way of action.

"How can you ask me that?" she said, as if he had hit her. He understood that she thought he was testing her.

"I've been out of the country, my dear. I can't explain where. It takes seven weeks to get a letter across the Atlantic, and very few came my way. Most people knew me as an American, but a

Tory. And there wasn't much serious talk about what Congress had offered Parliament, because as far as they were concerned Congress was illegal to begin with."

"You were in France!" she said. But he wouldn't tell her anything more, and so she fantasized, imagining him trying to raise money and guns and armies, a spy before there was even a hint of war. Never would she have imagined him to be so uncommitted that he hadn't bothered to read the journals or listen to the raging arguments, now half a year old, about what the Continental Congress had recommended in the wake of England's closing the Port of Boston: There were to be two things on which everyone agreed—nonimportation and the arming of citizens.

Tom thanked her for the information and passed the better part of the morning with her, waiting for the return of her father. Nonimportation was a principle he understood; since he was a small boy, there was always one boycott or another going on against English taxation. As for arming the citizenry—well, he believed in that too. Everyone had the right to bear arms. And when the threat of imperial force was on the horizon, especially with representatives of the Empire like the sergeant in the tavern, it was essential to maintain that right.

Still, there was no fire running through him. He had a grudge against the soldiers who'd beaten him yesterday; but in his heart of hearts, he felt himself just as English as they. Certainly he would refuse to buy English goods for the moment, but he couldn't decide how he'd react to a chance to *smuggle* English goods into a safe port for a healthy profit. This pretty young woman of Brooklyn, intensely patriotic, wild with a desire to separate from England, to create a land where women and men were equal in the eyes of the law, drew inspiration from a source unknown to him. She had something of Sally's madness, though less wise, less tempered. But he had none of it. It was absurd how he was lionized for deeds unnamed, for ideals never stated.

When Laker returned, he was dressed in a farmer's smock and an ancient broad-brimmed hat. He had similar clothes for Tom, and Tom quickly changed into sun-bleached and worn work clothes, boots far too large for his rather big feet. He balled his own clothes into a tattered length of canvas, tied to a pole which he slung over his shoulder. They joined a group of farmers—real farmers, he imagined, for their accents and leathery skins could scarcely have belonged to gentlemen—in a skiff loaded with shelled corn. There was little talk. Laker said they'd take him to the fish market, right on the East River waterfront, because no Brooklyn ferry went there.

"The gentleman won't have trouble," said one of the farmers, an older man with light brown eyes, looking at Tom with an admiration bordering on love. What exaggerated nonsense had Laker told them? Tom wondered. These men too had been moved by an ideal outside his ken. They assumed that he was one of their own, even if raised in a different class. Tom felt uncomfortable under all that protective adoration. "No one's going to harm this man, not while we're standing on our own two feet," the farmer added.

When the wind died, they lowered the small boat's sail and the farmers took turns rowing. No one allowed Tom to spell them; he had been injured for their common cause. They were across the choppy river in little more than an hour, but it was already past twelve o'clock when Tom was helped out of the boat into the mad confusion of the fish market. He thanked Laker, accepted the handshake of each of the farmers, and hurried off away from the river, looking for the wide break in the alleys and lanes that was Broadway.

Walking briskly, buffeted by cartmen, harangued by beggars, confused by the streets winding west and north and east, he began to feel the pain of his wounds. But he was comforted by the vision of Sally Woods. He knew that she would be far more responsive to him than ever before: not simply because of his plan for smuggling the guns, or because of the cove he'd found on the north shore of Long Island, but because he'd been wounded for her cause. What had moved the farmers would surely move her. Even Pierpont would be impressed. She would know that he wasn't simply a boy, a ruffian. When he would walk into Hull's in his disguise, and with his story, she would see him in an entirely new light. He was sure of this, and this certainty buoyed him, even as his head grew lighter, as the big boots he wore seemed to tread on air.

Many of the streets were hilly, and often he couldn't see

what lay ahead until he'd crested a winding little alley or a broad lane flanked with tiny shops and boardinghouses. Just before Broadway he turned west onto a side street distinguished by an old-fashioned front-yard garden before a three-story boardinghouse. Walking uphill, he came up to the house just as a fat milkmaid, carrying a yoke with two full pails, came over the top of the hill, running so fast that the milk sloshed over her apron and onto the muddy ground.

"The soldiers!" she said to him. "They're drunk!" As she ran past him, he saw the first of a line of red-coated English soldiers come over the hill, marching to a drunken tune. Through the fuzzy waves of pain, he saw the first soldier smile crookedly.

"Look here, farm boy, get your hat in your hands, hear me?"

The other soldiers were coming now, muskets thrown over their shoulders, smart new boots coated with mud. As in the tavern, he had a glimmer of political feeling: They were insulting him in his own land.

"I say, hat off for King George, you oaf!" said the soldier, and he knocked Tom's hat off his head, so clumsily that he grazed the bandaged wound over Tom's eyes and knocked him off his feet and into the garden of the boardinghouse.

"What did you do that for?" said one of the other soldiers, not angrily, just out of simple curiosity. Tom heard the answer as he slowly and painfully got to his feet.

"He didn't take his hat off for the King."

"The beggar!"

"You got to show them, right?"

"You showed him," said the soldiers, and in a moment the whole line of redcoats was down the hill, twisting off toward the river, all-powerful, singing, oblivious of the anger rising in Tom, and rising all about him as well. Maybe they wouldn't have bothered him if he'd been wearing gentleman's clothing, he reasoned, but he rejected this thought; his anger encompassed deeds perpetrated on all and any of his countrymen, farmers, beggars, merchants alike. John Collins hadn't been a gentleman, not by the clothes he wore. And he himself wasn't much of a gentleman, not by his manner, not by his instincts. But John Collins had been a fighter, a famous Indian fighter, and perhaps he would be famous too, a famous fighter against the English. He was an American, as John Collins of England was an American, as Mr. Laker was, and the farmers who'd rowed him across the East River, and Sally Woods, beautiful, wonderful Sally Woods.

He was weaving on shaky legs by the time he got to Broadway. A Jew in a black hat took him by the arm to the door of Hull's Tavern, and waited until he had attracted the attention of those inside. Sally saw him at once, and beat Pierpont to the door.

"I'm all right," said Tom. "They won't get away with it. We're Americans, and they're English, and that's all there is to it."

She was holding him, and he was aware enough to see the concern in her eyes, the relief that he was alive.

TWELVE

───◆───

Tom rested in bed for the better part of a week. He was eager to get out and run around the city, but Sally insisted on his remaining indoors, if not in bed, then in a stuffed chair. It rained, and the boardinghouse's bad candles provided inadequate light by which to read during the gray days. They brought him copies of the New York *Journal*, endless political broadsides from supporters of independence, a forty-year-old copy of the collected works of John Locke. He was very bored, but he was blissful.

"How do you feel?" she asked him, and he wanted to tell her the truth: He felt like pulling her severely elegant little body into the bed, like pulling away the silk scarf at her throat, like burying his face in the pale skin of her imperious neck.

"Very well," he said. "Ready to go out."

"Not yet. I'll be the judge, if you please," she said. "There's no urgency. Everything's been delayed, as I've told you and told you. And not because of you, but because of the problems with the arsenal."

"But you go out. Every day."

"There are meetings. I go with Pierpont."

"To the Sons of Liberty?"

"Yes."

"Why not to the Daughters? I would think that Pierpont would go to one and you to the other."

"What I do doesn't concern the Daughters. This is an action by the Sons, and I am helping them, though I am female. Just like you're helping them, though you are a rogue."

"You say that almost as if you like a rogue," he said. Throwing off the covers, he moved quickly out of bed, standing before her in his nightshirt, a shawl about his broad shoulders.

"Get back in bed."

"Do you really care about my health that much?"

"Yes. You are essential to getting the guns to Connecticut," she said.

Tom laughed at this, and pulled her into his arms. He attempted no passionate kiss, because this had long since met with failure, when his desire for her had led him to make a fool of himself in his father's house. But he wanted to hold her, and she allowed this, and he believed that she cared for him, even if it was not the way he cared for her.

"The people have a right to bear arms," he said.

"You're such a faker. And so handsome."

"I've never been in love, you know," he said.

"I'd much rather we discuss something less humorous. I've told you that I'm an old lady, passed over and by, and all you care about is my patriotic fervor."

"If you were a Tory, I'd be a Tory."

"That's not funny. And not what I like to hear at all," she said, suddenly angry. "I'm afraid for you, and for all of us, if that's all you care about the country—an old maid with long black hair."

"Were you in the tavern when I hit that sergeant? Did I do that for you?" He walked over to the creaky chest of drawers in the corner where his clothes—farmer's rags and gentleman's bundle—had been crammed into drawers. "Turn around, please, I want to dress."

"You're not getting dressed, you're staying in bed."

"Turn around or it'll be too late," he said, removing the nightshirt and pulling on his underclothes.

"I should leave the room."

"Not while I'm dressing. Think of the scandal. You would be

ejected from the Daughters of Liberty. Pierpont would challenge me to a duel. We might be sent back to England for trial." He had pulled on his pants and shirt, and had begun to smooth out his white cravat. "All right, you may turn around again."

"I would like to go to England, actually," she said.

"You? Of all people, I never suspected you would care enough to chance that trip."

"When I'm an American, and we're our own country—then, I mean. Don't think I don't have feelings for England. It's not all crystal clear. If Parliament weren't made up of such fools . . ."

His suit was wrinkled, but of fine broadcloth, in a youthful tan color. She had not seen it before. As he pulled on riding boots, the boots he'd worn while exploring the north shore of Long Island, she admired him wordlessly. He wasn't serious, but he was certainly dashing. She had never seen a handsomer young man, she thought.

"Are you quite sure you're well enough to go out?"

"It's stopped raining. I want to see the arsenal. I want to get a shave. I want to have a bowl of Madeira."

"You will certainly not have a bowl of Madeira!" she said. "You'll drink good New York City beer, or you'll suffer through a cup of coffee! If you don't pay attention to the boycott, who will?"

"I was only joking," said Tom. He attached his purse to his belt and picked up his hat. "After you, my lady."

The boardinghouse was a two-story wood structure, within a block of the magnificent King's College. But the area in which it stood was anything but magnificent. The great city was, for all its newness, as rigidly divided into neighborhoods separated by class as London or Paris. Tom, as a well-to-do young gentleman, had always stayed at Stoutenberg's handsome boardinghouse on lower Broadway. Sally and Pierpont usually stayed at the town house of a family friend, or went to one of their country homes—"country" meaning an idyllic acre overlooking the Hudson four miles from the Battery. While their boardinghouse was relatively clean, and certainly free of any visitors who might know them or their families, it was in that damned land west of Broadway, suitable only for the impoverished, the students of the college, and the five hundred-odd prostitutes who lived in warrens facing the west side of the King's College building.

"I'm taking off my bandage," said Tom as they walked into the garbage-strewn street. She began to protest, but thought better of it. They didn't want to attract attention from soldiers, not on March 17, 1775, with the city coiled up around its angry factions, every one of them ready to explode. A few days ago, a group of Tories and British soldiers out of uniform had stormed the office of the *Journal*, after it had printed its definition of a Tory: "A thing whose head is in England, and its body in America, and its neck ought to be stretched." But no great damage was done, and the *Journal* continued its campaign to call men to examine their consciences, even as the New York Assembly refused to ratify the proceedings of the Continental Congress. Among the students of the college, fights were frequent, tempers wild. The population of prostitutes, famous all the way to Massachusetts for refusing to entertain English soldiers, seemed to be patrolling the streets in a patriotic spirit. The Sons of Liberty were arguing over whom to send to the Second Continental Congress, since the New York Assembly seemed no longer a part of the country the Sons longed to form.

"There's a barber in the next street," Tom said, starting to cross over to the north side of the alley.

"I know a better barber," she said.

"What do you know about barbers? Even at twenty-eight, women don't need a shave."

"He's a Son," she said. "And you might as well meet him."

Like many of the cheaper shops in New York, the barber's shop was simply the front room of his family's small home. Still unfashionably west of Broadway, the barber attracted a clientele of working-class patriots and a few students from the college. Because of the late morning hour, the barbering room was deserted except for two small children, scampering about the great chair with squeals and laughter.

"Women aren't allowed," said the barber, coming into the room with a happy look. He had a foreign accent, too slight to place.

"No jokes, Jacob," she said. "I bring you a serious young man."

"Are you growing a beard, sir?" said the barber. "Or trying to disguise your face?"

"I'd like a shave and a hair wash," said Tom peremptorily. "And as there's no one here, I'd appreciate it if the lady may be allowed to wait."

"A very serious young man," said the barber, hurt by Tom's tone. He shooed out his children, and followed them into the kitchen for hot water.

"Jacob is a Son!" Sally said. "You were very rude."

"I didn't like how he looked at you."

"Don't be ridiculous, Tom! He's only friendly."

"That's what I mean," he said. "Too friendly, if you ask me." He thought it strange that a German would be a Son of Liberty. Most of the German population in New York was Tory, simply because King George, born and raised in England, was the scion of a German house. But he calmed down when Jacob returned with a bowl of Madeira.

"Where on earth did you get that?" said Sally, very annoyed.

"It's all right, it's not imported, it's smuggled."

"Nonimportation is nonimportation!" she said. Tom sipped the wine; it was very good. "I mean it, Jacob! That's not right, it's not in the spirit of what we're trying to do."

"What are we trying to do?" Jacob said. "Have no more fun?"

Tom saw the small blond man wink at him as he honed his ancient razor. He was an adventurer. This was his new country, and as much as coming here had been a dare, taking it over from its masters would be one too.

"This isn't a question of fun," said Sally. "We're all trying to do the same thing—bring about independence. And in that time, we can't give way to silly, inconsequential things."

"The wine is excellent, my friend," said Tom. "I haven't enjoyed such Madeira for a long time. To your health, Jacob!"

While he shaved Tom's week-old beard, Jacob explained about the problems with the arsenal. There were suddenly more troops in New York than anyone could remember. Weeks ago, the barracks held one hundred men. But suddenly, sensing trouble, the barracks master had called in reinforcements from the troops stationed on the islands in New York Harbor. Bedloe's Island was supposedly swarming with fresh recruits. And

Governor's Island, only five hundred yards from the tip of Manhattan, was sending over troops every day.

"What has that got to do with a single, unprotected warehouse for rifles and ammunition?"

"It's not unprotected," said Jacob. "No one ever said it was unprotected."

Sally's face reddened a bit. "It's not your responsibility, Tom. I've told you that. Pierpont's told you that."

"Careful, sir," said Jacob. "I don't want to cut you."

"Just a minute," said Tom. "Once and for all, who is taking those rifles out?"

"It's not your affair, not that part of it," said Sally. But Tom insisted, and she finally had to admit: "Pierpont. Myself. Jacob."

"That's all? What about the Sons of Liberty? I thought there were hundreds of Sons in New York."

"This is for Connecticut," said Sally. "The Sons support the move, but could only ask for voluntary assistance. *They're* going to attack the fort at the Battery."

"You're all crazy," said Tom, finishing the bowl of Madeira, and wanting only to run out of that room and not stop running until he was somewhere safe, and sensual, and selfish. But he willed himself to be still. Jacob carefully finished his shave, and at once began to wash his long thick hair.

Sally kept on explaining: There were more troops than they'd anticipated, but that problem would be overcome. The lucky thing was that the guns were still there. All the trouble in Boston, and the threat of more trouble, kept the New York barracks master busy supplying General Gage in Massachusetts. The New York merchants, even the patriots, were undeniably happy about the lumber, nails, shovels, and spades being bought locally and sent to New England. "The point is that there's a great deal of activity in and around New York right now. Some of that creates a problem, some of it gives us an opportunity. Right now there's a heavy guard on the new arsenal, because there are too many soldiers in New York with nothing to do. But soon we'll have a chance."

"You and Pierpont and Jacob," said Tom. "Two thousand guns."

"I have a wagon," said Jacob.

"Good," said Tom. "A wagon is very useful." He fumed in silence until his hair was washed and combed. Slowly he got up from the barber's chair and turned to face Sally. "Do you understand what New York City is? It's a little tiny island under the guns of the British. It's a camp town. If the navy didn't come here, half the city would be bankrupt. But it comes here, it is here, it brings soldiers, sailors, force of arms. If there's ever a war, they could blow this whole city away in a few minutes. All those ships, all those cannons—it would be target practice. So before you say anything else, just remember who you're fighting, please. The strongest, most powerful navy and army in the world. Our navy and our army, until the day we break away. And you plan to do that with Pierpont and Jacob and Jacob's wagon. I thought you said it was all worked out. Getting the guns wasn't the problem. I must have been crazy to listen to you. Are you trying to get us all killed? Is that what this is about? Simple suicide?"

"I've already told you," said Sally, speaking as coldly as she could. "The taking of the guns will be our task, and we are not afraid of failure, because we know what is at stake."

He couldn't talk anymore, not at that moment. Anger ran through him, and an unfamiliar fear: Here was an enemy that he couldn't expect to vanquish. For it was clear to him that he couldn't let them do anything on their own. What could Jacob possibly do that he couldn't—or Pierpont, or Sally? They were as weak and as ineffectual as he in dealing with armed men guarding a warehouse belonging to the British government. And he would have to join them, no matter what Sally said. To do otherwise was to admit his fear was greater than theirs, his courage of lesser quality; and how could he shrink back from danger when the woman he loved was rushing to meet it? No. No matter what she said, he couldn't agree to stay behind now that he understood what their action was to be—a blind and clumsy display of patriotism. And more than that: an adventure for Jacob. A chance for Pierpont to show himself a man different from his born-rich Tory father. An opportunity for Sally to show the world why she had chosen to be an old maid.

What would it be for him then? A chance to show Sally that he loved her? Surely she already knew what power she had over him. Angrily, he took her out of Jacob's shop, into the nicer streets near Broadway.

"Look at all the trees," she said.

"What?"

"The trees. Look how they plant trees along all the streets, the better streets. It makes the city one big garden."

"Don't talk to me about trees. I've been to New York. I know there are trees. They help drain the ground in wet weather. And give a little shade when it's too hot to live. But don't dare talk to me about trees."

"You look far better now that you've been shaved."

"What do you care how I look?" he said. Without thinking, he touched the scab over his eye where he'd removed the bandage, which had suddenly begun to throb. "Don't say things like that. Just tell me what you want. You don't have to flatter me or pet me. I'm not your puppy."

She said nothing to this outburst, because she knew it was justified, at least in part. Sally had been trying to make conversation, to ease the tension begun in the barber's chair. He must be made to see that all would be well, and to that end, she had indeed been manipulative. But she hadn't been trying to manipulate him when she'd mentioned how good he looked after his shave; that had been spontaneous. And she was not often spontaneous. Everyone who had thought that her decision not to marry three years ago had been a whim, a sudden madness, had been wrong. She had thought that out, logically, coldly. Marriage had offered advantages, but she had weighed these against the weight in her heart. She had felt nothing, and refused to imagine that emotion would blossom forth with children, years of life together, or a reading of the same books. Her only regret was in having caused such a scandal, in allowing marriage plans to be announced, in letting herself become yet another young woman whose family decided what was best for her. No. Her handpicked husband had money, breeding, position; but he hadn't ignited her passion. And even if such coarse thoughts were inappropriate in Sally Woods of Fairlawn, Connecticut, she would not suppress them. That he was a half-reluctant Tory added distaste to her general lack of desire; but it was lack of sensual feeling more than politics that had finally decided her. And even this decision, about desire, sensation, love, had been thought out, weighed in the balance of her life.

"Does your head hurt?" she said.

"No."

"The arsenal is north of the common. I don't think you can walk that far."

He didn't answer her, just continued toward Broadway. Sally wanted to suddenly tell him to stop. She would have liked to explain to him that she found him very nice, far nicer than she'd originally thought. Not simply because he was handsome and brave, but because he was showing her his hurts, his wounds; beyond all the bravado, he wanted to be loved. And if she didn't speak now, it was because she was afraid what might come out. It would be impossible to love him, she told herself, not in any way that he would find satisfying. He had grown up a motherless child, son of a tyrannical father, addicted to fighting, traveling, whoring. She knew enough to know not to offer him the love of a sister, a mother. And what other kind of love could she offer him? Without thinking, she smoothed her black hair, wondering what they looked like together: brother and sister, husband and wife, man and mistress?

A red-and-gold coach swung east out of the alley of a Dutch mansion, its coachman swinging his whip at a trio of beggars blocking his way. "Did you see that?" he said, his eyes wild with fury.

"Of course," she said. They were probably a fat old couple, prosperous and sleek, terrified that mob rule would take over their city. Many of the town's older burghers, no longer actively involved in shouting matches with New York's Sons of Liberty, were following the Bloomingdale Road out of the city, preferring to sit out the tense time in their country seats along the Hudson River. Soon enough the British would put the whole city under martial law, they thought. Let any of those hothead Sons of Liberty speak their minds then. They would find out soon enough how treason was punished!

"It's good that they're being scared," she said.

"What's good? That they whip a beggar who probably can't even speak English?" Tom started to cross over to where one of the beggars still skulked, opening a ragged cloak to bare the skin that had been hit by the coachman.

"Wait," she said. "Listen."

They were on the solid sidewalk along lower Broadway, looking north to St. Paul's, with the sun pulling out of the clouds and sitting squarely over the island at midday. Sally had heard a drum, and now looked toward City Hall, expecting to see a show of strength from the latest troops in Manhattan.

"What is that?" said Sally.

There were two drummers, skinny boys in the uniform of the local militia. They led a procession of perhaps two dozen, going north from City Hall along Broadway. Sally and Tom walked briskly to catch up to them, fascinated and appalled. All along the great avenue, shoppers and shopkeepers, bewigged merchants and disheveled British soldiers rushed to find a place in the rapidly growing crowd of spectators.

"Who are those women?" said Sally.

"I'm not sure," said Tom. "Thieves, whores, murderers. I've seen this before, you know. You can't blame this on Parliament. This is New York's own City Hall."

Behind the drummers walked two women, both younger than Sally. They were bareheaded and barefoot, dressed in the loose drab clothing of farmers. Behind them walked a half dozen officers of the law, and after them a small body of burghers—perhaps their accusers, or their sentencers. A crier called out their crimes to the populace: "Grand larceny," he shouted, and he shouted out their names and their punishment.

"What does that mean?" said Sally.

"That they stole something," he said. "But we're not going to go there."

"Where are they going? I couldn't hear. I couldn't even hear their names. Imagine walking barefoot on the cobblestones, with all those people."

"I said let's go," he said, and he took her arm and turned her about, so that the two of them had to struggle against the crowd rushing after the sound of the drum. Tom had come to New York often enough to know what would happen, even if he hadn't managed to hear the crier: The women had stolen something, a bit of silver perhaps, and their master had discovered it. Grand larceny meant that it was valuable enough to disgrace them in public, to harry them along Broadway all the way past the jail, on the north end of the common, where the whipping post stood, a constant reminder of the law. The women would be whipped publicly; each of them would be given thirty-nine lashes, enough to render them unconscious, and probably permanently disfigure their backs, and possibly break their health for years to come. When they came to, they would be thrown onto a wagon, for their penalties included exile from New York City forever.

"Where are you going?"

"Away from here," he said, and as he moved her through the crowd she felt all the power of his belligerence, his anger, ready to explode at any moment. He didn't speak again until they'd walked out of hearing range of the crowd, and stood on the promenade at the very tip of the island, facing the bay. "Your revolution won't mean a damned thing unless it does away with that."

Sally knew what he meant. "That" was the exploitation of the poor, the heinous punishments meted out by the mighty to the weak. But she couldn't understand why the sight of two criminals, female or not, angered him so much. He was not a minister, a man of peace. On the contrary, he was a brawler, and she often felt that his words of support for their cause were founded on air. "Why are you so angry?" she said.

They were at the windiest point on Manhattan Island. She could see tears in his eyes as he squinted out at the vast harbor, with hundreds of sailboats shifting about in the wind. He still had a boy's head of hair, thick and glossy, alive with highlights as it whipped back from his high forehead, the bruise over his eye shining like a mark of courage in the beautiful face. Wild ducks flew by, a raucous flock excited by something outside her understanding. Close to shore were men in small boats, fishing for clams and oysters. From out in the harbor one could see great estates on the neighboring islands, fields of corn in New Jersey and Brooklyn, the dense woods skirting all about the perimeter of the bay itself, save for the manicured tip of Manhattan. From the paved promenade, Bedloe's Island was most clear—a twelve-acre wasteland housing British troops. Even the nearby Governor's Island, where the governor used to enjoy country life on his estate, had become a depository for the British army.

"Everything I do is a lie," he said. "I should never have been born." He didn't turn his head to look at her, and Sally waited, afraid to speak or to touch him. "Everything is wrong in this world, can't you see that? Not just British taxes, not just the rich against the poor. Every law is wrong, every militia, every whipping post. I should have lived here a hundred years ago, when it was just forest, and England didn't send over packets every other week in the year. That's what America should be. Wild, a wilderness, without laws, without sidewalks and cobblestones."

"Tom," she said. He didn't turn his head. For no reason at all, she took hold of his shoulders and pressed them, and then he turned, and his eyes ran through hers, demanding knowledge, insisting that her touch, her lips, her every gesture be true. Sally kissed him. He hesitated only a moment, his lips shut for the smallest part of a second, and then he had thrown over objections, worries, thoughts. Alone on the promenade, he held her so tightly she could scarcely breathe. Without thinking, he drove his tongue between her teeth and ran his hands over her neck, her breasts, her thighs as they stood there in their stiff broadcloth, a twenty-four-year-old boy who had made love only to whores and a twenty-eight-year-old woman who had never been brought to physical passion, not by men, not by books, not even by her own hand.

"Come," he said. "We'll go back to the boardinghouse."

"Why?" she said.

Tom didn't answer. He was so wild with passion he could barely walk. He would not think of what was about to happen. Tom was in love. He held Sally's hand. Rifles, revolutions, laws, punishments were forgotten. They passed a dozen marching soldiers, street vendors selling cold meat pies to the students of the college, a French fencing master taking advantage of the sunny weather in front of his ramshackle school. But they might as well have been passing the wax figures at Vauxhall Gardens for all the concern they had for anyone outside their mutual universe.

The boardinghouse landlady spoke to them, noted that they were holding hands, asked Tom how he was feeling. But neither of them responded. She could think them brother and sister, husband and wife, student and prostitute. They were up the stairs quickly, through the door to the small low-ceilinged room where Tom had been convalescing. He bolted the door.

"What are you doing?" she said. He took off his cravat and his jacket, and crossed the little room in three steps. They sat down together at the edge of the bed, and she held his hands and kissed them. "I don't know if this is right," she whispered, but her body ignored her words, her hands were about his neck, she kissed his eyes, she pulled his head onto her lap and stroked his thick hair. Tom turned his head and pulled hers down to meet his. They kissed, and he rolled his long torso on top of hers on the soft bed, placing his yearning body against his love. Through his shut eyes, he felt her heart race; he felt her catch the madness running through him.

"Let me help you," he said, pulling away her heavy cloak and loosening the bow of her painted calico dress.

"I don't know," she said again, as if this would somehow make everything all right. She felt like a dreamer, twisting through a world of forbidden pleasure, saved from damnation because none of it was real. Through the open window came sounds of horses, wagons, heavy loads on the way to the west side warehouses; but the curtains which shut out the light slowly seemed to shut out everything else as well. They were in a bolted-up world of intense privacy. It was dark, and their desire, intense, urgent, obliterated all else.

He was clumsy with her, but she had no way to judge what was clumsy, what was swift, what was sure. This was a new world, a world she had tried to ignore most of her life, a world whose importance she had always denied. But her body had never denied its importance; nor her spirit; nor her dreams. So intense were her sensations now, so remarkably acute to every nuance of pleasure and pain, she felt as if she had been holding back the very essence of life itself. Sally didn't feel so much an end to frustration as she did an awakening to something so obvious, so patently right, that she had never taken the trouble to examine it, to understand it. It was like living a life with one's eyes shut, and suddenly being told to open them. It was as if she had spent a thousand nights looking straight out at the horizon, all the while a harpsichord played heavenly music, music she never thought to notice. But all the while it was there, with her, a part of her.

And Tom was nothing like a new husband, tentative and respectful, as virginal as his bride. He was clumsy, yes, but not inexperienced. He loved a woman's body, to look at it, to touch it, to kiss it. In the Orient he had learned the virtues of delaying one's pleasure, of leading up to it with delights of another order. He took off her clothing, tearing her caraco jacket, letting her long hair loose all over the bedsheets. There was time, more time than anyone knew. The urgency was very fine, it was delicious, but it would remain so while he took off his own clothes, while he moved her astonished hand about his chest, his belly, his genitals. It was dark, but their eyes were wide now, they could see each other's pale bodies, could look at and worship silently what they touched.

"I didn't know," she said, but the words were in her brain, not on her lips. She kissed him as her body moved in a way it had never moved before. Everything was instinctual, correct, loving. And she did love him; her body told her this; her body ran with the knowledge, ached with the knowledge so that it was a vast perfect pain. Sally remembered vaguely words he had spoken: something about wild, about wilderness, about laws. Yes, this was illicit, and right, more right than anything she could have ever imagined. He kissed the inside of her thighs, he touched her never-touched pubic hair. This had been the least-known part of her body, the animal part, the part to ignore; and now it was seen as nothing less than the center. Not for the sake of generation, but for the sake of pleasure. How could she not have known this? How could she not have known how perfect was his hand there, on her, inside her, his lips and tongue gently caressing her breasts, breasts she had covered, breasts whose existence were insignificant to her life? Now she lived for his touch. Now she listened to the music. Now she opened her eyes, and all she could see was desire, and desire was pure, and passion was noble, and everything else in the world was dross.

"Not yet," he said, and though his fingers only brushed her clitoris, though his teeth were too hard on her nipples, though her body yearned for a gentle scratch at the small of her back, it made no difference. They were rushing downhill, the wind at their backs, the snow pristine and clean. Their bodies wanted each other, at once, for a moment that would please, please last forever.

Tom entered her, and it was different than it had been with all the prostitutes, all the women he had loved in such a different way. Not simply the physical passage, not merely the fact that her cries were real, but the raw wedge of feelings cutting through his brain was more powerful than anything he'd ever known. He felt as if he were entering a body that was as much his as his own. He felt as if he were coming home, entering a house, a life, a being that could not exist in and of itself. When they were together, he felt his spirit soar, he felt the madness leave him, the anger, the incompleteness. He felt that everything that was bad in him fled his earthly frame, so that he could join with her in love, and this love was whole and clear and perfect.

Afterward, he slept on her still body. Sally had no desire to sleep. She watched him. He smiled. His lips were red and full, and he breathed through his smile, easily, with the confident rhythm of childhood.

Slowly, she touched a finger to her own lips, she pressed a palm to her breasts. Yes, this was true. They were on a bed in a boardinghouse in the city of New York, and had just made love. She would have a child, she thought. There would be a revolution, and she would be pregnant, in disgrace.

Tom stirred, his muscles stretching, then relaxing on top of her. What difference did it make? How could she be disgraced if he loved her? She shuddered at the return to reality, at the sounds coming through the open window, at the questions of time, discovery.

"Tom," she whispered, so he would not yet wake. She kissed him, and his lips moved; she touched his freshly shaved neck and moved the heel of her hand along his powerfully muscled back.

He woke slowly, happily; or perhaps he didn't wake fully at

all. He woke to her caress, and he moved slowly, easily through the ethereal atmosphere of their dream. They held each other, and the press of reality lessened, then fell away altogether. Once more they were alone, joined in a bit of space outside of time. There were no noises through the open window, and when the March sun sank into the Hudson, there was no more nor less light in their self-enclosed room.

THIRTEEN

———◆———

They were dressed and quiet in the room, looking at each other by the light of four candles when Pierpont knocked on the door. The knock had been expected. Their feet were long since back on the ground. Sally understood that she was different than she had been when she'd woken up that morning. Tom quite clearly saw that his life had changed: He would marry this woman, he would father her children, together they would bring family into a new world.

"Pierpont?" Tom called out, his voice sounding a bit strained to Sally. He had unbolted the door as soon as they were dressed, but he walked to open it nonetheless. Sally wondered if her brother would see the change in her eyes, in the color of her skin. The room smelled of passion; the candles lit up the stuff of their mystery.

"Tom, how are you, my friend?" said Pierpont, coming into the room with false heartiness and closing the door quickly and firmly. "Sally, you're here—thank God." As he approached the candles, she saw how white her brother's face was, how worried. And when he went to her for a sibling's embrace, he faltered, and sat down heavily on the freshly made bed.

"What's wrong, Pierpont?" She could see the exhaustion in

his bloodshot eyes, the fear in the way he held his arms close to his body. This was nothing to do with herself and Tom. He was oblivious of their joy, even though he had for a long time worried over their mutual attraction.

"It's tonight," he said.

"What's tonight? You don't mean the rifles? What happened? What's wrong?"

"Did you tell Tom?" said Pierpont. "About Jacob? The plan?"

"Yes."

"It's all right about Jacob," said Tom. "I'm going to help. I'm going to be there when you take the rifles."

"That wasn't our agreement," said Sally. "That wasn't supposed to be part of your risk."

"It's my cause too," said Tom, and Sally knew precisely what he meant. It would be wrong to try to convince him not to help them. Besides, she wanted him at her side. Even if she was afraid for him, she wanted him with her; she had become selfish in her love.

"If Tom wants to come," said Pierpont. He paused, put his face in his hands, cleared his throat. Then he made a great effort to be clear and forthright. "Tom, tell me the truth—how do you feel?"

"I'm perfectly well. I'm as fine as I ever was."

"Would you kindly tell us what your news is?" said Sally.

"There's a riot going on at the Fields. The Sons were having a meeting, at the tavern next to the Fields, and twenty, maybe thirty soldiers pushed themselves in. The fighting's going on still. Soldiers are coming up from the fort, and coming down from the common. Everyone's going to be at the Fields tonight. Jacob's got his wagon."

"But what's wrong with you? You don't look well."

"I didn't think—I didn't know it would be like that," said Pierpont. "The soldiers. When they came in, I couldn't really believe it was happening. They were like animals. I wasn't even hit, and I was so frightened, I thought I'd choke to death. I ran. I was a coward. And there's so much at stake now, and what can I do? I never realized I'd be afraid, but I am."

Tom crossed the room and turned his back to them. They weren't thinking, and he would have to think on their behalf.

Pierpont would be useless, Jacob would be useless except for his wagon—but Sally could be a great help. He had readied no boats, and neither he nor Sally had eaten since early that morning.

"Pierpont!" said Tom, trying to sharpen the man's attention. "What else? Why does it have to be tonight?"

"New Haven. The British are coming from New Haven—that was the talk of the town today. They're going to watch over the Sons here. They're going to make it impossible to move anything on the island, and anything off of it."

"Who's at the arsenal now?"

"I don't know. I only know there were six earlier today, drilling in front of the little warehouse. But the barracks is near. They'd only need a shout to bring on a hundred of them."

"Not if the riot at the tavern keeps up. They'll all be there."

"The riot will keep up. The Sons—the others—aren't cowards."

"Stop that talk," said Tom. "Coming here was more important than getting your head broken. Where's Jacob? Did you get to him?"

"Of course," said Pierpont. "He's getting his wagon. He might be here already."

"Do you have weapons?"

"Jacob has a musket," said Pierpont.

"There may not be anyone there," said Sally. "Maybe we can just walk in and take them. Just like that."

"Mess your hair up, Sally," said Tom.

"What?" she said, but he was already upon her, quickly and gently ruffling the beloved black hair. "Stop that, Tom. What on earth?"

"Leave it alone, Sally. Pierpont, see if Jacob is here yet."

"You want me to go?"

"Look out the window, Pierpont," said Tom, deciding that Pierpont must not come with them at all. As the frightened young man crossed to the curtains, Tom squeezed Sally's hands. "I love you," he whispered.

"What do you want with my hair?" said Sally.

Pierpont spoke up, his voice strained. "I see the wagon. I don't see Jacob, but it must be that he's there. It's the only wagon in the street. It's dark."

"All right. Good," said Tom. "Sally, you have to look in trouble. Like you were attacked. Bandits, you know. When we're outside, you can tear your cloak against the wagon."

"Why?" said Pierpont, not afraid for his sister, whom he loved with all his heart, but for himself.

"I'll be a diversion," said Sally to her brother. "You and Tom and Jacob won't come up till later."

"I don't understand," said Pierpont. "If you look as if you've been attacked, they'll alert the barracks. Everyone will come out. Even the ones at the tavern will come back if they see a young woman's been attacked. And then what are we supposed to do? I never realized. It's not thought out, is it? I still think there might be another way. Even from Connecticut. There are smugglers who bring guns in. I've heard that rifles can be bought right under the noses of the British in New Haven. We could drive there from Fairlawn. Take our silver."

"Pierpont," said Tom, "listen to me. You're not going to come with us."

"I didn't say I wouldn't come," he said. But his voice was bright with promise. "I'm willing to come. I've admitted to being frightened, but I swear to you, I won't disgrace you."

"Pierpont, listen," said Tom. "You're needed for something else. Something just as important as what we have to do. You've got to get to Brooklyn, and right away, at any cost."

Sally understood that Tom was getting rid of her brother, and she thanked him for it wordlessly, her eyes moving across his serious face. But Tom wasn't only trying to make it easy for a man who had discovered himself to be a coward. Pierpont really was needed to find Walter Laker and convince him of the urgency of their need; once again the gentleman who had helped pull Tom from the burning tavern on the Brooklyn waterfront would have to gather the farmers and the skiff which had spirited him across to Manhattan more than a week before. Now their task would be far more dangerous, because once the rifles were stolen, the East River would be alive with British ships, even in the middle of the night.

"His name is Walter Laker," Pierpont repeated slowly, regathering his dignity. "I know Ferry Street a little."

"Take the ferry from Peck's Slip—if there's none running, you'll have to hire a lighter, or anyone who's up and around.

You've got to get across, because they have to be back for us
and waiting. It has to be done immediately. Run if you can do
it without attracting attention. And if no one will take you
across, steal a boat. His house is near where the Peck's Slip
ferry comes in. But somewhere on Ferry Street you'll find a
man who knows Laker's house. It's not a city like London, you
know. It's not much more than a wild village."

Pierpont had found a deserted warehouse, with its own rot-
ting dock, a mile north of the active East River wharves;
the company it had served had gone out of business due to the
success of patriotic nonimportation. Tom had never seen the
dock, or the warehouse, because he had not been allowed out of
bed. But Pierpont assured him that Jacob would be able to
find it.

"We go then. You first, Pierpont. Don't talk to Jacob, just
go."

"Don't worry about me," said Pierpont. "I won't disappoint
you." He kissed his sister and shook Tom's hand. "She'll be all
right, won't she? It's not that dangerous, do you think?"

"She'll be all right," said Tom. "Go. Now."

Pierpont looked at them both one last time and left the room.
He was so nervous, he forgot to close the door. Tom went to it,
shut it silently, and turned to Sally.

"Are you well enough for this?" she said.

"Will you marry me then?"

"What sort of a question is that?" she said. "We might be
dead in a few hours. Just tell me if you feel well enough for
this."

"What if I were to tell you that I wasn't? That what I wanted
to do was run off, to another boardinghouse, and find passage to
England as soon as the next packet leaves? That I wanted to go
with you to London, that we would live there? We would be
alive, and together, and we would forget all this?"

"I would say no," she said.

"And that's only one of the reasons why I love you," he said.

"I feel that it's me making you do this," she said.

"Of course it is, silly. I love you. We're going to live together.
Whatever we do will be together. You're my life." He started to
embrace her, but she held him off for a moment, and he added:

"And of course I'm a patriot. I wouldn't miss this rifle smuggling for the world."

They kissed, and their bodies remembered what they'd shared that afternoon, and shuddered in pleasure. For a moment Sally forgot what they were about to do. This was the man she loved, the man who was already her husband, the man who would give her children, who would live with her and grow old with her and give meaning to her life.

"We'd better go," he said.

"Yes," she said, and her smile started up within her, for she felt his spirit, anxious to help her cause. It suddenly mattered not at all why he was a patriot: whether for the sake of a future country, or only for love of herself. In either case, he was willing, he was strong, he would succeed. She wanted to tell him that their fates would run together, that she would no longer criticize his lack of politics, for she knew that he was capable of great loving. His heart was good. She could not feel what she felt for someone who was ignoble, selfish, cowardly. Beyond all his boyish arrogance was kindness, generosity, true heroism.

"It'll be all right," he said. "And a bit exciting." He took her arm and they left the room and went down the stairs and out the front door, once more ignoring the landlady's greeting. Tom felt his English dagger in its sheath under his jacket, belted tightly to his left side. He was very worried for Sally. There was not a doubt in his mind that she wouldn't do what he told her, and do it as well as anyone could; but there was a doubt whether the two of them would live through the night.

Jacob spotted them and called out: "Good evening, my friends!"

"Don't talk," said Tom to Sally, and as they climbed onto the bench next to Jacob, he said: "No more talking. Whisper."

"Here?" laughed Jacob. "In the middle of five hundred whores I got to act like a ghost? Look here, mister, you might be a very important man where you come from, but in the Sons we're all pretty much equal."

Tom drove his elbow into the pit of Jacob's belly, and the man doubled over in pain. Sally started to interfere, but she was separated from Jacob by Tom, and thought better of it. Tom handed her the reins. "Let's go," he said, and Sally snapped the reins too hard, and the old mare lurched forward.

"I'm sorry I hit you, Jacob," whispered Tom, "but unfortunately, you are not being sufficiently serious. This is a matter of life and death for all of us. When I say whisper, you whisper. Or I'll kill you. Do you understand?"

"Yes, I understand. You're a crazy man," said Jacob. Shaking his head, he took the reins from Sally and turned the wagon west, toward the Greenwich road.

"Where is your rifle?" whispered Tom.

"What's that?" said Jacob in a loud voice. "I can't hear you."

"Are you trying to be funny?" said Tom. "Sally is going to be risking her life in a few minutes, and you're trying to be funny."

"They can't hear us at the arsenal, they can't hear us at the fort, and they sure as hell can't hear out on Bedloe's Island. And no silk-stockinged bastard is going to tell me how to talk. That's not why we're stealing guns. You are not in charge here, right?"

Tom was angry enough to murder him. Only Sally's presence at his side prevented him from slipping free his dagger and bringing it to the barber's cleanly shaved neck.

"Jacob," said Sally, speaking in her normal voice, "this isn't a question of gentleman and laborer. We're all equal, we're all on the same side. But please. For me. No trouble. Let Tom do what he has to do. And that means letting him lead, do you understand?"

"Let him apologize then," said Jacob.

"I apologize," said Tom, not even thinking. The horse had picked up speed, running downhill. The old New York custom of hanging lanterns from every seventh doorway had been all but abolished in the last few years. In the congested part of Manhattan, whale-oil lamps lit up the night with romantic fervor; lamplighters paid by the city attended to them at the start of evening, and extinguished them at the break of day. But here, on this quiet west side road, the few houses prosperous enough to burn candles outside their door did so. The candles cast little light, but lent a spirit of adventure to their trip. It seemed to Tom like a glimpse into the past—before lamplighters and paved roads and endless soldiers in barracks.

They were taking a roundabout way to the little arsenal.

Jacob turned into a country road, and then turned again onto a narrow, filthy road leading back into the city, through the Negro neighborhood about the Collect Pond.

"How far are we?" whispered Tom.

"Half mile," said Jacob.

"Stop the wagon when we're within hailing distance of the arsenal."

"How the hell am I supposed to know that in the dark?"

"Jacob," said Sally, "I thought you and Tom were going to be friends."

"It's dark," said Jacob, but he whispered the words. There was a half-moon, and no clouds, but the lantern on the wagon illuminated only a few feet of dirt road. When Jacob extinguished this—without any urging from Tom—the half-moon barely shined through the abundant trees shading their path.

"Do you think," whispered Tom, "that there is any chance they can hear us yet? Any chance?"

"I don't know," whispered Jacob. "Not yet. Maybe now." He slowed the old mare to a walk, and then stopped her altogether. "The musket's loaded and under the seat. Do you want it?"

"Can you use it?"

"Yes, and I'm very good with it, too," said Jacob.

"I want you to try to estimate twenty minutes," said Tom. "If we're not back by then, and if you don't hear any shouting and screaming and gunshots, then come on up to the arsenal. Just drive at a normal pace. Put your lantern back on. You can be bold as you please, as if you're out for a normal drive."

"A normal drive in the middle of the night with an empty wagon," said Jacob. But he wasn't afraid. That was important. Tom knew that he would come, no matter what danger presented itself. "What if there is shouting and screaming?"

"Then come right away," said Tom. "Come with the musket on your knees, and drive like hell, and get us out of there."

"It'll be a pleasure, Mr. Williams," said Jacob.

"Good luck, Jacob," said Sally. He was already taking out the musket from under the seat.

"You too. The both of you," said Jacob.

He watched as Tom ruffled Sally's loose hair once again, and tore at her cloak, and picked up a clod of earth and smeared it across her shoulders, and softly spotted her cheek and forehead with dirt. "All right," said Tom. "We have to go fast."

He took her hand, and they set off along the dirt road that was part of Manhattan, but far enough to the north and west of the common to be deserted at this dark hour. Tom picked up the pace, and he could hear Sally's breath laboring. But that would be fine. She should look and feel as ragged and worried and out of breath as possible; her beauty would do the rest.

Suddenly, from up the road came the sound of tramping feet and singing, a faint rhythm of hearty male voices, growing in power moment by moment. Silently, Tom and Sally stepped off the road and into the trees.

"Le-Ro! Le-Ro! Lil-li-bur-le-ro!" sang a company of men.

"What is that?" whispered Sally. "What are they saying?"

"It's an old army song. It doesn't mean anything. It gives them courage in the dark."

He could see the first soldier now, blowing up out of the dark into the pale moonlight. The song forced a smile onto the lips of the soldier, who could be no more than eighteen, his skinny frame trying to fill out the brazen red uniform.

"Le-Ro! Le-Ro! Lil-li-bur-le-ro! Lil-le-bur-le-ro! Bul-le-na-la! Lil-le-bur-le-ro!" A dozen men sang, their faces glistening with sweat in the cool night air. Most were tall men, very young, with pale faces and husky frames. All carried muskets. Tom could sense their fear, shameful and out of control. Only their voices were brave; they seemed like men shouting at ghosts, daring them to come forth in the black night. They passed by quickly, and Tom hoped that Jacob would have time to pull off the road.

"Let's go," said Tom, but Sally hesitated.

"Those men," she said. "What if they come back?"

"They're not going to be back for a long time. Someone must have sent for them to help with the tavern riot. They'll probably find some trouble and end up drinking the tavern."

He urged her to go even faster. "All you have to do," he whispered, "is go to the guard, call out to him, cry out to him for help."

"Where will you be?"

"You're not to think about me. Just about the guard. Getting him to believe you."

They kept up the fast pace for what seemed like ten minutes but was only three. A light in the distance stood out through the bleak March trees. "Shouldn't we stop?" Sally said, trying to catch her breath.

"No!" said Tom. "Hurry now. You're to keep running until I tell you to walk. And then you walk alone, and walk fast, and cry out like I told you."

The warehouse was new, and badly built, a clumsy structure of wood planks with a misshapen roof. It was no more than six feet high. Two tall posts supported whale-oil lamps illuminating the single sentry standing at ease in front of the locked door. A dozen yards away were the tents of the British army, housing men until they could be properly quartered in the homes of New York citizens. A hundred yards past these makeshift barracks was an old farmhouse, its white, weathered exterior forbidding and silent in the moonlight.

"Wait," said Tom. He held her hand, and willed himself to be calm. They were fifty yards from the sentry, across the dirt road, and behind an ancient oak tree. "I'm going first. You count slowly to ten, like this—one and two and three—like that, all right? Count to ten, and then run and walk and stagger across the road and collapse right into his arms."

"They might be in the tents."

"Sound asleep, we hope. They might all be south of here, fighting the Sons. No more talk. I'm going."

"Wait," said Sally. She pulled him into her arms and kissed him. It was strange that now that the moment of danger had arrived, the moment for which their first meeting had taken place, the moment of dedication to the patriotic cause, he seemed surer, more eager than she to go ahead. He let her go quickly. "I want to kiss you one more time," she said.

"No," he said. "We'll kiss in a few minutes. We'll kiss again. It will be easy."

"I want to," she said, and took him into her arms, and they kissed, and her passion infected him with its taste of danger and foreboding. He held her, he tried to let his strength pour from his body into hers. She wasn't afraid, he knew, but she

believed in the possibility of failure. He didn't want to kiss her
with the idea that they would never meet again on this earth,
but she took no strength from his embrace. On the contrary, she
let him go with doubts, grave doubts as to whether she was
committing a folly; she might be responsible for the death of
her lover, her brother, Jacob.

"That's it," he said. "You look terrible. Make believe you're
onstage at the John Street Theater. Everyone is watching you."
He turned her about and squeezed her shoulders. "Start counting. I love you."

Sally turned round to look at him one more time, but he was
already across the road, bending very low and running silently
in his riding boots. It was too late to stop him. He vanished into
the dark outside the pale of light cast by the lamps. "One," she
said to herself. She had forgotten to count, and now she hurried, panicked at the idea of being late for her lover's plan.

Tom had gotten within twenty-five feet of the sentry, slightly
to his rear. He breathed deeply, slowly, on one knee behind a
small bush that offered little cover, the dagger in his hand. If he
had suddenly coughed, the sentry would have heard, and probably would have seen him; but Tom didn't believe it possible to
make a mistake. He couldn't imagine that the lone sentry would
be able to discover him, ready his musket, and fire accurately
into the night. The twenty-five feet between him and the sentry
seemed like a paltry few steps. He felt invincible, breathing in
strength from the brisk March winds.

Sally began to run. She had counted to eight and, certain that
she had started too late, crossed the road, and let out a sigh so
that all the woods could hear. Tom watched, his heart beating
with sudden ferocity. He tried to still his quivering body, but
couldn't; he needed the release of action, and action was only
seconds away.

"Who goes there?" said the sentry, raising his flintlock musket to his arm. Tom wondered if the weapon had a rifled barrel,
with the spiral grooves inside the barrel making the bullet spin
with deadly accuracy, even from as far away as one hundred
and fifty yards.

"Help!" said Sally, and her girlish voice calmed the sentry, so
that he no longer sighted along his barrel into the dark, but
simply held the gun ready, waiting for her to come close.

And Sally came on wonderfully, exactly as Tom knew she would. She stumbled, she fell on her hands, she walked, she ran, she arrived in the lamplight pale and beautiful, a damsel in distress.

"What happened, miss?" said the sentry, lowering his musket and taking a step close to where she'd stopped, holding on to a lamppost for support. "Are you all right?"

"Help—five men—Negroes—they tried to—" Sally couldn't go on. She opened her huge eyes in perfect innocence, not knowing when and how Tom would appear, a lovely apparition. It was incredible to her that the man reacted precisely as Tom had predicted, lowering his guard, hostility and violence converted to concern and flirtation.

"Where, miss?"

"Far," she said. "I ran—help me—"

And she collapsed, eager to complete her act, her full weight falling into the soldier's open arms. But the soldier let her go almost at once, and a terrible sound came from his throat—powerful, full of fear and surprise, of a moment's duration—and somehow the man was flat on his back, his hair pulled back in Tom's hand, a dagger held against his throat.

"Not a sound or I cut you—right here," said Tom, his voice so flat and sure that Sally believed him once again capable of any vile deed. He had come around from behind and taken hold of the man's hair the instant Sally had fallen against the sentry; he had flung him to the ground on his back with nearly enough force to break it.

Sally came close, standing straight and brushing off her dirty clothes.

"Just answer yes or no. Is there anyone in the tents?" Tom stayed behind the man, the knife held to his throat, his grip on the man's scalp constant. He tried to roll his eyes up at Tom to see him, but of course this was impossible; the man was in shock and finding response difficult. "Are the soldiers here?" said Tom.

"No," said the man.

"Are you alone?"

"Yes, sir."

"Where's your key?"

"Key, sir?"

Tom pushed the knife's edge into the skin of the man's neck, cutting him.

"He doesn't understand," said Sally.

"Quiet," said Tom. "Soldier, the key to the warehouse. Where is it?" To Sally, he said, "Search him. Go through his pockets."

Sally did as she was told, but almost immediately she heard the clatter of hoofbeats and a badly sprung wagon, and she and Tom froze.

"Don't move," he said to Sally. "It might be Jacob."

It was. The barber slowed his horse and jumped down from the still-moving wagon. He was wildly excited, but his eyes shone with power. "We have five minutes, maybe six. They're coming back."

Later on he told them what had happened: The marching soldiers, singing their century-old battle song, had given him plenty of notice to hide horse and wagon north of the roadway. But minutes later he heard much louder singing, and a great deal of laughing. The reinforcements sent to the tavern were already coming back, and had met this latest group of twelve men with derisive comments about the Americans they'd taken care of that evening. Jacob had no idea how many would be coming back now—maybe twenty-five, maybe fifty; but he knew that it would take them a good deal longer than his racing horse to get here.

Tom let go of the soldier's hair and pulled him to his feet, keeping the knife against the man's throat. He walked him to the door of the warehouse. "Key, I said," said Tom.

"They're coming back," said the terrified man, not as a challenge, but as a reminder to his own sanity. Tom threw the soldier against the door, stunning him. Slowly, the man sank to the ground.

"Not like that," said Jacob. "Together."

He and Tom threw themselves at the door, once, twice, three times, while the soldier tried to get back on his feet. Sally held his fallen rifle, but she had no idea what to do with it. "Don't move," she said to the soldier. "I'll break your head." Obediently, the soldier remained on the ground. The door finally splintered, and Jacob kicked a big enough hole in it to get through and inside. Tom continued to kick at the door, until it broke away from the lock and swung open on its hinges. Then he picked up the soldier with great force. "Move," he said, and he pushed the man into the warehouse. "Get the wagon, Sally. Bring it as close as you can."

He followed the soldier inside, and turned him about and punched him squarely in the jaw. "You really are a wild animal," said Jacob. The soldier fell against the back wall, and was finally, blissfully unconscious.

Tom didn't bother to justify the blow—to explain that he needed the soldier out of the way, and unthreatening—but simply joined Jacob in lifting the long and extremely heavy boxes of rifles and ammunition. Staggering under the clumsy weight of one of them, Jacob made it to the open doorway and slammed the box to the ground.

"I hope you don't break them," said Tom.

"If you'd listen to me, you'd help me with these instead of carrying them on your own," said Jacob.

The blond barber was still incensed over having been hit, still angry over the rude way the young gentleman had treated him in his shop, even after the bowl of Madeira.

"I'll listen to you," said Tom.

And they threw themselves at the boxes, each holding up an end, and sidled clumsily through the doorway to the wagon. Even in the dark and the confusion, Tom knew that there couldn't possibly be two thousand rifles in the warehouse. There weren't more than forty or fifty boxes, and if the boxes were as heavy as one hundred pounds—they were certainly no heavier—there couldn't be more than seven or eight rifles in each.

"Can I help?" said Sally from her perch on the wagon's bench.

"Listen for singing soldiers," said Jacob.

But neither Tom nor Jacob heard a thing. The boxes were heavy, and of very rough wood, and the tension of what had preceded this heavy lifting was beginning to catch up with them. Still, Tom tried to deny the possibility of fear.

"You have a family, don't you, my friend?" he said.

"Those were my children you saw in the shop, and I have two more besides." He lifted a box with Tom. "But save your strength for this."

"Tell me when you think we should go," said Tom. "There's no time for all of them."

"We'll make time," said Jacob.

Somehow, they drove each other on, picking up the great weight of the boxes, staggering under the loads to the small doorway, raising them to the level of the wagon, and dropping them for a moment of relief. Tom was certain five minutes had passed. His heart raced, as if he had been running for an hour. The exertion was bringing tears to his eyes. For a moment he stopped thinking about Sally, about Jacob, about the unconscious soldier. Life was simply a race to bring boxes across the space of several yards in the night, before the dark exploded with violence.

"I hear something, I think," said Sally.

Jacob wouldn't stop. "Come on," he said, urging Tom to hurry with yet another box. He was exerting his own power now, weighing his strength and courage against that of the young gentleman. They slammed down what Tom assumed would be the final box, but Jacob urged otherwise. "I don't hear them. And they're on foot." He was back in the warehouse, and Tom followed him, concentrating on his fatigue, not his fear.

"One more, that's all," said Sally. "We have enough."

Enough for what? thought Tom. Once again, he was lifting his end of a box, numbers racing through his brain. Rifles were anywhere from ten to twenty pounds, but most were about twelve. They'd lifted thirty boxes at the very most. Would they bring even two hundred and fifty rifles to Connecticut? That many would be a miracle—and they'd hoped to steal two thousand.

"They're coming," said Sally as they dropped the box. "I'm going. If you don't want to come, you stay. I'm leaving."

They could all hear the singing and laughing of a company of men. Jacob said, "We have time for one more. Come on." He went into the warehouse, like a madman. Tom knew that he could leap into the wagon and snap the reins, and somehow find the way to the East River. But he followed, of course. He picked up his end.

"I accept your apology," said Jacob.

"Go to hell, you crazy bastard," said Tom, but Jacob thought this was a charming statement. They hurried the last box into the wagon and threw themselves into the back. Sally urged the horse forward, clucking her tongue and snapping the reins. Jacob climbed over the boxes and into the front. "Let me," said Jacob, and he slowed the mare down and drove them slowly into the dark road, even as the song of the soldiers seemed to overwhelm them, a black and destructive wave of ill fortune.

But they were never seen. The soldiers stumbled about for minutes more before coming upon the open warehouse and their half-conscious mate. Jacob didn't run the mare until they were under way for ten minutes, driving with great caution without a light on the narrow road. But finally he turned right, toward the south, and then left, toward the river, and though they were still quite a bit north of Wall Street, they were in a city: Houses appeared, candles and whale oil burned, a drunk cursed at them as he crossed the road near a just-closing tavern. Only a few streets had been built to have easy access from the west to the east side of the city; Wall Street, for example, had once been a great stockade of logs and planks to try to keep out the Indians to the north in the time of the Dutch rule. When the stockade was pulled down, they'd created an east-west thoroughfare. Jacob knew the city very well, but it was dark, and he was tired, and their daring unsettled him. A great house appeared on the right, and he couldn't tell the street from the dark shapes flanking it; he had thought them already past the residential area, closer to the water.

"I hope we're not too far south," he said.

"All I can tell is that this is New York," said Tom. "And I want to get home."

He had joined Sally and Jacob on the bench up front, and now Sally touched Tom's cheek and whispered: "It's a lovely shave you got this morning."

"The paper mill," said Jacob suddenly. "Thank God, I know where we are." They had entered a narrow street lined with shops and small factories, but as the horse and wagon picked up speed, almost dangerously, the great concentration of warehouses and ship chandlers that characterized the waterfront was all around them. "I know exactly where we are."

And Jacob did. Though the moon had slid behind a layer of

clouds, and the buildings towered hugely above them, dark and identical with foreboding, he drove on without hesitation, the only vehicle on the late-night streets. Soon they felt the river's presence, its ancient scent as pure as when nothing but wood-lands lined its banks. Jacob turned away from the waterfront street and went north through a labyrinth of shipmakers, mar-kets, sailmakers, and taverns. "We turn here," he said softly, as if speaking out a prayer. The wagon turned into a much seedier street; here the warehouses were smaller, without windows and signs. A tavern stood behind a carpet of weeds. But toward the end of the block a much grander structure rose, a ware-house with its own dock, waiting patiently for the ships that never came.

"Do you see them?" said Jacob.

"No," said Tom. "But they'll see us if they're out there."

And then all three of them saw the light of a lantern floating above the black water. It was the farmers' skiff, with its sail down, floating at the end of the dock. Pierpont had found Mr. Laker, and Mr. Laker had found his friends. More than the image of the lantern in the water, more than the sight of Sally embracing her brother, more than the rush of fellowship he felt at Jacob's parting, Tom would remember the look in the eyes of the farmers on the skiff when he entered their circle of lantern light. They were the same men who had rowed him across the river from Brooklyn to Manhattan, the same silent, serious men. Laker had already given them the idea that Tom was, if not a Son of Liberty, then something even more revolutionary. When the farmers helped them load the skiff with the heavy boxes of guns, their admiration was boundless. When they looked at him, he felt none of the embarrassment he had felt before, when they had cast him in the role of a hero simply for getting into a tavern fight. Now their admiration was not misplaced: He had stolen guns for the revolution. He and Sally and Jacob and Pierpont and Mr. Laker and Mr. Laker's pretty daughter back in Brooklyn were all a part of this revolution. When the boxes were all loaded and the skiff pushed off silently into the swift current, Tom felt surrounded by family. He felt safe. Though there were British ships north and south of them, though all of them could be hanged for the cargo they carried, for the deeds that had been committed that night, Tom felt as if a great weight were lifting off his shoulders, not as if danger was closing in all about him. He held Sally close, listening to the easy stroking of the oars. They would row a little farther away from the shore and then turn north and east, not for the coast of Brooklyn or the north shore of Long Island, but for the great Sound itself. There they would raise their sail, and hope for a good wind, and at dawn they would hide, all of them together. Neither Mr. Laker nor the farmers were about to do things halfway. They were all of them fighting the same fight. Tom would have to find some way to get his horse out of the stable in Brooklyn, but that was a small matter. All that counted was that he was with the woman he loved, and that they were going home.

FOURTEEN

───◆───

It took two days to sail to Safe Haven.

The farmers, used to sailing with impunity across the East River or along the coast of the north shore of Long Island, refused to believe that English sailors would challenge them on the Sound. And though they had left behind a mad scramble along the New York waterfront, they weren't there to watch the searches, confiscations, and harassment in the wake of the theft of the rifles.

It was Pierpont who finally asked Tom where precisely it was that they were going. Even if no one stopped them on the Sound, how was one supposed to unload boxes of British rifles on carefully policed docks?

"We'll go right to my house," said Tom. "After dark, up the Saugatuck, we'll pull up the boat to our little dock, and we'll carry the boxes into the house."

"What about your father?" said Sally.

"Perhaps he'll surprise us," said Tom.

Tom guided them about the dangerous shoals, the beautiful outcroppings of rock in the moonlight. They rowed noisily, busily, but there was no one to hear them as they entered the river and fought the current, turning about wildly. At midnight, they tied the skiff to the end of the dock downhill from the old house, where a lantern burned before the massive, impenetrable door.

Tom left them and walked silently onto the land. Two English mastiffs tore down the hill, eager to kill in defense of their territory. When they caught Tom's scent, their barking changed from truculent to ecstatic, from watchdog-mad to puppy love.

Isaac stood at the open door with a musket pointed at the night.

"Get my father," said Tom.

"I could shoot you, sir," said Isaac. "Maybe I can't see you."

"Please," said Tom.

"What are you doing waking him in the middle of the night? He's an old man."

But Isaac went to wake him, and Tom walked into the house, watching Isaac's candle retreat down the long hall, leaving him in the dark. His father appeared in half a minute. "Have you been drinking?"

"No, sir."

"The sloop from New York came in at noon. It's past midnight."

"I didn't come in by sloop from New York. I need your help, Father."

"If you wanted my help, you shouldn't have woken me in the middle of the night, you fool. Have you no sense at all? Even if I wasn't your father, wouldn't you use a little courtesy, if only to get what you want? How on earth am I going to leave my fortune to a wild crazy fool like you?"

"Father," said Tom, "there is going to be a war. I have stolen guns in New York from the British, and I've come here to hide them. Will you help me or won't you?"

"Where are they, these guns?" said Abe Williams, his mouth wide with wonder. He looked at his son as if he had never noticed him before.

"A skiff. At our dock."

"How many?"

"About three hundred rifles. They are for Connecticut. For the Sons of Liberty in the event of an uprising."

"I am not a revolutionary," said Abe Williams. "I don't want war."

"You may not have a choice," said Tom.

"Why did you do it?"

"Because I believe in it."

"In what?"

"I don't know," said Tom. "This house. Being born to this country, this freedom. What does it all mean if we're dictated to? If we are taxed, controlled, ruled by a power that has become foreign to us?"

"You're talking nonsense," said Abe Williams. "We're Englishmen. You and I are as English as anyone." But his words were no longer spoken severely. He could sense his son's fatigue. He could feel his own resolve weakening. "There were some confiscations at the docks yesterday. Smugglers. These are dangerous times."

"Father, they are waiting in the boat. I need an answer. I need your help."

"And what if I don't help you?" He could still scarcely believe that his son had taken an action that wasn't simply willful, selfish, or angry. Only two days ago, Abe had donated money to the Sons of Liberty, to help send supplies to blockaded Boston. But he wasn't sure why he had done this, though at the time he had told himself it was strictly good business: Safe Haven was a patriotic town, and it was bad business to be politically unpopular. "Never mind," said Abe Williams. "I suppose there is no choice. You could be hanged, and it would be my doing. You'd better hurry. That boat must be out of here long before first light."

Though his father scowled, Tom felt his love. Abe Williams was helping his son, not the revolution, and this was what Tom had hardly dared dream.

The boxes were unloaded, and Isaac served Mr. Laker, the farmers, and Sally and Pierpont hot coffee and cold meat pies. The heroism was infectious: Abe felt as if he had joined the Sons, as if he had made his first commitment to something besides business and marriage in his eighty years. Tom's gratitude and respect made Abe's last month happy. He died suddenly, on April 23, 1775, letting a saucer of Dutch tea crash to the floor, his hands clawing at his cravat, as if for air.

A day before, a messenger had brought the news of the battle at Lexington, Massachusetts, reading from a scroll at the marketplace:

"To All Friends of American Liberty: Be it known that this morning, April 19, before break of day, a brigade consisting of about one thousand or two thousand men landed at Phipp's farm, Cambridge, and marched to Lexington, where they found a company of our colonial militia in arms, upon whom they fired without provocation, and killed six men and wounded four others. By an express from Boston we find another brigade are on the march from Boston, supposed to be about one thousand."

Abe Williams had lived long enough to leave a legacy. The patriots of Safe Haven and Fairlawn had been training for the last month with the new rifles, and they were good weapons, accurate and quick-loading. When George Washington passed through Safe Haven on June 28, 1775, on the way to take command of the forces of the United Colonies of North America, many of those newly trained patriots joined him. Among them were Pierpont Woods, who was afraid but determined, and Thomas Williams, who was afraid too, for the first time in his life. He had married Sally Woods on the first day of May, and had left her pregnant in the house of his fathers. Tom had become committed, after a fashion, but his commitment to the liberty of America was as nothing compared to his love for his wife. Only the unspoken knowledge of how that love would fade if he did not go off to war had allowed him to leave her.

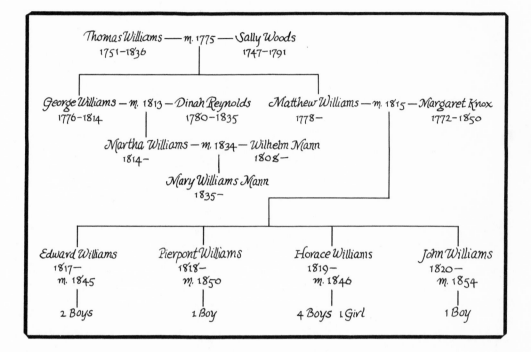

Thomas Williams — m. 1775 — Sally Woods
1751–1836   1747–1791

George Williams — m. 1813 — Dinah Reynolds   Matthew Williams — m. 1815 — Margaret Knox
1776–1814   1780–1835   1778–   1772–1850

Martha Williams — m. 1834 — Wilhelm Mann
1814–   1808–

Mary Williams Mann
1835–

Edward Williams   Pierpont Williams   Horace Williams   John Williams
1817–   1818–   1819–   1820–
m. 1845   m. 1850   m. 1846   m. 1854

2 Boys   1 Boy   4 Boys 1 Girl   1 Boy

The Family of
Thomas and Sally Williams
1775-1855

Tom Williams and his brother-in-law, Pierpont Woods, followed Washington's camp for the better part of a year. They returned to Safe Haven in March 1776, to look at George Williams, all of five weeks old, and to nurse their exhaustion and disappointment with the progress of the fighting. Pierpont proved his courage decisively by getting shot in the back at the Battle of Long Island in late August of that year; it took him a week to die, and during that time Tom decided he'd had enough of war. He helped his conscience by smuggling messages into and out of British-occupied New York, but with the birth of his and Sally's second son, he found himself thinking more of family than of country. Tom had been to China, and he knew that the end of the war would bring an enormous increase in the China trade; and long before the Treaty of Paris was signed, three Williams ships were halfway home from the Orient, loaded with spices and silks, the beginning of a trading relationship that would last for four decades.

Sally died young, at forty-four, succumbing to pneumonia during the miserable winter of 1791. Tom mourned her in his fashion; he never married the French émigrée with whom he'd been having an affair in New York. Instead, he threw himself

into the task of raising his boys to be men, even when it was
apparent that he would have little influence on hard, teenage
souls. George, the older son, was thin-skinned and myopic. He
loved liberty as much as his mother had, but he was also a
deist, and a bit of a coward. He disgraced himself at Yale by
refusing to fight a student who had insulted his family name.
Matthew, two years younger, was almost as eager to fight as his
father had been. He never made it through Yale either, but only
because he had no aptitude for philosophy. Matthew wanted to
enlarge the family's holdings; he wanted the family to make its
fortunes in shipping, in furs, in speculating in land. While
George married a pauper's daughter of great beauty and strong
religious convictions, Matthew married a stout young heiress
from Boston and began producing boys at a prodigious rate.
George returned to the Congregational Church in time to celebrate the birth of his daughter Martha, lusty and green-eyed
and eager to cry. Matthew built a brick mansion in Fairlawn,
leaving his older brother to suffer under the shadow of their
parents' roof; his four boys grew up to be tall, straight, conscious of their father's sense of family destiny. During the second war with the British, George was determined to prove his
courage, if not to himself, then to his young wife. Dinah begged
him not to go, urging him to believe that his duty was with his
wife and his three-month-old child. But George had become
obsessed with joining the army, partly because Matthew was
not going to do so; he was far too busy with his business affairs.
George volunteered for six months active duty, and was sent
west for training. Two months later they received word of his
death during the fighting with the Creek Indians. Dinah Reynolds Williams was a widow, charged with the care of an infant. She accepted her lot as a trial from the Lord.

Tom Williams grew old and sentimental. It was better to
live with his daughter-in-law and granddaughter than to live
alone, but he was often irritated by the sloppiness about him.
Dinah couldn't bear to keep servants in the house; she felt it
was a mark of vanity to do so. But neither was she any kind of
housekeeper. As her daughter, Martha, grew up, the child
began to cook for Tom. She loved her grandfather, and couldn't
understand how her Fairlawn relations could feel sorry for her.

It was true that they had no servants, and that her grandfather had lost a good deal of money by continuing to sail his ships when he could no longer get full, profitable cargoes. But there was still a comfortable amount of money for extravagant gifts, books from Boston and London, pretty dresses, furniture for her dollhouse. When she had grown into her teens, Martha loved the old man and her religious mother even more than before. It didn't matter to her that the Williams name had come to be more associated with Fairlawn, and the mansion and the dynasty built by her Uncle Matthew. It was far more important to Martha that her mother gave charity to the poor, and that her grandfather never fired his useless shipyard employees.

When she was twenty, she met and ran off with a German immigrant. Wilhelm Mann was dramatically handsome, but Martha was convinced that she had fallen in love with him for his good heart and wild ideas. He cared deeply about so many of the same things she did—the rights of women and black slaves and Indians—and wanted to devote his life to good works. They returned to Safe Haven, married and wildly in love. The townspeople were surprised that even so saintly a woman as Dinah Reynolds Williams would take her daughter and her non-American husband into her home; and that Tom Williams, the old patriot, could stand the sight of a German in his ancient house was even more incredible. It would have been far more appropriate for the disgraced descendant of John Collins to be sent off with a few dollars and her new husband into the western territories.

For months, many townspeople would shake their heads sadly while passing by the old house on the Saugatuck, even when they could see the infamous German out chopping wood, or repairing the side of a decrepit outbuilding. A year after the marriage Martha's mother died; she'd had consumption for six years, and the slow illness had suddenly hurried her to her end. Old Tom Williams died a year later, at the age of eighty-five. The gossips were strangely satisfied; it was easy to draw the conclusion that the union of Williams blood with that of the immigrant had killed off two of Safe Haven's most distinguished citizens.

But even though Martha and Wilhelm Mann added insult to

injury—not only did they inherit the home of John Collins, but they made it a home of radical upheaval—the town of Safe Haven had to accept them. Though they were vociferous in their support of causes unpopular in a small New England town —pacifism, temperance, universal education, abolition—no one could erase the fact of Martha's roots. Even though she'd married a German, everyone knew that her Americanism and patriotism must somehow stand beyond criticism, just as her family history in Safe Haven went back to before there was a country or a state or even a settlement.

Martha and Wilhelm had a daughter. Mary had her father's thick blond hair, her mother's green eyes, her great-grandfather's temper. But she had little sense of family. Her father had a German accent, and she despised it; her mother wanted to free every slave in the world, and she loathed this. She had no use for a family tree, for an old house visited by Negroes, religious fanatics, and Utopians. In 1855 Safe Haven was old, and Mary Mann was twenty and beautiful, and she wanted to live in a new hotel, with indoor plumbing and servants in starched uniforms, and be as rich and famous as Jenny Lind. The South could keep its slaves or eat them, for all she cared; the North could secede from the South or gobble up Canada and Cuba; her parents could spend their last penny ministering to madmen and drunken Catholics and runaway blacks. All Mary wanted was to be an actress; to be universally adored.

PART THREE: 1855

A House of Refuge

FIFTEEN

Mary Williams Mann sat on the projecting porch of the old house built by John Collins more than two centuries before, and wondered about petticoats. There were pleasure craft in the Saugatuck, and a brisk northeast wind led to more than one impromptu race between the sailors. But she hardly looked at the river, or at the ancient oaks, or at the pair of chipmunks foraging about the kitchen wall. She had on three petticoats. Her voluminous skirt—green and red and layered with lace trim—was quite attractively puffed out from her high, tiny waist; but there was room for four petticoats, or five. Mary knew that her mother would think such thoughts petty, unworthy of a noble soul; but she disagreed violently with her mother.

The door connecting the porch to the house opened behind her, and she heard the fat old Negro servant call out her name, the broad Southern accent underlined by its hateful arrogant tone: "Mary, your young man is here," she said.

It was never "Miss Mary," of course, not in the house of Wilhelm and Martha Mann, not in the home of the abolitionist, pacifist, temperance-crusading do-good laughingstock parents of Mary Mann.

"He's not my young man, Leah," said Mary, not deigning to

turn her head to the servant. "And I wish you wouldn't refer to him in that fashion."

Leah simply slammed the door for answer. She was a religious woman, and was certain that the Lord had sent Mary to her saintly parents as a trial. But she was not a saint, and she was certainly not a slave, and no one was forcing her to be polite to the twenty-year-old hellion. As she opened the door for Franklin Colson, the son of the local furniture factory owner, she tried to insinuate by her gesture that nothing but trouble waited for him on the dilapidated old porch.

"Thank you, Leah," he said, his nervousness spilling into his speech. He was handsome, he was rich, he was a college graduate in a fine new frock coat. Leah wanted to shake him by the lapels: *That ain't nothing to be scared of, boy*, she would have liked to say. *That's just something to avoid.*

"Hello, Mary," he said. "I know I'm early. I'm sorry. It's hard to know how long it takes to get here, what with the farmers coming to market. There was a lot of traffic on Main Street. And the bridge isn't fixed right yet. There was a real delay there, actually."

"If it wasn't for the bridge delay, you would have been here even earlier, then," she said.

Franklin turned red, and Mary's heart went out to him. He was a fool, of course, in love with her, or what he thought was her. He was twenty-six and awkward, and she was beautiful, more beautiful than any other girl in Safe Haven or Fairlawn, more beautiful than the actresses on the stage in New York City. This was Franklin's opinion, at any rate. Mary was more critical. There were more beautiful women than she on the stage, but perhaps their beauty had been helped by the gaslights and the magic of cosmetics.

"I'm flattered that you came so early," she said, to make it up to him. "It shows that you're interested in getting to the party on time."

"No, it doesn't," he said. "Forgive me. I don't mean to contradict. But I don't care about the party. Not one bit. You know that. You know why I'm early."

"Would you like something to drink?"

"No. I really wanted to talk, just talk."

"Can't you talk and drink at the same time?"

"No, I can't!" Franklin laughed at his own vehemence, crossed the shaky expanse of porch, looked out to the river, and then turned about abruptly. "It's hard for me, because of—just looking at you, Mary."

"It was very much like a play," she said. "When you turned round. And the river in the background. But the speech. How on earth am I supposed to know what you're talking about? Go on. Looking at me?"

"You're beautiful," he said.

"Franklin, I appreciate the compliment," said Mary. She stood up and approached him, and the words that he'd been groping for vanished altogether. "But as long as we're both ready, and you don't want a drink, why not get an early start? It's April. It might rain in an hour."

"May I talk to your parents?" he said.

"My parents?"

"Your father," he said, as if this would elucidate his previous remark. "I suppose your father is the one, even with all the talk of women's rights and so on. Yes, it's still the father."

"My father would laugh at you," said Mary.

"Oh, no, surely not—"

"He'd think you an old man. And he's nearly fifty."

"But in matters like this, it's beyond politics, it's a question of tradition—"

"Franklin," said Mary, "my father would laugh at you if you asked him for my hand in marriage."

"I don't believe that he would act in such a manner," said the grave young man, astonished that the words had been spoken: her *hand in marriage*.

"It's my hand," said Mary. "There are many things on which my parents and I disagree, but certainly my father and my mother would think it absurd for *you* to ask *them* about *my* wants and desires."

"Your parents are truly extraordinary," said Franklin, swallowing hard. Was it possible that she wanted him to ask her? To just say the words? "My parents aren't for antislavery, of course, but that's primarily because of their Southern upbringing. Intellectually, I rather think they're for emancipation with compensation to the owners, but they'd never say that in public, you see. Because of the factory. Everyone would think Father wanted to get more cheap labor into town, whereas nothing could be further from the truth. He hardly ever hires an Irisher or a German—I don't think he's about to hire a free black."

"No, I do not want to marry you," said Mary, taking his arm and walking him back into the house.

"I'm sorry, did I say something?" he said, wondering if he had uttered some nonsense that had not registered on his brain.

"You were about to ask me to marry you, and I wanted to save you the trouble. You're very nice, and I'm sure you'll be a wonderful husband, but I am never going to marry. Never."

"I will never marry anyone but you," said Franklin.

They were in the dark hallway where a score of early family portraits had once hung; but the dour-faced children of John and Virginia Collins now hung in new frames in Fairlawn, in the mansion of Mary's great-uncle, Matthew Williams, still robust and acquisitive at seventy-seven. There were portraits still, but they were of the poor side of the Williams family— George, the weak-chinned hero of the War of 1812, and his lovely wife, Dinah, dead a few months before Mary was born. But she looked nothing like her beautiful grandmother, or even like her ivory-skinned mother, still youthful at forty-one. A portrait of her father as a young man, newly arrived from Germany, captured the planes of her face, the independent tilt of her head. There was no portrait of her mother; Martha Williams Mann had decided it too vain to sit for one's portrait. She would not leave a legacy of her physical beauty, but of good deeds. Mother and daughter were both green-eyed, but even this lent them no resemblance: Her mother's gaze was steady, open, the green of an ocean of compassion; Mary's green eyes were jealous, bright with a boundless desire.

"Of course you'll marry," said Mary. "Stop moping, please, it's not becoming. I like you very much, but that's the end of it. And watch what you say about Irish and Germans—my father is a German, as you know perfectly well."

"I didn't mean him—" began Franklin, once again turning red. Of course he had said something remarkably stupid only a moment ago—his father didn't even hire Irishers and Germans, he'd said. "Please, Mary. You must forgive me. I don't think of your father that way. Your whole family—no one considers you or any part of you as anything other than pure American. Safe Haven is your family. Everyone else is a newcomer. Please say that you forgive me. I was an oaf, an absolute buffoon."

Mary stopped him at the end of the hallway and took hold of his arms. "Kiss me," she said.

He stared at her as if she'd gone mad. But she moved closer to him, bringing her lips to the corners of his mouth. She kissed him quickly, pecking at him like a bird. Franklin Colson could hardly respond; he was wondering if this meant that she did love him, that she would marry him, that only his stupid comment about Germans had angered her. But then he felt the passion rise up in him, clumsy and swift, and he brought her slender form crushingly to his chest, and he kissed her lips hard, without thought, full of love and desire.

"Mary," said a woman's voice, and a red-faced Franklin pushed away from his love as if she were on fire. It was Mary's mother, Martha Williams Mann, dressed in a wide-sleeved scarlet gown of excellent fabric that was at least twenty years old, and twenty-five years out of date. She was distracted, looking at her daughter without anger, but with concern. "Mary, I'm sorry, but I must ask your young man to help me."

"Help with what, Mother?" she said. Franklin stared at the women, unable to understand why he was the only one embarrassed at being caught in such a compromising position. Mrs. Mann pulled her cashmere shawl tightly about her shoulders. "We're about to go to a party."

"What party?"

"Uncle John's, Mother," said Mary. "In Fairlawn. You didn't want to come, don't you remember?"

"Of course, of course, child," she said, as if the very act of thinking about her Williams cousins was beneath contempt. "Listen, please, Mary, I must ask your young man to help me, and to swear himself to secrecy, to absolute secrecy."

"No, I don't want him to," said Mary. "I don't know what you need him for, but I don't like it, it's not fair, we're expected in Fairlawn."

"This is more important than Fairlawn and your fat cousins who live by the sweat and blood of other men." Mrs. Mann never got angry at Mary, but she often got angry at the world. She wanted something done now, something that would ease some tiny part of the world's pain. There would be no reasoning with her. "You are the son of the factory owner, are you not?"

"We've met before, Mrs. Mann—I've gone to the Lyceum—I've heard you lecture. And your husband."

"Are you for slavery or against it?"

"I am against it."

"Good, I won't ask another question. Come. I need you to drive your carriage. My husband's gone off with his, and this is a terrible emergency, a terrible emergency."

"Mother," said Mary, "you can't ask Franklin to commit a crime."

"Emerson himself said he wouldn't obey the Fugitive Slave Law," said Mrs. Mann. "Are we to do less than Emerson?"

"Emerson isn't doing anything but talking," said Mary. She turned to her love-struck companion. "Don't listen to her. I don't want you to help. I'll be furious if you help her, do you understand?"

But Franklin didn't understand. He couldn't imagine that the daughter of Wilhelm and Martha Mann was anything but a fiery antislavery advocate. Surely she protested now to protect him from danger, from getting involved in their defiant actions against antiquated laws.

"Of course, Mrs. Mann," he said, holding his head high. "I'm very happy to help you. My carriage is at your disposal."

"Mother, what is it for? What is it about?"

"Come and you shall see," said Mrs. Mann.

She asked Franklin Colson to drive them toward the waterfront, not yet giving their precise destination. Mary truly didn't know that they were about to pick up a fugitive slave; after all, her mother's causes were so many, and the recipients of her charity so various, that they might be en route to a madman, a murderer sentenced to death, a wife escaping her husband. But soon enough, the key words slipped out: Mrs. Mann began to rail against the Congress, against the cowardly U.S. marshals afraid to defy the law. "In Massachusetts there are no more attempts to catch runaway slaves—none, do you understand? The people have been heard. But here, in Connecticut, in our own town, there are people who would gladly surrender slaves to their masters. People hate free blacks so much that they'd rather see them dead than treated like human beings."

"Is it a slave that we're going to help?" said Mary.

"We're going to the station to pick up some freight," said her mother with a little-girl smile. Even at her most serious, she couldn't help but be charmed by the Underground Railroad's use of railway terms. No one imagined this to be a subterfuge. The Underground Railroad—that vague outline of routes and stopping places for runaway slaves, helped out by Quakers, abolitionists, and all sorts of men of good will—was perhaps more potent in its fame than it was in reality. People who would no more help a terrified slave family en route to Canada than they'd jump into the next clipper ship for China still knew all the jargon: A "line" was a route; a "station" was a resting place, or refuge, where the runaway could hide and recoup his strength. Fugitive slaves were called "freight," and, of course, those men and women of the "Railroad" who broke the law to help the fugitives called themselves "conductors."

"Why is it an emergency?" said Mary.

"Because the federal marshals are searching the stations for freight."

"How do they know where the stations are?"

"Everyone in Safe Haven knows who's an abolitionist," said Mrs. Mann. "Everyone knows where the abolitionists live."

Mary tried one last time to reason with Franklin: This was not his fight, she explained, but that of her parents. He could be sent to prison for breaking the law. His parents would be furious with him. His father might even disown him. But Franklin simply smiled, glad to be on sure ground. This was not a question of love talk, of being shocked by a kiss. This was a chance to exhibit courage, to drive a carriage with skill and speed, to keep his Colt revolver at the ready under his seat.

"Everyone knows where you live, Mother," said Mary. "I don't understand what you're planning to accomplish." A dozen thoughts, selfish thoughts, ran through her. There would be no party for her after all, and she'd so looked forward to showing off her dress and figure to her four young and handsome uncles, all of them married to women of some fashion, none of them half so pretty as herself. Franklin had been recruited to take her there only because he was so eminently presentable in her Fairlawn relations' eyes. And now anything might happen. Franklin might be shot, her mother might be held overnight in jail again, the newspapers would once again demand an end to illegal agitation. And what of the new play coming to town? She'd never get a chance to see it, not if her mother's escapade blew up in their faces. If only her father had been home with their dilapidated carriage!

Safe Haven's business district had been built up around the waterfront for generations, but in the last decade, a new, quieter business district had centered around Main Street on the opposite end of town. There, women could shop for cloth and clothing, men could go for a shave, children could buy sweets on the way home from school. Lawyers, physicians, apothecaries all moved their offices from the waterfront to the more genteel town center, and though waterfront property was still expensive, the area itself had become run-down, busy with bars and rough sailors and three cheap boardinghouses. It was strange to see the elegant masts of magnificent clipper ships, anchored out in the Sound like some fairy vision, floating against an outline of unpainted warehouses, weather-beaten old sailors begging for coins, and the occasional gang of young toughs from nearby Irishtown.

"Where is this station, on a boat?"

"No, Mary," said her mother. She directed Franklin to turn down the street fronting the water. It was Sunday, and though long after the main church services, it was unheard of to see men unloading a farmer's old skiff. Mary knew at once that they'd found their station.

"Turn down to the pier," Mrs. Mann said. Mary felt the approach of danger, strong and clear and wild with terror. She turned about to look for the U.S. marshals who must be lurking about, but all she could see were a few families looking at the boats along the water from their wagons and carriages. "All right, stop," said Mrs. Mann. "Mary, stay with the carriage."

Mrs. Mann jumped down and motioned for Franklin to follow. They walked down the pier to where two husky workingmen were unloading barrels in the sea-scented breeze. They hardly looked at them, but both of them smiled. One of them spoke, without turning his head. "The freight's landed," he said.

"Let it out," said Mrs. Mann.

"It ain't safe," said the other one. "Suppose somebody sees?"

"Hey," said the first workingman. "If Mrs. Mann says let it out . . ."

"Right," finished the other workingman. He grabbed hold of the lid of the largest barrel on the pier and lifted it off easily; it hadn't been nailed shut, because the barrel contained a living, breathing human being. "OK, boy," said the workingman. "Hurry on out, it's all right."

The "freight" lifted himself out of the barrel and stepped lightly onto the wood planks of the pier, shivering in the slight chill. He was a brown-skinned field hand, with light eyes and a freckled nose, and in his hand was a knife, ready to be used without hesitation.

"Come on, brother," said Mrs. Mann to the black man. "We'll get you some clothes and some food real fast."

"He killed my wife. It was him, not his missus, but I would've killed her too. I would kill anyone who would do that. I don't care about dying anymore. I figure it's the Lord who got me this far, and the Lord who guides my hand, so don't go thinking I'm afraid."

Franklin Colson was afraid. The spectacle of a black man with a knife, barefoot and filthy in threadbare blue-gray work clothes, uttering incomprehensible threats in a clear Southern accent, was uniquely threatening, more so because he was involved in the crime of his escape. That his eyes were bloodshot, his massive shoulders quivering as if just relieved of an enormous burden, that his entire frame seemed as capable of collapse as of murder, added to Franklin's fear. He understood now that Mary had warned him truly. What had he gotten himself involved with?

"Help him," said Mrs. Mann.

"What?"

"Franklin," said Mrs. Mann, "he's falling down." She went for the black man's arm, holding on to it without fear of the knife, and Franklin urged himself forward, to do as much as Mary's mother. The knife fell from the man's hands, and Mrs.

Mann reached for it with great speed, whisking it away beneath her cashmere shawl. "That's all right, brother," she said to the black man. "We're going to let you sleep, we're going to let you eat, we're going to take care of you. You've come to a safe place, brother. A safe place."

Franklin and Mrs. Mann held the stumbling man on either side and hurried him off the pier. Franklin was sure that the occupants of half a dozen conveyances had seen the black man, had wondered about him, had taken note of his presence and would be eager to investigate. As they helped him up into the carriage, he suddenly came to life in their hands.

"Let me go," he said. "I can do it. The Lord's giving me strength. 'The Lord is the strength of my life.' Yes. Psalms, Twenty-seven. I am not a bad man. We would have gone together."

Mary moved as far away from the man as possible, but his eyes found hers almost at once.

"It's all right, brother," said Mrs. Mann. She told Franklin to drive, and he spoke softly to the horse, clucking his tongue as if this would somehow minimize their danger.

"Who's she?" said the black man.

"That's my daughter, and your friend," said Mrs. Mann.

"No, not my friend," he said. He turned away from Mary finally, and shivered in his damp rags. "What did I say?"

"Nothing I understood, but it makes no difference," said Mrs. Mann. "You're going to a safe place."

"You don't know what I've done."

"Yes, I do," said Mrs. Mann. "I know everything." She called out to Franklin to turn north, and then sharply east on the narrow dirt road that led to the great estates of the factory owners of Safe Haven and Fairlawn.

"Where's the station, Mother?" said Mary.

"You'll know it when we're there, child."

"What did he do? He said he did something."

"He's a runaway from the most vile institution in the world," said Mrs. Mann. "That's all we need to know."

"No," said the black man. "I killed a man. I'm a murderer. But it was a time to kill, do you understand, a time to kill, and the Lord wanted it done. It was good in the eyes of the Lord."

Mary heard the words and recoiled, more in anger at her mother than in fear of the man. She never doubted the man for a moment. He said he was a murderer, and she knew at once that this was true; her mother's "emergency" was not simply to help a runaway slave along the Underground Railroad into Canada, but to help a murderer defy the law.

"Rest a while, brother," said Mrs. Mann, looking briefly and calmly into her daughter's eyes, measuring the extent of her anger. "You're more tired than you know."

"You took my knife," he said, but not angrily. He was not afraid of Mrs. Mann; he was eager to believe in someone's decency, and he felt her goodness like the fulfillment of a dream.

"Where do I go at the fork, Mrs. Mann?" said Franklin.

"Left," she said, letting the black man's head rest on her shoulder. He shivered a last time, and slept. As the carriage horse strained against the sudden upgrade in the dusty road, Mary spoke:

"Are we going to the asylum?"

"Yes."

"Mother, you can't be serious. The doctors will see him. The nurses, all the attendants outside—someone will talk."

"Your interest in the man's welfare is well founded, child," said her mother, without a trace of cynicism. "But this is not a sudden whim, do you see? It's all been prepared, thought out. This is the best way."

"What is the best way? You don't mean to leave him there?" Mary moved a fraction closer to the carriage door. The man's stench was frightful, but worse than that was the fact of his beauty. His brown face had relaxed its vigilance in sleep, so that the profile was no longer defiant, taking control, but shockingly childish, dependent. He had a short nose and broad African lips and long, feathery eyelashes. His ears were small, perfectly shaped, a gentle touch in a body of great strength. She could see him on the stage—noble Othello, of course, crushed by the revelation of his unjust murder of beautiful Desdemona. This slave, this murderer, this black man had the strength and the trust and the desire to be great, and to fall into an abyss crafted from passion. "The man said he's murdered. I believe him, if you don't."

"Slavery is the great murderer, child. This man is a good man, and he will be helped. We will all help him."

"Mother, this isn't just the Fugitive Slave Law you're breaking. Not if he's murdered. You're aiding a murderer, you're sharing in his crime."

"His master raped his wife," said Mrs. Mann softly. "Not once, but repeatedly, over a period of months. There was nothing he could do, no law to which he could appeal. If he wanted to commit murder, it was a holy murder, a murder against the abomination of slavery. His master's wife became jealous. The master spent too much time with the slave woman, and so she gave her extra work when she came in from the fields. She beat her for the slightest reason. One day the slave woman struck back. One of the conductors told me that she killed the master's wife, another one said that she recovered. It doesn't matter. She had hit the master's wife, and it was serious, and she was flogged, and the overseer, a black man, listening to his master, killed the woman. Perhaps not deliberately. But it makes no difference. Slavery, do you see? She was beaten to death. This black man killed his master and ran off. There are some parts of the Railroad who want nothing to do with him. But you can see that's wrong. I know you can, because you have a good heart, child. He killed his master, and all that matters is that he gets to safety, that he is able to live his life as a free man, among free people."

Mary heard her mother's words through the filter she always placed before serious words: It was a speech onstage; her mother was a character, not a human being but an incomplete image of one. Her mother had moved her. Often, Mrs. Mann was capable of that. She and Wilhelm Mann were famous for their speeches at the Lyceum in Safe Haven, their ability to whip up a crowd to a frenzy of indignation. But it was not real to Mary. Not completely. Her mother was good, of course, caring nothing for money or prestige or fancy clothes. She gave away all the money earned by Tom Williams's daring investments in mills in Massachusetts, in whaling voyages traveling to the Fiji Islands and beyond, in fledgling railroad lines just beginning to turn a profit the year of his death, 1836. But money was coming back now. Mary didn't know how much, but imagined it to be considerable, as her father had no job other than political and social agitation, and her mother was constantly being lauded by hospitals, churches, and orphanages for the family's patronage.

The asylum was another example of her parents' largesse. Where other people were embarrassed or revolted by madness, her parents saw only oppression. The great revolution in treating the mentally ill that began in the 1830s—when the competition for the mad members of wealthy families became intense —reached Safe Haven in 1840, when Mary was a child of five. No longer were the mad to be kept confined, often chained and treated with clumsy bloodletting or immersed in cold water, simply as a means of containing their spirits. Doctors emerged as heroic figures, becoming famous in a single burst of newspaper reports: The mentally ill could be cured! Asylums, special regimens, expensive techniques were all that kept the insane from the joys of mental clarity. That such techniques were practical but unavailable because of a lack of funding was an abomination to Mr. and Mrs. Wilhelm Mann. Like other donors in the Northeast, they contributed generously to an asylum just outside of Safe Haven, built under the auspices of a Dr. Marandino from Cambridge, Massachusetts. Though the state of Connecticut provided more than half of the funds for the building of Dr. Marandino's asylum, a good part of the annual budget was provided by private contributions. When her parents were not raging against slavery and war and alcohol, they were urging their brethren to "free the insane" through donations to therapeutic asylums.

"No, Franklin, drive around the back. I want to go to the doctor's house first."

"I don't understand, Mother," said Mary. "What can you possibly do with him here? This won't get him to Canada."

"He can't go to Canada. Too dangerous. They're hunting for him. This way he'll disappear for a while. Until it's safe. Imagine the day all the slaves are freed. No one will be looking for anyone anymore. He'll be free."

"If he'll be free the day the South frees their slaves, he'll be an old man then." But she understood her mother's plan. The asylum employed free blacks, more than a dozen of them. Dr. Marandino had been against this, of course, because it became nearly impossible to hire good American or even German nurses with black men walking the grounds. But Mrs. Mann had insisted, and her donation was large enough to force the doctor to accede to her wishes. There were too few places that would employ free blacks for her not to have insisted.

Franklin was driving the carriage past the main building when the black man woke with a start. "What?" he said, as if someone had addressed him, and Mary could see that his eyes had fastened on the asylum, rising to four stories on a plateau overlooking the neighboring farmlands. "Where are we?" He was quite angry, and his hands were coming alive, clenching and unclenching with such speed that for a moment it seemed possible that he was a candidate for admission as a patient to the asylum before them. But of course, such a privilege was reserved for the rich. Even the best efforts of men and women like the Manns couldn't get the impoverished insane out of poorhouses, workhouses, and prisons.

"It's safe," said Mrs. Mann.

"No," he said. "It's not safe." But he calmed down a bit as the carriage left the asylum, with its lovely portico supported by dignified columns. One of the doctors had looked up from a book on his lap, as he sat out on the great porch, attended by a black servant.

"You're not in the South," said Mary.

"What?" said Mrs. Mann. "Of course we're not. You know that, don't you, brother?"

The black man didn't respond for a moment, as if he was not quite through sloughing off his dream. He looked at Mary, and his light eyes held her hard green eyes, trying to see if he had misjudged her. But there was no feeling there. He felt her discomfort as well as her disdain. "Yes," he said, turning back to Mrs. Mann. "I was dreaming, and then I woke and saw the big house."

"It's all right," said Mrs. Mann.

"Did you really kill your master?" said Mary suddenly, so that he had to turn once again to the beautiful white girl.

"Yes, ma'am," he said.

"How did you feel?" she asked. "When it was done?"

"Mary, don't bother our friend when he's too weak to think straight."

"It felt good," said the black man. "Like it wasn't me. It was right, ma'am. 'It is God that avengeth me,' ma'am. That's Samuel. Second Book. It felt good."

"What's your name?" said Mary.

"He has a new name," said Mrs. Mann. "You're not to use your old one, do you understand?"

"Where I'm going—they don't know? It's not a station?"

"No," said Mrs. Mann. "But they'll leave you be. You're just a free black from South Carolina. Your master freed you because you saved his daughter's life. I have your papers."

"But what is he doing here then, Mother?" said Mary, more and more intrigued by the drama of the moment. He was handsome, a murderer, a bible-quoting avenger—this was certainly better than seeing another black minstrel show. But now she wanted the order of the stage, the artifice that she craved in her own life. "Look at his clothes, his eyes—how can anyone think he's anything else but a fugitive?"

"It'll be taken care of," said Mrs. Mann.

"What I'm saying is," said Mary, "if you mean to hide him, he has to learn to play his part."

"Stop here, Franklin," she said, and telling them all to stay still, she let herself out of the carriage and walked the few steps to Dr. Marandino's two-story house. Mary had a glimpse of the doctor, dark and handsome, with a pair of spectacles in his hand as he left his house to greet her mother, and then draw her inside.

"You all right back there?" said Franklin from the driver's bench, turning his head slightly toward them. Though he had been at all times close enough to take part in their conversation, he had restricted himself to his driving, and to his thoughts. He wanted to ask Mary why she had kissed him in the hallway, why she had said she'd never marry, why she had allowed him to take her about Safe Haven for the last few months. But there would be time for those questions. He felt virtuous. With each minute spent in the service of Mrs. Mann, he was earning a larger piece of gratitude from her daughter, he thought. Certainly, he would be allowed to kiss her once more that day, to hold her in his arms without the interference of her mother.

"Yes, sir," said the black man. "It's all right. I won't eat anybody up. I'm black, but I'm not crazy."

A moment later, Mrs. Mann left the house. "Come on down,"

she said. "The doctor knows you're a fugitive, but not what you've done. You're just a runaway slave is all he knows. Your papers are with him, and your name is Moses. Moses Barker."

Moses jumped down, without turning back to Mary. "Thank you, ma'am. May the Lord bless you."

"Hurry on in, Moses," said Mrs. Mann. "You've got to get some food, and get out of those clothes before somebody sees you."

The black took two quick steps to the house before he stopped and slowly, easily turned round. Perhaps the white girl wasn't bad, he thought. He found her eyes again, and this time they were more open, and he smiled at her, broadly and naturally. "Thank you too, ma'am. May the Lord bless you too for all your kindness."

As they drove away, leaving him there among the mad, Mary was struck by the force of his sincerity. It was not often that people found her kind—save for her mother, who could see no wrong in her—and she found it unaccountably pleasant to be thought of in that fashion. Quickly, she drifted away from her mother's talk, from Franklin's queries about the party in Fairlawn; she was imagining a character, up there on the gaslit stage. There, before the hushed dark masses, she stood, blonde, beautiful, and ennobled by struggle. Moses Barker had avenged the killing of his wife, had murdered and escaped, his dignity intact, and if Mary Mann wasn't moved by his pain, she was moved by his story; she was moved by the part he might play in the drama of her life.

SIXTEEN

As they approached the house, Mary heard the pleasant sound of horsemen overtaking them on the soft April ground. Without thinking, she turned about to look out and see who the riders were.

"No," said her mother. "Ignore them."

"What do you mean?" said Mary, a bit irritated. But her mother placed a hand on her knee.

"We were out for a drive to look out at the waterfront," she said, speaking up so that Franklin could hear.

"Yes, ma'am," he said.

"You want to go on the stage, you might as well learn to act now," she added. Mary started, and then she saw the two strangers slow down to their own speed and hail Franklin. They wore dark blue frock coats covered with dust, and their beards and moustaches were unkempt. She couldn't hear what they called out, but Franklin slowed down, and after a moment they stopped, hooves, wheels, springs all relaxing into silence two hundred yards from the drive to their house.

One of the men asked Franklin his name and the names of his passengers, and where they were going on such a fine Sunday. Before he could answer, Mrs. Mann spoke.

"I have a better question. Who are you?" she said.

"Federal marshals, ma'am," said the second man, looking politely at Mrs. Mann, so he would not have to stare at her remarkably beautiful daughter.

"Slave catchers, you mean," said Mary.

"No, miss, you have us wrong," said the first marshal, very offended.

"Well, you're not from these parts, are you?" said Mary. "And you're covered with dust, and you look like slave catchers, you both do." She could feel her mother's approbation, and battened on it, like an actress feeding off the audience's praise. In a black-haired wig, she could play Eliza, the beautiful mulatto heroine of *Uncle Tom's Cabin*, bringing an audience of two thousand to tears. "You should be ashamed of yourselves, bothering innocent people with your filthy questions. That's my house, and we're going there, and you had better let us be. Come on, Franklin!"

But Franklin didn't snap the reins. The first marshal spoke again, more slowly. "That's your house—the Mann house?"

"Yes," said Mrs. Mann.

"The abolitionist Manns? Your husband is Wilhelm Mann?"

Ordinarily, Mary would have bridled at any description of her house or family as "abolitionist." She preferred the milder "antislavery." But she was not through acting, not at all. She had seen the record-breaking dramatization of *Uncle Tom's Cabin* at Purdy's National Theater in New York—it had run 325 performances—and it had confirmed all her dreams about the stage. Though her parents had found it puerile, they admitted it might create some good feeling throughout the country about the plight of the slaves. That the melodramatic play was difficult to get produced in New England, in spite of its immense popularity with readers of Mrs. Stowe's novel and theatergoers alike, added weight to the Manns' belief that the play had a worthwhile political message. But all that was unimportant to Mary. She had watched the pain etched in the lovely face of the actress portraying Eliza as she fled across the ice-choked Ohio River, clutching her infant to her breast, bringing the cruelty of slavery home to the enraptured audience more than any fiery words spouted by her parents. How wonderful to imagine Lola Montez in the part! The marshals who had spoken so sharply to her mother just now were nothing less than spiritual brothers of Simon Legree. She would answer them in kind, she would bring the audience to its feet in a chorus of "Hurrahs!" and "Hi's!"

"So you're not slave catchers, are you?" said beautiful Mary, drawing fire from Moses Barker's eyes, from the brutal whipping of Tom by Simon Legree, from her overwhelming desire to scream forth emotions she herself did not possess. "Then why do you call us abolitionists? Why do you stop decent people in front of their own homes? What do you know about my father, or my mother, other than that they are kind and giving and good to everyone? You monsters, get away from us, get away from us, or the wrath of God Himself will strike you down!" With this, the fledgling actress burst into tears, leaving her audience torn between laughter and remorse.

"What did I say, miss?" said one of the marshals. "I've only asked if your house is the house of the abolitionist—"

He stopped speaking, because Franklin Colson had removed his Colt revolver from under the driver's bench and had leveled it at the first man. "You. Show me your papers. Slowly."

"You can't go around pointing guns at federal marshals," he said.

"Franklin cocked the gun. "You've upset my dear friends," he said.

"I'm sorry for that, young man," said the second marshal. "But even an impartial man would see that we've said and done nothing wrong. It's not as if we've abducted you at gunpoint."

Mrs. Mann was the first to understand. "You're lying, aren't you? You're not federal marshals. You don't have papers."

"We are not exactly federal marshals, no. But we are working with the understanding of your local authorities, Mrs. Mann. Perhaps if you would ask the young man to lower his gun, I'll explain."

"Don't, Franklin," said Mary. "If they make a move, shoot them."

"They won't move," said Franklin.

"This is ridiculous. We're not even armed," said the first man. "Please, let me explain. We're looking for a runaway, yes, but we're not slave catchers. This isn't just a nigger. This is a killer. A big black killer, dangerous, a menace to all of us, and we're only doing our part. This has nothing to do with abolition. This has nothing to do with slavery."

"How much do you get for him?" said Mrs. Mann.

"We're not doing this for money, ma'am."

"You are both an affront to my eyes, and to the eyes of my daughter and our friend. Leave us. We have seen no runaway, and if we had we would never tell you about him anyway. Now go. Go before Franklin decides to shoot you."

They rode off quickly, and for a few moments no one spoke. Franklin finally returned the gun to its position under the driver's bench, and turned about to face Mrs. Mann. "Shall I drive on to the house?"

"Yes, thank you."

"Are you all right, Mary?" he asked.

"Yes." After a moment she added, "You were wonderful, Franklin." It was what she imagined the feeling must be between actors once the final curtain has come down.

Wilhelm Mann waited for them in front of the house, his walking stick cradled in his arms. He was blond-haired and blond-bearded, with pale skin and enormous brown eyes. It was easy to understand how Mary's mother had fallen in love with him, for all his rough clothes and awful accent. He had a commitment to liberty equal to his wife's, but he had none of her easy temper, her willingness to believe in the goodness inherent in human beings. Wilhelm Mann was more like an Old Testament figure, quick to damn, to shatter the tablets before an unworthy, restless people. And where Martha saw only what was best about her daughter, Wilhelm saw Mary's vanity, selfishness, and lust with perfect clarity. But Wilhelm saw more than this as well. He remembered his adolescence, arriving from Germany with an embittered old father, caring nothing for his parents' revolutionary ideas. All Wilhelm had wanted was to shed his accent, to be loved and accepted by his new country. And for a while his good looks, his charm and industry, his excellent English, led him to employment in the new manufacturing companies in Hartford, New Haven, and Bridgeport. At twenty, he was adept at business, and saw how factories would replace the shipping industry as the lifeblood of New England, and urged expansion and efficiency on his employers. But the money and the clothes and the pretty girls couldn't make up for the insults to his national origin, and to his growing sensitivity to corollary bigotries and hatreds—anti-Negro, anti-Irish, anti-Catholic, anti-Indian. He flirted with religion, joining the American Home Missionary Society, and at twenty-two he quit his job and went west to preach the gospel to Indians and immigrants. But Indians and immigrants alike proved disappointing. They had little fellow feeling, and less patience. The Indians wanted guns or liquor, while the immigrants wanted the Indians driven off their land, or dead. The exigencies of frontier life led him to put aside his bible for more practical matters—education, sanitation, fortification—and he fell afoul of the missionary authorities. In a month, he had returned to New England, to a loudly voiced disenchantment with organized religion, to meetings on behalf of salvaging the culture of the Indians, to lectures given by the most extreme of abolitionists; it was at an abolitionist meeting that he found Martha Williams, and fell in love with her. Even when Wilhelm Mann was at his most angry with Mary, he remembered his former attraction to business, to religion, to goals that would allow him to join the multitudes, rather than face their contempt. Martha had nourished and sustained his idealism; perhaps someone would bring their daughter's decency to the surface.

"Willy!" said Martha, jumping down from the carriage. "The freight got in early, and you weren't home—"

"Not so fast, dear," said her husband. He looked with deliberation at Franklin Colson, and then at his daughter. "Weren't these two to go to your rich relations today?"

"They helped me, Willy," said Martha. "Mary was wonderful, and Franklin was very brave. He pulled a gun on two slave catchers."

"What on earth are you talking about?" said Wilhelm Mann. "Come on, let's go in. I don't like to hear such things, not when you're too excited to make sense of it. Come into the house, all of you."

They sat in hard-backed chairs that had been in the house for more than eighty years; only Mary's maple rocker, made in Boston, and prettified with a simulated crotch-grained mahogany seat, was new. All sat facing the enormous cold hearth, the center of the house, and Wilhelm spoke toward it, as if addressing the ghost of John Collins.

"They attacked the Universalist Church an hour ago. It's been burned to the ground. No one was killed, but many were injured." Slowly, he turned his eyes to where Martha sat, and reemphasized it for her, so she would understand that there was nothing good to be gleaned from the information. "They were animals. Carr was speaking. He's not even an abolitionist —he's a Weld disciple, wants emancipation to be gradual, wants those inhuman flesh peddlers to be compensated for the loss of the human beings they will no longer own. Someone hit him with a bottle. I got the minister out of there, and even before everyone was outside, the place was in flames."

"How many were there?" said Martha.

"A mob. It's difficult to count a mob, but they were at least one hundred. They wore bandannas over their noses, some had on burned-cork blackface—I didn't recognize anyone. But most of them could have come from anywhere, from Norwalk, Bridgeport, anywhere."

"Perhaps," said his wife, "perhaps it will work against them. For them to have attacked a church—it might sicken people to the whole movement."

"No! Martha, listen—please," said Wilhelm. "For once, try and understand that there was nothing good about this. Bad people attacked good people, and bad people won the day."

"I think what Mother's saying," said Mary, "is that when they attack the church, abolition grows stronger, more defiant. And the pro-slavery people are made to look like fools."

"Not like fools, Mary, like murderers. And that doesn't help abolition, it hurts it." He was looking at her sharply, as if wondering why she was suddenly so interested in the rights of slaves. As if to reprove her, he added: "The troupe of players from New York that was going to put on *The Drunkard* here was thinking about putting on *Uncle Tom's Cabin*. They were at the meeting, two of them got hurt, one of them a woman, and now they're not the least bit interested in doing *Uncle*

Tom. They don't want to get killed. It's as simple as that."

Mr. Mann was not through lecturing either wife or daughter. Once again he hammered home his basic points: that the world would not grow meek and pleasant through meek and pleasant action. Right action meant striking back at bigotry and hatred with force. Garrison was right. If the Constitution supported slavery, tear up the Constitution. If the Union supported slavery, secede. If the Know-Nothing party swelled up in xenophobic strength, it was best to strike down the men of the party with fists as well as words.

"Is the play going to go on?"

"What?" said Mr. Mann. Mary had interrupted his tirade. He looked at her, as if coming back from another world. "Did you say something about a play?"

"I asked if the play is going to go on? It's scheduled for tomorrow at the Museum."

"First of all," said Mr. Mann, "it is not a museum, but a theater. If the good burghers of Safe Haven want to call their theater a museum, they may, but I won't, and neither will my child. Particularly since she is so anxious to join up with good-for-nothing actors. Second of all, how dare you interrupt me with such nonsense? When are you going to learn a sense of proportion?"

"I'm trying to fight, Father," she said, not at all bothered by his vehemence. "You were just saying how one must fight, not just talk. Well, what about *Uncle Tom?* Maybe it can still be put on, maybe I can help convince them—"

"Stop being foolish, Mary," said her mother, very kindly, reaching out to caress husband and daughter with her green eyes. "Your father and I have a lot to discuss. Perhaps you would like to help Franklin out of this hilarious atmosphere?"

"I am not being foolish," said Mary. "I wasn't foolish today, was I? Father says we should fight. I want to fight. Let's see to it that *Uncle Tom* gets put on in Safe Haven. It's put on in New York, it's put on all over the country. It's a disgrace that towns like ours can't put it on because they're afraid of the mobs."

"You don't understand," said Mr. Mann. "Plays don't amount to a blessed thing, and besides, no one's going to put it on, and no one is going to come to it."

"Of course they will," said Mary. She stood up, and Franklin got up at once. "I will see to that. I will volunteer my services. This is quite important, Father. Perhaps we can influence people, perhaps we can win more people for your way of thinking."

Mr. Mann tried to explain that he didn't think the same way that Harriet Beecher Stowe did. But he couldn't know that he was talking into the wind. Mary was riding a wave of confidence and strength that had begun in the carriage with Moses, and was leading her now to the ancient inn on Main Street, where George Washington had naturally slept, and where the players from New York, wounded and all, must be stopping. It was the only inn in town.

Mary left a few paces ahead of Franklin, who was still making his polite farewells to an oblivious Mr. and Mrs. Mann. Martha was anxious to discuss the situation of Moses in the asylum, the threat of bounty hunters and slave catchers visiting local abolitionists, the contribution that they must make at once for the reconstruction of the Universalist Church. Wilhelm wanted to spend the money elsewhere—to double their contribution to Garrison and his radical paper, demanding over and over again nothing less than freedom for slaves, regardless of the cost, regardless of the consequences. And perhaps they would discuss Mary, too: Was it possible that she was changing, maturing into a woman who cared for the rights of others?

"Do you know the play?" Mary asked Franklin once he had joined her on the narrow driver's bench of his carriage.

"What play? *The Drunkard*?"

"No, of course not. *Uncle Tom's Cabin*."

"I've read the book."

"Your parents never took you to New York to see it?"

"They wouldn't have to. I'm perfectly capable of doing that on my own. It wasn't so long ago that it was running. It's just that I hate the trip, it's such a bother, and really, I've read the book—it was quite good. But I've seen *The Drunkard*. That's some play. You'd make a fine Mary Wilson—you know, the girl whose husband starts to drink, and they're going to lose the house to that awful old lawyer. What was his name—Cribbs?"

"Of course it's Cribbs—Lawyer Cribbs," said Mary Mann. William Henry Smith's *The Drunkard* was probably the most popular play in New England, since its first appearance in Boston, in 1844. Mary had seen it at the Safe Haven Museum, at Boston's Museum, at New York City's Chatham Theater, and a year later at the Park Theater. She had seen it in Hartford and in Providence, and she had seen it four times at Fairlawn's Museum of Natural Phenomenae. Like any young woman of her interests, she knew Cribbs's famous line: "Nay, then, proud beauty, you shall know my power." And she remembered perfectly the famous speech of lovely Mary Wilson, when she thanks the hero for ejecting the villain from her presence: "The blessings of the widow and fatherless be upon thee; may they accompany thy voice to Heaven's tribunal, not to cry for vengeance but plead for pardon on this wretched man." The characters in the play were as familiar to her as the true-life characters of the Revolutionary War; and more true to her than the always cited characters of the bible.

"Come on," she said. "Let's go to the inn."

"The inn? What for? Do you want to forget about going to Fairlawn?"

"Of course I do," said Mary. "I want to see the troupe from New York."

Franklin didn't attempt to dissuade her. The last few hours seemed more like a dream than a part of his life. Imagine taking out his gun to two strangers, imagine helping a black murderer hide in an asylum for the insane! To simply walk into the inn and demand to see the actors—that seemed a trifle by comparison. As far as *why* Mary wanted to do this, he would no more question this than he would the setting of the sun.

In a few minutes they'd turned off the dirt road onto the beginning of Safe Haven's Main Street, one tiny link in the chain of Main Streets and country roads that made up the hundred-year-old route from Boston to New York. They were still a half mile from the business district, but Main Street was already distinct from the surrounding network of dirt roads leading through woods and farmland. Here the street was planked with tarred wood, and citified gas lamps began to line the road at shorter and shorter intervals.

Unlike neighboring Fairlawn, which had begun around a church and been settled by a homogeneous group, Safe Haven had developed haphazardly. John Collins, a trapper, not a preacher, had been its first "citizen." The waterfront had been its centerpiece, not the Congregational Church. Three-year trips to China, to the Pacific whaling seas, had fueled the community's ardor, not a new religious tract or a better way to harvest crops. But since the War of 1812, Safe Haven had lost some of its roughness. While it was still considered "odd" by its neighboring communities, most of which had been founded, like Fairlawn, around a preacher and his church, it had begun to have the appearance, if not the history, of all the prosperous towns of the county.

The planked road gave way to cobblestones, just at the point where the sheriff's residence stood, a freshly painted wood structure with a wide front porch, and a hitching post. Franklin asked Mary if she'd like to stop there for a moment, just to tell the sheriff about the men who'd stopped them on the road, pretending to be federal marshals. But Mary had only one desire then, one impulse so strong that she could barely name it to herself. Her father had said a woman had been injured, an actress. What if she could get a chance to play a part, even if only in Safe Haven's tiny theater?

The cobblestones always lent a feeling of stateliness, of civilization, to the ride along the best part of Main Street. It reminded her of New York and Boston, of two-thousand-seat theaters with one-dollar box seats and twelve-and-one-half-cent back-gallery seats. They passed a lawyer's tiny office building, a modest drugstore owned by Germans, then the stables and adjacent lumberyard. Up ahead there was a little traffic—surprising on a Sunday—but then they saw that it came from the village green, where men and women in their Sunday best were coming from a meeting in the Congregational Church.

"It must be about the burning," said Franklin. "It's not meeting time."

"Do you think they care about the Universalists?"

"I'm sure Reverend Row does," said Franklin seriously. "You can say what you will about the Universalists, but they're still Christians, and Reverend Row has said that more than once. Perhaps they're raising money, to help them."

"Perhaps they're taking up a collection to ride them all out of town," said Mary. Her mother had belonged to the Universalist Church for a while; her father had actually been born a Catholic, though few people in Safe Haven knew that. It was always taken for granted that a former member of the American Missionary Society, a member by marriage of the old Williams family, must have been born in Protestant Germany. But neither parent had a thing to do with any church now, except to use their pulpits for lecturing on the evils of slavery. Mary had never been forbidden to go to church, but once the novelty of going there as a child with her schoolfriends had worn off, she was happy to be allowed to stay home, earning herself another mark of disapprobation from the community at large—and the envy of her less religiously inclined classmates.

Just beyond the church was the most imposing building in town: the courthouse. Very little of significance took place in the gorgeous brick structure. Fairlawn was the county seat, and its courthouse—built in Gothic style but of plebeian wood—tried most of the important cases in the area. But Safe Haven's courthouse was a mark of pride and prosperity. Few towns as small as Safe Haven, with its population of three thousand, could boast of such a grand place for a town meeting, or for a lawsuit between neighboring farmers, one of whose pigs had eaten up his neighbor's vegetable garden.

"May I ask how you propose to get to these people?" said Franklin. "I understand that they never like to be bothered by the townspeople. They need their rest for rehearsal and traveling from place to place."

"I shall tell them that I'm an actress," said Mary.

The theater—the Safe Haven Museum—was separated from the very old inn by a barbershop and a bookdealer. In a town that was otherwise shut down on the Sabbath, inn, barbershop, and bookdealer were a meeting place for those with something other than prayer on their mind. The bookdealer also sold rail and steamship tickets, and lent out books without discussing the rental fee until Sunday was over. The barbershop was open, because even the religious needed to look their best in the house of God, and though most of the shaving took place in the early morning hours, tradition allowed the shop to stay open, a meeting place for the tobacco chewers and newspaper readers.

As for the inn, everything could be gotten there on Sunday that one could get there all week; even whiskey was obtainable, quietly.

The rest of the cobblestoned road went on for a half mile past the theater. Here were the all-important general store, with its built-in post office, and staff of five full-time clerks; the two-room schoolhouse, with its fireplace as large as the one built by John Collins; the rickety old Lyceum, formerly used by theatrical troupes, but since the building of the Museum a place for lectures, fraternal meetings, and abolitionist calls to action; and then farther out, toward the end of town, the mayor's brick house, and a half mile past this, once again on the planked road, the home and workshop of the blacksmith.

But Franklin hadn't continued on the road, much as he would have liked to. Five miles away they'd be in Fairlawn; and driving up into the hilly section of brick Georgian mansions overlooking the Sound, they could be at Mary's uncle's home, enjoying the handsome setting, the beautiful clothes, the polite conversation of the wealthy. There, he would know how to talk, know how to lead. On the way home, in the dark, he would be able to kiss the beautiful girl at his side. And she, in turn, would have found in him something exciting, strong. Now, tying up in front of the carefully preserved inn, he felt as if he were sliding into quicksand. Actors were fast, handsome, clever. He had no equipment to deal with them. They would find Mary beautiful, of course, and she would find them fascinating. No one would think of him or notice him, except perhaps to make fun.

They were serving tea in the larger of half a dozen dining rooms on the ground floor of the inn when Mary and Franklin entered. Like her own house, the inn had been added on to for many years; there were rooms where two could dine, and one where thirty could. These were separated by heavy walls that had once been part of the exterior.

"Miss Mann, Mr. Colson!" said the innkeeper, coming to greet them with alacrity. Franklin's father often used the public rooms for business meetings, and put up visitors at the inn at his company's expense. And Mary's parents used the small assembly room for gatherings less volatile than calls for secession from the slave states. He would have pulled them into a pretty little room, poured them tea in delicate china cups, and gossiped with them until they made it clear that they wished to be alone. But Mary had hardly entered the inn when she caught the eye of a broad-shouldered, black-haired man with an extravagantly knotted red silk tie—on the Lord's day!—who looked at her as if trying to remember where he had last seen her. And then, to Franklin's dismay, the man spoke, his voice a magical projection of power and grace:

" 'She's beautiful and therefore to be woo'd, / She is a woman, therefore to be won.' "

"Do you know this man?" said Franklin with automatic gravity. But Mary didn't answer him. She took a step closer to the actors' table. An old man with a wig looked at her through spectacles; a middle-aged woman with a double chin turned deliberately from her approach to contemplate her cake plate; and the handsome man with the powerful voice rose and pulled out a chair.

"Ordinarily, I would not be so forward with a young woman I've never seen. But this is no ordinary day. We could have been killed. One must enjoy life when one is able, and your presence would be enjoyable to all of us. I am Charles Keats. May I introduce Mrs. Robinson, Mr. Parsil. Please, your friend too, he must join us as well. Innkeeper!"

"Was that *Henry the Fifth?*" said Mary.

"*Henry the Sixth*, I'm sure you mean—part one, in fact. My dear, when one has performed Shakespeare in Lowell, Worcester, Bangor, and Belfast, not to mention Lockport, Fredonia, Cahawaba, Columbus, and Canandaigua, it's quite a simple matter to remember the best lines from the best plays. And necessary, too. There are so many times when one must wing it. But you haven't told me your name?"

"Mary Mann," she said, and she turned around to motion over Franklin, who joined the large table, placing his gentleman's hands on its surface, waiting to be insulted for his lack of wit. The innkeeper brought old Mr. Parsil some more whiskey, and freshly brewed tea for the others.

"I like the name," said Charles Keats. "Very theatrical. Are you in the theater?"

"No," said Franklin. Keats was indecently handsome, with long aristocrat's fingers, a pretty mouth, deep-set brown eyes.

He was certainly as old as thirty, perhaps as old as thirty-five.

"I would like to be in the theater," said Mary. "I've wanted to be in the theater all my life."

"You poor child," said Mrs. Robinson. "All your life to be pining away for a chance to tread the boards."

"She probably doesn't mean all her life," said old Mr. Parsil, sipping his whiskey. His voice was preternaturally smooth, and though he spoke softly, every syllable he uttered could be heard from any corner of the large room. "Probably only since she saw her first play, she means. Junius Brutus Booth doing Lear. Or Charley's Romeo. He's quite a Romeo, in point of fact. It would be enough to make any young girl join the local thespians. What's the name of this town?"

"Safe Haven," said Franklin, a hint of anger in his voice. They were mocking her.

"The Safe Haven Thespian Corps!" said Mrs. Robinson. "Have you got it? Is that your troupe? Do you play the Lyceum whenever there's a county fair?"

"There's no thespian group in Safe Haven," said Mary. "Only professionals play here. And that's what I want to be. And I will be, even if you think it's funny. I know I can act. I'm only here because I thought you might need some help. My father said that some of your group was injured."

"Don't be absurd, my dear Miss Mann," said Mr. Parsil. "No matter what happens to us, we go on. Even with a broken leg, without an hour's sleep, without even any knowledge of the play—we go on."

"Julie is hurt," said Charley Keats.

"Charley!" said Mrs. Robinson. "She's only sleeping off her drunk."

"She was hit in the head," said Charley. "It wouldn't be the only time an amateur stepped in for a professional."

"What are you talking about? This child isn't an actress. Julie is going to be up and around. Charley, I'm not going to put up with it this time. If you and Miss Mann want to walk along the river and discuss the art of acting, that's fine—but this is not your troupe. It's ours together, and we're not going to make fools of ourselves."

"Are you quite through?" said Charley to Mrs. Robinson.

"Oh, Charley . . ." she said, but she had already given in.

"I have not had two words between myself and Miss Mann, and already you are imagining me casting her for the tour. I haven't even heard her perform."

"Listen to him," said Mrs. Robinson to Mr. Parsil. "He's doing it. He's really doing it." She shrugged and turned to look at Mary. "You'd be lovely in the tableaux. Very pretty you are, very pretty indeed."

"What are your speeches?" said Mr. Parsil.

"I have no speeches, sir," said Mary.

"Of course you have speeches," insisted the old man with the smooth voice. "You surely know Juliet, you surely know Mary Wilson, you surely know Eliza."

"Don't mention Eliza—please," said Charley Keats. "Old Eliza nearly got us killed today. What a crazy town. What insanity. Have you heard about the Universalist Church, Mr. Colson?"

"Yes, sir," said Franklin.

"In a crazy moment, I had agreed to put on *Uncle Tom's Cabin* here, after we'd let the town see *The Drunkard* for the five hundredth time. They kill you for that here, I didn't realize. I've played *Tom* in Texas, I've played *Tom* with *slaves* in the audience. And here, in New England, with no slaves, no cotton plantations, they burn down the church and damn near kill everyone for even mentioning antislavery."

"Don't say that, sir," said Franklin.

"I beg your pardon?"

"You've used a word that should not be mentioned in the presence of ladies, sir. I don't mean to be disrespectful, just to remind you."

"What the hell word was that—'damn,' do you mean?"

"Franklin, please," said Mary.

"I just don't like that sort of behavior," said Franklin.

"If you don't like it, you can leave then," she said. "I came here to see these people, and I won't have you confuse all my affairs."

Franklin stood up, suddenly furious. He wanted to hit handsome Charley Keats, but he'd have much preferred to hit Mary. "You can talk to me that way after what we've gone through today? It's scarcely possible that you can act this way."

"I want to be an actress," said Mary.

"Very well, then," said Franklin. "You may explain to your parents why it is that I didn't take you home." He took out his billfold to pay for the tea, but Charley Keats held up his hand and insisted that it wasn't necessary. "I would prefer it if you let me pay," said Franklin.

"We accept graciously, young man," said Mr. Parsil.

Franklin paid and left, ignoring the innkeeper's question as to the state of health of his father.

"Your parents," said Charley Keats after a long pause. "They won't object to your being parted from your companion?"

"My parents," said Mary slowly, looking up at his pretty-featured face with her own hard beauty, "object to nothing but slavery, prejudice, xenophobia, war, disease, and stupidity. To think about my coming home with or without an escort would never occur to them, never. It's just not worth their time."

"Well, my dear Miss Mann," said Charley, "if that is the case, perhaps you'd be good enough to show me the local theater. I mean museum, of course. The Safe Haven Museum." He didn't wait for an answer. He stood up, very tall, expecting to be admired. Mary got up as well, quite pleased that she wasn't smitten by the man. He wasn't after all, Edwin Forrest or William Macready, for whose rivalry twenty-two people had died in the Astor Place Riot of 1849. He wasn't a Booth either, not the famous father or the two young sons, both Edwin and John Wilkes reputed to be amazingly handsome, though neither had as yet any reputation as an actor. No, he was simply a handsome rake, very pleased with every word he uttered, every gesture he made. Mary was not in awe of him, and not afraid of him either. She wanted the world of the theater, but she had enough experience with life to know what was significant and what was not.

The Safe Haven Museum exhibited a dozen stuffed birds, several display cases of locally discovered Indian arrowheads, and an unspectacular specimen of native carving from the Fiji Islands. Most Museumgoers never noticed these items; like many other theaters in New England, the Safe Haven Museum was so named and so sprinkled with worthless trinkets simply to take the onus off its true function. The Puritans had closed English theaters two centuries before, and to this day the idea of players and plays, costumes and props and stage and stage lighting, was redolent of idleness, of sin. All the "museums" had "exhibition halls," the ostensible reason for their construction. They were theaters except for the stuffed birds in their lobbies, theaters in everything but name; even church deacons could attend the plays, so long as they were properly Bowdlerized and staged in a museum. Though all this was well known to Charley Keats and to Mary, he couldn't help mocking the system, simply to show off his wit and daring.

"These are marvelous birds," he said, once they'd walked over from the inn and entered through the unlocked front door. "Quite rare, I'm sure. Visitors must come from all around the world to see these treasures."

"These birds are as likely to get foreign visitors as your production of *The Drunkard* is," said Mary.

"Well said, Miss Mann," said Charley, caressing her with his histrionic voice. "Would you care to show me the rest of this marvelous opera house?"

"Why did you ask me to show you this place at all?" said Mary, standing her ground before the stuffed birds. "You knew what you'd find here. Are you actually so eager to see the stage you're going to see tomorrow anyway?"

"No," he said, his eyes glistening with villainous intensity. He seemed to believe himself in a play at that moment, and she recognized this, recognized its falseness, but didn't care. This was what she wanted, this power to change your mood, your skin, the shape of your eyes, the quality of your soul. "I wanted to see you alone on the stage. To look at you without the others."

"Fine," she said.

The April afternoon cast enough light into the exhibition hall to outline the two hundred-odd chairs. There were no boxes, no gallery, no pit. The amateur orchestra that played for the complaining touring companies usually consisted of four pieces, grouped in a dark corner of the stage. A huge chandelier, famous for dripping hot wax on the actors, hung over the stage's midpoint, and more efficient gas footlights ringed the stage's outer edge.

"Do you know how to get to the backstage?"

"Yes," she said, not at all worried about when he'd try to grab her, to force his fake passion on her unreceptive frame. Mary took him through a back door and up a pitch-black stairwell, groping for a lamp at the head of the stairs. She found it finally and asked him to light it, and he brushed against her, slowly and deliberately, but she didn't recoil. He struck a match and lit the lamp, and she asked him whether it was true that actors could go to the theaters in New York City free of charge, and always in the best seats. Charley smiled and explained that actors were welcome almost everywhere, but most especially in the theater.

"And did you ever see Booth?"

"See him? I've played with the old man. What a bastard." Charley put the lamp on a low table and followed her into the wings. She stuck her head out from behind the upstage curtain and turned around to look at the actor.

"But was he really that good?"

"Yes," said Charley. "Drunk, crazy, abusive—but the best." Even in the dim light she could sense his reverence for the actor, dead for three years. For a moment he had stopped pretending, had ceased building his speechless scene of love. "His King Lear. He was not acting, he had become the king. It was that simple. He was a terrible man, but there was no one who could touch him. He was terrible to work with, but it didn't matter a damn. We all watched him, just like the audience."

"And Lola Montez?"

"She's not an actress, just a whore—but beautiful—my God, more beautiful than any of her pictures. What else do you want to know? Who's better, Macready or Forrest? I say Forrest, but what difference does it make?" Charley came closer now, and took her hand. "There's a big world out there. Even the biggest actors can't be in New York and Boston the same night. There's work out there for those that know how to get it—there are towns like this one just as anxious to see a show as the high livers in New York. There's fourteen in our troupe. Do you want to give me a speech now—just to see?"

"Let go of my hands, Mr. Keats," said Mary. The actor smiled, as if to show his power over her, and let go. At once, Mary walked through the upstage curtain and onto the little stage of the Safe Haven Museum's exhibition hall. Keats watched her from the wings, in profile, by the light from the high windows of the hall. It had begun to drizzle. Mary froze into a pose—an immobile portrait of grief. Of the many scenes she had committed to memory, there was only one she was burning to do at that moment: Eliza, the mulatto slave girl, about to flee with her infant from bondage. Charley Keats knew that *Uncle Tom's Cabin* was a dreadful play; he was not insensitive to the poetry of Shakespeare's lines, even if he did not often do them justice. Still, he understood what the public wanted, and why they loved the melodramas of the day. Mary, playing to the empty house, was at all times posturing, demanding affection, begging for the crowd's attention. Never for a moment did she enter into the life of the paper-thin character; she remained always the beautiful blonde New England girl, portraying a mulatto for the purpose of sympathy and applause. But Charley knew what her effect would be on the audience. She would be an absurd Juliet, but with dusky make-up and black wig, she would be an enchanting Eliza. The house would respond to her request for love. They would give it to her, they would clap their hands and stomp their feet; and for a few moments at least, the men would cease spitting tobacco juice onto the floor, and even their women might quit cracking and spitting peanut shells.

When she had finished, he approached her from behind and put his hands on her shoulders. "Wonderful," he lied.

"Do you say that because you want to kiss me?"

"Yes," he said, and he turned her about and drew her to him, but Mary stiffened at the last moment, smiling her actress's smile.

"Will I have a part while your troupe is here?"

"We go on tomorrow."

"I know the play."

"We're not doing *Uncle Tom*."

"I know *The Drunkard*. If your Mary Wilson is injured, let me be your Mary Wilson."

"You can't learn the part in a day."

"I know the part."

"Perhaps you know the words." But she was smiling into his objections. She was happy to see real frustration enter into his artificial smile. He wanted her, and she was holding back, and Mary would make him do her bidding.

"I will work very hard," she said. "With your help, I can wing it." Charley smiled at her use of the theatrical phrase, derived from the wings of the theater, where the actors waited to go on stage. The true professionals, like old Mr. Parsil, like himself, often took over a part at the last minute, without any rehearsal, without knowing any lines by heart. Waiting in the wings, they would skim through the playbook, trying to make sense of their character while listening for their cue. When they went on, there was nothing to do but improvise, create a speech on the spur of the moment, based on stock speeches from a score of melodramas—pasting together tried and true words of menace, love, horror, as the sense of the scene demanded. And when the scene was mercifully over, they'd rush back to the wings and pick up the playbook where they'd stashed it and once again rush through the coming scenes, listening for the next cue.

"With my help," said Charley. "Yes." And he shut his eyes, and she allowed the kiss, only a tender brushing of lips, her heart as relaxed as his. "You're very beautiful," he said.

"You too, Charley," said Mary Mann. "But I'll only go on in *The Drunkard* if you promise to put on *Uncle Tom* at the end of the week."

"You'll only *what?*" said the actor, pushing her away as if she were on fire. But Mary held on to him, and looked at him promisingly in the lamplight. After a moment, he said: "*Uncle Tom!* You really had me there, for a moment. I thought you meant it. You're something, beauty. You're some special kind of girl." Then she initiated the kiss, and it was nothing like his. She remembered Moses Barker, how he had loved his wife, and how he had murdered to avenge her. No, acting meant nothing unless it was strong, unless it broke apart old feelings, swept up antique ways of thinking, unless it carried the weight of madness. Mary Mann would never be an actress in a nation about to pull itself apart, unless that acting was as strong as the love, the hatred, the urge for justice threatening to explode at any moment in every city and town. And so she kissed Charley Keats, handsome actor, a ladies' man on the troupers' circuit, and he found himself moved, he found himself forgetting his lines, he found himself as wild as any spectator before the most passionate scene in a powerful play.

SEVENTEEN

———◈———

Mary walked home in the light drizzle as darkness blew over Main Street like puffs of black clouds over the gas lamps. The damp made its inexorable way through her solid Connecticut-made soles, and by the time she'd trudged the length of the cobblestoned road and begun the slippery tarred boards of the less civilized section of the street, she was soaked. Still, she quite enjoyed the walk. Three times she refused the offer of a ride from neighbors, enjoying the shadows cast by the gas lamps, the play of colors sent by the yellow light through wet glass. The wet air was fresh, as cleansing as the fact of spring, as enticing as the sense of a new career.

Keats hadn't given her a part, of course; that was too much to expect. But she would be allowed backstage tomorrow night, and perhaps during the week would be given a nonspeaking part in the curtain raiser that preceded *The Drunkard*. That was enough for her at the moment. She knew that she would be called on to do more, that their ingenue would be unable to go on as Mary Wilson, that somehow the company would perform *Uncle Tom*, and she would be Eliza. This was not simply blind optimism, nor was it a belief in her ability to read the future. Mary Mann was one of those people for whom the description "intuitive" must always be inadequate; she felt herself not actively searching for something that was about to happen, but rather open, relaxed, easy enough to accept the messages about her. When she walked the dark road, leaving Main Street and its lamps for the muddy thread of ground connecting the farms and houses near her home, she wasn't apprehensive. Danger had a way of signaling her. She wasn't nervous without cause, and usually her optimism proved to be an accurate presage of events. There had never been any doubt that she'd go on the stage; she felt the inevitability, she was open to the voices about her. It was not clear how, or when, or why. She could no more predict a successful career than she could fashion it out of the electricity in the air; but she could sense what was coming, and more often than not, what was coming would signal her. Her father had explained that what she described was unscientific, childish nonsense founded on whimsy and wishes and luck. If men accosted her on the road, and she was unafraid because she sensed that no harm would come, what did that prove? She simply wished to be let alone, and was, and ought to leave it at that, rather than trying to believe she had read the future. If she wanted to get a part in a play, and her good looks and assertiveness had landed her a seat backstage, it was likewise as foolish to imagine that she knew this would take place. In abandoning religion, her father had abandoned everything that was not logical, quantifiable, devoid of intangible guideposts.

"What about justice, Father?" Mary had asked him. "What's logical about justice?" And when he had attempted to explain about the social contract between human animals, Mary had stopped listening. He was not open to her way, and she would not be open to his.

The drizzle had almost stopped as she neared the front door of her home, and the hour's walk, at a brisk pace, had warmed her damp body. But her future in the theater, and her father, and the bowl of chowder that she'd soon be wolfing down, were suddenly forgotten. Mary felt danger, and it was coming from the house, the old house so full of memories and spirits and desires.

She walked to the front door, selected by Tom Williams's

mother before her death in 1751, and opened it as quietly as she could. Leah, the lordly black servant, hurried up to her with a grim face.

"Go to your room, girl," she said.

"You can't order me about," said Mary, but speaking softly, like Leah. The servant took hold of the girl she'd looked after since she was a baby and held her.

"You ain't going in there, there's trouble, girl," said Leah.

"Call me 'Miss Mary,' not 'girl.' You get worse all the time. Now let me go, or so help me, I'll scream."

"If you scream, I'll brain you, honey," said Leah. She was pulling Mary to the stairway when the sound of furious voices erupted about them. Two men were being ushered out of the small parlor, the room with the great hearth, and pushed into the hall occupied by Leah and Mary.

"Move, don't drag your feet!" Mary's father was saying, his slightly accented voice picking up an unfamiliar Germanic rhythm. "I want you out, and out now. Don't answer me back! Go!"

One of the men was the sheriff of Safe Haven, and his embarrassed eyes met Mary's in the hallway. The man with him was one of the two false federal marshals who had stopped their carriage that day. He was not embarrassed. His lips were tightly closed, and everything about him suggested danger, enmity, rancor. "Don't dawdle, you heard Mr. Mann," said Leah.

"Shut your black mouth, nigger," said the false marshal, and Leah let go of Mary long enough to slap the man across the face. She hit him with enough force to send him into the wall, and the man was so astonished that he swung back at once, not thinking. His fist grazed the black woman's chin.

"Sheriff, get him out of here," said Mr. Mann, his big bulk taking over the hallway. He took hold of the false marshal as he spoke, holding him by both shoulders. "You are not wanted here, neither of you, but you are still a man of law, at least in theory. Get this bounty hunter out of here."

"I am not a bounty hunter," said the man.

"Are you all right, Leah?" said Mary, reaching for the maid.

"Sure, child," said Leah. She was turned to Mary, and now

she turned about, to where the sheriff stood next to the false marshal, with Mr. Mann's powerful hands on the man, holding him in place. Leah didn't hesitate this time either. She swung her booted toe into the man's shin with all her force, and then she hit him in the face with the flat of her hand. She grabbed his long hair and pulled him, and Mr. Mann let go of him, and the sheriff didn't do a thing to hinder her fury. "You don't call me a nigger, slave-catching trash. You don't come where you ain't wanted, or you'll die the next time. Open the door, child."

Leah wasn't strong enough to push the man out the front door, but Mary helped. She felt the man's fury, his danger, and ignored it. Whatever she did now would make no difference in the way she'd be treated by the man in the future. He would loathe her, and if it was in his power, he would harm her. She pushed at the man from behind, she kicked into the backs of his bent knees, and she howled at him, more demonic than Leah. He fell across the threshold and out into the muddy night.

"Now you, Sheriff," said Mr. Mann.

"I'm sorry for all this trouble," said the sheriff, "but I'm here in the name of the law." He walked out quickly, and Leah shut the heavy door.

"Come in here," said Mr. Mann to both of them, not bothering to comment on their action. He turned about and walked quickly to the hearth room, where Mrs. Mann sat white-faced, knitting a sweater for the town's clothing drive. "Leah, you heard?"

"Yes, sir."

"What is it, Father?" said Mary.

Mr. Mann smiled thinly. "You mean you don't know? I thought your intuition would have told you."

"It did. I know there's trouble. And it's not intuition."

"There won't be trouble if we use our heads, dear," said Mrs. Mann, looking up from her knitting. "The sheriff is simply a cowardly sort, he's not a bad man—"

"Martha, please—he *is* a bad man," said her husband. "I wish you'd at least acknowledge that. Things do get bad. People are not only driven by circumstance, some of them are just bastards, and that's the truth."

"Would someone please tell me?" said Mary.

"They know Moses is in Safe Haven," said Mr. Mann.

"How do they know that? Did they see us? Do they know where he is?"

"No," said Mrs. Mann. "All they think is that we took him, but nobody saw us do it."

"But what did they want here? Are we in trouble? If they didn't see us take him, how do they know where he is?"

"Sit down, Mary," her father said, and when she'd taken possession of the rocker in her wet clothes, he explained. There was a good deal of private money and public fury chasing the fugitive. He was not simply a runaway, but a murderer, regardless of the extenuating circumstances. The Mann family didn't find him guilty of anything, but that didn't prevent the federal government from waking up to pursue the man. Moses Barker was a political issue, more than a criminal case. If the federal government had been occasionally lax in going after runaways, it could not be seen to be lax in chasing a runaway who had murdered. There were elements in the South who were beginning to beat the drums about this case, to scream about the North's complicity in allowing a murdering slave to go free; and there were elements in the North who were determined not to let this happen. Even among the conductors of the Underground Railroad, men could be found who wanted Moses apprehended. Someone had spoken of the route to Safe Haven, possibly for money, possibly out of a desire to see the man caught and the furor ended. The sheriff had come to them because they were known abolitionists, certain to be involved with the runaway if he'd actually gotten to Safe Haven, as his information stated.

"What do they think, then?" said Mary. "Do they think we've hidden him away?"

"I don't think the sheriff really cares," said Mrs. Mann. "I think he was just going through the motions because he had no real choice. We told him he couldn't search the house, and he didn't put up a fuss—not too bad, anyway."

"So they'll search the house another day," said her husband.

"That's fine, dear, since Moses is not *in* the house."

Leah interrupted, still standing in the corner of the room. "The child is soaking wet. I'll put up some chowder. You'd better get out of those clothes, Mary."

"You're right, Leah. She is wet," said Mrs. Mann, reaching out to touch Mary. Mr. Mann continued with his explanation and instructions, as if the state of Mary's clothes were not worthy of mention. "Why are you wet, child?" interrupted Mrs. Mann.

"I would like to finish," said Mr. Mann. "I want Mary to understand, and I want you to understand also, just precisely what we are up against."

"We both understand," said Mrs. Mann. "You really must give Mary more credit sometimes, my dear. And Leah is right, of course. She really must get out of those clothes."

Mary finally went upstairs to change. The rain had gone through the first two layers of petticoats, but not the third. She left the clothes without thought on the patch of bare floor between the area rugs in her large room, and brushed out her hair in the spotty old mirror. Her image allowed her to forget about sheriffs, runaways, laws. She remembered Charley Keats, and how she had commanded him with her theatrical kiss. Soon she would be on the stage, not only in Safe Haven, but in New York, on Broadway. A great anonymous sea of humanity would rise out of their places in the dark to acknowledge her, to applaud the way in which she'd moved them, the artistry with which she'd taken them to another world.

"Mary, child," said her mother, opening the door to her room. "Soup is almost ready. Are you all right?"

"Yes."

"Not worried about all this? Moses, I mean?"

"No," said Mary.

"Your father wanted me to explain. There is the fact that we are accomplices—accessories—we've helped a fugitive. That's against the law."

"You don't think they'd send us to jail?" said Mary, her voice calm, her eyes smiling. She knew perfectly well that such a thing was impossible. Even as she spoke, she felt the clear waves of the future before her. There would be the stage, there would be triumphs, there would be disasters in love and marriage; but there would be no jail.

"No," said Mrs. Mann. "They won't catch us. No one knows except Moses, and he won't talk, and of course they'd have to find him first. Dr. Marandino at the asylum could tell, but I trust him. He owes us a good deal—though that's not the reason I trust him. I think he's a good man. And Franklin. Of course he's a good young man, a very strong character. He's antislavery, even with that father of his. So there's really not that much to worry about, though they will certainly be looking after us. To try to catch us out. We mustn't underestimate them, especially those bounty hunters. Men are so often ruined by the love of money."

"I'm going to be in a play, Mother."

"What did you say, dear—a play?"

Mary told her, with some exaggeration—she would be part of the professional troupe of actors while they were here in Safe Haven. With any luck she would go on, have a good part, perhaps play in *Uncle Tom's Cabin*. Any other mother in Safe Haven would have been appalled at this revelation—her maiden daughter ready to sacrifice her good name on the stage. But Mrs. Mann was already drifting, her lips rising into a steady smile. There was something here, an idea, a chance to do good.

"How big is the company?"

"Well, there's fourteen, I understand. I would be the fifteenth."

"No free blacks, I suppose?"

"Well, I don't know. They don't advertise that way. I would imagine they don't have, it would be quite unusual, don't you think?" Mary started. "What is it, Mother? You want me to do something, don't you?"

"I must consult with your father."

"Tell me. Please."

Mrs. Mann hesitated, not because she didn't trust her daughter, or because she didn't think Mary would do what was right and good, but simply because she hadn't brought a plan together in her mind. "Look," she said. "Perhaps you can help. With Moses. I have to speak with your father. You wouldn't be afraid to be alone with him, with Moses?"

"No," said Mary, though she felt the danger as soon as she spoke. Not the danger of guns and jails, but something indefinable, eerie.

"Tell me, would you go to the asylum? Perhaps with Franklin? To deliver a message, or check up on him? I want to speak to Dr. Marandino, but I would think we might be watched, your father and myself more than you." Mrs. Mann paused. "It's good about the theater. I'm very pleased. They will forget about you, the bounty hunters. No one will be dogging your footsteps."

"I hope that's not the only reason you're pleased about the theater," said Mary. "You know how important it is to me. I'd like to think that you, if not Father, would be proud of me for getting a part on the stage, with real actors."

"I think it's good that you have such strong convictions, dear," said Mrs. Mann. "But I'm sure that a girl with your heart will not remain in the theater forever. There are too many other things in the world that you will be drawn to. But I'm proud that you're independent and courageous, and I wouldn't have expected anything less."

It was not the answer that Mary wanted to hear, but she wasn't upset by it. Her mother had flattered her, even as she had belittled her aspirations. And she needed her. This was something momentous in the Mann household. It had been unusual enough for her mother to have drawn her and Franklin into a "freight collection" on the Underground Railroad. But there was to be more now, something daring perhaps. The danger was not displeasing, because it contained a foretaste of approbation. She returned to the mirror and her beautiful image, and when Leah brought her the chowder, she accepted the maid's unusual kindliness toward her as her due.

Backstage at the Safe Haven Museum's exhibition hall was not the high point of Mary Mann's life. She was amused, of course, by the sudden changes in expression of the actors as they wandered through the upstage exit, their angry looks turning placid, their amorous cries cut off in stupefied grimaces two steps into the wings. Charley Keats looked even more handsome in his stage make-up and padded jacket, his chiseled features nightmarishly attractive in the gaslights. Julie, the actress who'd been slightly injured during the riot at the Universalist Church, was as pretty as Charley was handsome; she was a wonderful Mary Wilson in *The Drunkard*, bringing the tiny audience to their feet twice before the second act. Mary found the slightly tipsy Mr. Parsil the most amusing of all, waiting for his latest comments every time he exited and caught her eye backstage. "I wonder," he said at one point, unhappy with the audience's reception of his last speech, "who took the trouble to pull all those corpses into the theater and set them up tall in their seats."

As it were, there weren't too many bodies, live or dead, making their way into the theater. *The Drunkard* had been seen by nearly everyone over the age of five in the state of Connecticut, and the troupe contained no major actors. Too, there were meetings going on that week that concerned the attention of the public: meetings to raise money for the Universalist Church; meetings to denounce the influx of foreigners into the town; meetings to denounce the excesses of abolitionist activity. When Mary Mann was allowed to go on the second night the troupe performed, she was one of five bewigged and powdered women being chased about by a clown on wooden stilts in the curtain raiser before the start of *The Drunkard*, and only her deep sense of destiny allowed her to view the experience as magical and lovely. Long before *The Drunkard* was over, she was thoroughly bored with watching it from the wings. Even Charley Keats's absurd posturing could no longer amuse her. There was no talk of Julie's needing a replacement, nor of the troupe's putting on *Uncle Tom*. Charley asked her again if she'd like to have a private drink with him after the show. If not for her clear vision of magnificent parts in enormous theaters in the great capitals of the world, she'd have burst into tears; she'd have allowed herself the normal reaction of a twenty-year-old to a vast disappointment. But even backstage, or perhaps *especially* backstage, she was acting: She was the undiscovered great actress, momentarily buried in a backwater. It was really quite a wonderful part, quite insulated from the reality of the moment, turned only toward the future of bliss.

"Miss Mann?" said a young boy she recognized from town. He was all of twelve, and very much in awe of the costumed men and women backstage. "Mr. Colson says I should give you

this. He's outside waiting, Miss Mann." He gave her a folded
bit of paper, and turned on his heels and ran off, colliding with
beams, actors, and the badly lit back wall. The note was terse:
"Urgent that you leave, as soon as possible. Not for me, but for
your parents, and I shall wait out back until you come."

Mary asked Charley if she could leave, but he was almost
ready to go back on and couldn't pay attention to her. Mr.
Parsil was more sympathetic. "Got a young man waiting?" he
said. "Go ahead. We don't need you till tomorrow. You looked
good in the farce. Another year or two they'll let you say something onstage at the same time. Don't forget you owe us three
dollars—tomorrow."

Mary laughed at this last barb as she rushed outside, still in
her make-up, but in her street clothes. Not only was she not
being paid for her tiny role in the farce—payment would come
later, they assured her, for bigger roles—but she had to pay for
the adjustments and maintenance of the costume she'd worn
that night. As Charley Keats, Mrs. Robinson, and Mr. Parsil
split the management chores and fees of the troupe, she felt
especially chagrined at their treatment. Perhaps the costume's
adjustment and maintenance fee would vanish if she allowed
Charley Keats his "private drink."

She found the carriage quickly behind the Museum, and
hoped that Franklin hadn't seen her performance in the farce.
Without a word, she let herself up onto the driver's bench, and
smiled at him in the dark night.

"What's on your face?"

"Stage make-up," she said. "It's to look good onstage under
the lights." She paused, feeling his anger, and reached out to
touch his hand. "Hello."

"Stop," he said. "Don't play me for the fool again."

"I beg your pardon," she said coldly, as if she were hurt. But
she was not hurt. She was still playing, in spite of herself, and
she was certainly aware of it. He had rebuffed her, and now she
was enlarging the scene, automatically, eager to break down his
resistance, to make him as attracted to her as before. "If you
find it so repulsive to touch my hand, so be it."

"Look," said Franklin, "don't talk nonsense. Let me tell you
why I've come before seeing you makes me forget."

"You were angry the other night," she said, feeling his resistance fall apart. She knew she was not a bad person, and believed that what she was doing wasn't bad; Mary was drawn to saying the words, supplying the gestures, making him want her. "You were jealous, and I'm sorry for that. You know I want to be on the stage. But that doesn't mean I care a thing about actors."

"Mary, for the love of God—don't do this to me!"

"All right," she said. "What? Tell me what you have to say and get it over with. I can be hurt too, just as well as you." Deliberately, she moved an inch away from him and averted her eyes. And then an added touch, not thought out, but the natural instinct of the born actress—she crossed her arms and retreated into herself, shivering, though the air wasn't cool. She could hear his sharp intake of breath, as if appalled at the spectacle of her pain. He forced himself to get it out.

"Your mother—she told me where to find you—I didn't go in, you needn't worry about that. We have to go to the asylum."

"We have to go where?" said Mary, forgetting for a moment the scene she was playing with Franklin Colson. She remembered the beautiful black man, the man strong enough to murder, the man whom the state now wanted to destroy. "What are we to do there?"

"Your mother said you had to first agree to go."

"I agree."

"Well then—I agreed also—out of respect for your mother—and because I helped the man once, didn't I? My crime has already been committed. You can only hang once, can't you?"

He was acting now, trying to portray himself as brave. But he was such a bad actor, pathetically bad. Mary shook her head slowly, the blonde hair catching the pale light of the moon and the diffuse glow of street lamps, filtered by the humid air. "We won't hang, silly," she said. "They're not going to hang white people. Tell me what my mother wants us to do, tell me everything."

Franklin drove to Main Street and followed the partially lit road for a half mile before turning south onto a country road, twisting and rutted, shadowed by tall trees. He drove slowly, worried about his horse's familiarity with the dark road. When they spoke, their voices seemed to carry for miles.

Mrs. Mann, with the approval of her husband, had contacted Franklin and asked him to go with Mary to the asylum, to speak with Moses. Inmates were in bed by half past nine, and Dr. Marandino would be able to take them to Moses' room in the staff quarters. "We're not supposed to tell the doctor any more than that we're paying a visit to the man. He'll know it's unusual, of course, but he won't want to know more. He won't want to incriminate himself. That's what your father thinks, anyway. Your mother would tell him everything, but your father doesn't want to risk it. He doesn't trust everybody the way your mother does."

"He trusts you," said Mary. She had moved quite close to him on the bench, and she could feel his growing weakness.

"You're to speak to the man alone," said Franklin. "I'll wait outside his room somewhere. He'll be nervous, and we're not to upset him. They're going to get him to New York, someone will be expecting him, and he must be ready to leave Thursday night."

It was Tuesday night. "You mean in two days? How does he leave? Where is he going? How does he get to New York?"

"All we tell him—you tell him—is that he must be ready to go Thursday night. That's all. Someone will come for him, I suppose. It's too dangerous here in Safe Haven. Your mother is being watched, so is your father. They've searched two churches, they've been down to Irishtown. They're looking, and someday someone's going to think of the asylum, and by then he's got to be long gone."

"You're very good to do this, Franklin."

"I believe in antislavery."

"Yes, you do," she said. "But that's not the only reason you're doing this. All right? Let me say it, then. From me. Thank you."

"Why on earth did you want to get involved with a troupe of good-for-nothings like that?" he said. "I can't imagine anything less likely for someone like yourself. You're from the best of families, you're well educated, you're beautiful, you have everything. Even if you do want to act, there are other ways to go about it. Get a teacher, a coach, to come to the house. Practice your Shakespeare. Why would you even consider getting involved with actors—"

"How else can you go on the stage?" she said. "If you want to act, you need other actors to act with—doesn't that sound logical to you?"

"Please don't mock me, not now, not again."

"I'm not mocking you."

"I want to marry you."

"This is not the time nor the place," she said. "I would much prefer if we think of the task at hand, all right?"

"Why do you sound so cold now?"

"Because you don't have any consideration for what I want to do with my life, except as it's directly related to you—"

"Oh, not women's rights! Save me from women's rights! Is there anything your parents *aren't* in favor of? How about common sense? Are they for that? I'm in love with you, I don't want to take away your rights."

She had let him go far enough. Softly, she touched the back of her hand to his cheek. "Please, let's not shout," she said. "You know that I care for you. I don't want us to be making scenes all the time. If it weren't for what I want—and I do want to go on the stage—if I were everything that I am now, except not an actress, I would marry you."

"But you want to go on the stage," he said.

"Yes," she said, and she heard herself say the word and understood that she was serious at that moment, not acting. But neither was Franklin acting at that moment. He was dejected, frustrated, certain that their mutual happiness would result from her listening to his clear understanding of what they must do. They remained silent for perhaps ten minutes of slow driving.

"Is this where we turn?" he said finally.

"Ask the mare. This could be China for all I know."

He turned down an even narrower road, and for a few seconds it seemed as if they were descending into a dark depression. They were quiet, and watched the swinging lantern that so poorly lit their way. But then the horse began to labor up a hill, and they could see in the distance points of light across a meadow—the back end of one of the great estates near the asylum. As the road grew level, it widened out, and the moonlight was no longer obscured by overhanging branches. They sped up, Franklin staring straight ahead, and Mary shut her eyes, letting herself drift away from his bad mood. It was enough for her that he still loved her, regardless of his anger. She forced herself to think of the black man, of what she must tell him, of the drama she would bring to him on this quiet spring night.

They were arriving from the back end of the asylum, and came first to Dr. Marandino's house. Franklin left Mary with the carriage, walking to the front door of the two-story house, waving his stick and shouting at the watchdogs. Marandino came to the door quickly and held a lantern up to Franklin's face. Mary watched them talk at the threshold, and then Marandino retreated inside, coming back a moment later with his overcoat. Then the two men came over to the carriage, and Franklin asked Mary to get into the passenger compartment.

"Your mother didn't say where the boy came from," said Marandino, turning his head about to Mary as they drove on to the asylum. The gatekeeper's booth was empty, and they drove right up to the main entrance and waited for an attendant to greet them.

"If you're asking me, Doctor, I haven't any idea myself."

"I don't want to know, actually. I assume he's a runaway. That much your mother never contradicted when I suggested it, but I wonder if you'll feel safe—"

"Yes," said Mary.

An attendant came out of the house, his breath thick with whiskey and tobacco smoke. Dr. Marandino spoke to him sharply, and then he turned to Mary and suggested that it would be best for her to walk the rest of the way.

"You're sure you want to see him alone?"

"Yes, Doctor," she said. Mary was suddenly very awake. There was no danger for her that night, but there was something terrible about this place, something more than just the depressing fact of its unfortunate inmates. She recoiled from the doctor when he brushed against her; she was repulsed by the attendant who led her past the ghostly facade of the grand administration building.

"It's a little bit of a walk to get to the niggers," said the attendant, turning his pockmarked face about to her. The four-story main building had two wings, each of two low stories, with small windows crossed with thick wooden sashes, behind which were metal bars. The attendant unlocked a side door and took her inside one of the patients' wings. It was glaringly bright. The long white-walled corridor was lit with gas lamps at regular intervals, and there was a profusion of shut doors on either side of the corridor.

"Are they locked?"

"Yeah, and it's a good thing—you wouldn't want them wandering, miss. Take it from one who knows."

Mary could feel the anguish all about her, the deadening weight of permanent despair. The corridor was long, but not as endlessly long as it seemed to Mary; she began to feel as if it would never end. The lamps and the doors were all identical, and the harsh white walls reflected the barrenness of the trammeled lives behind the locked doors. She had a question she was about to ask—about their bedtime—but it was suddenly forgotten as a horrible cry broke out from one of the patients' cells.

"Come on," said the attendant, smiling at her discomfort. "That ain't nothing. You don't even hear it after a while."

But Mary heard it, all too clearly. It was the voice of a young woman; it could have been her own voice, though it spoke no language, made no sense. The cry wasn't a cry for help, or a scream of rage, or anything other than an expression of pain, a pain that expected no relief. It was impossible to tell from behind which door it came, because all the doors were melting together under the bright light, under the atmosphere of madness. She was out of breath, either from walking quickly or from confusion and panic. The attendant spoke to her, his ugly lips forming a question that she didn't hear.

"You all right, miss?" he said. And then he repeated his question: "What does a nice young woman like you got to do with nigger trash that comes here, miss? We all been wondering who this new one is. He's got a mean look but he ain't looking for trouble. I think the white man's got him a little panicky, if you hear what I'm saying."

"I'm Mrs. Mann's daughter," said Mary.

"Oh," said the attendant, his face turning from hers quickly.

"You're rich, then, and I ain't supposed to say nothing bad about all the free blacks she got taking away white men's jobs."

"Correct," said Mary.

"I wish she'd spend a little of that do-good money on some more money for us whites who work this place. This ain't the greatest job, believe me. That screaming was nothing—she's practically finished already. It's no picnic what I go through. I could tell you stories."

He took her up a narrow flight of steps at the end of the wing, leading to a long corridor, white-walled and brightly lit, but they had come up to the end and did not have any longer to walk. "This is where he's at, but there's others there. You want him out by himself?"

"Yes, if you can."

"I can do anything in this place—anything."

He started to take out his heavy key ring, but then laughed at himself, remembering that this was one of the few doors that was unlocked. He turned to her and said in a soft voice: "Miss Mann, walk down a little ways—you don't want them Africans staring at you in the middle of the night. They're probably half naked."

Mary did as she was told, walking slowly away from the door, looking at the white floor, the white ceiling, the burning gas in white sconces. She wondered who was imprisoned on this floor, who had committed them, who had made the decision to isolate them forever from the community of men. It occurred to her how easy it would be to play a madwoman: She would simply relax all her inhibitions and restraints, simply allow her anger free rein, her need to be loved to be expressed without words, her great fear of the world to come to the surface in one continuous howl.

The black man's face stared at her from six inches away. Wordlessly, he had come up to her in the hall, leading the half-drunk white attendant, and now he waited for her to notice. He wore a white uniform, and his light eyes were no longer bloodshot, but no less full of pain.

"Moses," she said.

"Yes," he said. "Hello, ma'am. Miss."

"Miss Mann," said the attendant briskly.

"Miss Mann," said Moses. He did not take his eyes off her, but his gaze wasn't insolent or inviting; it was curious. She had knowledge that he needed. He wanted to hear what she had to say, and to know whether to trust her. And once again he felt himself confused about the white woman. It was not usually difficult to know from a glance who was a good person and who was not.

"Where can we talk?" she asked Moses. He turned to the attendant.

"Where can we talk?" said Moses. "Sir."

"What's wrong with right here?" said the attendant.

"Would you like me to tell my mother about your attitude?" said Mary, beginning to act the heiress apparent. It was a way to forget about the pain in the black man's eyes, and the unsettling effect he had on her. Without thinking, she had held her breath, and her face reddened, and when she spoke, the words came out in angry staccato bursts: "How dare you drink whiskey while working in a medical establishment! How dare you question the wisdom of my parents—they will hire and fire whom they choose! Who do you think you are to look at me like that? Did you take me here of your own free will, or was it an assignment from Dr. Marandino? I want a private room to speak with this man, and I want it at once!"

The attendant shook his head slowly, as if continually amazed at the blows rained on him by the world. He unlocked an empty room, opened the door, and lit the lamp. "You want me to wait out here, Miss Mann?"

"You can wait at the stairs."

"If you need me, just holler."

The room was narrow and, like the corridor, white-walled and stark: a cot, an oak armoire without carvings, a straight-backed chair. Mary walked in first and sat down quickly in the lone chair. The attendant vanished from the open doorway, and Mary wondered if it would be all right to close the door. Moses remained close to the doorway. Softly, looking right at her, he said: "He can't hear us, Miss Mann."

"Are they treating you all right here?" she said, wondering why she had blurted it out. There was no time for this kind of talk. She had to deliver a message and that was all. Before he could answer, she continued: "Look, listen—two nights—Thursday—you must be ready to leave here."

"I'm ready tonight," he said. "This is a bad place, miss. I don't know if your mother knows how bad it is. I must tell her."

"I can feel it," she said. "It is bad. I heard a scream before. Look—what about you? Does anybody know?"

"No. The other black men—they think I'm running, but that doesn't matter, not to them. No one knows about what I've done. What time Thursday? What am I supposed to do to get ready?"

"I don't know," said Mary. "I'm only carrying a message. You're going to be picked up, and someone will take you the next place you're going to—it'll be safe. My mother said so, and she has nothing but your interests at heart."

He took a step closer to her. "Listen, miss. Please. You must promise to tell your mother. I've been working here, with the other black men, and they're as guilty as the white men here. It's not that they're cruel, but maybe they are that too—it's just that it's wrong. Tell her. It's as bad as slavery—as bad as the men who say it's the best thing for Negroes because they don't know better. Do you know your bible? 'Surely oppression maketh a wise man mad.' This place is oppression and worse. Tell her. Tell her not to support it, but to fight it."

"I'll tell her, but you must tell me what it is that they do."

There was too much to tell; Moses didn't know where to begin. Mary looked away from his beautiful face and saw the bars, hidden by the wooden window sash when seen from the outside, but always evident to the patients. He told her how they got the patients up at five in the morning, gave them medicine—usually laxatives—fed them a bland breakfast, then examined them, four at a time, though most of them had no physical ailments. They were pushed from one thing to another, never having time to think for themselves. They were made to sew or weave baskets for three hours without a break, then given wood to be sanded down laboriously, then put through a battery of exercises. "It never stops," said Moses. "Some of these people are crazy, and this makes it worse, much worse, they burst into tears all day long. And some of them aren't so crazy—really, just like most people, but sometimes they're in strange moods, but not that bad. But the work, the bad food, the living in cells, getting up at five, in bed at nine-thirty, not getting mail or visitors—nothing but work and bad food. And the doctor—the doctor says it's the cure, miss. And it's not the cure. Anybody can see that. It's the cure the way the whip is the cure to slavery, and you got to tell your mother."

"You're going to be safe," said Mary.

"I'm all right, no one's going to get me. The Lord got me this far—He has a purpose."

"You must have loved your wife very much," said Mary.

"Yes," said Moses. "As much as a man can love a woman, I suppose. 'Many waters cannot quench love, neither can floods drown it.' But it is important to love God best, important and very hard, because a woman can get under your skin, miss. You had better be going. It's not good for us to talk too much or they'll ask me questions, and sometimes I'm not clever. I will be ready Thursday night, for anyone who's coming to get me."

"Moses," she said. He stopped from turning to the open doorway and looked at her with his steady eyes. She was about to tell him that she admired him for worrying about others in the midst of his own troubles. But other thoughts were rising through this simple sentiment of praise: She wanted to tell him that she was admirable too, because she had become an actress, with a real troupe of actors, and perhaps would play the part of Eliza and bring home the horrors of slavery to the American people. And there was more, much more. She would have liked to express, somehow, how she was affected by his presence. It was terrible to admit, but she understood now that there were black people besides Leah who were capable of human qualities, worthy of notice. Had she seen him working on the docks, pushing a cart, she would not have seen him as capable of feeling, thought, discernment. But he was not merely visible to her at this moment, but growing in clarity, his personality etching itself in her mind. This was sufficiently shocking, of course—to suffer a revelation for which she had not been looking, a revelation that brought home to her the fact that Negroes were human, that humans must not be enslaved, that the hysterical values of her parents were appropriate, the only response possible to insane institutions.

But through all this confused thinking, a momently more familiar yet nameless fear grew. She sensed the danger ahead for her from this man, and knew that its threat was potent, and that all her presentiments wouldn't prevent her from blindly falling victim to it. He was waiting for her to speak, because she had spoken out his name, and she tried to snap out the words, an actress portraying a calm source of strength: "You're right, of course. I must be going. At once."

He looked at her strangely then, once again not understanding her shifting tones. Moses wanted people to be as clear, as straightforward as he was. He felt as if the person to whom he was speaking had changed, like a supernatural being, into another form right before his eyes. But this was not possible. He was tired. The white girl was worried. He would remember her as he hoped she was, brave and good, eager to help an unfortunate, one of the few whites who were not poisoned with race hatred and fear.

"May the Lord bless you, Miss Mann," he said, and he left her quickly, so that when the white attendant came to take her back to her carriage, he was back in his cell, hidden from view with the other black men.

EIGHTEEN

———◆◉◆———

Franklin drove Mary home, waiting for her to pass through the old front door before clattering off into the dark. Leah was asleep, but her mother and father were both awake, waiting for her in the hearth room with a pot of tea. Wilhelm Mann was pacing, unhappy with his wife's relaxed air.

"Do you see, Willy?" said Mrs. Mann. "Back safe and sound, not a scratch on her."

"Please don't be flippant," he said. "This is a bad time to be flippant. Mary, please sit down. Tell us what happened."

Neither one of them had remarked on her stage make-up, though the room was quite light and they stared at her, looking for signs of struggle. Mary poured herself a cup of tea, and allowed her father to interrupt her half a dozen times. He was eager to tell her of the increasing danger to the runaway—the railroad station was being watched, the Post Road was under informal surveillance, friends of theirs from as far away as New Haven had been questioned. Three Southern congressmen had brought up the escape of the murderer, not only before their colleagues, but before the newspaper audience. It seemed that no one except the Mann family was interested in saving him—

the South wanted him dead, and the North wanted him brought to justice so as not to confuse the antislavery issue.

"Don't be like that, Willy," said Mrs. Mann. "There's Franklin Colson, look how he's helped—"

"He's in love with Mary."

"Perhaps, but he knows his duty. And there are others. We're not the only decent people. And we've found someone in New York—"

Mr. Mann interrupted again, savagely: "Stop it, Martha. Be disappointed, for the love of God! No one in town, not one of our group, wants to help this man, that's the extent of their commitment. We're alone in this, because the others are no good."

"I disagree," said Mrs. Mann mildly.

"Well, don't disagree! They won't help him! Not because he's a murderer—every one of them knows that the murder was justified—but because there's a threat of a jail sentence hanging over their heads if they do help."

"Dear Willy," said Mrs. Mann, with such love and peacefulness that Mary thought her father might strangle her. "Listen. They're good people. It's understandable if they're afraid. Some don't want to touch Moses because he's killed, just for that— there are those who don't condone what he's done. Why fault the good people? We have to help him, and there's the New York conductor who's been good enough to take charge—"

"If we deliver him," said Mr. Mann. He willed himself to be calm. "Right to New York. Of all the conductors on the Railroad, we're the only ones who have to pick him up, put him in a station, and get him to the next place. The whole Railroad is rotten if that's what it's got down to."

"He's fine," said Mary.

"What?"

"I said, Father," she said, "that Moses is all right. You asked me but I never got a chance to answer. He's anxious to leave, but he's rested and strong."

"Good," said Mr. Mann. "That's the least of our problems, but it's good to hear nonetheless."

"Thanks for bringing him the message, child," said Mrs. Mann.

"There's something he wanted you to know, Mother. Something he feels very strongly about. I hope you'll at least think about it."

"What is it?" said her father.

"He wants you to stop supporting the asylum," said Mary.

Mr. Mann at first grew angry. How could their flighty daughter presume to plague them with such nonsense in the midst of their very serious problem? What did one Negro runaway from the South know about the enlightened methods of modern medical treatment of the insane?

"He said it was like slavery," insisted Mary, and she tried to recapture his anger and pain at the useless treatment of the suffering inmates. Mr. Mann sat down, suddenly exhausted by all the cares of the day. His wife knew what he was thinking, of course—even after all they had done for the world, the world dared *complain*.

But Mrs. Mann was infinitely patient. She explained to Mary the theory behind the asylum's methods. Mental illness could be cured, men and women could be lifted forever from their misery, if only the regimented methods of modern medicine were employed. All the dronelike work and scheduling that Moses objected to was part of the cure. Even the bland food, the absolute sameness of the daily routine, work, talk, examinations, were essential, because they removed all excess from the mind, relieved the patients of any chance for exaggerated behavior. No visitors were allowed, no mail, nothing but the rigid adherence to schedule, and the tranquil, unvarying landscape.

"Moses says it doesn't work," said Mary.

"*Moses says!*" said Mr. Mann, exploding again. "We've talked long enough about this field hand's criticism of modern medicine. What does he want—to go back to bloodletting and beating and being chained in an attic?"

"Willy," said Mrs. Mann, "we're all tired—it's senseless to argue this way. Let me ask Mary what she thinks, all right? You said you wouldn't rule it out absolutely."

"Ask her then."

Mrs. Mann hesitated, looking at her daughter with a sudden look of surprise. She had noticed the stage make-up. "You were an actress tonight!" she said. "Your face."

"Yes, Mother," said Mary, touched that she had remembered it, even after so long a while, and seen fit to comment on it. "It's make-up so they can see you better from the audience. All the actors do it."

"Yes, I'm sure. You enjoyed yourself—that's the main thing," said her mother. Mary felt that she was being dismissed, or glossed over; her mother had mentioned the acting, but couldn't really concern herself with the experience. There was something else on her mind. "It's about the acting that I wanted to hear," she said, but Mary knew that wasn't true. Her mother wasn't devious, merely solicitous when she had the time for it.

"The acting wasn't much," said Mary. "I was on in the farce, just for a little while. It wasn't anything really, no speaking, a clown—"

"Do you think," said Mrs. Mann, "that you could get Moses into the company?"

"What?" said Mary. Her mother barreled on. Not to act, of course, but only to travel. They were returning to New York by train. They were fourteen in the company, fifteen with Mary, sixteen with Moses. He would get lost with them. Theater people all looked odd, dressed extravagantly. Sometimes a company had a Negro in it, even if only as a stagehand. Why couldn't Moses travel that way?

"Do you mean that you want me to arrange it with the company? But why should they do it? What will I tell them?"

"Tell them they will get one hundred dollars when Moses leaves the train in New York."

"One hundred dollars!" said Mary. "You would give them that, Father? You really would give that much?"

"Of course, child," he said. "A man's life is at stake."

"And a principle," said Mary. She understood the difference between her parents at that moment—the difference between her mother's automatic desire to achieve goodness and her father's visionary theorizing. Her mother wanted Moses to live because he had killed a bad man and had escaped a vile institution. Her father wanted Moses to escape because it created anger and dissension between North and South, between the many factions within the pro-slavery and antislavery groups alike. He wanted dissension, strife; he hoped for sufficient fuel to lead to violent change. One man like Moses meant little to him, except as a symbol. He wanted an end to slavery, and this cause was more important to him than the lives of any thousand men.

"Of course a principle," said her father. "We cannot allow a cancer to live within the heart of this country and still call it a Union. We will either tear slavery out of the Union, or tear the slave states out of the nation. Tell that to your actor friends, if you think it will help. Tell them at the last minute, though, tell them when it's too late for them to sell the information to someone else."

"What if they say no?"

"They're actors—they won't say no to one hundred dollars," said her father. "And if they do, it's just as well. I'm not sure this is the right way. It might be dangerous. To him. To you."

"No," interrupted Mary. The danger would not come from the law. She was smiling now, feeling the easy part of the trip ahead. No lawmen, no jails, no chance of Moses being caught at all.

"Are you foretelling the future?" said her father with exasperation. "God save us from such planning! My daughter wants to be an actress, helps the Underground Railroad without caring a fig for the rights of blacks—"

"That's not true," said Mary. "I do care."

"Of course," said her mother. "Willy, I told you. Mary is more mature and understanding every day."

"Mary is a beautiful, spoiled young child of an old and wealthy family," said Mr. Mann, as if he were talking about a stranger's daughter. "This is a dangerous business that I don't think either of you fully understand. She must carry one hundred dollars, accompany a murderer and a troupe of actors for sixty miles of miserable train tracks, all the while hoping that no marshal wanders into their car. He must get away from Safe Haven—*he must get to New York*."

"He will, Father," said Mary. "I'll see to it."

Mr. Mann examined his daughter's painted face one more time. "Take a look at this, please," he said, and put the local newspaper in his daughter's lap. The lead story was about an escaped Negro killer from South Carolina. His name was Aaron Carter, and he was six feet tall, one hundred and eighty pounds, with thick lips and a vicious mien. There was a reward of one thousand dollars being offered by the citizens of the state of South Carolina.

"That's Moses?"

"Yes."

"Thick lips—vicious . . . Father!" Mary laughed. It was that simple to her. If her father wanted to agonize over the search and its threat, let him. She was going to bed.

"Your mother may find this hard to believe," said Mr. Mann, "but in my experience, there are more than a few men who would willingly give up one hundred dollars if they can make one thousand. If any of your actors read this description . . ."

"Good night," said Mary. "I have to get some rest. I'm going to a rehearsal in the morning."

Mary slept till eleven o'clock. Leah woke her abruptly, slamming down a breakfast tray on a low bedside table. "It's late, child. They're all up and gone," she said.

Who was all up and gone? she wondered, blinking against the harsh light from the small south-facing windows. She had spent the night dreaming of the long white corridors of the asylum, of the beautiful black face of the fugitive, of the clumsy trains of the New York and New Haven Railroad hurtling faster and faster toward the nameless danger welling up in her chest, her throat, her eyes.

"I have a rehearsal," she said, sitting up suddenly.

"Whatever you've got, you better go and do it fast, because your Mr. Colson is waiting for you downstairs on the porch. Been waiting for an hour."

She wore a striped silk dress with a voluminous skirt; it was her most expensive daytime outfit, and one that Franklin found "fast." But she wanted to look alluring today, not for him, but for Charley Keats. It was Charley who would help get Moses away, and he would do it for her more than he would for one hundred dollars.

Franklin was eating corn bread and butter, and crumbs were

(287)

all over his shirtfront. He was overalert, perhaps from drinking coffee for the last hour, and when he spoke there was an urgency to his voice that she found alarming. "I know," he said. "Your mother explained what you're about to do. I offered to do it in your place, not for you, but for Moses. I think it's an idiotic plan."

"Why did she tell you?"

"Because she wants me to pick him up from the road behind the doctor's house. She wants me to take the two of you to the station."

"You mean the real railroad station, not the Underground Railroad—"

"Yes, yes, yes!" he said. "I'm not using your idiotic code, I'm simply speaking English."

"You're rude this morning. Even for a man habitually rude, you're pretty bad, Franklin."

"I don't want you to go."

"Well, I appreciate your concern," she said. "And I hope you'll do what my mother asked of you. You've been very helpful to Moses so far."

"Aaron Carter. One thousand dollars. It's all over the paper. Actors can read, can't they? What in the name of Jehoshaphat do you think they're going to do when you ask them to help get a nigger out of Safe Haven? *Moses Barker.* Listen, they'll turn him in, and you too, and then what are you going to do? Act in a prison?"

"What time tomorrow night are you picking him up?"

"Seven-thirty. The train is at eight-oh-nine. I'll have clothes for him—gentleman's clothes—mine, actually. Your mother said she'd get a message to him. She doesn't want the asylum administration to know that he's going. There's too much talk in town about him already. All the newspapers say he's here or in Fairlawn. Everyone is looking."

But they would not find him, she knew. Carefully, she poured herself coffee from the silver pot, and contemplated the boats on the Sound. Franklin would have to be handled, as would Charley Keats, and this she would accomplish, she would have to accomplish. She sipped daintily, prettily, turning her lovely face to Franklin to fill him with a moment's desire.

She told him that she admired his courage, that it must take great ingenuity to get hold of the family's carriage at all hours without exciting attention, that someday the town would know just what sort of a man he was. "And no matter what happens between the two of us—as friends, as more than friends—I will never forget what you've done for antislavery. It's given me more insight to the strength of your character than I might have learned in a hundred outings to my silly relatives at Fairlawn."

He drove her to the Safe Haven Museum, and she stepped out of the carriage already in character—not for the small part in the curtain-raiser farce, but for the larger role she must play with Charley Keats. And this part she played superbly. She let her hand brush against his, she arranged for him to find her staring at his profile, and blushed at being caught; she explained the depth of her desire to appear on the stage as being related to her love for his acting. After the performance that night, she still refused to have a private drink with him—but she made it clear that such a drink would be acceptable on the following night, in the city of New York.

"You're coming to New York with us?" said Charley.

"With you—yes. If you can square it with the others."

"Of course I can. You're learning fast. And your parents have money to support you, I suppose. They *do* have enough to pay for your lodgings and such—"

She interrupted his pecuniary worries. Her parents had nothing but admiration for her new profession, and would stake her for whatever she needed to join the company.

"Well, good then," said Charley. "It's all settled. Perhaps you might share a room with Julie. Whatever, there'll be a place for you in New York. Not a grand place, you understand. We're actors after all, aren't we? It's wonderful how you've convinced your parents that you have a calling."

"There's a catch," she said. "They want you to do them a favor. And they'll pay you and Mr. Parsil and Mrs. Robinson a flat fee of one hundred dollars for your help. If you don't do it, I can't go. It's very simple, and I can't tell you until tomorrow, but I wanted you to know now. I wanted you to think about me tonight, and dream about the trip to New York." And there once again, in the dark wings of the Museum's exhibition hall, she kissed the handsome ladies' man and brought fear to his heart. He was suddenly terrified that her parents' task might be too great to accomplish, even for the great sum they offered. Wanting the blonde girl so badly, he thrust her away, and asked her to tell him what the favor was.

"You can do it, Charley," she said. "But I mustn't tell you. Not yet, not till tomorrow." When she left him there, stricken with lust, she felt as if she were walking out to a wave of applause.

Her father drove her home that night, and she noticed what terrible shape the seats of their carriage were in; but instead of criticizing, she allowed herself to smile. She was no longer the spoiled child who resented her parents' prodigal donations to charity. Mary's character was saintly too, at least for the evening. She loved the ripped leather of the passenger compartment, the shot springs of the chassis. There was a beautiful black man, a hero, who must be saved, and only she could save him. That his rescue involved a hopeless danger for her, an irrevocable loss, a violent change, was simply a price she was willing to pay. Very full of herself, her courage, her beauty, her artistry, Mary went home to her mother's care and her father's cautions, and an endless repetition of the plans for the evening of the following day.

NINETEEN

———◆———

The Safe Haven station of the New York and New Haven Railroad was even more surprisingly opulent for a town of three thousand souls than was its brick courthouse. It was only a little smaller than the magnificent Italianate station of New Haven, from which the twenty-mile-an-hour train of wood and steel cars originated, in its three-and-a-half-hour run to New York City. The company of actors, fourteen strong, was quite impressed. Though there were only four other passengers waiting for the 8:09 P.M. train to New York, the vast main hall seemed perfectly capable of handling a small army of travelers. There were two parlors off the hall, one for gentlemen, one for ladies, but this being a company of actors, there was little notice taken of these fine points. Actors and actresses ran in and out of the gaily lit rooms, glad to be on the way back to their home city. Men and women both chewed tobacco, and spat with expertise into the brass spittoons, cavorted on the upholstered sofas and divans, declaimed melodramatic lines in front of the gilt mirrors. Two Negro boys were on duty in the main hall, dispensing free ice water and selling hot tea and coffee and stale cake. There was an employee of the railroad selling tickets from a booth, though most people bought their tickets from the conductors on the train. He, like the conductors, wore no uniform, but had a little badge stuck to his coat; this gave him a certain authority in the station, and a certain obligation to minimize the pandemonium so common to travelers about to begin a dirty, tiring trip.

Charley Keats smoked a cigar, and was about to say something sharp to one of the Negro boys, caught up in open-mouthed contemplation of Julie, the company's ingenue, who was smoking a cigarette with considerable familiarity and ease. But he was too caught up, waiting for the sound of an approaching carriage in the dark outside the gaslit entrance. He didn't want to think too much about the strange Negro man who would be accompanying them; who must be greeted by himself and Mr. Parsil and Mrs. Robinson as a trusted old friend, if only for the benefit of the stationmaster with his tin badge of office. Mary had told him at five o'clock what her parents wanted of him. The sets had been torn down and packed up, and all that had remained to be done was overseeing the company's personal packing, including their costumes, and making sure that no one would be left behind in some waterfront dive—not with them due to go on in Harlem Village Saturday night.

"What is he, a fugitive?" he had said.

"We won't know, Charley," she'd said to him, her marvelous green eyes fastened on him as if looking for a flash of weakness. Charley had determined to show nothing but nonchalance, as she did. "It's simply a matter of acting, isn't it? We act that he's a member of the company. A Negro actor, useful in some plays —some companies do it. And the rest of the time, a stagehand. That's all we need say to the others. Only Mr. Parsil and Mrs. Robinson must know, of course, as they're in charge with you. And surely all three of you can act as if he were an old friend. I've seen you act far more difficult parts." And then she hadn't kissed him, as she had the night before. She simply took his hand and squeezed it, caressing him with her eyes. When he spoke to Mr. Parsil and Mrs. Robinson about what they would be doing only a few hours later, he shouted down their puny objections with violence. Were they so afraid of taking a train ride with a nigger? he asked them. Was that too damned much to ask in return for one hundred dollars?

Mr. Parsil and Mrs. Robinson had both understood what was happening: Their ladies'-man co-manager had fallen for another rural beauty, another too-young, unsophisticated blonde with large wants and desires that would affect the life of their company. But there was little they could do about it. They needed Charley's intoxicating voice and glamorous profile. They demanded seventy-five of the one hundred dollars they must split, however; it was kind of them to allow Charley to keep twenty-five at all, since he was "running the nigger" out of love or, worse, blind infatuation.

Mary Mann was anything but blind at that moment.

For many hours, she had felt a conflict building within her, but not one that would hamper her thinking or her actions. On the contrary, it gave an edge to all her movements, a sureness that she did not always possess. She understood that she was acting: Mary had played scenes with Charley Keats, with Franklin Colson, with her mother and father, that had convinced one and all of her purity of heart, her intense appreciation of their efforts, the enormous possibility of her learning to love them. But this knowledge of her acting came in tandem with her understanding that she was also serious, involved, *not acting*. While a good part of her imagined herself on a stage, playing her heroine's role to the gallery, observing her beautiful face streaked with tears over the fate of Moses the fugitive, a better part of her, a bigger part of her, refused to believe that she was simply acting. What she did to manipulate Charley, Franklin, her parents—that was acting; but her desire to help the black fugitive—part of this desire was real. Mary wanted him free, and not only for the approbation of the crowd. That was her conflict: She couldn't decide what part of her was alive to the melodrama, the surface look of the dark night, the train to New York, the handsome Moses dressed in Franklin's clothes, and what part of her was alive to real emotion. She didn't know whether it was possible for her to want him free simply out of goodness, for Mary didn't know if she was good at all. All the impulses that had pushed her to the stage had come from this desire to be loved, to be told she was good; but what the crowd might tell her in years to come would never be based on anything but fictions, speeches, fabrications she would bring to life through art.

"It's not too late to change your mind," Franklin had told her in the carriage as they waited on a silent road for the black man to appear out of the dark. "I would be happy to accompany him in your place."

"Of course you would," she'd said, automatically placing her hand on his, smiling into his eyes with the full force of stage love. "But that is not the plan, is it? And there is no danger for me, none, please remember that. I don't want you to worry, because I care for you. You know that now, don't you?"

"Yes," he said, as if the word had been wrung out of him by master torturers. But before he could elaborate, before he could begin to explain the full force of *his* love, Moses appeared, as silently as a bird lighting on a branch, a spirit ascending from the netherworld. She could feel Franklin stiffen as all her concentration turned from him to the black man. He wore his white uniform, luminous in the dark night, and he was out of breath, but not from fright. Something had touched him with joy, and she knew it had nothing to do with his escape.

"In the back," said Franklin, and Moses jumped into the passenger compartment. Franklin snapped the reins and the carriage lurched forward, a sudden eruption of noise against the still shadows.

"There are clothes there," said Mary, turning around from the driver's bench. "You must change at once."

"Yes, Miss Mann. Thank you. Thank you both."

She faced forward for a good while, listening to the black man's breathing behind her as he changed in the small space, fumbling with buttons and snaps. Franklin said that he thought the clothes might fit, and Moses grunted that they were the finest clothes he'd ever felt against his skin. Mary held back her questions, her desire to take another look at the man. She knew there wasn't much time to reach the station, and she didn't want to hinder their progress by saying anything that would worry Franklin. The danger she had always felt threatening to erupt in the presence of the black man seemed so obviously alive that she found it hard to imagine how Franklin could not feel it. She listened as Franklin told him tersely about the train trip, about his sitting next to Miss Mann, talking to no one, and getting off the train at Fourth Avenue and Twenty-third Street. A man would be waiting for him, a man who would know him as Moses.

"Fine, sir," said the black man. His breathing was no longer audible, his exertions having ended, and Mary wanted very much to turn around and see him in his new clothes. But she remained facing front.

"For the trip," she said, "you know you're supposed to be an actor."

"I just told him that, Mary," said Franklin, so suddenly cross that Mary resolved to remain silent until he had driven off, back to his father's mansion, and left her alone with Moses and the actors and the train. But it was difficult to maintain the silence. She liked to act upon her desires, and what she desired now was to hear the man talk. Mary wanted to feel the danger, hold it in her hands, look at it squarely, and she could not do this until she had grown closer to the man, closer to the threat he radiated, like the hot air about an iron. And then, an instant before she was about to utter an inanity about the weather, Moses spoke, his Southern-accented speech slow and crisp, and easy to comprehend.

"You must tell Mrs. Mann that I hope she will forgive me," he said. "I had to act, before I left that place. There were too many things that I couldn't allow, not while I had some strength to help. And the Lord helped, He always helps. 'Blessed are ye, when men shall revile you.' That's from Matthew, chapter five. I know your mother will not be happy, not at first, but if I am not a slave, I must help others to be free. It's what the Lord demands, truly."

"What on earth did you do, Moses?" said Mary, realizing at once that she should have allowed Franklin to ask the question. There was jealousy in the carriage, an angry force that underlined the unspeakable attraction that the black man exerted on the white girl. But this could not be the sole explanation for the danger Mary felt. No, something was about to take place, some event, something dire and momentous that would mark her for the rest of her life.

"I let them out," he said. "A dozen of them, men and women —the ones I know are all right. As all right as I am, Miss Mann. Their families put them away, because they didn't know what to do with them, but it's not right, it's not decent. There's indoor work for the patients from seven o'clock till bedtime— mostly weaving baskets and sanding down furniture and sewing —and just before I left, I locked another black man, a guard, in the closet and I set my group of people free."

Franklin was so suddenly angry that he forgot where he was and how little time there was left to get to the station. He turned round and shouted at the man: "Are you crazy? You dumb nigger! What kind of gratitude is that! You let the maniacs out! He let the lunatics free! You're running, and you let the crazy people loose in our town—and who's going to be responsible for that?"

He had his whip in his hand, and Mary, without thinking, grabbed his wrist. She was afraid he was about to horsewhip their passenger. "Stop it!" she said. "Stop talking and just drive on, there's nothing to be done about it! Just get on with what we're supposed to do. Let my mother know, and that's all there is to it!"

"I mean he's a runaway slave, for the love of God!" said Franklin, whipping the mare for the first time that night. They picked up speed, tearing about the curves much too quickly for the carriage and the darkness. "Telling us how to run things! Instead of being grateful! Instead of shutting up and doing what he's told—"

"Mr. Colson, sir," said the even voice from the passenger compartment. "You have helped me a great deal, and I am grateful, even if you have called me vile names and showed me the worst part of your nature. I want you to remember that I thank you. Even now. I did what I had to. You did more than your conscience told you. You were a true son of the Lord, you went far in His service, and even if you hate me now, I count you as my friend."

"He doesn't hate you," said Mary. "Franklin spoke in anger, but you know as I do that he's a good man, a good friend, no matter what he says."

"You're both of you crazy," said Franklin. "Crazier than the lunatics walking around Safe Haven. How many did you let out? A dozen! I hope to God there's no one gets his throat cut tonight by some maniac, because it's going to be my fault then, my fault and yours."

The carriage tore up the driveway in front of the station with enough noise to raise the dead. There were four minutes left before the train's arrival time, but Mary insisted that they hurry, that they run. She squeezed Franklin's hand, she smiled at him, but she knew he didn't accept her last scene; his eyes were hard, cheated. He looked at her as if to acknowledge her deceit. He could have as easily told her that she didn't love him, that she had used him, and that he was through being her fool. "Franklin!" she said. "Drive home safely!" Her last line didn't make her any more endearing.

She hurried away, eyes turned toward the entrance to the station, not even looking at the black man at her side.

"It will be all right, Miss Mann," he said before they entered the ornate structure.

"What?" she said, turning to him. His collar was crooked, his shirtfront askew, but his broad shoulders, his lovely face, his erect posture were remarkably enhanced by the gentleman's clothing. "What did you say?"

"It will be all right," he repeated. "For you, Miss Mann, and for me. There will be no problems. I would feel it if there were."

"You would feel it," said Mary, staring at him. As they entered the main hall of the station, she found herself overwhelmed by his words. He was like her, she thought. The man believed in being open to the messages in the air. But he was wrong, of course. She could read what would happen better than anyone. The danger was there, it was about to explode. He was beautiful, and she understood that a black person was not only a human being, one distinguishable from another, capable of pain, of nobility, of understanding; but more than this. A black man was a man, and capable of exciting her inchoate passions. No more, no less than a white man. Simply a man, as her parents had always told her, though even they might be appalled if they could listen to her thoughts. What if she could love such a man? Would that be a danger? A danger that would alter the straight-line course of her life? She wanted to touch him, hold his hand, feel the texture of his woolly hair. Mary wondered if that might explain everything. If she could actually bring herself to touch the African hair, feel her cheek against the Negro skin . . . could the revulsion bred into her since birth explain the sense of impending doom? If she could kiss the black man's lips, bring him close to her in the clattering train, she might confront the danger, bring it to instant fruition and drive away the fear of what was unknown, and therefore far more terrible. "You would feel it," she said again. "And you don't feel it now. So there won't be danger."

"There might be danger," he said, as if it were some sort of joke. "But there will be no problems. We will make it all right. I am certain."

He was happy, idiotically happy, totally unafraid. When he had come to them, crawling out of a barrel on the Safe Haven dock with a knife in his hand, he had been a different person. He was ready to kill someone. There was no notion of his power, or his trust in the future, even with all his quoting from the Bible. Perhaps the asylum had changed him. Perhaps by freeing the lunatics he had bought himself a place in God's heaven. Maybe the black man needed the reassurance of his idea of a good deed to justify his place on the earth.

"Mary!" She turned to the sight of Charley Keats, very tall and dashing in his linen duster, the long light coat worn over his overcoat to protect it from the dust and cinders of a journey by train. "Hurry, the train is coming."

"May I introduce Moses Barker?" she said sharply, reminding him of his promise to act.

"Moses—of course. I know Moses. I saw your *Othello* in Cincinnati! I'm thrilled to death that you're joining us."

"Hold him, Charley," said Mary softly. "Now."

The stationmaster was walking past them, looking curiously at the elegantly dressed Negro man. Charley hesitated for a moment, but then threw himself into the act. He hugged Moses as if they were long-lost brothers, as if the man in his embrace had no more chance of being a fugitive murdering slave than he did.

The station bell began to ring.

"Hey, who's this?" said Julie, the pretty ingenue, as Charley let go of the handsome black man. "We doing a minstrel show?"

"New member of the company," said Charley. "Let's get the hell on board."

"Listen to how he talks in front of ladies," said Julie to the black man.

"Pardon me, sir," said the stationmaster, coming right up to Moses, his manner urgent but not dangerous. "I didn't see your bags."

"They're with the company stuff," said Charley, thinking fast.

"Oh, an actor!" said the stationmaster, as if satisfied on some confusing point. One of his duties was to take possession of the passengers' baggage upon their arrival in his station. It was his obligation to ticket the bags and see that they were carefully placed in the baggage car, and that all passengers had duplicate baggage tickets. On board, long before the train would arrive in New York, a baggage agent would go through the train, asking passengers for their baggage tickets and determining where the passengers would like their baggage delivered in the city. Mary understood that a threat had been averted, that she owed a debt to Charley for his quick thinking. But as she boarded one of the old, filthy wood and steel cars, right behind Moses, she knew that the danger had not yet been exposed. She had not yet touched the black man, she had not seen the slightest look of sexual interest on his part, but she knew that the sixty-odd miles to New York would seem to last far longer than three hours; they would stretch out the way a nightmare does, when one is lost in a maze of one's own fabrication, when the nemesis that is self-created has all of eternity to plague you with perfect fear.

The members of the company boarded three different cars on the eight-car train. Julie followed Charley Keats, Mary, and Moses into the next to the last car, a cold cigarette dangling from her lips. It was an old car, about eight feet wide, with narrow seats of cast iron, the leather cushions burst in a hundred places. Perhaps sixty people could find seats in the forty-foot-long car, but in the dim light from four single-candle lanterns, only a half dozen men could be discerned.

"This is nice," said Moses, speaking softly but without any

attempt to be secretive. "Much nicer than the ones down South."

Charley turned about and looked at him as if he were mad. "Moses, old friend, come over here and sit by me!" he said with broad familiarity. He gestured to an empty seat at the rear of the car, where the lantern illuminated the peeling paint of the wooden walls. A man in a heavily soiled duster looked up at the actors curiously, his eyes lingering on Julie with the cigarette in her mouth.

"You looking for a match, honey?"

"I'm not your honey, pal," said Julie. "And you watch your fresh mouth, or I'll see that it's broken for you." She looked at Moses, as if he were her secret protector. Moses smiled at this, as if he had entered a fairy tale world where men traveled at high speeds through the dark, black and white men together, without distinction.

" 'The flesh lusteth against the Spirit, and the Spirit against the flesh,' " quoted Moses in his deep voice, but the tired passenger was more impressed with his solid figure than with his biblical knowledge.

"No offense, miss," he said. The train jerked forward, throwing Mary against Moses, and he held her arm instinctively, powerfully.

"I'm going to sit over here with Miss Mann," said Moses. "I have some explaining to do her, sir," he added. "Miss Mann?" He gestured to a seat in the middle of the car, and Mary sat down at once, her back thrown against the cushions with force.

Charley whispered something with considerable emphasis to Julie, and the two of them went to sit in the rear of the car.

"It's about the asylum, Miss Mann," said Moses.

The train sounded as if it were about to come apart. Everything was loose and rattling, and dust and bits of ash flew through the wide-open windows. Though the night was cool, there was nothing to be done for it but bundle up; without the ventilation of the windows, the passengers would not have been able to breathe at all. As it was, the wind howled through the windows, bearing cool country air and hot cinder dust, and the terrible noise of the wood-burning steam locomotive. As the train wound about a too-sharp turn, Mary remembered the last time she'd returned from New York by railroad; she'd left the train in Stamford, unable to bear her train sickness, the product of the badly maintained track and irregular grades.

"You don't have to explain about the asylum," she said, hating herself for forgetting a duster. Already she was covered with dust, her whole body rigid with anticipation of the next puff of woodsmoke, the next violent upgrade of the tracks. She was about to ask him how he knew the bible so well, whether he used to preach to the other slaves on his plantation, but she couldn't get the words out because a noxious odor, unexpected, strong, filled the car with enough speed to bring tears to her eyes. "Oh my God," she said, gagging. "What is that?"

"It's almost over," said Moses. "Nothing to be worried about. It's the grease on the axles. They must have put some more on in the last station. Comes from animal fats, the grease. Must be rancid, but it won't last. There. Better already." He inhaled for her benefit. "Why don't you close your eyes, Miss Mann? It makes things go faster, don't you think? I appreciate what you've done for me, I surely do, but it's not necessary to suffer, right? You can close your eyes, and we'll get to New York that much faster."

A tall man with a whiskey bottle in his fist walked past them down the dark aisle, filthy with cigar butts. He spat out some tobacco juice every few steps, and his relaxed, loose-jointed manner unnerved Mary. There was a little star on his vest; he was the conductor, and he didn't seem to care who knew that he'd been drinking. Mary willed herself to be calm: It was two cents a mile, and the fare from Safe Haven was therefore one dollar and twenty-one cents, and she had to pay Moses' fare as well. She handed him two dollars and forty-two cents, and told him to pay the conductor when he approached them.

Then she shut her eyes.

Not simply against the ash and the wind and the sight of the conductor, who might or might not have been alerted to the flight from Safe Haven of one Aaron Carter, a vicious Negro field hand. Nor against the newspaper that Charley Keats had in his hand at the station, which might or might not have contained a description of Aaron Carter, with the notice of a one-thousand-dollar reward. No, not just this. It was also against the danger building at her side, slowly, with infinite patience, as if it had all the time in the world to burst forth, rather than the duration of a train ride to New York.

"That's better, Miss Mann," he was saying. "Not much to see out the window, just a lot of blackness and a few little dots of light. Lanterns in the windows, pretty if we were standing still." The conductor came and went, smelling of liquor but surprisingly polite. He made no comment about the man's race. Within twenty minutes, they had stopped once at a small station and slowed down to a crawl to get over the rickety covered bridge outside Norwalk. Even in daylight the view from the bridge wasn't picturesque—just a lot of smoke blackening the wooden slats that blotted out sun and rain. She remembered a lengthy stop in Stamford, where more wood for the engine was loaded on, and an entire family of six boarded their car, an odd sight for the late night train. All six of them stared at the black man at her side, wondering if the bad light could be playing tricks on them.

"You'd better fix your collar," she told him at one point.

"Thank you," he said, always polite, eager to express his gratitude. She took a chance at looking at him, and was surprised to meet his eyes, to discover that he was not looking straight ahead, or out the open window, but at her profile in the flickering light. "Like this?" he asked her, shifting the stiff cloth about his neck.

"Where did you learn the bible?" she asked suddenly, as if this were the most important question in the world.

"From reading it," he said. Moses could have told her something of his family history, how his mother had worked in the big house, how his father had been sold down the river for insubordination. But why should the white girl be interested in the hierarchies of Negro life? He lived most of his life as a field hand, not as a butler or a porter or a footman. There were other field hands as educated as he, others as light-skinned. He himself hated such distinctions, marks of class specifically frowned upon by his Christian teaching. "It's the only book I read, Miss Mann."

The train screamed over a hill and around a curve, swaying and rolling like a clumsy boat in gentle swells. Mary swallowed hard, to still her nausea, and turned her eyes front, and shut them once again. "I think you're very brave," she said. "And very good. What you did about the asylum. I felt it there. I felt what you felt, Moses."

"That's because you're a young woman in touch with the Lord," he said. "You have a gift."

"What gift?"

"Goodness," he said. "Not everyone could be the Good Samaritan. One must be blessed to want to help others. It's like any other God-given talent. I know you're not like the others— not like Mr. Colson, or the actors at the station, or even like your dear mother. You have a gift, Miss Mann. You do what's right."

He's crazy, she thought, listening to the vibration of the train. Her gift was manipulation, not goodness; her mother was good, her father was good. She was an actress, she wanted fame. This black man with his easy reading of the future knew nothing about her. He felt no danger, where she felt it growing moment by moment. He imagined her a saint, when in fact she knew her life would be open to license and lust. She imagined the federal marshals taking him off the train, his arms pinned behind his back, his mouth open to scream out his pain. Charley Keats might run up to them, eager to portray his indignation: This man is our minstrel show leader. You should hear him sing "Zip Coon" and "Jim Crow." Go on, Moses. Give the marshals a little dance, show them your nigger walk.

"Miss Mann," said Moses, his hand on her shoulder, his lips twisted into a smile. "Please, it's all right." She had been dreaming, retreating from the train and her fears. Now the beautiful black man had woken her up, and she didn't know what to say, how to warn him. The danger was much closer now, she could feel it growing more defined, pointed at her as much as at the fugitive.

"Where are we, Moses?"

"I don't know, Miss Mann. You slept about an hour, I think."

"An hour. Well. We're closer then. That's good."

"Don't worry, Miss Mann," he said. In the dark, he reached out and put his hand on hers. She didn't look down at the hand, didn't try to fathom the meaning of the touch, but simply looked up toward the front of the car, left and right, at all the new heads that had boarded since she'd fallen asleep. There were many new passengers. Mary couldn't imagine what they were doing on board the night train. Who but actors and fugitives needed to get to New York an hour before midnight? Many men sat crosswise on the leather-cushioned benches, their booted feet on the seats, their silk hats halfway over their eyes. Idly, a man spat into the aisle; another belched loudly into the middle of the car. It was worse in the summer, she remembered. Men removed their coats and ties and boots. Some louts even put their bare feet out the open windows.

"I won't worry," she said finally, taking a chance to look at him. His hand remained where it was, lightly on top of hers, not squeezing it, but simply establishing his presence, his proximity, his kinship. She felt the warmth, and understood that it was meant in friendship, and repeated this to herself, remembering her parents' lectures about the brotherhood of man, how her mother had called Moses "brother," and swallowed again, shutting her eyes, feeling the danger growing closer, coming into her, becoming one with her body and spirit.

"You're very beautiful, Miss Mann," said Moses, speaking softly, his hand moving on hers in the slightest of caresses. It seemed impossible, as if she were dreaming this, as if he had understood what her fear was and was acting on it now, a way of torturing her, tormenting her flesh. She thought of all the forbidden attractions she had abandoned in the course of maturing—giving up her father, her young uncles, the married schoolteacher with his neat yellow beard—and wondered if this were only an extension of her desire to have what she could not, to want where there was no chance to be fulfilled.

"Thank you," she whispered.

The train bells began to ring, and the brakes were applied with screeching effect. What had she thanked him for? she wondered. Who would come now to take him away? She turned to look out the open window at the station lights, but she couldn't tell where they were, nor what day it was, nor where exactly they were going. Why wasn't Charley Keats there, showing them his newspaper illustration of Aaron Carter?

"It'll be soon, Miss Mann, and I wanted you to know," she

heard the black man say, speaking from an ether in the speed-
ing train. She watched his lips move, his large regular teeth
chewing the words. "Not since my wife died. I haven't seen fit
to remember love for a woman. No disrespect meant, Miss
Mann. You know that. But you inspire me. As Solomon said,
you are 'fair as the moon, clear as the sun.' I will never forget,
not just your outer beauty, but what's inside. No one will know
but me what I'm saying here. It will go with me to the grave. I
knew at the asylum. Before I wasn't sure. But when I spoke,
and when I told you about the pain in that bad place, I loved
you because you understood. You see things, you know what's
in the air because you have the gift."

Every sentiment seemed to send another shock wave of terror
through her thin frame. He was speaking to her of love, and
that was more than enough to condemn him in any part of the
country. Even if he hadn't been a slave, a fugitive, and a murderer. She had always imagined love scenes from what she'd
seen on the stage, and these ended with embraces, with declarations, with suggestions outside her ken. But now, in the
blackness, in the inferno noise of the railroad, with the black
man's hand on hers, she trembled at the threshold of knowledge. Her body responded to his touch. She felt her heart race,
not only from the danger, but from the fact of work-hardened
hands, from the sensation of his sexual being next to hers. This
man had murdered the man responsible for his wife's death.
Not onstage, but in life, not from some fabricated emotion, but
from something natural, inexorable, a violence that was the absolute reverse of the love taken from him. An image of her own
naked flesh now rose up in the back of her mind, impossible to
stop. She had touched herself, sinfully, and had felt the same
stirring in the blood she now felt, and with it the same shame.
It was impossible to put a mask over it, a stage face, a character: She saw herself naked, and next to her the unknowable
shape of a man, a man with black skin.

"You're very wonderful," she said. "I admire you."

She was speaking inaudibly against the din of the train. But
still, her heartbeat was loud as a drum, the danger already
there, in the car, and ready to tear him away forever. He said
something about love, or the bible, or the Lord. She couldn't

quite hear, and the fear had brought tears to her eyes, and because she wanted everything to slow down, it had all speeded up, the motion of the train, the frequency of the stops, the endless clanging of the bell. It wasn't possible, but they had come into the city, they were at Forty-second Street, and the conductor came through the car asking for the tickets he had sold them only a short while before.

"It's all right," said Moses again, and he let go of her hand and sat up tall, extending both their tickets. At Forty-second, the cars of the train were disconnected from the locomotive and from each other as well. Teams of horses were used to pull each car along tracks farther downtown; the city fathers didn't allow the steam locomotives farther south than the relatively quiet Forty-second Street area.

"Please," she said, not thinking, reaching out for his hand, certain that the conductor was about to tear them apart. Quickly, their car fell into line behind the others, pulled by horses along the Fourth Avenue tracks. The great buildings lining the avenue were sharply visible against the night sky. There was no more smoke, and far less noise. They flew down the deserted streets lit by elegant street lamps, by yellow lamps burning in the ground-floor windows of fancy shops. She could not be wrong. There was a hand that would reach out and grab him, a bullet that would sail through the dark; a police officer, a slave catcher, would come from nowhere and find him.

The whole line of cars stopped at Thirty-fourth Street, letting a few passengers off. The next stop, at Twenty-third and Fourth Avenue, was where Moses must leave, to be met by the next conductor on the Underground Railroad. But she couldn't quite believe it would end like that. She couldn't quite believe that the danger was of her own making, that she hadn't read the messages from the air.

And then, like the nightmare she had looked for, if only to prove herself correct, she saw the conductor coming toward them, two burly men at his back. The car was moving along the tracks to Twenty-third Street. Mary felt her whole body stiffen as Moses took his hand from hers and began to stand.

"You," said the conductor to Moses, no longer as respectful as he'd been on the trip. "Where's your baggage ticket?"

"I'm with the actors," said Moses evenly, standing and moving lithely past Mary's seated form. "But I'm getting out at Twenty-third. We all don't sleep together, you see."

"Glad to hear it," said the conductor.

And that was all. The men with him were porters. They passed their seat, and Moses stopped to look down at Mary as the train car braked behind the horses. "Farewell. God bless you," said Moses.

And he was gone. The man moved so fast that Mary didn't even have a chance to say good-bye. It seemed impossible that there hadn't been time for one last touch of their hands. It seemed a tragedy that she would never bring her lips to his, that they would never share a moment of love in any world beyond that of the train car. She worried about him, wondered if he'd be picked up safely, according to plan. But more than the worrying, more than the regret, she continued to be stymied by the danger that had promised to come, that had entered her being, that had made her clumsy with terror; she didn't understand where it was, what had happened to it.

Charley Keats came over to her as the train pulled into the Canal Street station of the New York and New Haven Railroad, and began to talk about Broadway being outside their door, about the saloons that were open, about the actors whom they'd see drinking and eating on the way home from their shows. When she gave him the one hundred dollars for fulfilling his part of their bargain, her hand was steady, and her eyes were alive with flirtatious power. Saturday night the company would be performing in Harlem Village, and all she had to do to join them was not take the train back home tomorrow.

"Say, are you all right, beauty?" said Charley Keats later that night. "You look a little bit worried."

But she was not worried. The danger wasn't there. She took Charley's hand, she had a sip of his whiskey, she tried a puff of Julie's cigarette in the late-night dance hall they'd all gone to together—the whole company. The next morning the Connecticut train left without her. Mary Mann had left home and become an actress.

It took her years to understand what had happened with the black man in the train to New York; what the danger had been, and what it had done to her. For Mary had read the messages in the air. It had not been imagination that had sent fear through her body, that had predicted a cataclysm that would affect her all the days of her life. She had met a man, and this man had called her good, and had loved her for what she was deep within the layers of artifice she'd constructed with such care. All her life she would be an actress, and never again would she meet a man who would know her for anything other than her beauty, her wit, her grace. The danger was real, and it had come to her. Mary Mann would never be loved, except by her fans, and they would know her least of all.

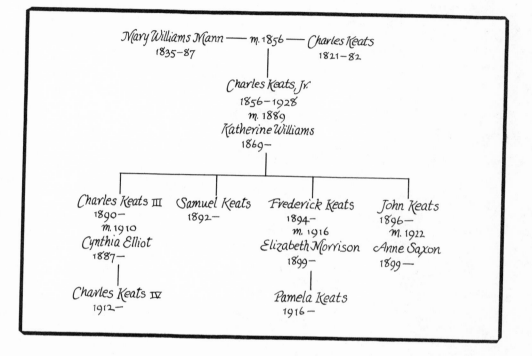

Mary Williams Mann —— m. 1856 —— Charles Keats
1835–87   1821–82

Charles Keats, Jr.
1856–1928
m. 1889
Katherine Williams
1869–

Charles Keats III   Samuel Keats   Frederick Keats   John Keats
1890–   1892–   1894–   1896–
m. 1910   m. 1916   m. 1922
Cynthia Elliot   Elizabeth Morrison   Anne Saxon
1887–   1899–   1899–

Charles Keats IV   Pamela Keats
1912–   1916–

The Family of
Mary Williams Mann and Charles Keats
1855-1938

Mary Mann stayed with Charley's company, and learned how
to act to suit the theatergoers of her day. She became a cred-
itable Mary Wilson in *The Drunkard* and a heartbreaking Eliza
in *Uncle Tom's Cabin*. Along the way, she broke Charley
Keats's heart. They had an affair, and it would have ended but
for her becoming pregnant. They married seven months before the baby, Charles junior, was born, and were divorced
with considerable histrionics at the time of the New York Draft
Riots of 1863. Because Mary had already become far better
known than her husband, she was able to give him enough
cash—three hundred dollars was the large sum that the federal
government required—to buy his way out of the Union Army.
She never saw "Moses" again, and never learned that he had
died in the racial violence directed against blacks in their little
neighborhoods in New York during the Draft Riots.

Mary's son, Charley junior, did not hamper her career. Only
Adah Isaacs Menken was more famous an actress during the
next decade, and when Mary took to wearing Adah's flesh-
colored tights and liberal décolletage while riding a prancing
horse in *Mazeppa*, there were many who found her even more
talented than the great Menken. Still in shock over the murder
of President Lincoln by the handsome son of the actor Junius
Brutus Booth, Mary went off to England's rich circuit of theaters, leaving her son with her ever-obliging parents. Charley

was ten when his mother left, and fifteen when she returned. She had made and spent a great deal of money, and been married and divorced once again, but this time without children. Charley junior, who had not seen his father since he was a little boy, and who had nothing but anger for his beautiful mother and her stage career, wanted only to be like his wealthy cousins in Fairlawn. There everything was orderly, from Christmas dinner to graduation from Yale to entry into a branch of the family's business. But the cousins who were his age were mostly second and third cousins, children and grandchildren of his grandmother's Williams cousins, and most of them looked askance at the sloppily run house in Safe Haven, the dangerously radical Martha and Wilhelm Mann, who were raising him. When his mother was in town for a brief visit, the cousins changed their tune; Mary Mann was a famous actress, and if her life style was bizarre, there was still some glory attached to knowing her. But as soon as she went off on tour, the invitations would cease, and Charley was left with dreams of vengeance and empire.

After his grandmother died, he went west, using a family interest in the Kansas Pacific Railroad to get a job in Abilene, where the cowboys drove cattle to ship east. His grandfather died two years later, but he didn't return east to claim the house in Safe Haven. Mary Mann's lawyers saw that it was boarded up, and when she passed through New York or Boston, she no longer visited Fairlawn or Safe Haven. She died at fifty-two, quite suddenly, after a performance in San Francisco in 1887. Charley junior hadn't seen her for years. Though he hadn't taken the trouble to claim his father's corpse when he died, five years earlier, he traveled to San Francisco now, and saw to it that a monument was built over her grave. He returned to Safe Haven, thirty-one years old and with the good looks of both his parents; he had not only become rich from the Kansas cattle business, but something of a roughneck, the product of years with cowboys and their women in frontier towns. Katherine Williams, the granddaughter of Martha Williams Mann's first cousin Edward Williams, and therefore Charley's third cousin, was eighteen and lovely. Charley wooed her in his spare time over the next two years. She fell in love with him at once, for his looks, his rough ways, his arrogance, his legends of the West. He loved her a little, but wanted her very much; she was a Williams from Fairlawn, and he wanted to bring that glorious part of the family back to himself, and to Safe Haven.

They were married in 1889, and the ancient house in Safe Haven was reopened and modernized in a halfhearted fashion. Charley felt the emotional force of the generations who'd lived there, but a part of him wanted a large brick house with open country acres, away from the waterfront and its workaday traffic. They had four children, and didn't move until the youngest was nine years old. Charley's investments in western Pennsylvania steel and in South Carolina textile mills had been made with the help of his august relations; but they had become Keats investments, Keats properties. They moved not to Fairlawn, where the Williams presence was too strong, but to Greenwich, where they bought an estate of twenty-five acres, and were much closer to the city of New York, where the newest Charles Keats, the Third, was anxious to invest, even as a teenager.

Junior, as Charles Keats III was called, was precocious, and often unlikable. He acted the aristocrat, was rude to servants and shopkeepers, and chased after girls of the lowest social class. He had theories about gold and silver backing the currency, about the entry of immigrants into America, about bankers and trusts and monopolies; most of these theories placed him solidly in the line of the most reactionary members of the Williams family, with the difference that Charley loved to ram his opinions down his elders' throats. He left Yale in his senior year and eloped with a stunningly beautiful Manhattan chorus girl, and fought his parents' fury with his own. They were forced to accept Cynthia into the family, because Charley took her everywhere they went—to the balls, to the country-house parties, to the great parties in Fairlawn and Greenwich.

Cynthia proved something of a calming influence on Charles Keats III. He became less rabid in his condemnation of "Jew bankers ruining the currency," of "Polack and Guinea trash pouring into the cities," of "warmongers trying to sell guns by killing American boys." Had he not been so spectacularly suc-

cessful in dealing in Manhattan real estate during the years
before the First World War, his influence and position in the
Keats family would have amounted to nothing. But his other
brothers were an odd lot, by his standards: Samuel became a
piano teacher in a second-rate conservatory, and never married;
Frederick married a historian and spent most of his time looking at ruins in Greece and Cyprus; and John married a half-
witted heiress, with whom he tried to spend every last bit of
their families' money by drinking and gambling and whoring
across the capitals of postwar Europe.

Since the end of the Great War, the ancient house in Safe
Haven had been open once again. Old Charles Keats II, nos-
talgic for a family history he knew little about, decided to use it
as a weekend retreat, a place to keep the family's two sailboats.
But of all his children, only Junior used the Safe Haven home.
For Charles Keats III, the ancient house had become a symbol
of the America in which he wished to live—a country without
immigrants, without a stiflingly powerful central government,
without an urge to adventure in foreign spheres. After the
death of his father in 1928, Junior retreated to the house at the
edge of the Saugatuck River more and more. He didn't mind
the presence of his indefatigable old patrician mother, or the
gentle criticism of his wife. After the crash of 1929, he grew
fatter all the time, both physically, from overeating, and emotionally, from feeding himself with praise at not being caught
in the stock market, as most of his Williams relations were.
Carefully, he invested in the underpriced stocks of 1931 and
1932, trying to forget about "That Madman" Roosevelt, and his
"New Deal," which he always called the "Jew Deal," blaming
this ubiquitous race for its planning and execution.

But as he grew older, and vastly richer, and the outside
world seemed more and more likely to threaten the rigid stability
and prosperity that he felt was his due, he had a new worry,
more disappointing than anything else in his life: his son, and
only child.

Charles Keats IV seemed incapable of right action. He had
been sent to the family's textile mills down South, and instead
of fighting the absurd demands of the striking workers, he'd
given in—and this in a country where millions were chronically

unemployed. Worse than this, in his father's eyes, was the son's interest in the theater—a throwback to his great-grandparents, and a decidedly unfortunate one. In 1938, the theater was filled with Jews, communists, and other agitators against the social order. Charles Keats IV wanted to be a playwright for precisely the reasons that his father wanted him to stay away from the theater: He wanted to shake up the complacency, the deep-rooted desire for isolation from the world, the deliberate blindness to the interdependence of man.

Even the house in Safe Haven was a point of contention between father and son. All the values that the father ascribed to the family, and to its roots in the ancient hearth, the son disputed. Charles Keats IV was only twenty-six, but he knew enough to see the history of his family, his town, his country, as one based on growth. From a people clinging to a vast wilderness, to one seeking to formulate equitable laws for an independent nation, to one insisting on a union of states where no one would be a slave, the country had grown from individual to collective responsibilities. And now, with the world at the brink of war, with dictators screaming their messages of hate and destruction, the son was certain that the American responsibility would have to grow; it would have to grow wide as the world.

PART FOUR: 1938

A House of
Old Tradition

TWENTY

———◆———

Charles Keats IV had a boyish quality that women found endearing. Heir to a fortune, Charley had raced cars and boats, traveled through the Yucatan with a gun in his belt, and weathered the rage of strikers in his family's factories over the last four turbulent years. But these manly accomplishments were part of a facade. It was easy for a woman to see through to a childish yearning. He liked to caress, not crush, he preferred milk to champagne, and when he was attracted to a woman, he didn't regard her figure, face, or style with a jaded eye; he looked once and was bowled over, infatuated, insisting on a miracle of love. His rumpled hair was boyish; his vulnerability, his eager smile, his innocence in a decadent world all gave him great credit with a certain kind of woman, often one far more experienced than he. But Charley often wished that he projected a different sort of glamor. He wished he could speak in short, sharp sentences, and look through hooded eyes at the world.

It was ninety degrees that day in New York, and hotter below ground, in the madhouse of Grand Central Station. He carried a suitcase in one hand, an ice cream cone in the other. On the platform, he caught sight of a princess, cool and blonde

and erect, holding the hand of what had to be her mother, as if
to bolster her against the aggressiveness of the crowd. Her
beauty was of precisely the sort that intrigued him. She wasn't
flamboyant. One could almost walk past her without noticing
the enormous gray eyes, the rigid lines of the mouth that was
beautiful in spite of its severe expression. She didn't want company, her eyes seemed to say; she had more than enough on her
mind to occupy her. Charley understood that he was creating a
fantasy of this girl, a fantasy built about her physical beauty,
her pulled-back hair, her simple silk clothes, her mother's hand
in hers. He wished he could meet her, but knew that he hadn't
the courage for this. Other men might have brazened forth a
few words, pretended to know her, asked if they could help
with the ladies' bags. It bothered Charley that while he created
a world for this girl to inhabit, she would create nothing with
his image. Even if she were to look his way, she would not
take great note of his good looks, not imagine a world of intrigue stemming from the ice cream cone dripping onto his
wrist. Perhaps if she knew that he was rich, she might look
twice. Or better yet, if she knew that he wrote plays, that for all
his boyishness he had a measured sense of the injustice and
misery of their fellow men, she might find in his figure something of stature, or of romance.

"Charley, you dog!" sang a voice so high-pitched and exuberant that it seemed everyone on the platform must turn to
look at him and the tall, attractive girl who came barreling
his way.

"Pamela!" he said, so astonished at seeing his favorite cousin
that he nearly forgot about the princess waiting twenty yards
away. "You're supposed to be in Europe."

"Charley!" she said again, crushing him to her, kissing his
forehead and messing his hair. "Give me that cone. What a
mess you're making." Pam opened her large mouth and de-
voured most of what was rapidly melting, and then she kissed
him on the cheek, to shock him with the sticky cold of the ice
cream. The train roared into the station, and the sudden noise,
the rush of the passengers to pick up bags and fight for a place
at the platform's edge, the continuing onrushing of Pamela's
words, all conspired to make Charley forget about the blonde

girl and her mother. But even so, he remained determined—not to speak with her, to meet her, but at least to keep her in sight.

"Where are you going?" said Pamela as Charley hurried to join the throng at the door to a car thirty yards away.

"It's less crowded," he said. "When did you get back from Europe?"

"Not Europe," she said. "England. It's different. It's an island. It's in a heck of a lot of trouble." She kissed him again. "Oh, you're the only Keats I like—except for my folks, of course. I have so much to tell you. Got any boyfriends like yourself back home for me?"

Charley finished the cone, grabbed his bag, and allowed Pamela to hang on to his free elbow as he pushed his way on board. "Warm," said Charley, looking around for the princess.

"Please, darling, don't go and talk about the weather. Not when I haven't seen you for months and months. Your father talks about the weather, but that's because he knows I'm going to hate everything else he says about anything. I can't wait to see him—I've got a few things to tell Mr. America for the Americans."

"Do you want to stand?" said Charley suddenly.

"What?" said Pamela, looking at him as if he'd gone a bit crazy. There were seats at the end of the car, and she pointed to them. "What's wrong with those?"

"Nothing," he said, and picked up his bag. A sleeping old man, well dressed but probably drunk, suddenly woke up. "Oh —wait." The princess and her mother were sitting up, as erect as statues, in the chair across the aisle.

"We can go to the back," said Pamela, wrinkling her nose at him.

"Oh, Pam, don't be so bourgeois," said Charley, helping the odoriferous drunk out of the chair and throwing his bag into the rack. Pam wanted the aisle seat, so Charley, pressed against the black window, had a better image of the princess in the window reflection than he did by staring deliberately over his cousin's head.

"You're quite right, Charley. It's unspeakably bourgeois to want to avoid sitting on top of a whiskey bottle." Pamela pulled a bottle and a paper bag folded around it out from under her seat cushion.

"You're wearing pants," said Charley, noticing for the first time. Pamela Keats, only child of his academic—and possibly socialist—aunt and uncle, was dressed completely in black cotton: pants, shirt, and scarf. She was twenty-two to his twenty-six, but had graduated from Vassar just two years after his graduation from Yale.

"Oh, it's the only thing to wear in the summer."

"I would think a skirt more comfortable."

"Everyone wears skirts. Little pale blue skirts with big straw bonnets," said Pamela. "I saw Lindbergh at a dinner party."

The train started up, and in the black window Charley could see the princess's hand go out to press her mother's knee.

"He's still a gorgeous glamor boy, I will say that, but he's far gone, he really is. A Nazi is what I'd call him, even if you wouldn't. Maybe you would—you're not as bad as the rest of the family."

She kissed him to show that she meant no ill will, and Charley felt a bit embarrassed, as if the princess might notice from the adjacent seat.

Charley spoke loudly, hoping that his intelligent voice might be overheard. "Why would you call the man a Nazi? Surely that's a bit rough?"

"Rough?" said Pamela. "Lord, it's rough to get back to America and listen to this. I mean the English are so reserved and polite, and they never seem to say anything unless you pull their teeth out, and they've got their own fascists running around half-cocked—but at least they know what a Nazi is."

"Don't think I don't," said Charley. "I read the papers, I follow everything. It's very important to me."

"Charley, you're such a boy!" said Pamela, messing his hair again, so that Charley wanted to throttle her on the spot. His cousin was loud and flamboyant enough to attract even the princess's attention, and he was determined to show the blonde girl that he was *not* a boy.

"Please don't call me that," said Charley, speaking slowly. "I have changed a lot since you've been away. I don't like to be thought of as someone of no account."

"Oh, darling, how could you think—?" said Pamela, kissing him once again. "I've always adored you and your boyish charm, and even if you are a little older than me, I've always felt like a big sister. It's not you, really, it's me. I'm so old in my head, don't you know that? But it's best to be boyish. You'll live to be a hundred and look like a teenager."

"Tell me about Lindbergh," he said, looking directly over Pam's head. The train pulled out of the tunnel and blinded everyone with the late afternoon sunlight, but Charley was certain that the blonde girl had finally looked their way.

"Well, everyone knows he's been to Germany, visiting their aircraft plants, being taken about like a hero," said Pamela.

"He is a hero," said Charley. "Whatever his politics, he is a hero."

"No," said Pamela. "What sort of nonsense is that? You're not a hero if you're a Nazi. I don't care how many planes you fly—you can fly upside down around the world—if you're a Nazi, you're an animal, and that's all there is to it."

"But Lindy isn't a Nazi."

"I saw the man," said Pamela. "Let me tell you. All right, he has his reasons to live abroad—I'm not saying he's a spy or anything. He's mostly been in France and England, and that makes sense, since he can't stand what the reporters do to him in the States. Maybe I'd go a little nuts if my baby was kidnapped and killed and then the newspapers took photos of him in the morgue. But that was six years ago. In 1938 you don't go around saying how great the German air force is."

"Is that what he said? Did you hear him?"

"Of course. I told you I saw him, didn't I? You don't think I'd pass up an opportunity like that? It's probably thanks to your exalted family that I even got invited to the party."

"Our family, not just mine."

"My father is an archeologist, yours makes steel for airplanes."

"What did Lindy say? You still haven't told me."

The conductor was calling out for tickets, punching them with bored efficiency, when the princess's mother spoke, with considerable fear, into her daughter's ear. Charley thought she spoke a foreign language, but couldn't be sure. The princess smiled, patted her mother's hands as if she were a child, and reassured her. She spoke, and now the words were clear but indecipherable. The princess spoke German.

"He's a racist, that's the problem," said Pamela. "Sees Germany and France and England as one big racial family. We're all brothers, he tells everyone, all the Aryan garbage that you hear in Connecticut today. Aryan Protestantism—what a joke. It's not just that he's an isolationist as far as America is concerned. He doesn't want anyone to look too hard at what's happening in Germany, or in Czechoslovakia, or anywhere else in Europe. His point is that the German air force can beat anyone, and that it would be crazy to have Aryan civilization—France and England, he means—fighting the other Aryans—the Germans."

Charley was about to make a couple of intelligent comments that would notify Pamela—and whoever else was listening—that he was perfectly aware of the Nazi menace, and though he was no communist, he was certainly not an isolationist, and didn't care who heard him. Why, he had just seen the Federal Theatre's adaptation of Sinclair Lewis's *It Can't Happen Here*. He would have told Pamela about the impact this antifascist play had on him, both as the son of an industrialist and as a fledgling playwright. But he had no time to speak.

"Tickets, please," said the conductor to the sunny space between the seats of the German mother and daughter and the Connecticut Keatses. And all of a sudden, the German mother became hysterical.

The car was crowded and very hot. The fans did little but circulate hot moist air about the closely packed bodies. But the bodies were bound for Westchester and Connecticut, and were mostly well groomed, soft-spoken, sedate. Everyone stopped talking at once, and all heads inclined slightly—it was not correct to stare obviously—as the conductor stood, red-faced, and waited for the daughter to calm her mother. The princess was no longer speaking German, but English, slightly accented, but crisp and correct.

"It is only the conductor, Mother. He is only asking for our tickets," she said.

"Conductor," said Pamela, her tone every bit as commanding as Charley Keats's father's, "please." The man leaned low over the black-clad young woman, and she said, rather sharply: "I think it would be best if you go away. Your uniform is disturbing her, I think. They probably are refugees, don't you see?"

"I need the ticket, lady," said the conductor.

"Are you crazy?" Pamela said in a low, urgent tone. "I said you *bother* them. *Go away*, the woman is not herself. I'll take care of the ticket. What's wrong with you?" She began to take out money from her purse.

"Let me," said Charley.

"I want to," said Pamela. "You weren't there."

But now the princess stood in the quiet car and extended her hand to the conductor. She already had tickets, bought at the terminal. "Conductor, please," she said. Charley wondered if she'd heard Pamela, if some of her glorious conduct had rubbed off on him. The conductor took the girl's tickets and turned back to Pamela.

"You don't call me crazy, lady. I don't care who you are, you don't go around treating people like that, all right?"

Charley paid for his cousin's ticket to Greenwich, and for his to Safe Haven. And then in the half hour left before Pamela's departure, he tried to listen to her tales of travel in England, France, and Germany. She was studying architecture, and had gone to sketch old cathedrals in France and new monumental structures in Germany. "Daddy's got an old friend in Berlin, a professor of archeology who lost his post in 1933. He's a half-Jew, whatever that means. It's all so backward. You can be a quarter-Jew, an eighth-Jew—it would be funny if it wasn't so serious. Professor Klein didn't want to leave because of his wife. She's an atheist—well, the important thing is she's got no Jewish blood. She's a doctor, and still working, but he hasn't worked, he can't use a library—by law he can't use a park bench. There are signs, 'No Jews on the park benches.' So don't tell me—"

"I didn't tell you—"

"Am I barking at you? I'm sorry. It's just that the change since a year ago is amazing. Paris last year was so full of life, and now it's ghastly. Poor. Refugees from the war in Spain, and of course endless refugees from the Nazis. Professor Klein's wife doesn't even like him anymore."

"How do you know that?"

"She asked me to help get him out. For his own good, she
said. But she means for her own good, and believe me, I can
understand her point too. It's like living in hell. They've taken
all his money, whatever was in his name, it's their right. Jews
lost civil rights in 1935. Just like that. I mean you're in Safe
Haven watching a monkey with a moustache in the newsreel,
but in Berlin it's real."

"Why do you keep talking about me? I'm serious, Pam. What
is it? I've fought my father tooth and nail on everything he
stands for. I work in the business without compromising myself,
and most of my time I spend working on my plays. What are
you picking on me for?"

"I have a Jewish boyfriend," she said.

Charley didn't know what to say; the transition was too
quick. "Well, that's nice," he said finally.

"He's absolutely brilliant. I met him in England. He's Vien-
nese. He got the hell out. Since the *Anschluss* it's over for the
Jews there. He's a student of Freud's. You know that Freud's in
England?"

"Yes, of course. He's Jewish too," said Charley.

"As is Einstein, branded a cultural Bolshevik, and now our
own national treasure. Still and all, my father informs me that
Uncle Charley is furious with his little niece."

"My father? What does he have to do with anything?"

"He supports my father and mother. And me too, in a small
way, though that's less important. He's threatening to cut them
off, no more stipend from the steel mills, unless their daughter
stops disgracing the Keats name. I'll speak to the son of a bitch
myself, don't worry, but I wish you would too. You are his
namesake, aren't you?"

"My father wants you to stop seeing this Jewish boy?"

"He's a man, and he's my lover," said Pamela. "He's beautiful,
and intelligent, and wants to help heal people who are in pain.
He has a broken nose from studying at the university in Vienna
before Hitler even dreamed of conquering Austria. And now
he's thirty-five, his father's department stores were taken over
by the government, and his mother committed suicide. I think
my poor Professor Klein will too, because he can't get the
money for an exit permit, and his wife won't help him. Say hello

to your mother for me, darling, and tell your father to try and join the human race. Don't be afraid of him. He's just a stupid fat man with a lot of money."

The train had stopped at the Greenwich station. Pamela stood and kissed Charley one more time. As she turned about, the blonde girl stood in the aisle, five inches shorter, very demure without lipstick or rouge, and tentatively held out her hand. "Thank you, miss," said the princess. "You were very good to want to help."

"Please, it was nothing," said Pamela. And then she had to walk quickly to the exit, blowing Charley a kiss before she stepped down from the train. Charley knew that it was his moment to stand up, at once, before the blonde girl could sit, and introduce himself, perhaps welcome her to the country. But the train started up almost at once. He had hesitated for a fraction of an instant, and as the princess regained her seat, he felt he had forever lost his chance to make contact with her.

Safe Haven was a half hour farther along the New York and New Haven Railroad tracks. There were frequent stops. Charley no longer had the safety of looking at the girl through the window's reflection, as the late afternoon sun continued to press its way to the west. He looked at her directly now, in profile, her attention completely on her mother and on their little bit of space. Pamela had a Jewish boyfriend, and his father disapproved, and she wanted him to read the riot act to his father. He was on his way to Safe Haven for a four-week vacation from the steaming city, to get a chance to work on his play on the screened-in porch overlooking the Saugatuck River. Charley tried to imagine bringing the blonde girl and her mother home with him to Safe Haven, introducing them to his parents. He smiled. *Refugees*. They might be communists, or even Jews. It would be different if his father were even a little bit pleased with him. But Charles Keats III was not at all happy with his full-grown son. He didn't like his haircut, his hat, his posture, his politics. The little work he did out of the Keats office on Wall Street was unappreciated; father never let the son forget that he was simply allowing the heir to familiarize himself with a business empire that the son had done nothing to create or sustain.

Charley stood up before the train had begun to decelerate for the Safe Haven station. He wondered where the princess and her mother were going to get off; perhaps New Haven. A Yale professor might meet them at the station, a friend of the family's, fluent in German. He had gone to Yale. Perhaps if he stayed on, waited for them to get off, he could offer his assistance, direct them to the university, to a tearoom. He could buy them iced tea and cakes and tell them why he hated fascism. Charley looked down at the top of the blonde girl's immobile head, as if a thought might leap up and grab hold of him, a connection that would bind them, an idea that he could use to find out her name, her country, her goal.

She turned so quickly that he couldn't pretend he hadn't been staring. But she didn't seem surprised to find him looking at her.

"Pardon me, sir," she said, her gray eyes steady, absolutely fearless. He held on to the seat back by his side, and tried to show by the concentration he gave her that he would like to help her, know her, offer her whatever she desired. "Is this the Safe Haven station?"

"Coming up?" he said. "Yes. This one. We're slowing down for it right now. Are you getting off at Safe Haven?"

"Yes," she said. He took down his small suitcase from the rack, and smiled at the mother, who seemed suddenly less frightened, quite willing to get to know this nice young man.

"May I, please?" he said to the girl's mother, indicating her suitcase.

"Thank you, sir," said the mother. She had her daughter's gray eyes, but they were not fearless. There was about them an inner absorption, a preoccupation with what was past and not present; she seemed to speak to him as if by rote, without interest, for he was not of her world. He was afraid to look at the princess too closely now. He needed to think. Safe Haven was his town. He had spent more years here than in Greenwich, as his father and mother had grown accustomed to what had once been a weekend house; all of them had enjoyed the association with the past, which their Greenwich home couldn't offer. Charley would most probably know the person who would be coming to pick the women up at the station. He would say hello,

exchange introductions at once; after all, he held the mother's
bag.

"May I?" he said again, turning finally to the daughter, offering to take her bag as well, but she shrugged, not smiling. It
was obvious that he had more than enough to carry with his
own suitcase as well. He followed mother and daughter out the
train door and onto the sun-swept platform. "Perhaps I could
offer you a ride?" he said to the mother. "You're not from
around here, I take it." He was talking too much again, too
quickly, was too boyishly eager, and knew it. A score of people
had left the train and stood with their backs to the closing
doors. As the train pulled away, generating noise and heat, he
saw a tall, thin man in rough working clothes running up the
platform steps.

"Mrs. Berger!" he called out. "Frau Berger!"

The princess's mother turned, but did not smile. She didn't
show the faintest sign of recognition. But the daughter was
obviously pleased, and relieved. She waved and called out:
"Yes, sir! Right you are! Right here, and on time!"

But it was a false cheer she was radiating. Even Charley
could see that. The thin man looked vaguely familiar; he had
seen him around town, but dressed very differently. Of course,
he remembered. His mother had said hello to him, and the man
had been quite unfriendly, surprisingly so. He was a banker of
some sort. With a name like Jones or Smith, or something
equally forgettable.

"Welcome, Frau Berger," said the man. "I'm William Hiram,
and I hope you'll excuse my clothes, but this is Safe Haven.
Very informal. Did you have a good trip?"

Charley could see that the man was as nervous as he. Miss
Berger spoke for her mother: "It was tiring, very hot. We're not
used to this American heat yet. It's very good of you to have us
out here."

"Please, don't even begin to say anything remotely grateful,"
said Hiram. "If you knew a tenth of what your father has done
for me . . ."

Mrs. Berger seemed suddenly very interested in what the
man was saying. She spoke rapidly to her daughter in German,
asking her a question. Miss Berger responded in English: "He

says Father has been helpful to him too, you see. I'm Lily Berger, Mr. Hiram." She turned to Charley, as if remembering him after a long time. "Oh, thank you. Please, we can manage the luggage now, I think."

"I'm Charley Keats," he said.

"Ah, yes," said Lily Berger. "Thank you, Mr. Keats."

He had had enough hesitation for the day. "Look here, Miss Berger. This may be none of my business, but I don't suppose you know many people in town, and I was wondering if I could take you to dinner one night."

"I beg your pardon, please?" said Lily Berger. For the first time since he'd been observing her, he noticed a flicker of shock in her beautiful face.

"Did you say you're Charley *Keats?*" said William Hiram.

"Yes."

"The son of—"

"Yes," said Charley, remembering the man's rudeness. His mother had explained that there had been some trouble at the country club. Hiram had brought in a guest who shouldn't have been there, and Charles Keats III had complained.

"Let me explain something to you, Keats, and I'll do it quickly, because my friends are tired. In polite society, you aren't considered properly introduced because you helped carry a suitcase out of a train. Thus Miss Berger's surprise at your bad manners. As for my bad manners, you may ask your father about the leasing of his warehouse on Front Street to the German-American Bund. Excuse us, Mr. Keats."

He was too astonished to answer. Afterward, he would think of many things he could have said, most of them predicated on the fact that he was not his father, but a different man. But almost in the instant that Hiram had finished his angry speech, he saw the little Ford convertible coupe, its top down; his mother was at the wheel, squinting toward the platform.

As Hiram and the two Berger women walked off, Charley had to fight off one last impulse to go after Lily Berger. Though he had spoken nothing but formula phrases to her, he felt as if he had been in communication with her since he'd first seen her at Grand Central. Now that she was named—Lily, no longer a princess—he would have difficulty forgetting her. Like a vague feeling of discomfort that becomes a cold, or a virus, only after it has been named, Lily had become full-blown, vivid. Lily the fugitive, Lily the German-speaking fugitive from the Nazis, Lily the well-brought-up aristocratic beauty, Lily the dutiful daughter, Lily the grateful thanker of Pamela, Lily the daughter of some unknown powerful man.

"Charley!" his mother called, honking the horn, laughing in her artificial way. Slowly, he picked up his suitcase and walked down the steps, forcing himself to look away from the Bergers, getting into Hiram's Cadillac sedan. "How are you, darling?" she said, kissing his cheek with her cold lips. Mrs. Keats started up the car at once, and jerked forward in an incompletely engaged first gear. "Warm, yes? You look fine, very fine. How are things at the office?"

"Under control, Mother," said Charley.

"You're still spending time with those theater people?" she said, only half a question. "Oh, well, things were different when I was in show business. But I've told you all that. I talk too much, and you should stop me. It's just that your father is so hard sometimes. Sometimes I think he resents me because I can't pull up a family tree. He knew perfectly well my family was poor, and that all I wanted was to dance in the line with all those beautiful girls."

"I ran into Pamela on the train."

"Our Pam! No kidding. I didn't know she was back. You know she has a Jewish boyfriend?"

"She mentioned it, yes," said Charley. "Don't we turn here?"

Used to taking orders, his mother turned the wheel with enough cheery abruptness to send the car screaming all over the road. "Sorry. Your father was going to send Max, but I wanted to meet you all alone."

"Pam says that Father is cutting off her parents—"

"She said that! The girl is certainly forthright. I'd be embarrassed, I should think, especially in front of my own cousin."

"Embarrassed about what? Being cut off, or having a Jewish boyfriend?"

"Darling, you don't think I care a fig about any of that nonsense? I may have spent twenty-eight years learning to act the Connecticut matron, but don't forget I was a New Yorker. In the business. You've heard of Gershwin—Mr. Berlin—don't forget George S. Kaufman. I'm not crazy. I had nothing against Jewish men. I found them exotic and fascinating, except for some of them who were a little too wild. But that's the show business more than the Jews. Oh, it was terrible talking to your father when we first got married. He has a thing in him. I suppose it's the bankers. He says terrible things about the Rothschilds, and I say, even if it's true, that's no excuse for the Nazis. But it doesn't matter. Pam will have to give him up. She'll just have to."

The ancient house had been freshly painted—white, of course—and the car turned abruptly up the driveway that had been lined with oaks since Martha Williams Mann had planted them during the Civil War. Charley felt a touch of home-coming. Here, at the edge of the river, where he had often walked with his grandmother, his father's mother, he had come to be fascinated by the family legend. Good people had lived in the house, and in his blood was the blood of saints as well as sinners, men of good will as well as bigots.

"How is Grandmother?" he said before she had parked the car.

"Not well, darling." His mother smiled at him. "Just one more reason why we shouldn't allow Father to get too excited. Come on, she's waiting for you. They both are."

But as he climbed out of the car, grabbing his suitcase and looking automatically to the river, he saw only his father waiting. Or rather, he saw his father in motion, waddling his way with a walking stick beating time in his open hand.

"I can't talk to you now," he said. "You should have come out yesterday, like I asked you to. I've got to get down to the water-front."

"Did you lease the warehouse on Front Street, Father?" said Charley. He had not even had the sense to say hello first, to ask his father how he was holding up in the hot weather. Charles Keats III opened the driver's door of the Ford and leaned on it heavily. He was very angry, his mouth open for air. "I'm only asking because I ran into William Hiram at the station."

"We don't talk to William Hiram, son—do you hear me?"

Charley put down his suitcase and almost laughed out loud.

He felt as if he were sliding down a precipice, out of control, already past any sort of fear. He had not seen his father for months, and for all that time he had imagined confronting him, besting him, demanding that he be decent and good and kind. But now, in place of the usual anger, the childhood dread mixed with embarrassment and loathing, he heard only a name ringing in his head: Lily. Charley wanted to grow strong, to be free, to join the generations that had preceded him with the purpose and power that had always marked the men and women of John Collins's house. But all his strength flowed in one direction now, all his desire was boyish, ineluctable, maddening. He felt as if his father's presence was diminishing into the humid air, that the house behind them was as insubstantial as a dream. Charley wanted Lily Berger, to see her, to meet with her, to hold her hand. He would not fight his father, he would not renounce his world, he would not do anything other than follow the impulse of his infatuation. In the heat of the day, in this quiet corner of Connecticut earth, Charley understood that he was retreating from the world, isolating himself from its problems, turning blind eyes to hatred. He let his lips smile, his eyes relax their violent glare. Lily Berger, at William Hiram's house in the town of Safe Haven. That was what he wanted. That was what his struggle would be.

TWENTY-ONE

"I must go see how Grandmother is," said Charley. If his father had heard him, he made no indication of this. Charles Keats III sat himself down in the Ford, his belly pressing into the steering wheel, and backed away from the house at great speed.

"Dinner is at seven, Charley," said his mother. "We're having a few people, but no one's dressing. It's too hot."

Katherine Williams Keats was approaching seventy. She owned the house in Safe Haven, and though her son was a powerful and assertive man, he never was able to convince her that she was living well on his bounty. Katherine Keats was rich in her own right. And though the house belonged to her as the legacy of her husband, Charles Keats II, she felt she had a double right to it. Her grandfather was Edward Williams, the grandson of Thomas Williams and Sally Woods. There were some question marks in the family tree, but no one could dispute the fact that her great-great-grandfather was a direct descendant of John Collins, the trapper who'd built the original house around the hearth that still stood, sturdy and vast, blackened with age. The Keatses had simply married into the family, she'd often told her grandson, the original Charles Keats being a ne'er-do-well who'd managed to snare the young and pretty Mary Williams Mann with his actor's profile. Katherine's great-grandfather was Mary Mann's grandfather's brother, she had begun to explain to Charley in her antique-filled room on the second floor. She pulled herself up to a more rigid sitting position in her four-poster bed, a late-eighteenth-century Hepplewhite tester bed of carved cherry wood.

"I'm not senile," she said slowly, enunciating every word.

"If you're not senile, why is it that you tell me the same story every time that you see me, Grandmother?" said Charley, taking her hands in his.

"In case you're forgetful," she said. Her smile was the self-conscious exhibition of a woman who'd been beautiful all her life. His grandmother's white hair was as long as a schoolgirl's, pulled into a careless chignon, but very clean and thick and lustrous. Her green eyes were tired, bored with poring over the daily newspapers and weekly newsmagazines, but there was about her body an alertness, a strength that seemed to belie her bedridden status. "Do you know who bought that chair you're sitting on?"

"No, and neither do you," said Charley. It was an arch-back Windsor armchair from about 1800, very uncomfortable and lightweight.

"My great-grandfather sat in that very chair," she said.

"It's possible, but what's the difference if he did or didn't? Grandfather could have bought it from a junkman in Westport and we'd never know the difference."

"Go to the secretary, Charley," she said.

"What? All right. Do you want something?" He opened the writing flap, glancing at the neat sheets of correspondence, copies of letters to friends and their replies over a half century. Often, she asked him to find her a special letter and read it aloud to her; her face would light up, as if his voice had brought back the moment the letter had been first opened, first read.

"No, close the flap," she said. It was a Sheraton secretary with satinwood veneer, but very uninteresting to Charley. He liked the pigeonholes inside, but the beautiful old wood was of a piece with the bed, the chairs, the tables—everything was at least one hundred and fifty years old and felt like it was about to crumble. "Third drawer, boy," she said. "Do you see the bible?"

"There's only a copy of *Gone with the Wind*," he said.

"I still haven't read that, isn't it disgraceful?" she said. "That's the third drawer from the top?"

"From the bottom," said Charley. He pulled open the third drawer from the top and found the leather-bound King James bible, nearly a century old, but hardly ever used. "Shall I bring it to you?"

"You catch on fast," said his grandmother. She took the bible and turned the pages at the beginning of Exodus. An envelope fell out into her lap. "Have you spoken to Pammie?"

"Yes. I was going to tell you. I didn't even know she was back. I ran into her on the train. She looked wonderful. All in black."

"I'm leaving you and Pamela the house," said his grandmother. "It's in the envelope, what my lawyer drew up. I want you to examine it, show it to Pamela, show it to your lawyer if you want. Your father is a powerful man. I don't want him to take it away from you."

Charley opened the envelope and saw a notarized, closely printed sheet of paper. But he couldn't begin to read it. He and Pamela were his grandmother's only grandchildren, but it was a mark of great uneasiness for her to be showing him a part of her will. She had been sick for a long time, until it had become a normal state in Charley's eyes. His lovely grandmother lived in and gave audiences from her antique four-poster bed. This was a condition that would go on indefinitely. "What are you telling me this for—I mean now?"

"I don't plan to drop dead for a while, Charley," she said. "That's not the point. I have four sons, four disappointments, two grandchildren, two bits of joy. That's what this is about. You need to know that he can only do so much to you, your father. He can take away your money, your livelihood, even your mother. But this house will be yours—and your cousin's— and no threat of his can change that. Your father can cut off his own brother's stipend, even though it comes from property that should be jointly shared by the whole family—but that's because he's the businessman, the only one of my boys who ever went after money. But Junior's changed. He's no good, and I say that even if he's my own son. Henry Ford just got the Grand Cross of the Order of the German Eagle. A birthday present from Chancellor Hitler for his seventy-fifth birthday. I told your father we should sell our Fords. He said that I shouldn't let myself be influenced by communist propaganda. He said it's only the Germans who aren't afraid of the future, who know that fascism is only a tool to prevent chaos. Charley, the house is yours. Do what you have to do, you understand?"

Charley wasn't quite sure what his grandmother wanted of him. It was not as if he didn't often contradict his father, walk away when he was spewing out venom. He supposed she knew about Pamela's Jewish boyfriend; Pam hadn't even asked him on the train about their grandmother, because she had probably already spoken to her, and at length. Perhaps he was being exhorted to support Pamela, but he couldn't believe that was all his grandmother meant; surely she knew he would support Pam's cause without being told.

He wandered down the renovated stairwell, pausing to look at the old photographs of Mary Mann, in her late forties, when her career was taking her to more and more distant points, in younger and younger roles. There was a ground-floor hallway of old portraits in oil that he had never found very interesting, but perhaps because of his grandmother's words, he found himself looking at familiar objects with a new concentration. He tried to see himself in the dull colors of eighteenth-century forebears, to imagine his life as an object of study in some future generation. Not an Indian fighter, a Revolutionary War hero, a radical fighting the forces of slavery, but an only child, a boy at twenty-six, afraid to look squarely into the future, or even into his own heart.

"Charley, come see what we've done to the kitchen," said his mother, interrupting his reverie in the hallway. But he had no desire to see a new sink, new plumbing, new electrical outlets in a room that John Collins had first staked out as a lean-to addition to a two-room cabin. His mother's cheeriness was not infectious, not at all. Charley wanted to touch the past, to feel the connections to his home that he didn't feel in the presence of his parents. He walked out onto the screened-in porch that looked out on the river, and then walked outside and down to the shore. As a boy, he had often followed the shore all the way down to the Sound, but in recent years many new houses had been built, very pretty waterfront homes on one acre for big prices—fifteen to twenty thousand dollars. The residents of these homes didn't like to see strangers wandering on their shoreline, particularly a tall, dark-haired stranger. But Charley didn't think of this. He hadn't been in Safe Haven in months, and he wanted a walk, and he wanted the river, and he wanted the Sound and its sandy beach.

And of course he knew that William Hiram's house was on Shore Road, just across the ribbon of asphalt from the beach, perhaps three miles away. Thinking of this made him walk faster. It would be enough to sit on the beach, his back to the water, looking up at the second-story windows winking over the water's edge. But after a half mile he had to give up his plan to walk down to the Sound along the riverside. Nearly every property line was delineated by a dock and a fence running from the water to the road. Short of climbing rusty chain link, or wading out into the precipitously deep water, he had no way of strolling where his ancestors had. Charley hurried up the hill from the water, staying close to a fence, hoping not to run into an unfriendly neighbor. He would go for the road and then hitch a ride to the beach.

"You," said a distinctly familiar voice. "What are you doing here?"

Disbelievingly, Charley turned around and saw Lily Berger standing at the side of a relatively new house, built in the colonial style, with a straw basket filled with flowers in one hand and garden shears in the other. "This isn't the Hiram house," he said.

"How did you know where I was going?" said Lily. "Did you follow us?"

"No—I—it was an accident coming upon you like this. I thought you'd be down at the beach. On the Sound. You know, Long Island Sound."

"You haven't explained how you found me," she said, putting down the basket of flowers, but holding on to the shears.

"It was luck," he said. "The most amazing luck I've ever come across. We're practically neighbors. Whose house is this?"

"It's ours," she said.

"I don't understand. You're not even—you're foreigners," said Charley.

"I assure you it's all quite legal. What's not legal is your presence on our property. I don't know how you found out I'd be here, but I think you'd better go right now."

"Wait," said Charley. "Please, I'm not an idiot, but you keep making me sound like one. As if English isn't my native language. You make me nervous—"

"And you make me nervous, Mr. Keats. You're not supposed to be here. I don't know you, and I don't know how you found me, and I want you to leave or I'm going to call the local police."

"The local police?" said Charley laughing. "They'd never bother a member of my family."

This was meant as a joke, but Lily Berger didn't seem to find it at all funny. Charley had no idea how seriously upset she'd become at seeing him in the garden of the furnished house purchased by her father's Swiss banker, through William Hiram, for nineteen thousand dollars, sight unseen. The house had been cleaned by an incompetent servant; that much had been clear at once to mother and daughter, if not to the genial Mr. Hiram. But worse than that remediable situation was the house itself, utterly without charm or distinction, furnished with rented beds and tables and chairs too bizarrely ugly for the Bergers to have ever imagined. They had not come for the view of the river, of course, nor for the ease of country living. Lily reminded her mother that here they would be free, not only from the hatred and harassment of the mob, but from the legislated hatred of the Nazi regime. But Hiram had referred to this young man as a Nazi during the drive over. And somehow he had found their house, and he seemed intent on staying here, looking at her as if she were a piece of meat in the butcher shop. "So here too the police work for you?"

"Not exactly," said Charley. "But we do support them at Christmas."

"Get out of here," she said, holding back tears of anger and fear. "This is my house, and I want you to leave! Go on!" She held the shears in front of her, as if she would stab him. "Move!"

"No," said Charley, thinking it a sort of romantic game. "You'll have to kill me, I'm afraid." Smiling, he took a half step toward her, and the beautiful blonde girl drove the shears forward, mindlessly. Charley held up his hand to protect his chest, and the point of the shears grazed his palm, drawing blood. "Jesus," he said. "You're crazy."

"I told you to leave," she said, dropping the shears.

"I'm bleeding," he said. "I don't believe you did that to me. Look at me—" He held up the bloody palm, and Lily took him by the elbow and steered him toward the house.

"It was stupid of you—" she said, but he interrupted her.

"Of me? Are you crazy? *You* stabbed *me!*"

"I didn't mean to. It was an accident," she said, and when he still complained she added harshly: "Just shut up, will you? Let me take care of it."

She was unfamiliar with the house, and could not at first find the medicine chest stocked with essentials by the woman whom Hiram had employed to ready the house for the Bergers. With quick, determined motions, she took hold of his hand, rinsed it with lukewarm water, then with water and soap, then examined the wound and determined that it was minor. "This will hurt," she said, and poured on the antiseptic, holding his squirming wrist in a powerful grip. "And be quiet. My mother is sleeping."

"Anything you say, Miss Berger." He watched as she applied some gauze and a bandage, content to have his hand under her care for as long as she liked.

"Why do you look at me like that?"

"Because you're the most beautiful girl I've even seen," he said stupidly, hating the words almost as much as she did. Lily hit him at once across the face, letting go of his just-bandaged hand.

"It's forbidden," she said.

"What? What did I say?"

"I think you should go, Mr. Keats. I'm sorry about the accident. It's not serious, but you can go, and you can stay off my property I think from now on, yes?"

"No," said Charley. "Wait a minute. You're crazy. This is crazy. Let me explain. Don't you want to know why I'm here, why you stabbed me?"

"That was a mistake, now please go," she said. But as she walked him outside, he insisted on explaining: He had no idea that she and her mother had bought this house on the river; it was simply fate that had brought him right up to her in the garden, and it was fate that had enabled her to stab him, simply so they would have a chance to speak.

"It's true I would have come here if I'd known you'd be here, but I didn't, you see," he said wildly. "Ever since I saw you on the train, I've wanted to meet you, but I was too shy. Not simply because of the way you look. Something else. There's some quality about you that I've never seen or felt or imagined before. I was afraid to say that to you, but not now. On the train, there was nothing I could do to tell you how I felt. You'd think I was crazy, and why would someone like you be interested in someone like me? But I thought I'd go down to the beach, the Sound beach, because Hiram's house is down there, on Shore Road, overlooking the water. And not that I'd have had the nerve to knock on his door, not at all. But I just wanted to go down there, because I knew you'd be there, and maybe I'd catch a glimpse of you, do you see? Maybe you'd even take a walk on the beach. But it was fate. I never got to the beach, your fence was in the way, I was coming up to go to the road, and there you were, and you even cut me with the shears. Please, just talk to me. I want to know you."

"I'm Jewish," said Lily Berger.

"That's all right," said Charley, realizing at once that it was an inadequate, even idiotic response. "I don't mean that it's all right," he said. "I mean that it doesn't make a difference. A person is a person, and I'm not one of those who make such a distinction about what religion—"

"Mr. Hiram said that you're a Nazi," said Lily.

"That's a lie."

"You're not a Nazi? You are telling me the truth?"

"Of course I'm telling you the truth. First of all, my father isn't a Nazi, not a real Nazi—no one is, not in America—and even if he were, what has that got to do with me? I'm not my father. I'm quite nice, really I am, I never would hurt a fly. I want to write plays. I'm a romantic, do you see, and I just wanted to get to know you, that's all. Just to know you, please.

(341)

Why are you crying? What did I say that you should be crying?"

"I'm Jewish," she said again, and the young woman's whole frame seemed to shake from some vast reserve of pain. Charley moved toward her at once, putting his arm about her shoulders, trying to comfort her. "But I'm Jewish," she said again. "It's forbidden. How can you touch me?"

What he had first seen as aristocratic aloofness, as the poise of a princess, was an absolute sham. She was not simply vulnerable, but someone who had been hurt, again and again. He remembered what Pamela had spoken to him about on the train: how Jews were forbidden to sit on park benches in the city of Berlin. But of course, there was much more to it than that; he read the newspapers, the bizarre facts that were somehow insulated from his consciousness by the newsprint, by the European dateline. Since 1935, Jews and Aryans weren't allowed to marry; perhaps they were not allowed to make love at all. Even a half-Jew couldn't marry a German. This was what she must mean by forbidden, he imagined, the prohibition against mingling the Master Race with the Chosen People.

"How can you stand to touch me?" she said, so softly that he almost couldn't hear the impossible words. She was not a princess, then; she was a fallen angel, a superior being far greater than anyone he had ever known, who had somehow fallen to earth, had somehow been made to think of herself as degraded and low and untouchable.

"I love you," he said, letting his boyish infatuation have full reign. How else could he explain that he wanted to touch her, that he wanted to hold her in his arms and allow her to cry, or to laugh, to attend to his wounded palm? She was troubled, yes, and he would attend to her trouble. He knew so little about her, not enough to understand his attraction, or to base it on something logical. She was beautiful, she was different, she was mysterious. On the one hand, she was far too good for him; on the other hand, she was so low as to be forbidden to the mainstream of men. She was a refugee, but she was rich; she was a stranger, a foreigner, but there was in the touch of her hand, in the scent of her hair, something familiar, something as natural to him as his own skin.

"You can't love me," she said, as if she might be speaking to someone else, another Gentile across the ocean, or perhaps to her own sense of self. "You can't love me," she said again, but Charley held her chin in his bandaged hand and gently brought his lips to hers.

Lily blinked against the tears, shivering, as if the boy in front of her eyes were transforming himself into a monster, an alien. "Let go of me," she said, softly at first, then much more loudly: "Let go of me! How dare you touch me! Who do you think you are?"

Charley backed away. He understood that she had accepted his kiss, had wanted his embrace. Some part of her needed love as much as he did; some beaten and desperate part of her psyche wanted him to reach out for her, to make extravagant claims of romantic passion, and for these claims to be true and undying. But this was a small part of Lily Berger, perhaps the smallest part. She had spent five years building a wall about herself, since 1933, when she'd been seventeen, and her best friend, a Christian girl who shared her first name, Lily Haupt-mann, who told her every last secret of her heart, had told her that the Jews were getting what they deserved. Later, there was another abandonment, far more cruel. The boy who had pledged his love to Lily Berger forever, fell out of love with her at once. Love had been replaced by fear.

"Are you all right?" Charley said.

"I shouted at you," she said. "I hope I didn't disturb Mother. I'm not crazy, please understand. I was just thinking about— what's there. Left behind. And my father. He didn't want to go."

"Believe me, I understand. You can tell me anything, and I will listen, and I will try to help you. If you want to talk, please do. If you want to be quiet, I'll just be happy listening to you get used to the sound of the river."

"You kissed me."

"Yes."

"You're a handsome boy," she said.

"I'm older than you, and you're more beautiful than anyone I've ever seen. In the movies too, I mean—"

"Stop," she said. "I can't listen to that kind of talk. It doesn't make sense to me. I only left a week ago. From London. We've been shut up there for two weeks, but it didn't feel any different than Berlin. There's a threat there too, you know. Not just war. Collapse. They have their fascists, they hate their Jews too. I've had to wear a star on my clothing. Wherever I was, people would stare at me. I can't imagine being beautiful—no, I *remember* being beautiful. When I was a little girl, a young girl with very long hair, carefully braided, and all the boys knew my name. But I haven't been in school since I was seventeen, not a real school. I've only taught in the Jewish school. I've taught little children German and English grammar, and many times Nazis waited outside with pebbles and stones to throw at our windows, or at us. I'm forbidden. Do you understand? I'm not a human over there, and it's my country, it's been my country all my life. Why did that nice man say you are a Nazi?"

"I'm not—please—it's just not true."

"Your father then. What is your father? What sort of a man is he?"

"He's not a Nazi, truly, he's not," said Charley. "He's a businessman, and he believes in a kind of powerful capitalism. He's not a fascist, but he has very little regard for people who aren't rich, for people who weren't born into the same circumstances he was born into."

"He hates Jews?" said Lily Berger.

"My cousin—you saw her on the train—she has a Jewish boyfriend. An Austrian. My father is against him, against the whole idea."

"If it's not different in America, I will not be able to stop my mother from killing herself," she said.

"It is different in America."

"They say—the Nazis—they say that the Germans are the guardians of the Aryan race. They must preserve its purity. The Jews are the greatest corrupters of this purity. We are Semites, you see," she said, running her fingers through her thick blonde hair. "A dark and nefarious race. We grow fat on the lifeblood of the West. We grow strong by corrupting the Aryans. My Uncle Jacob died last year of a heart attack. He was forty-three, and had been a champion fencer until 1929. In good condition.

His wife left him. He had married a Gentile woman, and her parents were able to convince her to leave. They had no children. The divorce was arranged without delay. He had owned a dozen office buildings in Hamburg and Munich, and when the Nazis confiscated his holdings, his wife had already left him, and all the money he had in the bank was sequestered, by law, except for five thousand marks. Two thousand dollars. That's not a lot of money, not for a man who needed hundreds of marks a week just to be able to bribe the local shopkeepers to sell a Jew medicine. His mother was sick. She's still alive now, you see, an old Jew alive in Berlin. But my uncle died. He had a heart attack. The day after his wife remarried. It was his first attack, and there was no warning, and they found him dead on the street, with his gold star pinned to his coat." She smiled at him, as if there was something scarcely credible about Charley Keats. "But this is America."

"It's safe here," he said, taking her hand into his bandaged palm. "You did a good job."

"What job?"

"The bandage."

"I tell you all this because your face doesn't look like it's ever seen a single bad day. You look like an American. Charley. That is so American. I want what you say to be true."

"That I love you?" he said.

"No, of course not. You don't know the first thing about me. I mean what you said about America—that it's different. That it's safe here."

"It is," said Charley. "Everything I said is true. Everything."

"How old are you?" she said, and when he had told her that he was twenty-six, she asked him where he had gone to school (Yale), where he was now employed (New York City, with his own studio apartment on West Eleventh Street), and what was his greatest goal, his grandest dream.

"To be a playwright," he said without hesitation. "Do you think you could ever love a playwright?"

"No," she said. "Not at all. Never. I could only love a man of action, a soldier, a fighter. Do you understand? Someone who would know what to do without just words. Someone who would have enough hate and strength to strangle Adolf Hitler."

Charley had an answer for this, a variation on what he employed to tell his father why there was as much glory and
power in writing for the theater as there was in controlling the
enterprises of the family business. He would have explained
why a play could move audiences to understand justice and
freedom in a way that no violent act ever could; he would have
told her that he was drawn to art not only from an aesthetic
impulse but from an urge to educate, to influence. Nothing
could be greater than to re-create the world according to his
own wants and desires, and to make others see that his creation
was best. But Charley had no chance to speak. The beautiful
princess was looking at him strangely, the tip of her tongue
caught between her clenched teeth; and then she took hold of
his hand, the one without a bandage, and brought it squarely
against her open mouth.

This was the single most sensual act he had ever experienced,
not least because of its incredible surprise.

Her gray eyes seemed to leap from one world to another;
from a life of restraint to one of utter abandon. Lily's hands
held his with unnatural force, as her tongue lightly touched the
surface of his knuckles, as her eyes bound his with a need that
had been masked until that moment. She let out a sharp little
breath, a puff of collapsing will. All this was the work of a
second, a half second, but it so shocked Charley Keats, so unnerved him, that he was left without words, without designs.
He looked at the girl, every bit as beautiful as she'd been a
moment before, her story every bit as poignant, his love for her
no less compelling.

But she had changed.

She had initiated contact, she had expressed a desire that
transcended any polite talk, any wild, clumsy attempt to get
her to find him attractive. In a moment she had radiated her
unmistakable desire for a love that was fundamentally sexual,
and this so shocked Charley that he couldn't tell if he was
terrified or repulsed. Or if, perhaps, a mistake had been made, a
terrible neurotic bump in space and time that would now vanish, that would be replaced by the princess, cool and distant,
in need of help, interested only in heroes.

"Charley," she said, and she let go of his hand and took hold of his head, and drove her tongue into his mouth. He wanted to flatter himself, to hold on to his dream image of this girl, to imagine that she had somehow discovered his true worth, had somehow been exposed to the finest part of his character, and understanding it at once had fallen in love with him, only him, and for the first time. But this made no sense. He tried to respond, to drive his tongue into her mouth, to caress her lips with his teeth; but he couldn't concentrate. Charley was overwhelmed. He could feel the racing of her heart, the heat of her body exploding on this very hot day, his tongue being sucked into her mouth and bitten, as if by a wild animal, a creature of the lowest moral order. Like many young men who had made love only to whores, his notion of romance and passion involved chasing a virgin and being rebuffed, held at bay. And Lily was a perfect image of romance: blonde, chastely dressed, the guardian of her mother, the heroine of a monstrous hate-filled regime. Now this image was shattered. Her hands moved to the back of his neck, her fingers drove into his ears, pulled at the roots of his hair.

"Lily," he said, but his voice was strange, trying to be sophisticated, or excited, or glad, but sounding instead like that of a small boy. "You're beautiful," he said, and did more of what she was doing to him. There, outside the new house on the Saugatuck River, he held her cheeks, he ran his fingers through her hair, he kissed her lips, her eyes, trying to remember that he had loved her without knowing this—that she was a woman who actually wanted what he wanted. He wondered if he would be allowed to touch her breast, if she would restrain him from moving his hands onto her waist, her thighs. It seemed like a dream that was half nightmare, half ecstatic fulfillment. He didn't want his infatuation to founder on repulsion for a whore; but what if she were not a whore, if they were simply experiencing passion, true passion, together for the first time? What if she were a virgin, what if she had never been in love, what if she had never kissed a man this way before?

"Don't call me beautiful," said Lily, out of breath and insistent. "Don't say that you love me, don't say that I'm wonderful, don't say anything at all."

And then she didn't say anything else, because the mood had

been broken. She let go of him, and turned away and walked across the lawn toward the house. He called after her to wait, and hurried alongside her.

"I'm sorry," he said.

"For what?"

"I offended you," he said, not knowing how. She looked at him sharply.

"You're surprised," she said.

"No, not at all."

"You're surprised that I kissed you," she insisted.

He felt he was losing her. This was a test, and he was failing. She was angry, and he didn't understand why. Charley felt a perverse excitement growing in him, a sexual excitement; he had to chase her, he had to hold on to her.

"I don't know what I am anymore," he said. "I don't know anything."

And now he pulled her into his arms, and it was *his* excitement that broke apart thought. He stopped wondering if she was good or bad, if his first impression of her was sullied by the fact of her sensuality. Charley wanted her. He kissed her, and didn't wonder who had touched her lips, he held her, and didn't remember the whores who had rented him their bodies.

"Yes," she said. "Oh my God."

He had brought his body so close to hers that her breasts were pressed into his belly, his genitals rubbed against her waist. His hands wanted to bring her closer. When he kissed her he wanted nothing less than to draw her inside his body, when he touched her he wanted nothing less than to make her flesh one with his. If he had stopped to think, he would have realized that he was no longer preceding an action with a question, no longer looking to past customs, experiences, ideas in order to decide what to do at the moment. He was much taller than she, and he lowered himself on shaking knees, he held her waist and then her backside as he drove his penis against her pelvis, feeling a thousand sensations through the layers of clothing, and not one of them was guilt. Later he would remember the time he had gone to the brothel in New York with three friends, and they had danced about the parlor with laughing whores, none of whom was the least bit happy; they had held the prostitutes in just that way as they danced. Later he would remember the arch way in which whores had smiled at him, suggesting that he was in some way making them excited, when all they wanted was to hurry him along and through and out. But though he held Lily now the way he had held whores, though she and he both wanted to move their passion along from the unbearable plateau at which it now stood, a remarkable thing had taken place inside the young man. He was ecstatic. He had forgotten shame, he had thrown away any Puritanical notions of moral turpitude. This young woman, whom he had seen for the first time only hours before on the platform at Grand Central Station, was a source of bliss. He had gone past infatuation, without turning it inside out or discarding it. He wanted her now, he wanted to make love to her, and he could scarcely stand up, he could scarcely keep the pressure behind his shut eyes from overwhelming his consciousness.

"Where can we go?" he said, and she took him into the house, both of them silent, intent on their soft steps, on their loudly pounding hearts.

Like so many houses on the river, this one had a rear porch, screened in, looking out to the water. There were chairs, there were tables, there was a couch covered with cheap cloth. He had a momentary shock, a stab that took him back into the real world, when she kicked off her shoes and pulled him to her; it rekindled in him the ingrained notion of her "badness." But he forgot this. Her lips parted, and his were there, urgent, and if she pulled him to her on the couch, he needed no prompting to join her, to relax his long frame alongside her elegant little body, silk-clad, and in ecstatic motion.

Then, instead of being tentative, he was very fast. He had many twisted ideas about sexuality: that passionate people were not only bad, but quick; that sophisticated loving was rough and hard and cruel. But it was not quite possible for him to put these wrongheaded notions into practice. While his passion was very occasionally penetrated by a stab of erroneous moralizing, it was continually overpowered by his infatuation. Love slowed him down. It was not possible to grip the beautiful neck with brutal fingers, to rip off her clothes in some 1938 vision of Neanderthal virility. Not with Lily. Fast at first, kissing her lips, pulling at the complicated buttons of her dress, kneading her belly and breasts as if he were a baker's assistant run amok, Charley found himself slowing down, falling into a place he had never visited. Looking into her eyes, feeling her sure hands easy on his brow and shoulders and chest, he let his passion join his love, rather than place it in opposition.

"Do you want me?" she said, very softly, and when he said that he did, he no longer thought of her words as the words of a whore; and when he called her beautiful, when he told her that he loved her, and she reminded him to say nothing, to stop talking, to just tell her that he wanted her, that and nothing more, he thought the words perfectly correct, without any possibility of sinfulness. Because he did want her, and he did love her, and this truth was so overwhelming that nothing else could take precedence in his mind. And so he stopped fighting, stopped trying to act according to a formula, either a sophisticated model gleaned from books and brothels or a moral one inherited from church and tradition.

She helped him remove her dress. It was the work of a few moments, and she allowed him to help her, because helping her was part of his vision. He wanted to love her, and the lovemaking was not just a little bit of dying, but a little bit of creating. Charley needed the feeling of control, even if the feeling was subliminal. He needed to reveal her nakedness, to revel in what he had stripped away. When he saw her before him in her underclothes she didn't strike him as salacious or sultry, but only as dear, impossibly lovable. He kissed the skin of her belly, he lightly touched the inside of her thighs. "You too," she said softly, and he found himself removing his clothes in the gently shadowed light of the porch, in the afternoon heat tempered by the river breeze. It amazed him that she seemed to enjoy the touch of his bare chest. She sighed, and there was no feigning her joy, her desire, as she drove her tongue along his nipples, along the chest hair, heavy with sweat. He was naked, save for his socks and undershorts, and when Lily removed her brassiere, her eyes were on his without shame or hesitation or anything other than the search for consummation. Charley removed his shorts and turned over on his belly, moving along the rough surface of the couch like a giant snake, his head raised not to strike but to kiss. He touched her breasts, small and firm and pale, and he placed his hand under her short half-slip, and Lily groaned, almost as if she were in pain. "Wait," she said, and raising herself slightly, she pulled off her slip and her panties and tossed them on the floor. "Take off your socks," she said.

Charley quickly did as he was told, and when he had dropped the second long sock to the floor, Lily pulled him back to her side, cradling him on the narrow width of the couch, and then gently pulling at his pubic hair. He was already so far removed from any previous sexual experience, where the whores had always dropped a few compliments about his youth and his beauty, and then saw to it that he was satisfied while they froze smiles onto their enduring faces, that he had no basis for comparison, no map in his mind about where next to tread. Like a foreigner in a land of endless promise, he made no hasty moves, not wanting the gorgeous terrain to vanish into the realm of dreams. And Lily guided him. Lily knew what she wanted, and she wanted him.

"Charley," she said, her accent making the name exotic, her light touch on his erect penis sending slow waves of ecstatic pain through the heat and the light on the porch. He was conscious of his own body, more conscious than he had ever been. For Lily showed it to him. Her tongue and her fingertips played with the muscles about his knee, felt the wetness inside his armpit, traced the outline of his small, perfectly shaped ears. Without thinking, he had begun to follow her movement, accepting the beauty of his erection, but also of his straining muscles, the taut skin of his abdomen scratched by her slowly moving fingernails. It was nice to be awake, and hot, and sweating; their heat radiated at each other, overwhelming the heat of the day, adding to the mutual atmosphere of abandon.

And Charley had abandoned most of the baggage he carried in his mind. He was hot now, and relishing the heat, and he loved his body and he loved her body, and he loved their bodies together. And he touched her now, not to excite her, or to excite himself, not to take something that was not his, not to indicate possession or conquest but simply to celebrate love, simply to love. He kissed her breasts, he brought his knee up between her thighs, placing his hand over her vagina, then kissing the dark blonde pubic hair, then allowing his fingers to sink slowly into her wetness, feeling her heart race, and wanting only to slow it down, to expand the moment, to build it into a universe without end.

And then she pulled back. "Wait," she said, lifting her eyes from the madness, opening her mouth for air. "Lie back, please. Please. You're wonderful." Charley didn't know how and why he was wonderful, but he accepted it; it was part of the love-making, part of the hot, warm universe. He was flat on his back now on the couch, more excited than he had ever been, but strangely calm; the consummation was no longer the goal. The goal was gone. He was already there, in love, making love, finding happiness. But a moment later he realized he'd been wrong. Lily was on top of him, more radiantly beautiful than any creature of the imagination. Strands of her hair were stuck to her wet forehead, her nose and neck and cheeks ran with sweat. But the gray eyes were steady, calm, inner-directed. She closed them, and moved herself onto his erection, placing him inside her gently, slowly, her mouth open but not issuing a sound or even a breath of air. This was better. Yes, this was a far better moment. This was indeed the best moment in his life, so suddenly blissful that he felt as if he would cry out, or black out from the heat, the pleasure, the rioting of his emotions. He forced himself to keep his eyes open. She barely moved now, but when she did, it was agonizing, it was as beautiful as a spectrum of colors in the back of the brain, everything flashing at once, but not erupting; everything held back, everything promised. Her eyes were still closed, but he was able to watch her pale, thin body, her wet, heavy head of hair, her open mouth and twisted lips, her slowly moving, gently rising hips. He felt a shiver run through her, and then another, a contraction about his penis like a powerful hand. But still she held back. She moved yet more slowly. She opened her eyes and looked at him through tears. Then her mouth twisted, as if in pain, and she cried out, and her body jerked, and she shut her eyes, and she clenched his shoulders, she clamped her teeth together, and then she smiled. "Oh, God," she said, and then she said it again, and her body shook, and her hips and her thighs pressed together violently, but there was no place in the world for her to hold steady at that moment. Lily began to move, like a puppet, like a demon, and the movements were from within, from the best part of her, from a desire that was immense, and from an ability to meet that desire, to ride it, to accept it, to be one with it.

Charley felt the beginnings of her pleasure, but couldn't recognize it. He had no idea a woman could enjoy what Lily enjoyed. He understood that an incredible reserve of joy and love was being released, that he was in some way a part of it, perhaps even at its center. But he couldn't follow the mad movements of her body. She shivered and shook like a woman who had lost control of her being; but Charley had lost control of his. He hardly knew what happened, only that he had come and that at that moment he was full of love, and a sensation of loss. For the moment was already dying. Even at the heart of their ecstasy, reality lurked, eager to remind them of the world. The sadness was overpowering. For Charley, the coming together of their bodies was the most emotional experience of his life. He literally could not imagine anything better than what had just taken place. He was still inside her, and her eyes were closed once again, and though she had come, he moved slightly, and this gave her a shock of pleasure, and her whole body quivered, a spasm of joy.

Lily bent at the waist now, and with infinite care lowered her head to his chest. They said nothing. She pressed her lips to his neck, but did not kiss him. Twice more her body shook, reacting to a pleasure that was slow in receding from her frail frame; these were aftershocks, not like the moment when they had come together, but short delicious reminders of his slowly diminishing penis inside her, and necessary: They made what had just passed seem possible.

She fell asleep like that, bent over on his body, his penis inside her, the sunlight moving westward across the screened-in porch, her mother sleeping dreamlessly upstairs. Charley did not sleep. He felt his heart slow down its mad pace even as his love grew. There was a danger revealing itself to him. He did not want to leave. It would be unbearable to withdraw from her body, from the ecstasy they shared, and from the gentle joy of proximity. What had begun as infatuation was now obsession. He didn't know a thing about this girl, he remembered, and now he knew that he didn't know anything at all—not about women, about sex, about his own capacity for bliss. This was bliss, and it had taken him twenty-six years to discover it. He would not leave, he could not leave.

"Oh, God," she said.

Lily was awake, and as she raised herself up from his chest, his penis was hard again, and her hips were already in motion, slow and agonizing, and there were tears in her eyes. She bent over once more to kiss him, and then pulled back, quickly, and she shut her eyes, and the madness was upon them once again. It was not better or worse than the first time. It was the same. They had discovered a mutuality of passion that was so deliriously full that it could have no gradations. There was simply the world, and then there was its obverse—this demonic netherworld that was yet holy and good and loving.

"Did you mean what you said?" he asked her a long time later. "That you could never love a playwright?"

"I didn't say that." She moved slightly, her back stretching out its muscles, and he wanted to crush her to him, to bring her inside him, the way he was inside her. "I said that I could only love a man of action. A fighter."

"Yes," said Charley. "Then I will be a fighter. I will be whatever I have to be for you to love me."

She didn't answer this, for she didn't think it possible for him to love her at all.

When they had dressed, they walked outside, down to the river, and she explained to him that she had had a lover, five years before, a German, a black-haired blue-eyed athlete who was kind, and strong, and decent. He loved Thomas Mann and Picasso and read *The Good Earth* with her in English. She had been seventeen. It was 1933. Albert Einstein fled to America. Her best friend abandoned her. And then her lover, beautiful and constant and true, went off to the university and wrote her a letter explaining why they could never see each other again. He had even taken the trouble to type the letter, to sign it with an initial rather than his own name, as if someone might confiscate the letter and incriminate him for having had a Jewess as a lover.

"I love you," said Charley.

"Go home," she said. "It's late, and you don't know what you're saying."

"I know what I'm saying, and I want my home to be with you."

"Listen to me," said Lily. "I don't love you. I don't even know you. We made love. That was what happened. Maybe I'm wild, maybe I'm bad, maybe I'm just a Jewess corrupting your soul. I've had one lover, and that was five years ago, and all that time I've lived with wanting love. Do you understand? I'm forbidden, I'm the foreign woman, I'm the one you'd better forget."

Charley took her in his arms, and Lily stopped talking, feeling his strength, his will. He kissed her. He held her close, and then slowly released her, holding her at arm's length, looking with amazement at a face he had never seen before that day, and now knew as well as his own. "Tomorrow," he said. "May I take you and your mother for a little tour of the town?"

"Not tomorrow," she said. "I want you to think a little. By yourself. Think of who I am, and what you want, and what is possible."

"Anything is possible," said Charley, still holding her. But he agreed to wait another day before coming to see her and her mother. And then they said good-bye quickly; and she watched him walk off along the water's edge toward the very old home that had belonged to fighters and lovers and passionate men and women for three hundred years.

TWENTY-TWO

———◆———

Charley felt cleansed. He was strong and handsome and intelligent. Whereas before sex had always left him feeling dirty, tired, depressed, he was now energetic, happy, eager to bring the world about him into sharper focus. At home, he looked at his mother, still pretty and vivacious, and wondered if she could have ever experienced the sort of love that was running through him at that moment. He didn't believe his father capable of love, not a great love that became the center of one's self.

"Have you been running?" said his mother when he'd come home. "You'd better shower up and change. Dinner's at seven."

A shower would be fine, he thought. And a dinner. And a long night's sleep in his antique bed, trying to bring back the image of the girl with whom he had just made love. He took his shower, feeling her touch all about his soapy body. They were not dressing formally, so he wore an open-necked cotton lisle shirt and floppy trousers. He stopped by his grandmother's room, still wet from the shower, eager to talk with someone he loved.

"What's happened to you?" said Katherine Keats, squinting at him over her reading glasses.

"I had a shower."

"It must have been quite a shower," said his grandmother.

"I'm in love," said Charley.

"Since this afternoon? You're sure it's not just sunstroke?"

"I'm sure," said Charley. He couldn't help remembering, even at that moment, the incredible passion so recently experienced. And it could be his again. He could make love with Lily Berger once more, and then again, and then a hundred thousand times more for the rest of his life. To bring himself back to earth, he asked his grandmother to tell him about how she met Charles Keats II, and how she had fallen in love with him.

"I was very young, and he was very experienced," she said. "And of course very good-looking, like all the Charley Keatses, even your crazy father, if only he'd lose weight." Katherine Keats launched into her story, talking quietly, as if afraid to lose her audience. She had already dined, alone in her bed, and soon his mother and father would join him in her bedroom for martinis, while she would have her after-dinner brandy, to hasten her to sleep. He tried to follow her story, but his concentration wavered. She had once been a lovely young woman, like Lily, but he couldn't quite bring himself to believe that she had been like Lily in bed. No, that would be impossible. There was not that much energy in the world. If everyone could experience what he had that afternoon, no one would work, sleep, fight, eat. No one would do anything but make love, endlessly, and the world would expire in a sigh of bliss. That was certainly not the direction of things in this house, in this town, in this country. He thought of the lover she'd mentioned, a nameless German boy five years in the past, when the swastikas had begun to wave supremely, with the full force of the government behind them, when Lily had been seventeen, and fresh, and a believer in the possibility of love. Either the German had not experienced one tenth of the emotional force that Charley had that day, or he was the world's greatest coward. No one could frighten *him* away from Lily, Charley thought.

"Are you going to tell me with whom you've fallen in love?" said his grandmother finally.

"Of course, but not at this moment. I don't know much about her," said Charley. "I think I'd like to bring her here, to meet you." He wondered what his grandmother would make of her, if she would be able to read past the aristocratic outlines to the sensual craving, the terrible need for love. They cut off any further talk of love as Charley's parents wandered into the large bedroom, Mrs. Keats carrying a silver tray. She handed the old lady her brandy, and shook the martini shaker.

"How are you, boy?" said Charley's father, hitting him squarely between the shoulder blades, laughing at his own exuberance. "What do we have to do to get you out for a weekend, anyway? You got something against the country and clean air?"

"He probably has a girlfriend in the city," said his mother.

"I hope so," said his father. "I want my son to be normal, right?" He hit his son again, to emphasize his paternal feelings. Then father, mother, and son drank their cold martinis in silence, while Katherine Keats observed them coolly over her brandy snifter.

"Junior," she said finally, looking at Charles Keats III without a trace of maternal affection, "if you're going to insist on breaking up Pamela from this Jewish friend of hers, you're going to have to find some other place to hang your hat in Safe Haven."

"What did you say?" said Charley's father, twisting his heavy body about from the front to the side of the four-poster bed. "Pamela has been complaining to you, has she? She'll regret it, let me tell you."

"No, no," said Katherine Keats mildly. "My granddaughter need not regret anything. Pammie came to me because I am the mother of her father, and the mother of the man who helps support her parents."

"Supports them," said Charles Keats III. "Not just helps. I do it all. And as much as I admire and love you, Mother, please don't forget that I am responsible for the comfort of each and every one of us, not just in this house, but in what we own in Greenwich, and the houses and cars and lands of all your sons. Me. Samuel doesn't take much, but he takes. John takes anything that's not nailed down. And Pam and her parents are a constant source of need. So if I want to make a condition—"

"Junior," said Katherine Keats, interrupting her son, "whose house is this?"

"I refuse to let you make yourself upset just before going to sleep, Mother," he said. "I think it best if we just wish you good night and go down to our dinner. We have guests, and I think I just heard their car."

"This is my house," said Katherine Keats. "And you are my son. And everything you have stems from me, if you want to know the truth. Your father did well, but he did better because of me and my family. You did well, but you were helped, not only by the fact of being born, but in a hundred other ways. I may be sick, but you're not going to blackmail your own brother's daughter because you have a little more money than he does."

"Finish your brandy, Mother," said Charles Keats III. "And go to sleep." He walked out of the bedroom, expecting the others to follow.

"I'll try and talk to him," said Cynthia Keats. She put down her martini glass, smiled awkwardly at her mother-in-law, and asked Charley if he was coming.

"When I'm through with Grandmother," he said, so that the lines of loyalty would be well established. After his mother had left, he smiled at his grandmother and then blurted out: "It's funny. The girl I'm in love with—she happens to be Jewish too."

"That's *not* funny," said Katherine Keats.

"You don't mind, do you?" said Charley, amazed at his grandmother's reaction. "I thought you didn't care about such things."

"Darling, Pammie is a crazy and delightful young girl. She runs around. I don't know a great deal about her private life, but I can imagine it. If she has a boyfriend who studies with Freud and happens to be beautiful and Jewish—well, no one is going to tell her what to do or not to do. But *you*. You fall in love. You marry. You have a different sort of obligation. I won't tell you what to do, Charley, but I will tell you that you should have fun now but don't ever marry a Jewish girl. It would be foolhardy. Don't misunderstand me. I'm not trying to force my opinions on you. I love you, so I'm telling you—don't marry out of your own class. For your own good. Now let me have a little peace."

A 1933 SJ Duesenberg—the car of Mae West, William Randolph Hearst, and the King of Spain—brought Dr. and Mrs.

Richard Bullock to the Keats home, ten minutes late for the "informal" dinner planned by Charley's mother. While a maid distributed drinks and hors d'oeuvres on the screened-in rear porch, the men talked a bit about automobiles. The Duesenberg was compared to a friend's Cord, with its 4.7-liter engine and elegant independent suspension; the Duesenberg's much bigger 6.9-liter engine could accelerate to one hundred miles an hour in seventeen seconds. Charles Keats III spoke fondly of his ever reliable Ford, but had a good word for his sixteen-cylinder Cadillac, which cost him nine thousand dollars at the height of the Depression, and was still in immaculate condition.

"I see a lot of Jews driving them," said Bullock pleasantly.

"You got Jews driving Bugattis," answered his host. "That doesn't mean the Bugatti's a bad car, right? It just means the Jews are making too much money. And it all starts with Rosenveldt."

Charley was trying his best to abstract himself from the conversation. Only hours before, he had been on another screened-in porch; the sun had descended as he'd shared love with Lily Berger. On a couch, looking out at the black night, the lightning bugs flashing against the screens, he remembered everything. He drank three martinis, and a soft visceral sensation, a memory of her touch inside his thigh, an electric prickling along his spine, made him look strangely at his fat father and his big-shouldered, crew-cut friend.

"Do you know," said Charley, "in New York, they make fun of people who think that Roosevelt's a Jew?"

"Naturally," said Bullock. "New York is a Jew town. They got the press by the short hairs."

"That's not the reason," said Charley with a sharpness new to the room. He stood up, and took a fourth drink from the maid, whose name he had forgotten for the moment. She was Max the chauffeur's new wife, and must have been twenty-five years younger than her husband. Charley's mother asked Mrs. Bullock if she'd care to see their newly remodeled kitchen.

"No," said Mrs. Bullock. "I'd rather stay here. I'm interested in your son's views of Mr. Roosevelt."

"You needn't use the name, my dear," said her husband. "Just 'The Madman' would be enough."

"I call him Mr. Roosevelt, Richard," said Mrs. Bullock. "You may call him what you like, but I call him by his proper name. I find your talking about him absolutely childish. If you want to criticize the man, criticize his policies. Either you call him a Jew, or you call him a traitor to his class. Which class? Make up your mind. Do you want to think of him as a secret Jew, a descendant of some Germanic criminal whom Peter Stuyvesant exiled to Hyde Park three hundred years ago—that story is too funny, really—or do you want to castigate him for going to Groton and Harvard and Columbia Law, inheriting pots of money, and then giving it away to the poor people?"

"My wife," said Bullock to Charles Keats III, "does not express my own views. Obviously."

"What views?" said Mrs. Bullock, her voice still rather mild. "I wasn't aware of any views being expressed. Just racial slurs and schoolboy prejudice—as usual." She stood up and placed her empty glass on the maid's tray. "This is a delightfully cool porch, Mrs. Keats. I'd very much enjoy seeing . . . the kitchen? I believe you said it was the kitchen that was just remodeled?"

"Bravo, Mrs. Bullock," said Charley, grinning widely, and holding on to her arm. "Don't go. You wanted to hear my views. All right. I'll tell you. I think President Roosevelt is practically a saint."

"That's enough of that rot," said his father.

"I would like to be heard, thank you," said Charley. "I am twenty-six years old and a great asset to your company, sir. I think you should be glad to hear the views of your son and only child. I think the President's signing of the Fair Labor Standards Act was enough to qualify him for sainthood among the poor workers of this country, but there's more to it than just that."

"I'm not going to listen to this," said his father. He stood up, lifting his great bulk with effort, and stomped over to where his son was about to make a drunken speech. More than anything else that Roosevelt had allowed, the Fair Labor Standards Act had alienated the factory-owning Keats. The idea of having to pay a minimum wage of twenty-five cents an hour, increasing over seven years to forty cents, was positively mind-boggling. It seemed to Keats that the whole system of free enterprise was being wrenched out from underneath him. And if he didn't quite believe the silly stories of Roosevelt having descended from German Jews, he was still eager to blame the Jewish advisers about "The Madman" for having pushed through communist ideology into the American government. "You're going to shut up right now, or you can just leave!"

"Secondly, though Mr. Roosevelt has since vacillated," continued Charley, standing his ground before his father's advancing shape, "I know his heart is in the right place. He's not neutral. He said he wanted to 'quarantine the aggressors.' We know who the aggressor is, don't we?"

His father took hold of him by the shoulders and shook him. "Are you drunk, Charley? I said to shut up, and when I say something, you listen. Right?"

Mrs. Bullock interceded on the boy's behalf: "Perhaps the Jews put something in the liquor, Mr. Keats."

"That's funny," said Mrs. Keats, trying to laugh. "I really think it would be best if we all had a little food in us. It's the liquor talking now—I've seen it a lot. He's really a good boy."

"He's a very good boy," said Mrs. Bullock.

"Thirdly," said Charley. "He's been very good with immigration. Since March. I read it in the *Times*. Even with all the crazies, he's keeping the refugees coming right up to full quota. Pamela's boyfriend might need a special visa—do you know anyone in the State Department, Father? Someone who doesn't hate Jews too much?"

"You're right. He's drunk," said Charles Keats III. "We'd better eat. Right away."

"I'm not drunk," said Charley, but his father had turned away from him, and only Mrs. Bullock was listening. "I'm just supporting Pam. She's my cousin. Loves a Jewish boy."

"They're very handsome," said Mrs. Bullock. "Do you like Paul Muni?"

"I am a playwright," said Charley, picking up a fifth drink and following Mrs. Bullock into the dining room. "I like all actors. They're much nicer than businessmen. Don't you agree?"

"Yes, dear," she said, keeping him from tripping over his own feet.

Over dinner, his father and Bullock scrupulously avoided eye contact with everyone else, even the maid who served them their poached fish. It was as if they'd decided to divorce themselves not only from Charley, but from the rest of the world. Together they went through the list of Roosevelt's anticapitalist crimes, dismissing German fascism with the idea that the real enemy was Japan. The fact that England and France had allowed Germany to begin the dismemberment of Czechoslovakia was seen not as shortsighted weakness, but as the strength to realize that England, France, and Germany were fraternally related, racially homogeneous, strong Aryan nations that must never fight one another.

"That's a lot of hooey," said Charley. "Would you pass the wine, please, Mrs. Bullock?" The maid brought over the bottle and poured it into Charley's glass. His father hesitated in his speech to Bullock, wondering whether to answer his son, and deciding finally against it. One didn't win an argument with a drunk, especially one sitting next to a Jew-loving liberal who was unfortunately married to his friend and fellow industrialist. Richard Bullock was actually quite important to Charles Keats III, and when he would later think about the disastrous evening, he would be very grateful to Mrs. Bullock for matching his son's humiliating words with opinions even more incendiary —especially since she remained sober throughout the evening. "And what about Spain?" asked Charley. "I suppose the Germans aren't the threat there either? I guess it's the Japanese who are bombing the women and children."

"There's bombing on both sides," said Bullock, answering Charley in place of his wife. He knew her opinions about the Spanish Civil War only too well. "The communists are bombing women and children, and they'll make slaves of all of us if we don't fight them now."

"Karl Marx was a Jew," said Charley drunkenly. "Did you know that, Dad?"

"Of course I know that," said his father. "If you can't behave yourself like a gentleman at the table, I suggest you go to your room."

"This is Grandmother's house," said Charley, his voice suddenly rising in volume. "Karl Marx must have been smart. I'm not a communist, but still, that's a heck of a theory, isn't it? And don't forget Freud. Do you have something against Freud, Dad?"

"I think you had better go—right now," said his father.

"Freud is Jewish," said Charley. "Pamela's boyfriend is Jewish too. He's in England. As a matter of fact, so is Dr. Freud. I just want you all to know," said Charley, stumbling to his feet, raising his wine glass to Mrs. Bullock, Mr. Bullock, his mother, and then finally his father, "I just want you all to know that I support Pamela Keats, daughter of Frederick and Elizabeth Keats, my own first cousin, the only cousin on my father's side —I have lots of cousins on Mom's side—I support Pam with all my might. That is a fact. I love Pam. This house belongs to Grandmother. And when she dies, it belongs to Pammie and me. Cheers."

Charley drank, and sat down heavily. The room remained quiet for a few moments, but his father knew the difference between drunken raving and a suddenly revealed truth from too-loose lips.

"The house belongs to you and Pammie," repeated Charles Keats III. "Is that what you said?"

"Yes, sir," said Charley. "It's all in writing. It's all legal, that's the truth. You can cut me off, but you can't throw me out of the house. And if you cut off Pamela—well, we're not going to be very happy with you living here then, are we, sir?"

"Tell me again, you miserable little bastard," said his father, getting up from his antique chair and knocking it over against the polished hardwood floor. "She's leaving you and Pamela this house? My house? Tell me, go on, *tell me.*"

"Charles!" said his wife, worrying more about the antique chair than about her stalwart son. His father had taken hold of his shoulders and pulled him back with great force, so that Charley's chair was also in danger of toppling, but with an awkwardly drunken Charley glued to the seat.

"I said tell me," repeated his father, and twisted the old chair so that his son fell out of it and went sprawling to the floor. Charley looked stupidly at the polished old wood, and smiled at the table legs and the summer shoes and the very pretty ankles of Mrs. Richard Bullock. He understood that his father was angry at him, very angry, but he was not at all worried. This was his house, not his father's; this was his floor, this ancient floor would be his and his children's. Somehow the anger was related to the Jewish question, he knew, but he had truly forgotten about Pamela, and about his grandmother, and about everything else other than his lust for Lily Berger and his perfect desire to go back to her, to be with her. "Get up," said his father, pulling at Charley's shirt collar and wrenching him to his feet.

The sudden shock to his neck angered Charley. It was like a rebuff. He looked at his father's fat face. "Don't hit me," he said.

"I didn't hit you, boy. You'll know when I hit you. I asked you a question."

Mrs. Bullock got up from her seat, pushing it back with great care and standing slim and straight and unafraid. "Richard, we seem to be in the midst of a family quarrel. Perhaps you and Mr. Keats can continue your discussion of financial contributions to fascist movements over lunch? I have a little indigestion."

Bullock stood up angrily, scratching his crew-cut head, his great potential for violence rising into the blood vessels of his cleanly shaved cheeks. "I've asked you," he said, "and asked you. Is it that impossible for you to stop calling me a fascist?"

Charley's mother tried to save the day. She got up too; she didn't want to address them from her chair, alone at the heavily food-laden table. "I really think it would be best if we all just sat down and tried to be calm. It's really the martinis. They're not like other drinks, you know. Right to your head—zap! You can't be responsible for what you say once you've had one, and we've all had much more than one. Really. Let's all come back to the table and have some dessert. Please?"

"You're quite a girl," said Mrs. Bullock to Mrs. Keats, and walked out of the dining room, en route to the cool night air.

"Please excuse my wife's poor manners," said Mr. Bullock.

"Oh, I do," said Cynthia Keats. Without thinking, she had gone to Charley's aid, helping him into a chair turned away from the table so that he could look at his father, red-faced and glowering, waiting for his son's response. But with Bullock still in the room, and his giddiness somewhat tempered by being back in a chair, he reached back in the memories of the day to strike back at his father, to question rather than answer.

"Is it true that you're leasing the Front Street warehouse to the Nazis?" he said.

"Who in hell told you that?" said his father. Bullock, who had been on his way out of the dining room, stopped in his tracks.

"Bill Hiram," said Charley.

"Bill Hiram," repeated his father, as if each syllable was a stab in the heart. "Right. He told you I had leased it. Did he say that—did he say the word 'Nazis'?"

"What's the difference?" said Charley. "I don't remember what he said. Just tell me, all right? Just tell me if you're leasing the place to the Nazis."

"Go ahead," said Bullock. "Tell him. Tell your son."

"The German-American Bund," said Charles Keats III. "It is not the same thing as the Nazis, is it then? It's a patriotic group. *American* patriotic."

"Your father," said Richard Bullock to Charley, "is leasing the warehouse to the Bund. As I am letting them use some country property of mine to hold drills on weekends. You're not that drunk, are you, young man? I mean you are capable of reason?"

"I'm capable of reason," said Charley.

"It's one thing to talk the kind of drivel that my beloved wife does, you understand, it's quite another to take the consequences of such talk." Richard Bullock's red face smiled, as if glad of the intense concentration given him by Charley. He pulled up a chair and sat next to his friend's son, knee to knee. Like Charles Keats, his presence was large, powerful; but unlike him, he was without fat, or a hint of any former or present attractiveness. He was trim, big, and ugly. "This has got nothing to do with your cousin, with someone's Jew boyfriend or girlfriend, with how you feel about the Spanish Civil War, or Chancellor Hitler's wanting some land—populated by Germans already—back from Czechoslovakia. This is just business. You know business?"

"I know business."

"There will never be a war between white, Anglo-Saxon

Protestant people and the Germans. It is not possible. The German-American Bund is an extreme sort of group, I admit that. But so were the Nazis in Munich. Most of the Bund members are lower-middle-class Americans, many of them born in Germany; but they see no conflict of loyalty. Outside the Bund there are millions of German-Americans, some of them three and four generations back, some of them proud of Hitler, others embarrassed by him. But they're there, you see. German-Americans, part of the reason we'll never go to war. When Germany takes what it wants in Europe, it will be stronger than ever. It might not be satisfied with the Sudetenland. Roosevelt will not be President forever, you know. There will come a time when we trade actively with Germany, two strong Protestant nations, Aryan nations, and when our steel industries will grow fat on the need to produce German armaments."

"I understand," said Charley, suddenly feeling quite sober. He turned to his father. "You're leasing the warehouse to the Bund so that one day you'll be remembered fondly by the Nazis."

"That warehouse is empty anyway," said Charles Keats. "It's only leaflets and uniforms, and they're providing all the maintenance."

"I don't know if I like your tone, Charles," said Bullock. "You make it sound like you're apologizing. These people must be regarded as friends. If you look down on them, they'll notice, they'll remember."

"So you're leasing the warehouse, Father, just in case the Nazis take over America. I think that's terrific logic. What do you think of that, Mom? Do you think that makes sense?"

Mrs. Keats didn't respond. She was torn between trying to bring Mrs. Bullock back into the dining room and running off to hide in the remodeled kitchen. Charley stood up, as steadily as he could manage, and walked over to his father.

"The Nazis are sick," he said. "They are inhuman. There is nothing good about them. They beat and kill people, and every civilized person in America loathes them."

"That is not true," said Bullock.

"Shut up, mister," said Charley. "I'm talking. This is my house."

JOEL GROSS

"I didn't realize your son was such a fool, Charles," said Bullock.

"Get out," said Charley. "Get out and get in your goddamned Duesenberg. Get out of my house."

"Why aren't you saying anything, Charles?" said Bullock, bristling in his chair.

"Charley," said his father, "you've gone far enough. Mr. Bullock is our guest, and he is a business associate of mine, and therefore of yours."

"Not mine, Father. I don't do business with Nazis."

"Then," said Bullock, "you won't have a great deal of business in a shorter time than you think." He stood up, looking as if he was trying to decide whether to knock Charley down. He swiveled about to Charles Keats III. "It's not enough, you know," he said. "I appreciate your donating the warehouse. But you vacillate. I'm not asking you to wear a swastika. But Father Coughlin favors the Bund, and he's no German. The Klan favors the Bund, and you can't get much more nationalistic and antiforeign than the KKK. You just have to acknowledge them. Henry Ford accepted Hitler's medal. Don't you think Henry Ford's a good American? I want you to contribute money, and it's not the amount that matters, it's the sentiment. I want your son to know that you're giving to the Bund, I want your wife to know, I want everyone in Safe Haven to know. So when we have our little rally, it will be legitimate. Not the work of crazy people. Just freedom-loving Americans who don't want the Jew bankers to control the American government, who don't want the communists to get us into a war with the only country willing to fight chaos and anarchy in the world today. I know those are your views, Charles. But I want *them* to know—and all your neighbors."

Bullock didn't wait for a response. Charley went after him, not wanting him to leave just yet. He was not as quick as he was when sober, and was bothered by this; something that Bullock had said needed to be clarified. "What rally?" said Charley, holding on to Bullock's arm.

"The Bund rally, son," said Bullock. "They're going to drill on Saturday, then on Sunday they're going to march down Main Street. It's going to be a 'Buy Christian, Jews Out of Safe

368)

Haven' rally. Pray for a sunny day." He brushed off Charley's hand and walked out, and there was no noise until they heard the Duesenberg start up its eight cylinders.

"I don't know how that marriage lasts," said Mrs. Keats.

Charley hardly heard this. Even the subtle change in his father's tone—undermined by Bullock's greater stupidity, perhaps—failed to interest him. A Bund rally. He had seen the tail end of one of these in Yorktown, in the German part of Manhattan. Men in green German army uniforms, complete with swastika armbands, goose-stepping like lunatics along Eighty-sixth Street, storm troopers without any weapons save their fanaticism, their hatred. He could not allow this. It would be obscene to allow Lily Berger to look at the hated caricatures that had already torn apart the first part of her life. And even if the Bund had gotten permission to stage their displays of race hatred in public halls in Manhattan, even in Madison Square Garden, they must still never be allowed to shout their madness on the main street of this town. Not in Safe Haven.

"Where are you going?" said his mother, but Charley just shook his head.

"Some air, I need some air," he said.

"I want you to know something," said his father, standing in his way. "Just hear me out. I'm not going to stop you from going out, I just want a second of your time."

"John Collins must be turning over in his grave."

"Just listen—"

"And Tom Williams—and Martha Mann—" He pushed his father, harder than he'd intended, and Charles Keats III reacted instinctively, with violence. He grabbed hold of his son and shoved him against the wall.

"You'll show a little respect, damn you," he said.

"I want you and Mom out of here," said Charley. "Go home to Greenwich. This is Grandmother's house, and she's not going to want any part of you. Tomorrow morning you pack up and go. This is one thing that doesn't belong to you, and we want you out."

"They have the right of free speech," said his father, still holding on to his son, pressing him against the wainscoting. He tried to explain a great deal in a short time, how Nazis weren't all alike any more than Democrats or Republicans were, how he didn't believe in violent acts against the Jews, but did believe he had the right to say that they were too powerful in controlling the finances of the world. All the rally was trying to do was show some support for conservative ideals in a world without sufficient structure. If a few Jewish merchants were frightened into lowering their prices, what terrible harm was there in that? No one was going to break their windows or make them wear gold stars stitched to their clothing. And all the publicity would make any Jews thinking of moving to the area think again—and that would be best for property values.

"Tomorrow morning you're getting out of this house," said Charley, and he pushed his father away, pushing with all his force, and hurried for the hallway and ran out the front door of the very old home. His mother called after him, but he ignored her voice. She had never wanted anything but peace in the house, peace at any cost; and that was too much to pay.

Charley walked quickly along the dark ribbon of roadway connecting the riverfront houses. He knew he was walking to Lily's house, but couldn't imagine any particular action to take when he got there. The night air cleared his head. With every step he grew less fuzzy and more angry. He remembered a hundred instances of his father's clumsy hatred, directed at servants, waiters, gas station attendants. Hostility always waited at the corners of the man's mouth, waiting to erupt. It was not just Jews that he hated, not just communists, servants, and the workers in his factories. He hated the smaller cars on the road, families with four and five children, regular churchgoers, atheists. It was evident that he hated Bullock, if only because he had seen the "weaknesses" of his son.

"This house," he remembered his father having once shouted at him. "Do you know what this house represents? Do you have any feeling for the lives lived in this space? Can you stand here and tell me you don't care about the ideals of your country, when everything your country stands for is written into these walls and floors and doors?" And what were those ideals? thought Charley. Did his father honestly believe that John Collins cared nothing for the outside world, that he would have had no opinion about the lives being shattered across the ocean? Could he imagine that Tom Williams would have allowed ersatz storm troopers to strut down the streets of his town extolling the virtues of order and discipline? Could anyone picture pacifist and abolitionist Martha Mann demanding the boycott of Jewish shops?

There would be a complete break with his father, perhaps with his mother as well. Not simply because he had fallen in love with a Jewish girl. Not simply because he wanted to write plays that would preach universal tolerance, that would tear down the mighty institutions of fascism and tyranny. He would break with his father because he had to affirm who he was, with whom he wished to be linked; his spirit was like his grandmother's, his heart was like that of the men and women who had lived in the old house in Safe Haven. Breaking with his father, he would deny the worst part of himself; he would affirm the best impulses of his soul.

He didn't know at what moment the flashing lights penetrated his consciousness. The road was winding and very dark, but there was a moon, and stars, and the lights from the houses. But suddenly it was very clear: an ambulance. No sounds, only the flashing lights, and it was up ahead, parked in front of one of the waterfront houses, and he knew at once that the lights had been flashing for many steps, perhaps half a minute, a near eternity of delay.

The houses all looked alike in the dark, but this one, in colonial style, freshly painted, with a police car and an ambulance in front, was the one where he had made love with Lily Berger that same day. He ran now, and his eyes reached for the front door, where two men carried out a stretcher, and he could see blonde hair falling over the side, tawdry in the flashing lights.

"Lily," he whispered, but then, as in a dream, she emerged from the house, right after the stretcher, talking to a man with a doctor's bag in his hand. It was very bad, a terrible thing to strike the refugees on their first night in Safe Haven, but he couldn't help but smile—it was not Lily on the stretcher. "Lily," he said again, but now he shouted it, now he hurried past the policeman, past her mother on the stretcher, past the doctor with his grave look. "Lily," he said. "Let me help you. I'm here, and everything is going to be all right."

TWENTY-THREE

———◆———

Charley pushed his way into the ambulance with Lily and the doctor, very conscious of his alcohol-scented breath. Lily had no eyes for him. She looked only at her mother, listened only to the doctor, spoke only about the length of time it would take to get to the hospital, ten miles away, in the nearest large town. Mrs. Berger was very pale, her breathing shallow and slow. Wrapped in the gray blankets of the ambulance attendants, she looked as if she already had one foot in the grave.

"There's nothing to worry about, Miss Berger," said the doctor. "She's in shock, but she'll come around very soon. It's very likely she'll be conscious before we get to the hospital." Whether to allay her fears or to simply fill the quiet of the ambulance, the doctor elaborated on his diagnosis: Mrs. Berger's shock was self-induced, a hysterical attack of anxiety that led to fainting. "Shock can come about when the circulatory capacity is suddenly expanded, so that in a moment, a half moment, there is not enough blood for the amount of roadway, so to speak. In psychogenic shock, you see, blood vessels in the muscles suddenly dilate, and the blood pressure falls precipitously, and therefore the pulse becomes rapid and weak, and the skin becomes clammy and moist—but it's not serious.

Just lying down, the blood will flow to the brain and she'll regain consciousness. The important thing is for us to determine why your mother is so anxious. It's quite unusual for such an attack to lead to unconsciousness. Usually she'd be a little lightheaded, feel a bit out of sorts. Have there been problems at home?"

"Mrs. Berger has only just arrived in Safe Haven," said Charley. "From Germany, via London. Her husband is still in Berlin. They're Jews."

"I see," said the doctor. "Well, I suppose that's sufficient cause for anxiety." He paused, as if this might be the place for a self-conscious laugh, but there were not even the beginnings of a smile. They arrived at the hospital without incident, and true to the doctor's word, Mrs. Berger was already stirring, German words bubbling up from her pale lips.

At the hospital, a private room was secured, and several doctors were consulted, but the case was both physiologically simple and emotionally complex. A blood transfusion was unnecessary. At one o'clock in the morning, Mrs. Berger asked to see Lily, and the doctors allowed her a few minutes with her mother. Charley took the time to call his parents in Safe Haven. His mother answered the phone.

"Mom, I'm OK. I'm staying over with a friend tonight in Norwalk," he said.

"Your father is worried half out of his head," she rattled into the phone. "I don't know what's got into you, into both of you. Didn't we always get over our little problems? We were all drunk, right? Let's just all be friends again, can't we?"

"We were not all drunk, Mother," said Charles. "You don't have to leave tomorrow, but if father is going to lease that warehouse to the Bund, then I meant what I said. You'll have to get out. I'll get a lawyer and see to it. Now, good night."

"But, Charley, I don't understand what's got into you. You were never so hotheaded—it's not like you," said his mother. But he repeated his good night, and went back to the hard bench in the hallway outside Mrs. Berger's room. A day-old newspaper from New York was folded up neatly on the bench, and he opened it, eager to forget about his mother's weak voice, his growing disappointment in his parents. The headline read:

GERMANY TIGHTENS PRESSURE ON JEWS. Underneath this, in smaller type: FREE USE OF SAFE DEPOSIT BOXES CURTAILED—276 APPROVED NAMES ARE PUBLISHED.

Charley shook himself, as if he had taken a few steps into a fantasy land once again. This was the *New York Times* in his lap. The date was right there, black on white, August 24, 1938. He had hurried through many such stories in the past. Cold-blooded reports of beatings and looting, of curtailment of civil liberties in the land of Goethe and Mann and Heine and Brecht, had taken their place amidst the other horrors of the Thirties. But this one little story was riveting, with Lily's mother in shock in the next room.

Datelined Berlin, August 23, the article detailed the latest strictures to be applied against the Jews of Germany: Jews no longer were allowed access to their safety-deposit boxes. Jews owning automobiles must have specially numbered license plates, identifying them as Jews for all to see. Jewish men must add the name Israel to their names, and Jewish women must add the name Sarah, so that all would know who was a Jew from glancing at a list of names. Thus, thought Charley, Einstein, should he care to reside in Germany ever again, would be Israel Albert Einstein. And Lily—she would be Sarah Lily Berger. As for newborn Jewish children, they would no longer be allowed "Aryan" names at all. The *Times* listed the new names allowed for Jewish babies, names like Bachja and Efim and Feibisch. Following this article was a smaller one, ITALY BEGINS COUNT OF JEWS, and Charley found his hand shaking from a kind of stupefied anger. No wonder Mrs. Berger was in shock. No wonder her daughter had an almost manic need for love.

"What are you doing here?" Lily said when she emerged from her mother's room.

"Don't you remember?" said Charley. "I came with you in the ambulance—"

"Of course I remember. Do you think I'm insane? I'm asking what you are here for. What do you want with us?" Lily's eyes were tired, but bright with intelligence and purpose. "Listen. This isn't the time or the place, but I must tell you. Forget about what happened today. Forget it. Forget the whole thing, do you hear me?"

"No," said Charley, and he pulled her into his arms and kissed her, one gentle, lingering kiss, not to shut her up, but to allow his own lips expression.

"I don't love you," she said. But he could feel her body against his, there in the antiseptic surroundings, in the middle of the night, with too much alcohol and coffee vying for control of his brain; he could feel her body, and it remembered the afternoon, it belied her words. Lily broke away from him and sat down on the bench. He joined her. "There are four doctors with her tonight. When New York hears about it, we'll have a dozen doctors in her room, German doctors who owe everything to Father—but there is nothing anyone can do for her. Nothing."

He asked her if anything had precipitated her fainting, and she looked at him searchingly, as if wondering if it would be possible to make him understand anything at all about her life. "Sheets," she said. "The woman who got the house ready didn't make the beds with sheets. There were just covers on the beds —quilts, you call them—but no sheets. Just the bare mattresses." Lily stopped talking, as if a door had slammed shut inside her head. She stood up. "I'm going to get some coffee."

"Let me get it," said Charley.

"No. You stay here. Do you want some coffee? I'll get it for you," she said. It was five minutes before she came back, but she was noticeably less agitated. She said that a nurse had been very nice about making her some of her own coffee. "It seemed she was very American," said Lily. "She said it was a shame my mother had gotten sick. And I think she knows who we are, that we're Jews, I mean." Charley sipped the coffee she'd brought him, watching Lily's coffee grow cold in the cup in her hand. "Is Connecticut like the rest of America?"

"In some ways, yes," said Charley. "It's a big country, very different in different sections, but it all rests on the same ideas. It all comes from independence—I don't mean from England— I mean independent spirit. We can be very nice, because no one is telling us how to be—we don't follow rigid lines."

"You must be tired, Charley."

"I'm all right."

"Were you drinking tonight? Liquor?"

"Yes."

"Because of what happened this afternoon?"

"No—because of my father. We had an argument. It was nothing to do with you. Aren't you going to drink your coffee?"

"We only stayed one night in New York," said Lily, gazing into the coffee. "That was a mistake. Mother can't move around too fast. I couldn't decide if it would be good to show her the museums, or if it would be better after she'd rested, and had gotten used to a new home. It's hard for me to keep making decisions. I'm used to having my father around. But when Mr. Hiram said the house was ready, and New York was so hot and humid, I thought it would be perfect to get out there right away, even if it was by train.

"Do you know that my mother is a famous artist? Perhaps I should say *was* a famous artist. It was just in Germany, after all. And her paintings are no longer exhibited, or sold, or talked about. Worse than anything for her was when her own circle— I don't know if you have this in America—a group of friends, artists, all meet to talk and criticize and have coffee and cigarettes and invite artists from other countries. Like a club. My mother's circle was together twenty years, since she was my age, even younger. They threw her out. They asked her to leave. They explained that it was the only way, they had no choice. It was not that they agreed with the Nazis, you see—no one agrees with them, but no one says anything back to them either. Ever since then my mother hasn't been the same. She doesn't paint, she doesn't look at pictures, she hardly reads the paper. She talks about the past. It's not the sheets, you know. It's not even that the servants weren't there, or even hired. My mother isn't like that—like a lazy aristocrat. It was the surprise. Pulling off the quilts, and there were no sheets on the bed, and there were no sheets in the closet, and it was such a little thing, you see, a little thing compared to everyone who's gone, dead, ruined, vanished. A little thing, but it was the first day in a new house, and she missed her own home, her own circle, her own country, and she doesn't know if she'll ever see my father alive again—and it happened because of the sheets."

Perhaps because of the late hour, Lily's defenses were down. She didn't object when he held her hand, so mild and innocent a physical claim in the wake of their lovemaking, and there were no more declarations that she did not love him and would never love him. Lily talked, freely associating from the lack of sheets in the Safe Haven house to the way her bedroom had been furnished in Berlin, to the pictures that had hung there, painted by her mother, to the little chair that her father had always occupied when he'd come to visit her in her room.

Charley enjoyed the hours there, waiting for dawn on the hardwood bench, beginning to get an understanding of her father's importance in German and international banking circles. He couldn't pretend to understand the society that had bred Lily, but it was comforting to know that she liked fast cars and Saint Bernard dogs, that money in any amount could not impress her. Her father impressed her because he was brave, because he was using his money and his expertise to bribe and coerce the Nazis to let out certain Jews from detention centers in their native land, to freedom in Switzerland, Argentina, America. What she liked about her father was his tolerance, his love of good books, his understanding of her mother's breakdown. She talked and talked, till her voice was cracking and she was drinking the cold coffee to stay awake. And over the hours, Charley felt his love grow, but with it, a return of the sickening sensation of sinfulness in the lovely girl; he tried to fight this, but he couldn't help finding something bizarrely incongruous in Lily. He alternately found himself wishing her a virgin, and then wanting to make love to her so badly that his lust was like a thirst, a terrible hunger. And to bolster both his desires, he told her again and again that he was in love with her, but Lily never took this seriously, and begged him to talk about something else.

In the morning, her mother was examined, fed, and allowed to dress and sit up. Lily wouldn't leave her alone in the hospital, so Mrs. Berger insisted that they all go home. In German, she asked Lily to introduce Charley, and Lily reminded her mother that he was the young man who'd helped them with their baggage at the train station.

"Mr. Hiram said that you were a Nazi," said Mrs. Berger pleasantly.

"No, Mother. Charley is a very nice young man, and he is a believer in freedom. He wants to be a playwright."

"Is the food in American hospitals always of such a type, Mr. Charley?"

"Just Charley, Mrs. Berger. I'd be happy to go into town and get you both a wonderful breakfast—"

"You didn't sleep, Lily," said Mrs. Berger.

"I'm all right, Mother. I don't need much. I'll nap when we get home."

"Are there sheets?" said Mrs. Berger. "You can't sleep without sheets on the bed. You're not a gypsy, Lily, no matter what they tell you."

Lily explained that Mr. Hiram was bringing over some of his own sheets, and that a housekeepers' agency was sending over some applicants to them later that morning. Charley called a car service in Safe Haven to drive over to the hospital, and as they waited for the car in front of the main entrance, Mrs. Berger asked if it was difficult to purchase eggs in Connecticut. "You see, Mr. Charley, my husband is a very important man in Berlin, but even he can't get eggs these days, because he has to wear that little Jewish star on his clothes, and so he is not allowed to buy them. Now does that make sense to you?"

It didn't make sense to Charley at all, and therefore, in the taxi back to Safe Haven, he suggested that they stop at an old-fashioned country store, just off the Post Road, where one could buy farm-fresh eggs and milk and cheese, and vegetables freshly picked from the garden. "Doesn't that sound lovely, Mother?" said Lily.

"We will be allowed to buy eggs, you think?" said Mrs. Berger cautiously. Lily reminded her of the omelette she'd consumed the other day at the Waldorf, of the three eggs she'd managed at the Ritz in London every day for two weeks. Mrs. Berger shook her head at the memory. "It's hard to believe. I can't even remember what an egg tastes like. My husband likes eggs too. When he comes to America, I shall bake him cakes, with scores of eggs. I will build egg whites into mountains."

"You from Germany, folks?" said the cabdriver, looking at his passengers in the rearview mirror.

"That's right," said Charley. "They're new in town, and can probably use some good old American food. Why don't you drive over to Roland's? We'll just be a few minutes."

"That ups the price, mister," said the cabdriver, but Charley said that was fine, and after a few minutes they turned off the Post Road and down a country lane. Roland's was in need of a good whitewashing, and its fence had been knocked down by clumsy drivers in several places. But it was essentially the same as Charley remembered it: a miniature one-story colonial house, all its interior walls torn down to make way for one enormous room filled with produce and groceries. Roland himself was an old man when Charley first came to the store. He had long since sold it to a newcomer to Safe Haven, a mean-spirited groceryman from Bridgeport, glad to be able to charge high prices to the inhabitants of the old homes and new mansions along the river and the Sound. Mrs. Berger held Charley's arm instinctively; it was obvious she was used to dependence, and eager to believe in a new source of friendship.

"Mr. Keats, Jr.!" said the proprietor's wife, stolid and big-nosed, her gray hair disheveled. "Long time we ain't seen the likes of you! We've got fresh corn today! Ain't seen your mother neither! We answer the phone, you know. We'll bring you anything you like!"

"What is this?" said Mrs. Berger, attracted to the only stack of reading material in sight in the store. Charley felt himself turning red, more from embarrassment than anger. Even from six feet away he recognized Father Coughlin's anti-Semitic newspaper, *Social Justice*, with its screaming noninterventionist articles and diatribes about the Jewish plot to take over the world. Throughout 1938 the paper had been running pieces of the scurrilous forgery *Protocols of the Elders of Zion*, purporting to be a blueprint for a Jewish cabal's rise to power. The issue on display in Roland's Safe Haven grocery had an article about "The Gold Standard Racket" on its front page, the print highlighting an illustration from *The Merchant of Venice*— Shylock about to try to collect his pound of flesh. "Look," said Mrs. Berger, glancing at the hook-nosed illustration of Shylock, an image all too familiar in German posters, billboards, and magazines. "This is all about the Jews again."

"Put it down, Mother," said Lily. "We've come to buy eggs, remember."

"Ah, you're German, yes?" said the proprietor's wife happily.

Mrs. Berger still had her eyes on the newspaper's front page, which seemed to place all the world's financial troubles on Meyer Amschel Rothschild and the devil, working in unholy union.

"What are you doing selling this rag?" said Charley.

"It's really not doing too well, Mr. Keats. I don't think I sold three copies."

"What are you doing selling it at all?" he insisted, and his tone of voice made it clear that selling such a paper was a crime as well as an affront. The proprietor's wife wanted only to smooth over the hot temper of the son of Charles Keats III.

"It's got nothing to do with me, sir," she said. "A man came in, my husband knows him, I don't remember his name. It was hard to say no to letting him leave the stuff on the counter, but if it bothers you, I'll just put it away."

"It bothers me a great deal," said Charley.

"Well then," said the proprietor's wife, as if that made everything simple and clear. She took the stack of newspapers and placed it on the other side of the counter, on the floor and out of sight. "Is that what you wanted then? All done, OK?"

But it was not all done. Eggs were purchased, along with milk and cheese and corn and tomatoes and lettuce, and Charley tried to reduce the pressure behind his eyes. But the anger would not go away. He hadn't slept, he'd been drunk, he'd been picked up by a pot of coffee, but fatigue gnawed at the corners of consciousness; there was a great need for sleep, for dreaming. There was something alien, unfamiliar, all about him. Roland's Safe Haven grocery had been vitiated by a hateful presence. He had come here as a small child and been given a sucking candy, a lollipop, a chocolate, free of charge, and the gifts had always made him feel special, loved. In place of a lollipop from Roland, he was now given a false respect by his successor. If Mr. Keats doesn't want to be upset by hate literature, well, we just take it away. But this wasn't satisfying to Charley. He wanted to know why it was there to begin with, why anyone in his town would allow such nonsense to be disseminated. And he could see how Lily and her mother seemed to have shrunk a bit. Trying to be happy with their bags of groceries, they were still diminished by fear; they recognized the possibility of what they had fled following them to America.

"I'm sorry again if that disturbed you, Mr. Keats," said the proprietor's wife. "I guess you won't be too happy about that rally, either."

"No," said Charley. And then, through his exhaustion, his anger surfaced: "What about you? Are you happy about the rally?"

"I'm not happy," she said. "But I don't want to make a federal case about it. It's too bad it's going to be here, but I don't want to get nobody mad at me, see? I can't afford it. Some of those characters play rough."

The taxi drove past Charley's house to get to the Berger home, but he didn't even think to point it out to Lily and her mother, to tell her of its great history. He was ashamed. It was not enough for him to know the difference between right and wrong; he wanted the whole town to know it. Lily asked him what the rally was about, and for a long time he couldn't even answer her. Then he told her the truth, quietly, because Mrs. Berger had become lost in her own thoughts, perhaps dreaming of an old canvas left behind in a Berlin she would never again enter.

"The German-American Bund is going to have a rally right here in Safe Haven, right in the center of town," said Charley.

"They are Nazis?"

"Yes, they are," said Charley. He had already reached a decision, but was afraid that telling it to Lily would make it sound as if he wanted to do it on her account.

"Mother must not know," said Lily.

"If she stays in and around the house, she'll never have to," said Charley.

"Thank you, Charley," she said when the taxi stopped in front of their house. "For everything. You're much nicer than I hoped." He watched her take her mother by the arm and walk slowly to their door. She didn't want him to accompany them any longer, and he was glad. There was much to be done, and he needed sleep; he needed it desperately if he was going to be able to think and plan and act.

"You're the Keats boy, then," said the taxi driver as Charley directed him back up the riverside road. "I'd give anything to take a look in that house of yours someday. It looks just like all the new ones; I guess they copied, huh?"

"You can tomorrow," said Charley. "Tomorrow afternoon, late, if you can make it."

"Are you serious?"

"Yes."

"I can make it. Sure. That's very nice of you. I mean I've lived in Safe Haven most of my life, and I've never seen the inside, you know, and you grow up knowing it's the oldest thing here. It is, isn't it?"

"Yeah," said Charley. "Look, don't misunderstand me. You can see the house. But I'm having you there for a reason. Kind of like an informal town meeting. Were you listening to what I was telling the young lady?"

"I try never to listen, Mr. Keats. It's not my business."

"About the Nazi rally," said Charley.

"Sure. I heard you. And I think it's a damned shame," said the taxi driver. He had pulled over the car in front of the old house, and turned about to look at Charley face to face.

"So do I," said Charley. "And I'm not going to sit back and let it happen. You come to the house, tomorrow afternoon, and there'll be others there, I'm going to get them, and we're going to talk this out, like free men, men who want to keep this place free and open for everybody."

"But what do you intend to do about it, Mr. Keats?" said the taxi driver. "I mean those guys come up dressed like storm troopers, and there could be hundreds of them, and they're all half crazy. What can you do about it? If it's called for, it's just going to have to happen."

"Oh, no," said Charley, feeling the strength of decision cutting through his fatigue. "It doesn't have to happen. The Bund is going to try to have their rally, but I am going to stop them. I'm going to stop them dead."

TWENTY-FOUR

A feeling of calm, of inevitability, took hold of Charley from the moment he left the taxi and walked to his house. He liked to imagine this security a link to the past: Men and women of his family—at least according to the legends of his grandmother—had always been able to look at dangers and problems with equanimity. It was a question of rightness, and what one was willing to lose to see one's moral vision fulfilled. Charley had no precise plan, but knew that he would have; he knew there would be danger, but understood that the danger was insignificant compared to the damage to his soul if he didn't face it.

His mother caught sight of him as soon as he entered the house, eager to ply him with coffee and questions, but Charley made it quite clear that he was going to sleep, and that he would be happy to talk with her after he'd awakened. "Didn't you sleep last night?" she said. "I thought you slept at a friend's house in Norwalk."

"I didn't sleep," said Charley. "I'm going to now."

"Wait," demanded Mrs. Keats, and Charley stopped, exhausted, before the stairs. His mother walked over to him, tentatively, as if wondering what to say, and deciding to say nothing at all. She took her son's hands and touched his exhausted face, as if remembering how tiny the hands had once been, how simple and careless her baby's face. Mrs. Keats embraced Charley, holding him silently, reminding him of the fact that he was still her child, that she had brought him into the world. "You know that your mother loves you, don't you, Charley?" she said.

"Yes," he said, and then he went upstairs and fell asleep slowly, his conscious mind trying to accept the idea that his mother could be strong, that she could be a person he could still love. Though he was exhausted, he didn't sleep well. He was afraid to confront his dreams. He didn't want to imagine what he would have to abandon—what loyalties, what loves— in order to be true to himself. When he got out of bed, he found himself wet with perspiration, still in his clothes from the day before, his dark stubble and bloodshot eyes looking grim in the old mirror over the antique chest-on-chest. Charley shaved, showered, and hurried downstairs, suddenly anxious to speak to his mother. He must try to imagine the world from her point of view. She was not only less intelligent than he, she had not been born into privilege. What she had gained through marriage could never feel as secure as a birthright. He could be firm, he could be angry; but he mustn't judge her by his own standards.

"Sit down, son," said his father as Charley walked into the remodeled kitchen.

"I was about to," said Charley. He smiled at his mother, standing next to the maid at a very long counter. His mother returned the smile automatically, but there was real concern in her eyes. She was begging him for peace.

"Some coffee, Charley?" said his mother. "A sandwich?"

"I'm starved, Mom," he said, and Mrs. Keats told the maid she'd attend to it, and when the maid had left them alone in the huge, gleaming kitchen, Charley sat down at the brightly painted modern table, directly opposite his father.

"I'll fry up some eggs, OK? And some home-fried potatoes?"

"Cynthia, I want to speak to the boy," said his father.

"That sounds fine, Mom," said Charley. She brought him some hot coffee, making a wide berth around her husband's chair, as if afraid he might lash out at her at any moment.

"I'm not going to waste a great deal of time talking about

how you frightened your mother and myself last night—you've been inconsiderate before, and I suppose that we should have learned to get used to your selfish nature by now."

"Very nice coffee, Mom," said Charley.

"Thank you," she mouthed silently. Quickly, she prepared eggs and butter and bread and potatoes.

"I've thought about what I wanted to say to you, so that there can be no misunderstanding. You are sober now, aren't you?"

"Obviously."

"You are perfectly capable of reason then. Any decision you make now will have nothing to do with being drunk or childish or whimsical, is that correct?"

"I'm not drunk, Father. And I've already made my decisions. Why don't you just tell me what you want to say? I'm ready for it."

"I am not a Nazi," said Charles Keats III. "And I hope you know that I'm not a coward either. You don't make millions of dollars in the stock market *after* the crash by being a coward."

"Then you're going to back out of leasing the warehouse to the Bund?"

"No," said Charles Keats III. "Not at all. You're not listening. I have not done anything wrong. This is what I'm trying to explain to you. I am not going to be coerced by childish threats or communist thinking. I am not a Nazi, no, but they are a political group, and they can have their say as far as I'm concerned."

"Then as far as I'm concerned, we have nothing left to talk about."

"Yes we do," said his father. "First of all, your job. You're fired."

"Oh, really? Didn't you hear? I quit."

"Second of all, the house. I have checked with my attorney, and with your grandmother's doctor. She is absolutely incapable of reason at this point in her life. Do you realize she's been bedridden for a year? That she sees no one but the immediate family? Any change in her will would be thrown out by the court. I'm her son, remember? I have precedence, and I have the legal power behind me as well."

"We'll see about that, won't we?" said Charley. "I have some money of my own, you know. I even have a good friend who's a lawyer, an Italian Catholic who went to Harvard Law. Do you think you could bear to sit in a courtroom with one of *them?*"

"What the hell do you want?" said his father suddenly. He was angry, but more than that, he was exasperated. His son had come from his loins, and he wanted him to be reliable, to be of the same mind as the father. It didn't seem like so much to expect. Losing control over his son felt like losing control over an arm or a leg. This is not to suggest that Charles Keats III loved his son, but in his own way, he did. "You're not going to tell your own father how to behave, do you understand? Just because you got yourself some new friends, and you and your grandmother think I'm prying into Pamela's life when all I'm trying to do is help her from making a mistake she'll never stop being sorry for, you're acting crazy. Do you want to lose your job? Do you want to know what it's like to be on your own completely, without any help from your family, is that what you want? To be a stranger?"

"Your eggs, dear," said Mrs. Keats, and she put the plate before Charley and then stood straight behind his back. "He'll never be a stranger to his mother," she said to her husband.

"I don't want you to get involved with this, Cynthia."

"I don't care what you want, Charles. Not about this. He's my son too."

"What is going on around here? What the hell is going on?" said Charles Keats III. He stood up, fat and coarse and full of thwarted power. "You don't think you can change my mind, do you, Cynthia? This is not something about which you have a great deal of knowledge, is it, then? My son the Jew-loving playwright, and my wife the Jew-loving chorus girl."

Cynthia Keats hit her husband hard, not slapping with her palm, but swinging with her fist. "You swore to me, you bastard!"

"What the hell did I say? I didn't say anything about *your* Jew."

"He wasn't *my* Jew, goddamn you. He was my boyfriend when I was nineteen years old—and his name was Jimmy, and if I ran into him today I wouldn't know it, and if I did I

(3 8 6)

wouldn't care—and you can go to hell, you can just go to hell!"

Charley watched in wonder as his mother, tall and slim and elegant, walked out of the kitchen, leaving the two men together, their conflict strangely muted by her outburst. "Your mother had a boyfriend once," said his father. "You heard. That's got nothing to do with anything. I mean when I met her they didn't even see each other anymore. That's not why I called her 'Jew-lover.' I called her that because of you and she getting together, talking a whole lot of nonsense that doesn't mean a damn thing." He was rubbing his jaw where his wife had hit him, and Charley asked him if he was all right. "Since when do you care?" said his father.

Charley didn't answer him. He knew he cared a great deal, but he had no desire to share this information with his father. "Look, Father," he said, "I'm not going to be fighting you on the house right away. I don't want to think further ahead than this weekend. But you should know that this is my house, in my opinion, and I'm going to treat it that way."

"No one's throwing you out, boy. I'm not the one who started talking about throwing people out of their own homes."

"You just fired me and disinherited me, that's all."

"Not officially, Charley. Jesus, why can't we just forget the whole thing?"

"Because tomorrow there's going to be a meeting here. My meeting. People from town, I don't know how many, but I don't want any trouble."

"It's your house, son. Have your meeting. What people from town? You mean from the club?"

"No, I don't think there'll be anyone at all from the club," said Charley. "It's not a social meeting, it's a political one. It's going to be mostly shopkeepers, I guess." He was thinking out loud now, planning what had to be done right under the critical eyes of his father. "I want the Jewish shopkeepers especially, if there are any. I think the barber is Jewish, isn't he? On Main Street?"

"I don't go to him," said Charles Keats III. He tried to find the will to be angry once again, to demand to know why shopkeepers were coming to their home, particularly Jewish ones. But he was tired of being angry. His wife hadn't hit him in a quarter century. His only son seemed to despise him. Charles Keats III remained convinced of the negative influence of Jews on conservative government in America, was absolutely positive that only Jewish interests wanted America to become involved in the coming conflict in Europe; but he was suddenly tired of his abstract hatred of a people he didn't know. If it were possible, he would start all over again, refuse the Bund the use of his warehouse, shut up his anti-Semitic feelings, and forget once and for all that his wife once loved a Jewish boy—a Broadway chorus dancer, not an international banker—and allow his son the free rein of his talents that his own father had given him. But it wasn't possible. Words had been exchanged, positions taken. A father could not back down before a son and still command respect. Charles Keats III grimaced. "You want Jews in this house, that's your business, boy. See how liberal your dad is?" He stalked out of the kitchen, and Charley finished his cold eggs and potatoes, relishing the love that had gone into their making.

The most difficult thing about the next three days was staying away from Lily Berger. Charley's kitchen-table confrontation with his father was on Thursday; that afternoon and the next morning he spent on Main Street, cajoling merchants to come to the meeting in the ancient house. Pamela and her parents arrived Thursday evening, an hour late for dinner, having had to change a tire on the Post Road on the way up from Greenwich. The dinner lasted till one o'clock in the morning, and there was no mention of Pamela's Jewish lover until after midnight; and then it was Pamela who brought him up.

"At least he's not a Negro," said Charles Keats III. It was his attempt to be humorous, but Pamela wasn't amused; unlike Charley, she didn't recognize her uncle's capitulation. "Look, Pammie, forget what I said, OK? Don't go on the warpath. I'm not saying you can bring him to the hunt club, but all that money stuff I spoke about—which shouldn't even be discussed around a family dinner table anyway—you can forget about. No threats, no actions, not even any comments. You're a big girl, and your parents can take the stick to you without my help, right?"

Uncle Freddie, Aunt Liz, and Pam slept over that night, and drove off right after breakfast. It was possible for Charley to keep his plans to himself, though he would have loved to see Pam's expression when she learned about his anti-Nazi action. She would have wanted to help, to enlist her friends, perhaps to get it into the newspapers. But this was precisely what Charley didn't want.

Friday afternoon, a total of fourteen merchants came to the house on the Saugatuck and sat or stood on the screened-in porch with the view of the river. There the descendant of John Collins explained how he felt about the German-American Bund rally on the main street of the town born in 1636 as a refuge, a haven. He showed them the ancient hearth, he told them what he knew of Tom Williams and Martha Mann and her daughter Mary, and explained that his father was of a different mind than he, but that family differences never prevented a member of his family from following his political beliefs. Charley spoke to them about his grandmother, born in 1869, and not free of prejudice; but she was willing to take a stand for freedom and decency even from her sickbed. He wanted very much to speak of Lily, or her mother and father, but was afraid to. Lily's pain might choke his throat; the memory of her beauty could fire the passion he was trying to suppress, at least until after the rally. He had to stay away from her, not confuse his anger at fascism and the world's acquiescence to its rise with his love. Charley's plans were amorphous, but the shop-keepers listened less to his plans than to his spirit. They had come out of curiosity as well as out of anger; some had come out of respect for the Keats family, for their power if not their politics. There were Yankees, Italians, Poles, Jews, even a Portuguese shoemaker who had read Jefferson. They were barbers, grocers, bakers, printers. Most were Democrats, but many had little real political affiliation. Their feelings were for the street on which they worked, and the town it served, and the freedom to carve out lives with work and promise and zeal. The Portuguese shoemaker quoted Jefferson: " 'I have sworn upon the altar of God, eternal hostility against every form of tyranny over the mind of man.' " And then he added his own wisdom: "They are a joke, the Nazis, what they say, what they want to do. But they are not funny. They are a bad joke."

"In that case," said Charley, "we'll have to make sure that no one who sees them laughs." Even when the lone nonmerchant guest, the cabdriver who'd wanted to visit the Keats home, suggested that it might very well be best if the rally was simply laughed at, Charley disagreed. For every person who laughed, there would be one who would be intimidated. It was not enough to stay aloof. One had to take a stand. And before it was dark on that Friday in late August of 1938, the Main Street merchants and the Keats boy took a stand, prepared a plan, and swore to act on it.

His father had gone into New York City that day, one of the rare occasions that he ventured into his office during the summer. When he returned, it was nearly dark, and the last of the merchants had left. He asked his son if he'd like to have a drink with him on the porch. Charley made the martinis while his father showered and changed. It was difficult for Charley to maintain his anger at his father whenever he sensed the man's vulnerability. Last night, giving in to Pamela, he had been trying to build a bridge to his son. Charley tried not to think about this, for he knew that his father's attitude toward Jews, Democrats, communists, and international bankers had remained the same. He had not suggested that Pamela might have a right to love whom she chose, but rather that Pamela's love affair was not worth alienating him from his only son.

"Is your father home?" said Mrs. Keats, joining Charley on the porch. "I thought I heard the big car."

"Join us, Mom," said Charley.

"All right," she said, though she was not happy at the prospect.

Her husband appeared a few moments later, his face uncharacteristically tentative. He carried his briefcase.

"I've a present for you, Cynthia," he said.

"Oh," she said. It was impossible to take her eyes from his. The spectacle of her husband apologizing was amazing enough to vanish at the slightest provocation. "Thank you, Charles."

He opened his briefcase and took out a small box, wrapped in gilt paper. She came over to where he stood and took it from his hands. "This is very nice of you," she said.

"You're pretty nice," said Charles Keats III. She tore off the paper and opened the box, and was momentarily speechless. Inside was a diamond bracelet, obviously very expensive—but something beyond this excited Cynthia Keats.

"And I have something for you too, Charley," said his father.

"Are you serious?"

"Yes." He took out a long brown envelope from the briefcase, while his wife tried on the bracelet.

"It's so beautiful, Charles," she said. "I can't believe you went back to him. Is it the same one?"

"Of course. How many like that do you think you have in New York?"

"It's from Kalman. Mr. Kalman, a jeweler on Lexington Avenue. I saw it in his window. He's Jewish, and he was charging a great deal of money for the bracelet, and your father didn't want to have anything to do with the man. They often like to bargain, you see, and, well . . . it seems like a long time ago."

"The envelope is for me?"

"Yes," said Charles Keats III. "As for Mr. Kalman, he wasn't so bad. You were right, he wanted to bargain. I bargained. I think I did pretty well. I've got some Yankee peddler in me, I guess."

Charley took the envelope and untied the string that held down its flap. There was a legal document inside, printed on half a dozen pages, the kind of paper that never failed to confuse Charley. But now it was suddenly crystal clear. It was a lease, a commercial lease, and he saw the address of the Front Street warehouse, and the name of the German-American Bund had been typed in as the lessee.

"Your present cost almost as much as your mother's."

"I'm not sure I understand," said Charley.

"I hope you made the martinis dry, son," said his father. "That's the original. I bought the lease back from them. They're out. The warehouse is empty. You can use it to store fish now, or Jewish prayer shawls. Whatever the hell you want. God, it was a hell of a hot day to do business in New York."

Because his son seemed too stunned to move, Charles Keats III poured his own martini, and backed his way into a seat on the couch. He was embarrassed by the outpouring of confused good will directed his way. Mrs. Keats had had more time to recover from the shock of her present, and she bent low over the couch and kissed her husband on the mouth, her clumsy hands nearly upsetting his drink.

"Thank you, Father," said Charley softly from the other side of the porch. Then he said it again, more fervently, still not understanding that he had achieved a victory, or indeed how and why his father had come round to doing what Charley had wanted.

"I just kind of figured it would be hard to replace a bum like you, seeing how President Rosenveldt is doing such a terrific job getting all the unemployed back to work."

"I was hoping it might have been because you realized that the Nazis were exactly the opposite of everything you hoped and believed," said Charley.

"Well—we won't quibble, son," said his father, drawing his ex-chorus girl wife down onto his enormous lap. "The fact is, those Bund guys are pretty scary. I had to give them a hell of a story—and a hell of a check. They acted like I'd been bought off by the Jews or something. Remind me to stay off Main Street on Sunday."

"Sure," said Charley.

"You're not still going to be there?" said his father suddenly.

"Yes, I am."

"Well," said his father, trying to smile. "I would have thought you'd be satisfied. I mean they're crazy, I agree, you win. I'm not saying Rosenveldt's not a madman and the Jewish bankers aren't trying to drag us into intervention in European affairs— but people like that, the Nazis I mean, they're going to march no matter what you do. I'm saying you were right. I was wrong to get involved with them. It was stupid. If we had a decent man in the White House instead of a communist-loving madman, I would never have been drawn into listening to Bullock. But the rally. Son. Look what I brought you. Their lease. There's no taint on the family. They've got their permit, they're going to march and scream a little, and then they'll get back in their cars and go back to New York. It's not our affair anymore. OK?"

"I'm not angry at you anymore," said Charley. "I really appreciate what you've done. But the rally is my affair. And there's nothing you or anyone else can say that will change my mind about it."

"This isn't like when you went camping in the Yucatan, you know."

"I know."

"They're crazy, Charley. I'm worried for you."

"I'll be all right," said Charley. "But if you want to worry, go right ahead. It's nice to know that your father cares."

"Get me another drink, son," said his father. "And quit all the sentimental stuff. I wouldn't want to lose my appetite so close to dinner."

Then there was only Saturday to get through, and Charley realized, the moment he woke up Saturday morning, that he could not possibly stay away from Lily another day. She didn't know of his plans for the rally, but she would know that he hadn't seen her since Thursday, hadn't called on her to inquire about her mother's health, or if they had had word from her father. He dressed quickly and ran down the stairs in unlaced shoes, taking his breakfast of juice and muffins before anyone could wake up and delay his purpose.

The Cadillac was gone, probably being tuned or washed by the chauffeur somewhere out of earshot on the quiet morning. He decided to take the Ford instead of a bicycle, just in case Lily and her mother wanted a ride. The top was down, and as he backed the car out of the new garage, he felt suddenly joyous. There wasn't a thing wrong with going to see Lily now. Even if she had metamorphosed into an Episcopalian, he would still stop the rally tomorrow. She had been a catalyst, but the reaction had taken place within him, and was proceeding all on its own.

He arrived at the Berger home in less than two minutes. In spite of a thousand differences in their lives, they were neighbors. Regardless of the fact that he had made love with her the first day he had ever seen her, she was as decent and good as anyone in the world. It didn't matter that the world was about to explode, perhaps ending the way T. S. Eliot suggested, "not with a bang but a whimper." Charley was quite at peace, because he was following his heart. He knocked on their door, though it was only half past seven in the morning, and Lily answered it herself; a sleepy-eyed maid joined her a moment later. "Go back to sleep, Rose," she said to the maid, staring at Charley Keats through her omniscient gray eyes.

"I've missed you," she said, as if this were an admission of guilt.

They drank coffee, sitting on the couch on the porch where they had made love, and the sun grew big and hot and violent with the promise of a new day.

TWENTY-FIVE

———◆———

The greatest changes in the look of Main Street since the Civil War had been the conversion of utilitarian objects—the hitching post in front of the sheriff's residence, the water trough in front of the blacksmith's—into decorative items. Safe Haven's main thoroughfare was relatively peaceful for a town of ten thousand. The introduction of the automobile hadn't marred the tranquility of the town as much as it had that of larger towns and cities; and the happy growth of the great trees lining the street, giving more shade than there had ever been during the summers before the internal combustion engine, added a sleepiness to Safe Haven that hadn't existed when the town was smaller and younger. This was also due to the change in status of the community as a whole. It was not that Safe Haven had become an adjunct of New York City, a village brought into commuting range by faster trains, though this was true to a minor extent. Rather, it was the notion of the residents that their town was charming to look at, because it was old. The cobblestones placed there a hundred years ago were left, not because they were the best way of paving a road, but because they were part of what was old and authentic about the town. There were plaques everywhere now, designating the age of the

Congregational Church, the date of the erection of the local theater, the distant years that the Safe Haven Community Center had been used as a courthouse.

Many of the most mundane shops were housed in shells one hundred and more years old. The old inn attracted tourists from both New York and Boston, eager to sleep in canopied beds and walk along the shady sidewalks that seemed to carry the weight of three hundred years. Because many of the buildings on the street had been built at the same time, their different wares were somehow less important to the visitor than their similarly aged wood and brick and clapboard. Though real people shopped and banked and had their hair cut on this street, it had the look—particularly on a Sunday, when the stores were closed—of a stage set, a Hollywood vision of preserved idyllic America.

It was a street where one expected to see Fourth of July parades, with flags and Revolutionary War-era fifers. And although the town had its share of German-Americans, many of them came from families who had lived in New England for two centuries. There was no more allegiance to Germanic ideals among the people of the town than there was to the planet Mars. Many of the "German" families in town—the Manns, the Schmidts, the Schlitzes—had lost sons in the Great War, and could no more read the German-language Bund newspaper than they could scream the Bund slogans: "One Nationality! One Bund! One Führer!" That the rally had been permitted to take place at all had been more because of the Bund's fascist ideology than its German chauvinism. Richard Bullock, who had one German grandparent, cared nothing for Germany; but he had helped bring the rally to Safe Haven because he was a genuine anti-Semite, antidemocrat, racist, and fascist. He wanted to prove that the Bund cry, "Free America!" was a cry from the heartland, and that it meant that the United States would not go to war because of Jews and communists and scheming bankers. And when he saw the neat rows of Bund members, standing tall and still at the east end of Main Street, waiting to begin their goose-stepping parade early on Sunday morning, he saw nothing incongruous about Nazi regalia on an all-American street. Bullock wanted the connection. He wasn't looking to frighten anyone except Jews and communists; what he mostly wanted was to impress. There was something stirring to him about the black trousers and gray shirts, swastika armbands, and swastika stickpins holding black ties in place. The storm troopers weren't all blond, but they were big, and many wore their hair and moustaches in imitation of Chancellor Hitler. They wore their uniforms well, with a fanatic intensity of purpose that everyone would recognize from the newsreels of Germany. He didn't want the storm troopers to conquer Safe Haven; rather, he wanted Safe Haven to acknowledge the reality of the Bund. His own neighbors would see that their aims were to keep America from fighting overseas, to keep the Jews out of the town, to prevent communists from influencing the young; surely these were goals that no one could argue with.

But the Bund district leader, a frizzy-haired giant of a man from New York, had different goals from Bullock. Richard Bullock had made it possible for them to get the parade permit, for them to have a place to drill; but his goals were too hazy, too theoretical. The Bund leader wanted action. He knew that a single smashed window had more impact than a hundred shouted words. Unlike Bullock, he was a German nationalist; like most members of the Bund, he was looking forward not only to anti-Semitic pillage, but to a true Nazified America. He wanted to impress too, but more than that he wanted to strike fear into the hearts of everyone, Jew and Gentile alike. That was how Hitler had come to power, and the Bund took their orders from the Nazis in Germany. As the Bund members waited silently for the start of the parade, their leaders looked with contempt at the dozen police officers ranged at wide intervals along the empty street, as if to protect unpopular marchers from an enraged populace. Well, there was no populace in evidence, and if there had been, the Bund would not have been afraid; it would have been the other way around, he thought.

"Thanks again, Dr. Bullock," said the Bund leader. "We shall not forget your help with getting us a chance for some country air."

"You can start anytime," said Bullock. A few moments later he left the uniformed storm troopers and walked briskly down a side street to where he had parked his Duesenberg.

The Bund leader issued a few sharp commands, and the neat

rows of uniformed men broke apart to pick up their flags and banners. The first row of men carried the red and gold swastika standards; the second row carried smaller banners—the Italian flag, the German flag, the German-American Bund flag, and a single American flag, waving in their midst. Behind them were men carrying placards: FREE AMERICA! and AMERICA FOR THE AMERICANS! and SHALL AMERICA BE JEW-RULED? and BUY CHRISTIAN! The men were impatient to move down the street. This was not Yorkville, and many of them would be glad when it was over. They liked to strut, but unlike their leaders, most of them preferred to avoid confrontation. And for all their pseudo-Americanisms, the Bund members looking down Safe Haven's Main Street saw no welcome glimmer of the fatherland.

The leader prepared them. A drum roll began. The placards and banners were raised high. Those men with free hands returned the leader's Nazi salute, and then, as the leader swiveled about with precision, they prepared to take the first steps along the empty street.

A lone man was walking down the center of Main Street, directly toward the Nazis, taking long easy strides. He carried a large American flag, which waved briskly in the open spaces of the street.

"Who the hell is that?" said one of the policemen.

"That's trouble," said another, readying his billy club. He didn't know whether he had a right to grab the man off the street before he provoked an argument. After all, he didn't see what was wrong with carrying an American flag, and bearing no hateful slogans.

"Let's get him out of here, fast," said the first policeman.

The Bund had begun to march, and their leader, goose-stepping like a marionette, was trying not to smile. The stupid man with the stupid flag would soon have his head cracked for his trouble. Even if there weren't a hundred men at his back, he would have gladly confronted the man alone. One word, one blow, one thrust, and he would be lying in the dirt where he belonged.

"Nazis out!" came a shout from one of the closed shops, and as the storm troopers turned their angry heads to the source of the sound, another shout came from the opposite end of the street. "Nazis out!"

Up and down Main Street, deserted only a moment before, the doors to a dozen shops were opening, and men came out, carrying American flags and shouting. "Nazis out! Nazis out! Nazis out!" The policemen who had begun to run to the lone man with the flag stopped in their tracks. There was danger all around now. It might begin at any moment, it might come from any source. "Hey you, buddy," said one of the policemen, shouting across a dozen yards to where Charley Keats marched, "get the hell out of the street. You don't got a permit. Move it out of there!"

"I don't need a permit to carry the American flag," said Charley.

"There's a parade coming," said the policeman stupidly, because the Bund leader was only a few yards away.

"I'm stopping it," said Charley. "I'm keeping the sons of bitches out of my town."

The policeman couldn't argue. From the storefronts behind him there were more and more people shouting, women and children clustering around the flags carried by their husbands and fathers, and though they stayed well out of the line of the parade, there was no telling what could happen next. The Nazis could turn to the right, they could turn to the left, they could charge into Rosenberg's dry goods store or they could maul Charley Keats and his flag, and all the police had were pistols in holsters and puny little clubs. No one had been shot by a policeman in Safe Haven in twenty years.

"You, kike-lover, out of my way," said the Bund leader to Charley. He had stopped, and the men behind now marched in place, their heavy boots beating an eerie rhythm on the cobblestones.

"I have a better idea, punk," said Charley Keats. "Take your clowns and take a walk, back where you came from."

The Bund leader threw an excellent punch, a right uppercut into Charley's chin that knocked him off his feet, and forced the young man to let go of the American flag. It was clear that the law had been broken. But even the merchants and their families were so stunned at that moment that they quit their rhythmic shouting. The policemen didn't know if they should remove Charley from the street, now that he was lying in it, or arrest the Bund leader. But as the storm troopers continued marching in place, their lips revealing neither surprise nor gladness, Charley began to get up by himself.

"If you get up, I'm going to knock you down," said the Bund leader.

Charley heard this quite clearly, and feeling that he had already been taken unfair advantage of—having been hit without warning, while his hands had been occupied with the flag—he felt not at all bad about going from his knees into an enraged charge, butting the man in his solar plexus. As the Nazi doubled up in pain, Charley stood up and raised his fists.

It was at that moment that the gunshot rang out, and all eyes turned to the fat man coming up from behind Charley on Main Street. The storm troopers, some of whom had been ready to jump on Charley in defense of their leader, abruptly stopped their marching in place. No one moved except the Bund leader, who was slowly gathering his breath and his strength. He looked at the fat man with the rifle, who had just fired a bullet into the air.

"The first one of you Krauts makes a move towards my son is a dead man," said Charles Keats III. Charley felt his heart beat wildly, felt the blood rush to his ears. He was suddenly so happy he could barely contain his joy. "And what the hell is wrong with you men?" his father said to the policemen on both sides of the street. "Get out your goddamn guns. What good are they doing if they're not in your hands?"

The Bund leader didn't imagine that the maniac's commands had anything to do with him; and if they did, he would not let the threat of a bullet deter him from breaking the young man's nose. But as he threw another right toward Charley, the young man stepped to the side and hit him with all his force, a right hook that was aimed at the man's chin, but missed. Charley's blow went into the Nazi's neck, and nearly broke his windpipe.

The fight might have been over if Charley had been aware of how badly he had accidentally hurt the man. But the blow was the work of a moment, and yards away was a sea of men with swastikas, and all about him were the merchants of Safe Haven, holding on to their flags while the ancient trees looked down on them, as if from a vista of centuries. He had thought of Lily Berger that morning, when he had woken up and remembered her love, and how he had felt when they had brought their bodies together, how deep was the joy, how perfect the passion. He had something of that same passion now. He had connected to some source of energy that was usually out of reach. Like the sexual world revealed to him by Lily, he was suddenly connected to a line of action that was as old as man. There was a man who was attacking him, and he must stand his ground; he must destroy him.

Yes, and his father was here, and the men of his town, and the dimly realized ancestors who had preceded him.

Charley hit the Bund leader again, a left to the side of his head, and another left, a jab, hitting him lightly in the nose, in the mouth, and then a powerful right to the point of his chin, and the staggering man fell down, flat on his back, looking as if he were dead.

"I'm going to kill you," said Charley, and he was no less full of violence than Tom Williams had been, no less certain about what was right and what was wrong than Mary Mann or Virginia Collins. He was crazed, but it was the craziness of purpose, the genius of action that had long been denied him. This was not a play he was writing, not an exacerbating discussion with his father, but an immediate reordering of the world. He was out of control, in the sense that he didn't know how he had moved the few yards past the unconscious Nazi to the first line of stunned storm troopers. There was no practical plan to the way he swung his fist, first at one gray-shirted belly, then into another Hitler-moustached face. Charley could barely remember the rhythm of his well-learned punching sequences, the product of college boxing and a body bag in his New York apartment. His fists and legs and head moved of their own volition, and moved well, keeping him from harm and inflicting damage to those in his way; but he was not listening to the conflicting information about him. As the policemen moved in, as his father fired another shot in the air, as the merchants screamed out their hate, the young man was in control of only one thing—desire. He wanted to push the men back, away; he wanted to rip away evil, to obliterate it; he wanted not to murder, but to overcome by the sheer force of passion. And he had passion. This he knew; he learned it once and for all. Though he was born to privilege, of an old family, with prospects as rigid as law, he had the passion of his ancestors. He wanted, he lusted, he demanded; and he won. The sea of Nazis broke. They picked up their leader, they pushed away the howling young madman who chased them, they turned around and walked away, hurling slogans to hide their shame.

Not until the street was clear of the uniformed men did Charley relax in the grip of the two policemen who held him. "You OK, son?" said his father.

"Nazis out," said Charley.

"They're out," said his father. "How do you feel?"

"Good," said Charley. "And right. I did what had to be done." And then whatever force that had been holding him up vanished, and he would have fallen if not for the men who held him. But he didn't pass out. He remained very still and quiet, and as his father drove him away, he relished the August beauty of Safe Haven, he longed for his bed in the house on the Saugatuck, he dreamed of getting back to his home.

EPILOGUE

———◦◼◦———

Early in 1939, Lily Berger's father was murdered in Berlin.

The plans that had been made for her marriage to Charley Keats were postponed. The details of the Bergers' personal tragedy were not overwhelmed in Lily's mind by the catastrophic war in Europe. On the contrary, each news item added to her sense of depression and loss. Her mother remained weak in spirit, and suffered from severe headaches. Mrs. Berger's doctors recommended a move to Los Angeles's dry, warm climate, where the large contingent of German émigrés might help the self-imposed isolation of both mother and daughter. Lily and her mother moved to California in 1940. Charley visited them three times, the last time in December 1941, a week after the attack on Pearl Harbor. By then he had been engaged to Lily for three years.

Charley enlisted in the army the first week of 1942. He was killed in 1944, during the Allied landing on the beaches of Anzio, Italy. Lily learned of the death from Charley's father. She mourned for him as if he had been her husband. She never married. In 1947, Lily and her mother moved to Zurich. Lily studied medicine, and became a pediatrician at the age of thirty-six.

Katherine Williams died in 1958, at the age of eighty-nine. Her son, Charles Keats III, died a few weeks later. Cynthia Keats returned to living in Greenwich, and watched in considerable dismay as the fortune left by her husband was dissipated by his brothers with little thought. As stipulated in Katherine Williams's will, the ancient home in Safe Haven went to Pamela Keats, as poor Charley hadn't even outlived his grandmother.

Pamela was very glad to get the house. The Jewish boyfriend who had so angered her uncle years before was now hardly a memory. He too had lost his life during the war, fighting with the British army in North Africa. She was married in 1948, to a bespectacled veteran by the name of Paul Collins; but this Collins was from a Massachusetts family, and was not related to Pamela's famous ancestor John Collins.

Paul Collins, like Pamela's mother, was a professor of history. They had three children, two boys and a girl, Charles, John, and Evelyn. John was the youngest child, born in 1958, only two months after they'd moved into the inherited house in Safe Haven. Indeed, it was the inheritance and its wealth of associations that prompted Pamela to name the boy after the legendary Indian fighter; Paul thought it a bit silly. He would have preferred to name the boy after his own mentor, a famous professor of history at Yale.

Pamela began to take an interest in the Keats family's business, particularly their holdings in New York City real estate. Her father had no interest in business, and both her uncles, Samuel and John, were essentially frivolous men. By 1964, both these uncles had died, and Pamela began to work full time from an office in the Safe Haven house. She was very successful. There was not only more than enough money for a comfortable Connecticut life style, money for college and cars and clothes, money for paintings and books and trips to faraway places— there was money for the founding of a family fortune.

But by 1982, none of the children seemed especially interested in entering the world of business. Charles was thirty-one, a musician living in Los Angeles. Evelyn was twenty-eight, a married lawyer with two children of her own. Her husband was

a first-term congressman from the state of Illinois, very interested in any financial aid available from his wife's family, but
solely to further his political ambitions.

As for John, the youngest, there was little hope that he'd
show any interest in business or politics. Like his namesake, he
liked to travel to faraway places; like his ancestor Tom Williams, he had a quick temper, with little patience for fools. At
twenty, he'd been suspended from Harvard after being arrested
during an anti–South African apartheid demonstration. He had
gone to the demonstration only to be with a girl from one of his
classes, but once the police had urged the demonstrators to
move, his sense of injustice had been ignited—not for South
Africa's blacks, but for his own freedom to demonstrate any
beliefs in his own country. He was twenty-four in 1982, and
had traveled in India, Afghanistan, Australia, often by bicycle,
sometimes on foot, working at odd jobs for his passage money
across the waters sailed by his ancestors' great ships. Recently
he had taken an interest in agriculture; he had told his mother
about plans to go to Central America, to work with poor farmers. John insisted that this desire had no political component.
He was being selfish, he said. To live among people he could
help would be personally gratifying, at least for the moment.

His mother understood this selfishness perfectly, even if his
father did not. She found it easy to imagine him penniless and
drifting for most of his life, uncommitted to their business, to
any affiliation with a political party or ideal. But she found it
just as easy to imagine him working at her side, or taking over
her place at the head of the family's finances; or standing up at
the village meeting and speaking out in indignation at wrongs
and excesses in the local or national government. John could be
an idler, a saint, a financier, or a leader of men; but she was
sure that he would be what the world needed, what he himself
would want to become.

Sitting in front of her enormous hearth on a cold night, the
burning wood carrying too much heat out of the poorly insulated old home, Pamela and her husband sometimes felt the
emptiness of a familiar space vacated by children. But there
were ghosts to console them, a long line of them back to the
seventeenth century. And whatever the waste of wood cost

them in money and hard work, watching the fire dance in the old hearth was worth it; here was the reminder of a foundation, not just of a family, or a town, or even a country. The fire from the hearth reminded them that what was well built would last; that as long as the house would stand, good men and women would live to inhabit it; and from its heart would come the spirit of strength and passion and love.